MAI

BOOK 2 OF THE SINISTER SERIES

TONY MARTURANO

a Different Angle

Published in the United Kingdom and the rest of the world by
a Different Angle 2023

Cambridge, England

A catalogue record for this book is available from the
British Library

ISBN
978-1-7397694-3-7

For my mamma, Anna, who sparked my love of writing by gifting me my first mechanical typewriter. Thank you for always being there and for keeping the dream alive.

I love you x

Tony

"Under the fiery glow of a malevolent star, the spawn of Satan shall emerge from the depths of the earth to enslave all of humanity, reducing mankind to nothing more than mere slaves to his dark rule."

– Cameron Carmichael.

Steven Rochford
Passenger Experience Team
Stansted Airport

Dear Steven,

Subject: RESIGNATION

Please accept this letter as official notice of my resignation, effective immediately.

As you know, I still have holiday days remaining. In addition, you previously agreed that holiday due to me from last year could be carried over, though you later denied this. Regardless, there is still plenty of leave remaining which means I shall not be working my notice.

Please be so kind as to forward my final pay care of my lawyer, Roger Mitchell. He can be reached at the firm MORGAN, THOMAS & MITCHELL, located in The Shard, London.

Please address any queries you may have regarding this letter to him also. If you feel unable to carry out my request, please provide your reasons in detail so that he can pursue this matter on my behalf.

In closing, I would like to thank you for all the opportunities you have afforded me during my employment. Regrettably, I cannot. My late father always told me that if I didn't have anything kind to say then I should say nothing.

Yours sincerely,

Sophie Cooper

DELIVERED BY COURIER

My dearest friend,

By the time you read this, I'll be gone. I know this may come as a bit of a shock to you and I am so very sorry. I hate leaving you and Damon like this, but I love you both so very much that I just know if I come back to Cambridge, I will definitely change my mind. And yes, that may well be a good thing, but I won't know until I try.

I hope you understand.

I'm taking the train from London to France and then from there to Italy. In total, it should take me around 13 hours to reach Venice. Seems like a long time, but it will give me plenty of opportunity to think and it means I don't have to see the inside of an airport! LOL!

I love you, Janay. You and Damon mean the world to me, so please don't' see this as a reflection of our friendship but only for what it is: my need to explore this new life that fate appears to have carved out for me. Hopefully I'll rediscover parts of who I used to be along the way.

I have to go now as my lawyer is going to arrange to have this letter specially couriered to you! He also arranged my ticket on the train—that I'm going to miss if I don't run—while also taking care of a few other things for me.

I love you with all my heart. Give Damon a BIG squeeze and a kiss from me. And I PROMISE to send you my number as soon as I get a new phone and then maybe you can both come visit once I'm settled in!

All my love,

Sophie xxx

1

HOME

WEDNESDAY. LATE MORNING.

Sophie wiped the tear from her cheek. The symbolic poetry of the act was not lost on her. It was the first time such sorrowful tears had revisited her since her father's funeral. And yes, she had concluded, no matter the deception or the motivation, the man who had raised her and made sure that she wanted for nothing, was, for all intents and purposes, her father. As for the woman who used to tuck her into bed at night… well, she simply avoided thinking about her. All the potential truths she could imagine about her were ugly, albeit for different reasons.

A fresh start. That is the sentiment with which she had boarded the train in London. And it was this belief that she would carry with her during her time here.

A quick internal check told her that she was all right. Her stomach was still in knots, and she was feeling somewhat lonely, but otherwise she was okay. This was, after all, a unique opportunity to write a whole new chapter of her life. Or some such rubbish. It sounded much better when Doctor Krauss said it.

Oddly, her psychiatrist had been very supportive of her decision to uproot herself from everything she knew to travel to a foreign land where she barely understood the lingo.

But you've been learning Italian, haven't you?

Yes. But that was just to help at work.

History has taught us that human adaptability flourishes in the face of adversity. And you, my dear Sophie, are the very essence of this.

How the man had drawn that conclusion was beyond her. She was a wreck of bundled neuroses who was forever afraid of her own shadow, someone who had spent most of her life cowering behind a fantastical and horrific juvenile delusion rather than face the truth: that she had been abandoned both by her biological parents and by one half of her foster parents. If she really was as strong as the doctor suggested, she'd be more like Victoria. Victoria had come from a broken home and hadn't experienced anything near to the privileged life that Sophie had, and still she took shit from nobody.

And yet it is you who are abandoning everything that is familiar, including your friend, behind whom you have hidden all these years, to embark on an adventure hundreds of miles from the boundaries of your comfort zone.

Okay. So maybe Krauss had a point. After all, she did appear to have undergone some kind of a metamorphosis since her father's funeral, as much as she still couldn't believe it. She appeared to have overcome a lifetime of obsessive compulsions, had quit her job and her best friend, and was now master of her own destiny.

Somehow all of that just made her feel worse.

She lingered on the thought of her friend, Victoria, for a few seconds. She hated how things had ended between them and planned to get in touch with her as soon as she had the chance. Despite this, she was surprised to discover that she didn't feel as badly about their fallout as she had expected. Was this all part of the process of moving on? Had her lifelong friendship just evaporated into the memories of her former life? Was it that simple?

Sofia DaTerra. That's who she was now. A countess, no less.

And hard bitch, apparently.

She swiped another tear and tried sending Janay another message, but it kept failing. She hadn't been able to contact her since she boarded the first train at London St Pancras. She'd tried again in Paris and several times once she'd changed to the overnight sleeper, but still, the message wouldn't go through.

High-pitched whirring startled her as she felt the train slow before coming to a gradual stop.

Was this it? Was she here already? She had been so absorbed by her thoughts that she hadn't even noticed her arrival.

She looked out of the window, but all she could see were train tracks and a concrete column. Where were the signs? This must be some kind of stop along the way, she thought, before catching sight of the sign a few metres down the platform.

VENEZIA, SANTA LUCIA.

Oh, what have I done?

Her stomach lurched and she readied herself for the onset of a panic attack. It had always been like this. Any kind of stress was soon followed by palpitations, sweaty palms… and yet nothing happened. Yes. She was feeling nervous, apprehensive even, but her breathing remained steady.

"You've lost your mind," she muttered to herself over and over, continuing as she reached up to retrieve the small suitcase from the overhead rack.

It was an impulse buy, along with other clothing essentials. Jeans, a couple of shirts, sweaters, underwear, and a black beanie hat, of all things. Her hair felt like a mess, and she'd decided to hide it until she got the chance to do something with it. A beanie hat seemed like the most logical thing and Victoria had told her on several occasions that she looked cute in them, particularly with her hair spilling out down the sides of her face. Victoria would have most likely frowned at the rest of her clothing choices, but Sophie was opting for practicality over style.

She'd never been any other way. Even as a child, she always behaved as if she were much wiser than her years and was often bullied because of it. Her peculiar maturity naturally made her different from the other children. Doctor Krauss explained that it was most likely a reaction. *An attempt to reclaim some of the control you lost when your mother abandoned you.*

That said, she did have a crazy moment back in London when she considered buying herself a floaty dress and one of those giant floppy hats. She had imagined herself in glorious monochromatic vintage cinematic chic, leaving the train in a delicious cloud of perfume like one of those femme fatales. The image was swiftly replaced with a colour snapshot of her being blinded by the hat, tripping on her dress, and falling arse over tit. Knowing her luck, it would be filmed, and she'd become one of those TikTok sensations but for entirely the wrong reasons.

No. She was happy in her jeans and trainers. And the mirror the compartment door made was telling her that the hat was a good choice. She used the reflection to tidy the strands of platinum blonde hair around her face before refocussing on the metallic glint of braces that belonged to some boy gawking at her from the other side of the glass.

She smiled at him as his younger sibling slapped him out of his stupor with a giggle. Then she took a deep breath, slung her bag over her shoulder, extended her case's handle, and slowly merged with the stream of passengers shuffling down the train corridor towards the exit.

Her heart thumped to the cadence of her every step and she found herself imagining that it was the drumbeat to her funeral march.

Really? Pull yourself together. Just think of this as a holiday. It's just a holiday.

Only it wasn't.

Now, as she waited for the loud two-point-four American family featuring her metal-mouthed teenage fan to leave the train, she thought about how completely underdressed she was. Maybe she should have bought that dress after all.

Light suddenly flooded in as the nearest train door yawned wide open before her. Three steps down. They appeared much steeper than when she had boarded, and she paused. Should she pick the case up and attempt to leave with it or get off first and then reach back for her belongings?

She must have been considering this for more seconds than was acceptable since her obvious reluctance to leave the train was already prompting impatient sighs from the passengers waiting behind her.

Move!

And yet she couldn't

The bag felt heavy on her shoulder despite only holding her wallet, a paperback book that she'd picked up on impulse and barely looked at since, and that unopened packet. It was this that was weighing her down. Yes, it was still unopened. And that's exactly how she wanted it to stay until she reached her destination. It was her *get out* clause should she choose to abandon this madness and catch the next train home.

Open only if you wish to submit to the terms of the will. Roger Mitchell's words echoed in her mind.

"Prego signorina, prego." Sofia looked down the steps and into the chestnut eyes of a man with a mop of curly black hair. He was nodding at her case.

"My case?"

"Yes. I help."

"Oh, okay. Thank you. Thank you so much."

The man reached up and took first the case and then her hand, holding it as she negotiated the steps.

"Oh, grazie! Grazie!" she said, feeling for the very first time in her life like one of those proverbial damsels, despite her jeans and trainers. If she could have rolled her eyes at herself, she would have. Since when did she become so bloody helpless? Still, on a positive note, she'd been here but minutes and was already courting attention. Flirting isn't something that came naturally to her, but she'd seen Victoria in action enough times. Apparently, batting your eyelashes was very effective.

The handsome stranger gave her a lopsided smile. She probably looked like she had something in her eye. Then he nodded, bidding her a good day as a giggling girl waved at her before linking arms with him.

"Bravo. Bravo," she said, kissing him on the cheek before they disappeared into the shoal of people, leaving Sofia alone once more.

But not for long. Her loud American travelling companions hadn't made much progress. They were busy oohing and aahing about the Santa Lucia train station, explaining how, according to their guidebook, it was located at the northern edge of the historic city on the Grand Canal—or *Canale Grande*—and was built all the way back in 1861 when Venice was under the control of the Austrian Empire. It is just a twenty-minute walk to the *Ponte di Rialto* or twenty-seven minutes to *Piazza San Marco,* which Sofia thought was good information to have.

Sofia followed them. They obviously knew where they were going, and she wanted to see what other nuggets of wisdom she could overhear while swimming in the river of humans migrating upstream towards the exit.

The wind funnelling in from outside and blowing across the platforms felt cold on her face and was no doubt turning her small nose a shade of rouge and colouring in the freckles on her cheeks. It smelt of grease and a medley of other fragrances. Trains whirred, shoes shuffled, luggage wheels clicked as the crowd chatted animatedly, yet she could still hear that somewhere, someone was whistling the melody to "O Sole Mio."

She smiled. She didn't know why, but there was something about being among her fellow passengers, united in a common destination, that, for the first time in a while, made her feel like she was part of something. Like she belonged here. Like she was… home.

There was a large bottleneck at the end of the platform as arriving passengers merged with other travellers milling around the station.

Sofia paused to take in the architecture. The station was much more modern than she expected, nowhere near as gothic as she had imagined. There were the usual information screens mounted on walls, restaurants, snack bars, and a litany of general souvenir stores.

High above, the public address system blared an announcement in Italian which prompted a trio of girls to rush by in a cloud of excited squeals. Nearby, a group of people were crying, others were laughing, while some were even chatting in Cockney accents, instantly reminding Sofia of what she had left behind for a moment.

She made her way through the crowds to the concourse and into the main station, which was dimly lit compared to the view that she could now see through the giant double exit doors. The further she walked forward, the more the station fell away and opened to a giant canvas painted in another century.

Concrete steps led down to the station's piazza and then to the dazzling water of the canal. On the opposite side, more steps climbed through large white pillars to the entrance of *Chiesa di San Simeon Piccolo,* as narrated by the American group, who had flowed with her out of the station. It invoked an involuntary gasp from Sofia, who recognised the church by its unmistakable giant green dome that was pearlescent against the backdrop of a clear blue sky. She had seen images of the church on so many posters at work and to be standing across from it was *awesome,* to use one of the American family's favourite adjectives.

Oddly, the view reminded her of home once more, of her father and the endless travel shows they had watched together. For once, the memory was bittersweet and not downright gut-wrenching, her emotions likely soothed by the feeling of winter sun on her face as she arched her head back and squinted upward. It was like the embrace of a long-lost relative.

Sophie Cooper may well be a stranger to Venice, but Sofia DaTerra felt like she had indeed come home.

Contessa, you mean!

The thought made her smile again and after several minutes of standing in a trance, the weight of her shoulder bag reminded her that she should keep moving. She descended the steps to the piazza and reunited with the Americans.

She had no idea where to go from here. What she had already concluded, validated by her unofficial travelling companions, was that the modern-looking bus shelter in front of her, with the orange sash that read *Santa Lucia Station,* was Venice's equivalent of a bus stop. Only instead of a motor bus with wheels, here, she would have to wait for the equivalent, known locally as a *vaporetto* or boat bus, since *there are no motor vehicles in Venice because it's built on water, you retard!*

Billy! Don't call your brother that.

Yeah, Billy!

Sofia watched as the young boy punched his brother's arm, prompting instant retaliation, and smiled. She wondered what it might be like to have a brother, or a sister for that matter, although right now, she'd settle for just knowing who her biological family were.

And just like that, the smile disappeared from her face. She focussed on the task in hand. *I'm in Venice! I'm in bloody Venice!* She wanted to scream it out loud but that wasn't her style, and she found herself thinking about Victoria and Janay, both of whom wouldn't have cared. How she wished she was more like them. She missed them.

She rummaged in her bag for her phone, but when she tried to message Janay, it failed again. Then, after considering it for a few seconds, she tapped out a tentative message to Victoria.

IN VENICE. MISS YOU.

She deleted the message then tapped it out once more, her thumb hovering over the send button for several seconds before pressing it.

MESSAGE FAILED.

"Shit." Something obviously wasn't working despite the man at the store telling her she was all set. Roaming switched on and everything.

She'd need to call the phone company as soon as she was settled in.

But for now, the joyful smile returned as Sofia looked across the canal once more to the buildings that surrounded the green church. They were an explosion of colour, reminding her of the multicoloured beach huts of the English coast but on a much larger scale, featuring a whole series of arched balconies and windows overlooking the Grand Canal.

A couple of young men in t-shirts and shorts crossed her line of vision and smiled at her.

She smiled back and awkwardly yelled, "Buongiorno!"

"Ciao, bellezza!" the men called back, their appreciative smiles and waves instantly dragging a curtain of heat up her face. So, this is what it felt like to flirt.

She was grinning again and anybody watching her would probably think she'd lost her mind, but who cared? She was a stranger in this gorgeous city, and nobody would be interested in her.

Nobody but the rather distinguished-looking man with a grey beard who was making a beeline for her. He was dressed in what looked like vintage clothing: corduroy trousers, waistcoat, and flat cap. It was only after she concluded that she didn't recognise him that she noticed he was holding a piece of cardboard with something scribbled on it in thick black pen.

Contessa Sofia DaTerra.

He waved the card at her and, like a pair of cat eyes tracking a lively treat, she followed the words back and forth.

That's me!

She was never going to get used to that name. But she certainly was going to try.

Reflexively, she nodded as the man approached her.

"Buongiorno, Contessa," he said, taking off his cap and revealing strands of thinning grey hair plastered to his scalp. *"Sono Armando,"* he added in a gravelly voice that suggested he had smoked way too many cigarettes. The man kept his eyes lowered, like he was in the presence of nobility.

"Si prega, Contessa," he said, looking over his shoulder to one of the boats bobbing up and down on the water and then back at her. He hastily picked up her case, stopped just short of wrestling the shoulder bag from her, then carried them both down the steps to their waiting transportation.

Sofia followed to what looked like a pristine brown speedboat. It had a cabin at one end with enough room to seat around four people. She watched her escort place the luggage inside before turning to offer her his hand, eyes still lowered. She accepted the invitation, climbing aboard and immediately taking a seat inside the cabin.

Seconds later, the engine started, and the stranger carefully manoeuvred the boat out into the canal, slowly passing the so-called bus stop where the Americans were still queuing with the other tourists. She resisted the urge to wave and call out, opting instead to secretly thank them. They had unknowingly made her journey easier with their idle banter that she realised had helped to calm her anxiety.

Moments into the journey and now feeling an unusual surge of confidence, the newly named contessa decided that she didn't want her first glimpses of Venice to be from behind a pane of glass, so, somewhat awkwardly, she left her seat and moved aft of the boat to a tiny observation deck. There, on wobbly legs, she clutched onto the railing, strands of hair flying about her face, as she watched the waters of the Grand Canal churn in their wake.

Il Canale Grande was the main artery through the medieval city of Venezia. It was overlooked by a spectacular array of colourful gothic and classic buildings dating back as far as the 13th century, many of which were elaborately decorated with portraits of gods and noblemen. Sofia recalled from one of the travel programs she used to watch that it was how citizens projected their status and wealth. And if she was awestruck in the 21st century, she could only imagine how visitors must have felt hundreds of years earlier.

The waterway was busy with other vaporettos and taxis, as well as gondolas brimming with tourists. In a somewhat bizarre fusion between present and past, some were ferrying people in ostentatious costumes of ornate detailing that was matched only by the vibrancy of their colours. Sofia was particularly captivated by a trio of two women and a man dressed in violet damasks of layered lace, trimmed with die-cut ties and beads. They were wearing white masks so she couldn't see their faces, but when they saw her, the man bowed, and the women curtsied.

As gracefully as she could on the swaying boat, she instinctively returned the gesture, grinning from ear to ear as she suddenly realised. It was the middle of February. *Carnevale!*

Venice's world-famous carnival took place each year for approximately two weeks until Shrove Tuesday, known locally as *Martedi Grasso.* The most famous feature of the event, besides the masquerade balls and the parades, were the intricate, colourful gowns and the masks of all inspirations and designs, all fashioned on the lavish and colourful splendour afforded to the nobility of the 18th century. The age of Casanova and great painters like Giambattista Tiepolo and Canaletto.

Some of the passing boat captains nodded or smiled at Sofia. Others opted for the more traditional approach of yelling, *"Ciao, bellissima!"* and *"Buongiorno, signorina!"*

It took Sofia a few seconds to realise they were yelling at her. "Me?" she mouthed. Then, "CIAO! BUONGIORNO!" she called back, waving excitedly.

She breathed in deeply. She had heard tales of Venice smelling badly, particularly during the summer, but all she could smell was ocean salt, algae, engine fumes, and the occasional waft of fried food that made her tummy rumble.

Venice smells just fine to me.

She imagined the Americans narrating, what she had already learned elsewhere, that the very body of water that she was floating on used to be part of a swamp to which many Northern Italians were forced to flee to escape the savagery of Attila the Hun. In fact, Venezia was nothing until those settlements went on to prosper, transforming the city into a major economic hub and home for the arts.

Now, centuries later, this stunning city had become a major tourist destination with over twenty million people swarming to its various lagunas each year. It was a staggering statistic considering that the number of local residents of Venice was just over a quarter of a million.

And now you are one of them.

Sofia smiled as she was filled with optimism for her new life. Of course, she had no idea how it was going to unravel, but to her surprise, she was looking forward to finding out.

After ten minutes or so, the boat's engine relaxed and slowed as the driver expertly steered the craft around the oncoming traffic and began to reverse. Sofia turned, following the direction of the boat, and her mouth fell open. They were reversing into a somewhat dilapidated wooden dock. Some planks were missing, leaving aged timber struts jutting out of the water like gapped teeth. Yet it wasn't this that caught Sofia's eye. What was making her skin tingle was the three-storey building towering over them. She instantly recognised it from the photo.

Palazzo Rosso. The red palace.

Unlike the jetty leading to it, the building appeared to be immaculately maintained with a fresh coat of deliciously deep crimson. As per the picture, it featured at least eight arched windows on this side of the house, large and symmetrical, two of which included ornate terrazzo balconies. They were highlighted in white paint, sealed with dark red shutters, and framed by a verdant coat of ivy.

The building was fronted by a flower garden filled with a vibrant kaleidoscope of winter roses and an orchard of naked trees that supported a canopy of vines weaving around a pergola. The photo did not do this magnificent building justice, Sofia thought, as Armando unloaded her case and then turned to her.

"Prego, Contessa," he repeated, eyes still lowered.

"Grazie," she said, tilting her head to make eye contact, but the man had already hustled up the dock and ashore.

Sofia looked up at the building and sighed.

She had arrived.

2

THE RED PALACE

WEDNESDAY. NOON.

Access to Palazzo Rosso was via a stone archway leading to a small piazza of dwarf trees and rambling ivy. Straight ahead, a bridge led over the canal, to other vias and the heart of Venice. To the right, a set of steep stone steps ran up and across the back of the palace.

Armando—who Sofia estimated must be in his early seventies—had removed his cap and was waiting at the foot of the steps.

"Up here?" Sofia asked.

The man nodded, "*Si. Prego,*" and then returned his eyes to his feet.

Sofia was glad that common sense had prevailed and she had chosen to wear her jeans and trainers. She couldn't tell for sure, but there were at least twenty steps to the top.

Although there were tourists using the *calli*, it seemed much quieter and calmer this side of the Grand Canal, in stark contrast to the hustle and bustle of the main thoroughfare.

Sofia had heard so much about the calli of Venice. These narrow streets or alleyways were a common feature of the city's unique and intricate network of waterways. They line both traditional buildings and old architecture and provide a maze-like atmosphere for visitors to explore. And now she was just across the bridge from one.

With a smile, Sofia climbed the steps to the raucous call of seagulls overhead, who seemed to cheer her. She paused on the sixth step when the clock of Piazza San Marco announced that it was noon. The sound filled Sofia with renewed excitement. She couldn't wait to tell Janay that she could hear the Campanile from her room! How cool was that?

Room? It's not a hotel. It's my new home. It was as she was considering this that the most peculiar thing happened. An apple. A large red delicious apple, gleaming in the sunshine, came rolling down the stone steps to greet her. Then another. And another.

She instinctively caught the first and then the second before looking up. There was someone crouched down at the top of the steps, hastily gathering the runaway fruit and placing it into a large black floppy hat.

From her slender back profile that revealed long black hair cascading over a figure-hugging white dress, it was obvious that it was a lady. She was wearing red heels. Designer, no doubt, of the kind Victoria would worship but that Sofia would have to be paid to wear.

"Grazie," the lady said, standing to her full height. *"La borsa é rotta,"* she added, turning to Sofia while clutching her hat turned

makeshift bag to her bosom.

She was beautiful. Stunning, in fact, in that thirties movie siren kind of way, with milky-white skin smoothed over high cheekbones beneath almond-shaped hazelnut eyes. She had accented them by maintaining thin eyebrows and complemented the look with immaculately painted red wine lipstick.

"*Grazie*," the woman repeated with a big smile, holding out her floppy hat for Sofia to deposit the rogue apples into while looking her over. It was a fleeting glance, but Sofia noticed it and was back to reconsidering her wardrobe once more.

Stop it!

"Um, prego?" she said with a thoughtful frown.

"Oh, you're English!" the woman declared, juggling the apples with one hand so she could push a lock of luscious black hair from in front of her eyes with the other.

"Oh, wow, so are you!" Sofia exclaimed.

"Born and bred. Northern lass," she said with an exaggerated inflection that would have otherwise been undetectable.

"Oh wow!"

"Thank you so much for these," the woman said, clutching her hat. "The bag just fell apart and, you know… they went tumbling down."

"Oh, it was no problem."

"Are you lost? Can I give you directions to somewhere?" she asked.

"Oh," Sofia looked around, almost as if reminding herself why she was there. "No. I...um…I think I live here," she said, turning, looking for the entrance. She assumed it was the big wooden door behind her.

The lady laughed as if Sofia had made a joke, but then, noticing the bemused look on the young woman's face, she stopped and, with an incredulous whisper, asked, "Here? At Palazzo Rosso?"

Sofia shrugged awkwardly, still not quite believing it herself. "Yes. I think so. Just arrived."

"Oh, my… well, that's wonderful! That's truly wonderful."

"It is! Oh sorry… I am Soph-ia."

"Soph-ia?"

"Well, back home I was Sophie. Here, I… well, I'm Sofia. Sofia DaTerra," she added, holding out a hand like she'd spoken those words many times before.

The woman drank her in as if she were a long-lost daughter and then pulled her into a squeeze before emerging and declaring, *"Sofia, che piacere!"* Noticing the look on Sofia's face, she repeated herself in English. "It's a pleasure, Sofia. It really is. I'm Aurora. Welcome. Welcome! The boys will be so excited to hear that we have a new neighbour."

"Neighbour?"

"Yes. I live just across the way," she said, pointing towards a narrow bridge. Sofia noticed that her nails were flawless, painted to match her lipstick. And, once again, she was reminded of Victoria.

"Wow. I didn't realise that these steps led elsewhere."

"Well, only across the bridge to my humble abode. It's not as magnificent as yours, of course. More suitable for the hired help than a contessa," Aurora said with a smile.

Sofia forced an awkward laugh but then realised. "Oh, you know about me?"

"I'm sorry?"

"You know about me. The whole contessa thing."

"Well, I don't know of you specifically, but I do know that the ladies of Palazzo Rosso have always been contessas. The title comes with the property."

Sofia remembered. "Oh yes, of course," she said, hoping she didn't sound too paranoid. "So, we're going to be neighbours," she added quickly, eager to change the subject.

"Yes. Fancy that, eh? Two Brits in the heart of *La Serenissima,* sharing the same steps, like shared driveways."

Both women paused as Armando reached the top of the steps, panting. He gently deposited her case, removed his hat, and nodded respectfully at both women.

"Buongiorno, Armando," Aurora said.

The man nodded again before scurrying off.

"He doesn't talk much," Aurora said.

"No, I've noticed," Sofia agreed.

There was a pause. A wood pigeon cooed. Crows cawed. Boats hummed in the distance.

"So, Contessa DaTerra. Do you have a key?" Aurora asked.

Sofia looked at her bag. "Yes, I do," she said, retrieving the envelope and feeling the weight in her hand once more.

Open only if you wish to commit to the terms of the will.

"Is something wrong?" Aurora asked, noticing her reticence.

Sofia forced a laugh. "I…um… no, it's just… I'm feeling a bit nervous," she admitted to the stranger.

"Well, of course you are, darling. This is the beginning of a whole new adventure for you," the woman said sympathetically. "I know how I felt when I first got here. Scared shitless."

Sofia laughed. She hadn't known the lady two minutes but hearing her say a vulgar word seemed odd for someone so stylish.

"But then I just thought of my divorce settlement, and it made me feel so much better. You'll be surprised how a healthy bank account does wonders for your confidence," Aurora added with a wry smile.

Sofia walked over to the door that was twice her height. It looked more like one of those big castle doors made of thick wood, lashed together by bars of steel. And yet it wasn't this that caught her attention, but the thing attached to the front of it.

She'd never seen anything like it before. It was an ugly thing. Like one of those gargoyles she'd seen dangling off buildings. Had

Aurora not been standing behind her, she would have most likely recoiled from it.

The life-sized intricate wood carving was a head and face of some kind of male imp creature with what looked like three horns sprouting from his skull, with the middle one a metal rod. The thing appeared to be grinning at her in such a malevolent way that it sent a shiver skittering down her spine. And what was that sprouting out of its scalp? Was that… real hair?

"Il Burlone," Aurora offered.

"I'm sorry?" Sofia said, unable to take her eyes off the thing.

"It's the joker. You know, from a pack of cards. This one here is a Venetian variation. Part joker, part gargoyle. They're pretty common in Venice. It is said they ward off evil spirits."

"Oh right," Sofia said. "That's different." She still thought it was ugly.

Aurora patted her on the arm. "Don't worry. It's just an ostentatious doorknocker. You'll get used to it."

Sofia wasn't sure about that. The thing didn't appear to have eyes, only blank planed wood that made it look like its eyeballs had rolled into the back of its head, yet it still seemed to observe her somehow and the packet in her hand.

She looked at the tear strip, waiting to be ripped open, for what felt like the hundredth time.

She wished the lawyer hadn't said anything to her. He made the whole thing sound so much more dramatic. She probably wouldn't be thinking twice about it had he not made such an ominous statement. Her heart was in her throat, for crying out loud, and her palms were already clammy in anticipation.

Just do it!

She felt Aurora take a step closer as if eagerly awaiting her decision. The cold breeze was back too, stroking her hair, coaxing her to step inside to bring the sounds of the ancient city with her: the melodic hum of its people, its laughter and chaos, and the upbeat notes of an accordion far away.

"Oh, sod it," she hissed, tearing the strip and pulling out a large metal key. It was heavy. Rusty-looking. Like it was literally centuries old. No wonder it weighed so much: It was solid bronze.

She checked the envelope for any additional instructions. There were none.

"Okay," she said, stepping forward. Avoiding eye contact with the watching grotesque, she found the keyhole and pushed the key into it with a loud clunk. It produced a large clanging sound as she turned it, as if she were opening giant rusty gates and not a front door. She half expected a hiss and a cloud of dust to escape from it, as if she'd just breached the seal of an ancient sarcophagus. Instead, the birds that had watched proceedings from their perch on the roof screeched and flew away in a loud flutter of wings, startling the two women. The voice that was singing in the distance stopped and the world went momentarily silent.

The Countdown had begun. 10 days left.

The two neighbours looked at each other for a few seconds and then laughed.

"Would you like to come in?" Sofia asked. She had no idea what to expect, but the thought of having somebody to explore with appealed to her.

Her neighbour looked at the door with fleeting eagerness but then said quickly, "No. No, my darling. Thanks for asking, but I think this is something you should do on your own."

Sofia nodded but must have looked crestfallen.

"That said," Aurora quickly added, "you must come over for dinner. Only if you don't have other plans this evening, of course."

"Other plans? You're the only person I've talked to properly since I've got here. Armando and I haven't quite been able to have a real conversation."

"Then it's a date. You go take a tour. Get settled in and all, then see how you feel."

"Thank you, Aurora. That's very nice of you."

"Think nothing of it. Dinner is normally served around eight. The boys are going to be so excited," she added enthusiastically, before taking a step backward as if she'd suddenly remembered she needed to be elsewhere.

"Yes. Eight sounds lovely. Thank you so much."

With that the woman turned and hurried away. Sofia watched her expertly navigate the uneven stone path in her heels and shook her head before turning back to the door.

She took a deep breath and pushed on it. It was heavy and resisted at first. She almost thought that it hadn't unlocked properly, but with a bit of an extra shove and despite it creaking in protest, it yielded.

Entering Palazzo Rosso was like stepping into another world, painted in the colours of opulence, built with walls of history.

She found herself in what looked like the inside of a dome chapel with ornate white columns. They rose to an intricate ceiling fresco of a mythical creature—half muscular man, half beast—reaching for the giant oculus that flooded the space with light. Flanking her were two wall niches. One exhibited a stone statue of a muscular and well-endowed male who wore a crown and carried a spear, while the other was of a beautiful naked female, also crowned and holding a bow and arrow. Sofia was in no way an art connoisseur and yet the intricate detail of both the sculptures was not lost on her, nor was the beauty of their respective nakedness. In fact, she was surprised to discover that she rather *enjoyed* it.

She raised an eyebrow at herself and moved swiftly on.

But Sofia didn't get far before she had to pause once more to take a breath. The grandeur was unlike anything she had experienced before, beyond her visits to stately homes. She had emerged from the entrance into what looked like a ballroom. The spacious room with its high ceiling was fantastically opulent and could easily fit her old house twice over inside. It featured large crystal chandeliers and a ceiling painted as a sky filled with flora and fauna. There were gilded walls of ancient frescos, cornices of gold, and a marble floor of crimson and white check.

To her left, like a giant rococo-inspired art installation, was a sweeping staircase of ornate gold that spiralled both up and down to the next floors.

It was only when a cold chill prodded at her cheek that Sofia realised, she was gawping. She had no idea how long she had stood there taking it in.

She turned. Directly ahead, two giant double balcony doors filled the space with daylight. They were festooned with velvet red drapes that swayed in the breeze. Nearby, a clutch of deep red upholstered sofas had been strategically placed diagonally so as to face each other and the view.

Sofia crossed the room, stepped out onto the balcony, and caught her breath. She was looking over the terrazzo orchard below. Beyond that was the bustle of Venice's Grand Canal lined by a technicolour of historic architecture, with one side stretching as far as the eye could see into the distance and the other leading to Antonio da Ponte's unmistakable Venetian landmark—formerly, the only way to cross the Grand Canal for over 260 years—the Rialto Bridge.

Sofia threw a hand to her mouth to stifle an excited squeal before allowing herself a furtive jiggle of a dance. But a sudden memory of her father called an end to the impromptu festivity. Alan Cooper would have loved this place. He was all about travel and history. She imagined his reaction to seeing this view and her heart swelled. *Don't mind if I do.* She could hear him speaking those very words as if he was standing beside her.

Suddenly, Sofia's balloon of excitement deflated, and she came crashing back down to the balcony once more.

What good was this place if she didn't have anybody to share it with?

You will, she thought positively. After all, she'd been in Venice barely a couple of hours and had already met her neighbour and fellow compatriot.

Back inside, she paused to take a closer look at the frescos.

It was odd. She hadn't noticed it before. She must have been so awestruck that she missed the detail, but the frescos… well, not only had they spread to some of the walls, but they appeared to have changed which, of course, was ridiculous. And yet she could have sworn that the ceiling was a depiction of a beautiful blue sky when she came in, but now it appeared to have morphed into a gloriously colourful display of womanhood. Females of all shapes and sizes. Rich, poor, clothed or nude. Gold hair, black hair, auburn, and white. Damsels and warriors. All were depicted in a variety of settings. It was a visual celebration of both the fragility and strength of the female of the species. And it was stunning.

She absorbed the creative spectacle for several minutes, enjoying the intricate detail while half expecting it to change again. But it didn't, of course.

Near the staircase was a sideboard of a kind she had never seen before. Made of heavy dark wood with baroque markings, it was clearly from a different century. Yet it gleamed as if it were new, as did the crystal vase of white roses and the silver stand laden with a bounty of exotic fruits. Giant black grapes winked at her under the light. She couldn't resist plucking one and popping it in her mouth. It was deliciously sweet and so fragrantly juicy it was almost as if she could taste its purpleness.

She was reaching for another when she noticed the canvas hanging high on the intersection of the staircase. It was a portrait of a rather striking lady, with white hair artistically piled atop her head, dressed in a beautiful crimson ballgown. Her pose was regal, with her hands crossed at the front, and she donned an enigmatic smile as if she knew all the secrets of the world. Nobility for sure. Probably a former contessa. Maybe a relative of some kind. Maybe distant. Maybe as close as a grandmother. She made a mental note to research. Although a quick glance at her phone told her that there didn't appear to be any Wi-Fi in the building.

She didn't linger. There was much to explore. That, and she found the painting a little creepy. Nothing obvious. It was just the eyes again, like the gargoyle on the front door. It felt as if they were watching her, following her around the room as they peered out of that gold frame. As if she wasn't an artist's rendition but a real person trapped inside there.

Sofia crossed in front of the stairs and paused at the door of another spacious room. It housed a large heavy-set banquet table at its centre with room enough for twelve people. It was resplendent, the wood glimmering in the light. Someone had obviously scrubbed and polished every surface to an immaculate standard. The air was thick with the scent of lavender, the waxed surfaces rich with it.

The walls were gilded gold. The ceiling was a series of frescos of handsome sailing boats navigating the waters of the Venetian lagoons.

Beautiful. And yet, again, she couldn't help but feel a stab of loneliness. The table looked so big.

You can fill it with children!

The thought just popped into her head. Of course, she'd need a husband first. *Hey, you can dream.*

She left the dining room and stopped at the stairs as clouds passed in front of the sun, casting elongated shadows over the walls, momentarily animating the frescos. For a second, she thought they might change. But they didn't.

She looked down the steps into the darkness below and then up towards the light as that chill whistled through the curtains.

She paused and looked around the space. It was empty. Somewhere, a clock ticked loudly. Boats hummed outside, reminding her again that she wasn't alone in the world.

She glanced at the darkness below once more but chose to grab her case and climb the steps instead, eager to see where she would be sleeping tonight.

She followed the curve of the balustrade, tracing fingers over the elaborate swirled carvings until she reached the top to realise that it wasn't a corridor but a wide gallery that overlooked the ballroom. She had a vision of herself standing there, dressed in an 18th century ballgown, fanning herself while watching the dancing below. She laughed. Yes, she'd read way too much Jane Austen.

The sumptuously lavish décor continued with more frescos, gilded walls, and cornices trimmed in gold.

She realised that the artwork up here mirrored the piece on womanhood below except this featured the male of the species. One particularly unusual image was of a naked muscular man sprawled on a bed with his head in the lap of a semi-naked female in flowing robes while around them a group of children of all ages, sexes, and sizes looked on.

Sofia had no clue what the imagery was supposed to represent—fertility, maybe—but something told her that Aurora might know. She would invite her over for drinks sometime.

It appeared that the palazzo was ultimately a gigantic luxurious townhouse in a city where land was quite literally at a premium.

This place must be worth an absolute fortune!

There were three spacious rooms up here. The first led to another impressive space of golden chandeliers, with parquet tile peeking out from under an ornate pink, red, and gold floor tapestry. The room contained a giant bed and sumptuous couches upholstered in delicate floral fabrics of greens and pinks. The next room was similar.

At the opposite end of the hallway was what could only be the master bedroom. It exuded regal elegance with its gleaming marble floors etched with hieroglyphic patterns, polished wood walls, and ornate gold panelling. The room was awash with light from the circular glass ceiling, revealing a pale blue sky painted with white fluffy clouds.

Sofia gasped, feeling as though she had discovered the private chambers of royalty in an ancient castle. She half expected to be ushered out by an attendant and returned to the lower public viewing galleries at any second.

Was this real? It couldn't be, could it? She felt underdressed just walking into this room. It was like something out of a fairy tale. A gothic rendition of one, perhaps, for the panelling that lined the walls was resplendent, yet dark and heavy.

A giant bed took up one side of the room. King-size maybe? Bigger? Sofia wasn't sure. It sat on its own platform reached by three steps. The whole area was wrapped in a large alcove of intricate wood carvings. She was about to go over to inspect it in more detail when movement on the opposite side of the room caught her eye. White gold leaf voiles swayed languidly in the breeze.

She crossed the room and looked out. It was the small piazza with an archway to the dock on one side and the bridge to the rest of the city on the other. A couple floated down the canal in a gondola. A group of four girls giggled as they paused on the other side of the bridge to take a selfie. Italian folk music from one of the nearby houses sailed on the wind.

One of the girls spotted her looking down from the balcony and waved. She waved back and was overwhelmed by a sudden pang of loneliness. She missed Janay and regretted once more what had happened between her and Victoria.

She pulled out her phone. Full bars! She didn't hesitate to find Janay in her contacts and ring her number. But the line kept dropping. She tried again. Same, so she tapped out a message instead. *IS ANYBODY THERE?!*

MESSAGE FAILED.

"Shit!" she hissed.

That's when she heard them. She first thought it was more people in the square below, but when she looked down there was nobody there. It was strange because she could have sworn that she heard talking and giggling and yet… that's when she realised. The sound wasn't coming from outside but inside the palazzo.

Slowly, she turned around and, pushing the voiles aside, stepped forward.

"Hello?"

It took a while for her eyes to readjust but gradually the room came back into focus. It was empty.

"Hello?"

Nothing.

She took another step forward. "Hello? Is anybody in here?"

SLAM!

She yelped. Hand to her chest. Heart in her throat.

It's okay, Sofia. It's just the bedroom door in the draft.

"Oh shit," she laughed nervously, as she caught sight of her reflection in the full-length mirror before pausing to admire it. Oh, it was stunning. Like most of the furniture in the room, including the nearby vanity desk with cushioned seat, it was fashioned from wood. Yet it was somehow different, and she felt immediately drawn to it as it stood proud in the dimly lit room.

It wasn't as ostentatious as the other furniture. It looked heavier. Darker. More gothic. It was nonetheless beautiful in its simplicity, with simple markings carved into the wood frame. Sofia smiled and was about to ask it who the fairest of them all was when she noticed the reflection of the bed in the background.

"Oh my…" she breathed. How could she have missed them? And yet there they were, sculpted into the wood panelling of the alcove. A dozen or so, carved with such meticulous detail they looked real, like they had simply fused to the walls.

She turned from the mirror and walked over.

At first glance, they gave the impression of typical cherubs, but on closer inspection they were more like figures of children of all ages, sexes, and sizes, with some chubby and others slender. The elder ones were defined and muscular, some with wings and others without. Each one was a miniature work of art, capturing every aspect of their subjects' innocent and playful nature. From chubby cheeks to dimpled chins, each had his or her own expression, with every line and curve expertly fashioned to give the illusion of life. They were angled to face different directions all around the room. Only two of them were leaning into each other, with mischievous expressions on their faces, as if they were sharing the most intimate of secrets. Others were more solitary, aloof, gazing at the bed, upward, or out towards the balcony and city beyond.

Above them, carved in the wood panelling of the ceiling as if tending to their offspring, were the naked forms of a man and a woman. Surrounding them all were equally intricate carvings of leaves, acorns, and other symbols of nature. Each leaf was sculpted in such detail that it was almost possible to see the veins and the curve of the stem. All of these carvings were arranged around the figurines in a harmonious and beautiful way, completing the dramatic overall effect of the grand canopy.

The whole thing was so realistic that Sofia expected one of the figurines to blink at her.

Just the thought of that sent a shiver down her spine, but she shrugged it away. Palazzo Rosso was enormous, intimidating and, yes, a little creepy.

Okay, a lot creepy.

But if she was going to last here, she needed to start with the right mindset. So, she tore her eyes away from the carvings and made her way across the room to another door.

The bathroom. It was just how she expected. Gorgeous. Resplendent. There was a claw copper bath and a walk-in shower. A giant hanging mirror reflected the light from a large circular window which she imagined must look out over the stone steps to the front door. The window was too high up for anybody to see inside or for her to see out without climbing onto something, but Sofia could hear voices and see shadows cast on nearby buildings, which she found oddly comforting.

Palazzo Rosso was everything she had hoped for and more. It was regal, ostentatious, bourgeoisie, and very much gothic in places. And it might feel a bit lonely right now, but she was confident that would change as she settled in and started making friends. Who knows, maybe even a boyfriend if she was lucky.

She looked at herself in the gorgeous mirror and reminded herself that she hadn't just checked into a fancy hotel. This was to be her new home for the foreseeable future. A thrill rippled through her, and she grinned at her reflection.

She turned the claw tap on the sink and the water sputtered before hissing itself clear and steady. She watched it circle the basin. Oddly it didn't seem to wet it, as if the thing were coated in some kind of repellent.

She ran the water over her fingers. The pressure was good. She'd freshen up and go for an exploratory walk, maybe even have a bite to eat. Afterwards, she would attempt to contact England once more.

She splashed water on her face. One, two, three times and then screamed. For there, in the mirror, was the unmistakable reflection of someone standing in the doorway behind her.

3

FUGITIVE

GREENFIELDS, ENGLAND.

WEDNESDAY MORNING

What am I looking at?" Detective Inspector Patricia King asked, cringing at the stench of smouldering wood and…

She didn't even want to consider what the other acrid stench was because she'd already attended more *cruel and unusual*—as her new partner would put it—crime scenes in the last week than she had during her entire time on the force.

They were standing in front of the charred remains of the stables at Greenfields. They'd only visited this place a few days ago. Now, it looked like the smouldering remains of a gigantic bonfire in the middle of a field.

"A neighbour on the nearby farm saw the flames in the early hours of this morning and called it in," Detective Sergeant Jayson Butler narrated, producing a notebook from the inside pocket of his suit jacket.

King thought the man took himself way too seriously with all the power dressing, but then again, he was young. And, as much as she hated to draw the comparison, she wasn't much different when she first started. Hungry. Eager to be taken seriously.

"Please tell me this was an accident," she said, eyeing the plumes of smoke snaking up into a grey slate sky that was spitting rain. Around them, firefighters gathered their gear. The inferno had flamed fiercely but quickly, burning itself out before they had even arrived.

"The fire burned unusually hot, apparently. Incinerated everything, including the horses that were stabled here."

"Any accelerants?" King asked, frowning, and wiping the back of her hand over her nose, as if the action might in some way expel the stench that she could feel permeating her clothes, hair, and skin.

"Well, no, that's just it. The fire service hasn't found any evidence of foul play. Early indication is that it was an accident, although we won't truly know until the post-mortem findings are in."

"Body count?"

"Two so far. Not much left of the bodies to be sure, but preliminary thinking is that it's a male and female."

"Mr and Mrs?"

"Most likely. Again, hard to tell without DNA analysis. Fire crew seem to think the point of origin was most likely one of those oil lanterns."

"Oil lanterns?"

"They found several of them in there. If you remember, they were hanging on hooks inside. I thought they were just ornamental."

"You remember that?" King asked.

"It's my job."

"Ornamental? Is that even a word?" King asked with a scowl. Butler smiled wryly.

"Any ideas why no spread?" King nodded at the nearby trees that led into the woods and then to the back of the house.

Butler rocked his head. King no doubt already had a theory, but he played along. "Yeah, it's odd, but not unheard of. There's quite a gap between here and those trees. And to the back of the house. Also, I did a quick check. Bit of a weird one. The weather forecast had it as clear with a touch of frost. And yet last night, an hour or so before the fire, nearest weather station reported gale force winds and rain for this area. Didn't last long though."

"Obviously not, since it didn't seem to have any effect on the fire," King said pensively.

Butler nodded.

"What about the friend that was supposed to be staying with them. The timid one. Whatshername?"

"Cooper. Sophie Cooper. Twenty-one."

"Yeah, her."

"Well, this is the interesting bit."

"More interesting than a couple and their two horses roasting to death?" King said flatly.

"Well, depends on your point of view. And there were three horses in there, not two."

King turned and gave the younger man a pointed look.

Butler cleared his throat and explained. "There was a third horse. It was found wandering in the woods. We've arranged to have it picked up by a local sanctuary. They should be here—"

"We were talking about little Miss Cooper," King interrupted.

"Right. It would appear that little Miss Cooper has left the country," he said with a lift of the eyebrows.

King frowned. "When you say *has left the country,* you're not talking Scotland or Wales, are you?"

"Nope. According to her friend, she talked about leaving for Italy to claim some inheritance she'd just come into."

"What kind of inheritance?"

"A house."

"A house?"

"No. Sorry. Not a house. A *palazzo* were her words," he said, reading from his notes. "They had agreed that she was going to go see her psychiatrist, but—"

"Wait. Her psychiatrist?"

"Yep. And it gets better. She's been seeing this bloke for the best part of her life, apparently. Lately, she'd also been struggling with the recent death of her dad."

"Struggling. Struggling how?"

Butler rocked his head and was about to speak when he was interrupted by a sudden horse whinny that visibly startled King. He suppressed a chuckle and, as casually as he could, said, "That's the horse that got out." He nodded at the animal that was watching all the activity from a distance.

"Do we know how it escaped?"

Butler shrugged. "No. I expect that one just bolted the moment the fire started."

"But not the others?" King asked.

Butler shrugged.

King nodded as they both gazed at the beautiful horse with fluffy white feet and glorious mane.

"Yeah, so, Cooper's friend, Janay Evans, said that they had agreed that Cooper was going to see her doctor before making any rash decisions, but instead she just never showed. The friend got worried and called us. And then, this morning, she received a handwritten note from Cooper where she said she had to leave. Evans hasn't heard from her since."

"Do we know the name of this psychiatrist? And why exactly she was seeing him?"

"We do. He's name is Krauss. Albert. But I'm not expecting him to say much. Doctor-patient confidentiality and all that shite."

"Okay, hold on. Let me see if I've got this right. Cooper, this twenty-something-year-old girl—the same one that looked like she wouldn't say boo to a goose—just happened to live next door to the girl that was brutally murdered and across from the man who had his penis bitten off, as well as the parents who've had their baby abducted. She was friends with the posh bird whose husband cheated on her with that estate agent, both of whom we believe met their demise here along with a couple of their pet horses on a night when she was expected to be staying over?"

Butler nodded.

"The same one who has now mysteriously left the country in a hurry without so much as a word to her best friend beforehand?"

Butler made a face.

"Have we tried contacting her?"

"Yep," he said with another knowing face.

"Go on," King prompted.

"Her phone's dead. Friend said she bricked it by dropping it in the bath."

"Convenient. What about this inheritance thing? Does it check out?"

"Still looking into that. Friend says she went to see a London firm of solicitors. She was coming back from there that night we met her."

"Have you—"

"Already called. Waiting for a call back."

There was a long pause as both the detectives considered what they had just pulled together. Nearby birds tweeted, unaffected by the tragedy before them. Flecks of black soot attempted to fly away from the scene of their creation but were washed down by the drizzle.

King cleared her throat not because she had anything to say, but because the acrid stench of burnt wood and flesh was starting to trigger her gag reflex.

"Are you thinking what I'm thinking?" Butler prompted.

King bit her lip. "It's all a bit sus, but circumstantial at best. Doesn't mean I wouldn't love having a chat with her. Keep trying that lawyer and then get me a contact at Interpol. I want to know what our options are."

4

LA SERENISSIMA

VENICE. WEDNESDAY EVENING.

Her dress rustled as she made her way down the red velvet steps and through the crowd. There were people everywhere. All dressed in their finery. All exhilarated by the anonymity that his or her mask afforded. They were free. Liberated from the burden of command and released from the shackles of social inadequacies.

Anything was possible here. Tonight.

And yet all she could think about was him. She could sense him standing behind her. Feel his heart thrumming as one with her own, surging through the fibres of the carpet and spreading through the minerals of the stone to touch her. To stimulate her body in a way that took her breath away.

The sensation was sensual, delicious, moreish as it kissed the nape of her neck and tickled her inner thigh.

With an enigmatic smile on her immaculately painted lips, she lifted her gown off the floor and made her way forward, passing faceless people flowing in the opposite direction as she descended the steps to the two red doors.

He was still following her, of that she was sure. The pulse emanating from the heat of his body was much stronger now. She needed, wanted, yearned for him. Right here. Right now. And yet she didn't dare turn to lay eyes on him. Not yet. It wasn't time. But soon. Very soon.

She clutched the gold handle of the door on the left, pulled it open and stepped through into a narrow footway lined with flowers. The scent was rich and intoxicating while all around her the bells of the Campanile tolled loudly, urging, and beckoning everyone to Mass.

It was time to pay homage. It was time for everyone to go. Shoes clacking, robes rustling, mouths whispering.

"It's time."

Sofia's eyes snapped open. Somebody had spoken those words. A man. She wasn't dreaming. Was she?

No. At least not completely. She was in Venice. There was no mistaking the sounds beyond the balcony, the slosh of the water against stone and that ubiquitous call of seagulls.

She was curled up on one of the couches in the ballroom that, while clean, smelt musty and damp, like those seaside cottages she'd stayed in as a child.

Dad.

Without moving from her position, head lying on folded hands, she watched the flickering rainbow reflection of the water shining in through the balcony doors as it danced off the walls. It was beautiful. Mesmerising.

On a giant coffee table in front of her was a spread of sliced bread with an assortment of cheese and meats. Carafes of water and wine stood nearby.

She sat up. She didn't put that stuff there. The memory filtered back and invoked a groan.

The creepy housekeeper turned out to be nowhere near as amiable as Armando the caretaker. The woman, who must be in her late sixties, had all the attributes of Mrs Danvers of Du Maurier's Rebecca and was scarier, even. At least that's what Sofia had concluded, as unkind as the thought probably was. But the woman did sneak up on her in the bathroom, all dressed in black with her hair scraped into a cruel bun and one good and one filmy white cataractous eye glaring. Scared the bloody life out of her.

Worse, the woman didn't even say anything or give her a smile. Nothing. She just gave Sofia a disapproving look before skulking back off into the shadows.

Maybe she wasn't the housekeeper after all. Maybe she was some crazy ghost haunting the place. It was a flippant thought, of course. The woman had been wearing an apron and carrying a mop and bucket.

Nonetheless, the incident had spooked her so much that she'd grabbed her bag and run out of the place. She'd had no clue where she was going, but as long as she was out in the fresh air she hadn't cared.

It was only after she'd put some distance between her and the incident that she realised just how ridiculous she was being. It was understandable. Palazzo Rosso wasn't your average home. It was an imposing and somewhat intimidating place to arrive at without so much as a tour. After all, if she was honest with herself, she recognised that she had a somewhat fantastical mind. It didn't consciously feel that way to her but, as Doctor Krauss would say, that's the fastest way for one to become unravelled from the moorings of reality. Or some sort of similar rubbish.

How would she ever cope without the man, she wondered. It scared her a little. But at the same time, she was excited by the challenge of mastering her own mind rather than having someone manipulate it into something manageable for her.

She admonished herself. The thought was much harsher than she'd intended. Oh well, it was there now.

A pale blue sky and lots of wintry sunshine had soon lifted her spirits. She came to love having no clue where she was or where she was going. It felt like a whole new adventure and Sofia—and perhaps even old Sophie—loved every second of it.

Most of the time she simply used the technique she'd learned with that American family. She lingered around groups of tourists and listened out for any nuggets of touristy information, such as how Venice got its nickname.

Did you know that the title of 'Serenissimo' was first given to the Doge and the Signoria before it was extended to cover the whole Republic of Venice? With Serenissimo being the masculine form of the word and Serenissima, with an a, being the feminine form. From the outside world Venice was also seen as a *serene* place, free from all the turmoil affecting all the other cities at the time.—

Yes, that's all very fascinating, Margaret, but can we go get a cup of tea now? My feet are killing me!

Sofia's strategy of listening in to other people's conversations meant that she unfortunately had to witness a few more explosive domestics.

It was at this point that she decided to simply follow the crowds over bridges, down and up stone steps until the majesty of Piazza San Marco opened up before her. It turned out it was much closer than she thought.

It was an emotional moment. She had seen the place mentioned so many times on travel shows, online, on posters, and, of course, at the airport's arrival and departure screens. To find herself standing there in person, as a resident, was beyond overwhelming.

She spent several minutes ogling the iconic Torre dell'Orologio and marvelling at the Basilica. It was decorated with Byzantine art treasures which, she overheard, were part of the booty brought back by Venetian ships after the fall of Constantinople. And, of course, there was the jewel in the crown: Palazzo Ducale, or Doge's Palace, and the Bridge of Sighs. She considered going inside but the visit would have constituted the realisation of a lifelong dream. She wanted to savour every moment and decided that she'd come back. After all, she had plenty of time.

And so, it was onward with a visit to one of the world's most beautiful bookshops, the workshop of a family of artisan mask makers, then finally, a museum, before stopping off at a café for an espresso and fritole. She'd seen them in the window. The traditional sweet fried pastry ball dusted in powdered sugar was a traditional treat during Carnevale, so she felt she should make the most of it.

At one point she had to check herself to make sure she wasn't daydreaming again. She was behaving nothing like the neurotic introvert she'd known all these years. In fact, she didn't feel anything like her usual self. And she loved it.

She spent the rest of the day mingling with the crowds and photographing random strangers in their spectacular carnival costumes. She even conversed with some of the locals, albeit with some difficulty.

Several hours later, she somehow found her way back to Palazzo Rosso, happy but thoroughly exhausted.

Now, as the Campanile chimed the top of the hour, she thought about Janay and Victoria.

She had attempted to reach both of them while she was out, eager to share all her adventures, yet, once again, she was unable to do so. But it was no problem. She'd visit an internet café tomorrow and retry from there instead. There was obviously something wrong with her phone.

Now, as she watched the rainbow reflections dim with the setting sun, she stretched and considered what to do next. She might venture back to the square. She might even—

"Oh shit! Dinner!"

She looked at the clock. It was seven fifteen.

She raced up the stairs, down the corridor, and into her new bedroom. She had no idea what she was going to wear. Everything she brought with her was practical. Most of it was creased and she had no clue if this place even had an iron. She wondered if the housekeeper was still in the building somewhere. Maybe she could ask her. Maybe she would take care of those kind of things for her?

She pulled the doors open to the wardrobe—it was a huge heavy-set thing of dark wood and intricate carvings—and froze. Her suitcase was gone. All of her clothes were now hanging neatly off wooden hangers along with an array of other items she did not recognise.

Dresses. Gowns. Blouses. Skirts. Coats. At least two dozen items in a range of colours. She was no expert—fashion was Victoria's thing—but they looked stylish in a vintage-chic kind of way. Victoria would have gone mad over it all.

She pulled a few items out and held them to her body. She could be imagining it, but it appeared as if all of these things were in her size. Had somebody shopped for her?

She looked around the room as if the anonymous benefactor might be sitting nearby, waiting for a fashion show. But she was alone. Though it didn't feel that way.

It was weird. Although the building felt cavernous and empty, she never felt completely alone. It was a peculiar feeling. Both comforting and terrifying.

But she shrugged the sensation off and turned back to look down towards the foot of the wardrobe. Sure enough, boxes. A whole row of them. Full of shoes. And these were definitely her size. Somebody had definitely been shopping for her. But who?

Time was ticking.

She pulled out the one thing that seemed a little more her speed: a black lacey pantsuit. Most of the footwear had heels so she opted for a pair of ankle-strapped wedges.

She threw everything onto the bed and ran into the bathroom, stripping as she went.

5

LIGHT & SHADOWS

VENICE. WEDNESDAY EVENING.

The sun had already bid farewell to Sofia's first Venetian day by the time she was pulling the palazzo's heavy wooden door shut with a loud echoey thud. She looked out at the vista before her and smiled. Fiery red rooftops glowed in the afterlight like hot embers, before slowly fading to grey. The air smelt sweet, like the end of a summer's day, but that ever-present cold wind was still patrolling the area, blowing across the surface of the canal and funnelling through narrow passageways up to the stone steps, to play with Sofia's freshly brushed hair like the fingers of restless children.

It was as she was trying to get ready that Sofia realised that she didn't have any of her creature comforts with her. She needed to change that, so she made a mental note to ask Aurora at some point during the evening for some advice on where best to shop for such things.

In the meantime, she had settled for using a pretty but unusually heavy hairbrush that she had found on a silver tray on the vanity desk in her bedroom. It was there alongside an array of other beauty accessories, including perfume bottles that appeared to be untouched.

Was it all hers? She needed to talk to the lawyer. For now, she told herself that she was borrowing those things, as much as it pained her to do so. She was no expert, but the vanity desk alone must be worth a few thousand. It was made of wood with fanciful carvings and painted silver. It looked like the real deal. Which was why she couldn't truly relax. Like a child in a stranger's house, she was perpetually terrified of dirtying or damaging something. An act that would no doubt put her on a warpath with the housekeeper from hell.

Sofia had no idea as to the customary gift one brought to a neighbourly dinner in Venice. Aurora was undoubtedly a woman of style and bringing her the bottle of Italian wine from a brand she did not recognise that she had found in one of the kitchen cupboards somehow felt inadequate. Even so, it was exactly what she was carrying. It was better than going empty-handed, after all.

She crossed the crest of the steps and looked down into the dimly lit gloom of the via below and wondered what it would feel like to take a tumble down there. The mere thought of fragile flesh impacting against cold stone sent a shiver down her spine.

Sharing steps instead of a driveway was something Sofia had never experienced before. She liked it. Especially when she had to cross the tiny narrow bridge over the canal. It was like crossing a drawbridge to a fort. Particularly as, instead of the usual garden lights, her path appeared to be lit by lanterns.

The front door continued with this theme. Not unlike Palazzo Rosso's, it appeared to be made of solid wood, bound by black metal rods of steel, and branded with a series of unusual symbols she couldn't decipher.

It was lit by two burning torches that completed the medieval look, though Sofia—or perhaps more Sophie—couldn't help but wonder if placing naked flames outside your front door wasn't a bit of a safety hazard.

Really? You're worried about bloody health and safety?

Sofia shook her head at herself. That was what working at the airport had done to her; everything needed an on-the-spot risk assessment.

Ugh. Work. She hadn't really thought about that place since sending Steve that letter and had no intention of starting now. Despite the odd pang of apprehension about her decision to leave England and her old life, she was happy. There. She had admitted it to herself. She had had a wonderful day and, for the first time since her father's funeral, she was allowing herself a real moment of happiness. Was that so wrong?

She spotted a red rope and tassel hanging out of a hole in the wall. She pulled on it, expecting to hear a bell clang somewhere, but there was nothing except an odd fusion of rhythmic percussion and Celtic music, pushing its way out under the door and rushing off to join the many merriments she could hear coming from other parts of the city.

A minute or so passed. She half expected to hear bare feet slapping on stone as someone approached the door but there was nothing.

She spun around, sensing something. Night was fast devouring the last dregs of daylight, yet it was still bright enough to see that the path behind her was empty. Strange. She was sure she had felt someone standing right behind her. But she was alone.

She pulled the rope again. Twice this time. She was eager to get inside, but when that yielded nothing, she stepped back from the building. There were small windows on the ground and first floor. It almost seemed as though they were painted black, but this could only be an illusion. It was obviously just dark inside, everywhere but upstairs where she could see that one of the windows was glowing amber. There *was* someone inside.

"Aurora?" she called up.

There was singing on the streets below. Laughter. Music. But no reply from anybody inside the house.

She considered leaving. Aurora had obviously changed her mind. But first she walked forward and thumped on the door. As she did so, she noticed that, now that daylight was almost faded away, the symbols were clearer somehow, brighter, as if glowing under the flickering torchlight.

She moved in for a closer look before drawing in a sharp breath. The carvings, underlined by an iron bar, were of a group of naked horned beings, seemingly defiling a clutch of naked females as well as the occasional male. The detail was astonishing, more akin to a painting than something that had been carved into wood. She almost expected one of those things to turn and look up at her with lustful eyes.

She snatched her head away. One of them just did! It moved!

She blinked and refocussed. *That's silly.* It was just a trick of the light and her own overactive imagination. She knew exactly what this was about. It was about everything else here. She was the proverbial fish out of water, and she was already starting to manufacture reasons why she shouldn't remain.

Well, I am. I'm staying.

Frustrated, she tried turning the loop handle. It clicked and swung open with a loud atmospheric creak.

The chamber music was much louder now and a bittersweet fragrance of burning incense welcomed her.

"Aurora?" she called, trying to raise her voice over the music that she now realised was coming not from the second floor but from a doorway across the dimly lit entrance lobby.

There were no electrical lights in here. Everything appeared to be lit by the amber glow of flickering candles. They burned and glinted off the ornate gem-encrusted chandelier above her head and from the pewter candelabras set upon tables that were seemingly carved out of the natural shape of tree trunks.

"Aurora?" she called again.

Nothing.

"Aurora! It's Soph-ia!"

Her voice was loud and echoed around the walls. They were adorned by ornate wood panels featuring more carvings she couldn't identify—not that she particularly wanted to—and frescos of unrecognisable characters in woodlands and on riverbanks.

Her frustration was already dissipating, absorbed by the undulating shadows, and giving way to nervousness. She was, after all, venturing inside the inner sanctum of somebody else's home. She wasn't afraid though, she told herself.

Why would you be afraid?

Her heart, on the other hand, was already reacting to the fact that she had entered such a dark place without permission and was thumping against her ribcage, urging her to turn back.

I do have permission. I was invited.

No. You just let yourself in!

And yet she stepped forward.

"Aurora!"

She had barely got the word out of her mouth when her attention was drawn to the end of the hallway, to more undulating shadows and something else. Laughter. It was faint but loud enough to be heard over the music.

She took another step forward but stopped when she saw the

stairs to the next floor. At first, she thought it was a trick of the dim light, but when she moved closer, she could see that it wasn't, and the sight quite literally took the breath from her mouth.

It was a masterpiece and could only be the elaborate result of a film set created to be one of the most magical of fairy-tale movies. The thick branches of a naked tree, reminiscent of Jack's beanstalk, snaked up the side of wooden steps to create an elaborate natural handrail that disappeared into the ceiling. The effect was so realistic that Sofia felt compelled to reach out and touch it. There was no mistaking its texture. It was a real tree, confirmed by the heady aroma of terpenes and the musky fragrance of tree bark.

The realisation brought a smile to Sofia's face as she ran her fingers over the abrasive surface only to suddenly snatch them away.

She reached out once more. Slowly. Tentatively. Yes! There! Did she imagine that too? No. It was there. Faint, perhaps, but perceptible. A tiny current running through her fingers, up her arm, and through her body. A thrum like a lifeforce. The very same one she had experienced at Greenfields.

Loud laughter startled her, and she pulled her hand away once more.

Now, her eyes fully accustomed to the gloom, she made her way further down the entrance hall and crossed to an open doorway where the amber light glowed brighter.

She stepped inside to find herself standing in what looked like a giant observatory. Overhead, a giant cloth studded with twinkling lights appeared to have been fashioned into an oval shape, resembling an eye. It was only when Sofia spotted the now ubiquitous glow that she realised. It wasn't a piece of cloth at all but an oval window to a juvenile night sky, studded with stars. At its centre, like a queen bee in her hive, was the unmistakable glimmering coma of the comet. Sofia had completely forgotten about that thing. Right now, it looked like one of the most beautiful gems she'd ever seen. Still, there was something about it that unsettled her, and she must have drawn in a sharp breath or something because a voice suddenly spoke from inside the shadows.

"Ah, there you are. We've been expecting you," it said.

Sofia squinted through the candlelight to see Aurora's milky pearlescent shoulders peeking out from her velvet kaftan, her long black hair spilling, like ink, down her back to the base of her spine. She was sat in front of a large canvas, painting, although Sofia couldn't see what from her angle.

All around, the shadows ebbed and shifted as if the woman were performing to an audience.

"Please. There's nothing to fear, my lovely."

Sofia forced a laugh. "I...um...I'm not afraid."

"And yet you continue to view the portent as something evil."

"Portent?"

"The comet."

"Oh" was all Sofia could say. It seemed as if the woman had read her mind. Given the peculiar setting in which she found herself, it sent a skitter of a chill over her skin. "Well," she said, swallowing, "things haven't gone too well for me since it showed up."

"And yet here you are. A contessa of her own palace, no less, in the beautiful city of light and shadows. Please, come in. Don't be shy, my dearest Sofia. You are most welcome here. Most welcome."

She continued with her art.

"Painting by candlelight, as many of history's most renowned artists did too, is one of my favourite pastimes." Her arm moved over the canvas in short strokes.

Sofia tentatively stepped forward.

"Did you know that Sofia means wisdom in Greek?" Aurora

asked casually, eyes still on the task in hand.

"No, I didn't," Sofia responded with a shake of the head, as if the woman, her face still turned toward her canvas, could see her.

"Yes, it does. And Aurora means dawn. My favourite time of the day: the periphery between light and darkness."

Sofia stepped around her host, and, like a developing photo, the painting slowly came into view.

Two heads. Two men. Both had short hair though one was darker than the other. Blond hair was painted above a round face with pointy chin and neat, elvish-like ears. Black hair crowned a square face with a strong jawline and small ears. The figure of blond hair had a slim yet defined naked body, with an arm resting on one leg and a cheeky grin on his face. The man of dark hair possessed a thick muscular body, nude and leaning back onto a delicate chair, his two strong arms rippling. He had speckled stubble on his face and a lustful glint in his eyes.

"Wow," Sofia said, marvelling at the detail in the painting. "This is amazing."

"You like it?" Aurora asked.

"I love it. They look like ancient gods."

"Or demons," Aurora mused.

Sofia laughed. "Now that you mention it… definitely naughty little devils!"

"Good evening, Sofia."

The sound of men's voices greeting her in perfect synchronicity made her jump back, away from the painting, as if it had spoken to her.

"We are over here," said an amused voice in perfect English, but with an Italian inflection.

It took Sofia a few seconds to establish that the voice was not coming from the easel but from beyond it. She took another step forward and peeked around the canvas. Her eyes widened.

The two men in the painting were actually in the room, posing against a backdrop of red velvet and gold cushions. Both were naked.

Reflexively, Sofia shielded her eyes with her hand, as if wanting to spare the men's modesty. In truth, she was protecting her own.

Aurora laughed out loud. "Oh, isn't she adorable? It's just nakedness, Sofia," she chuckled with great enjoyment.

"I...um..." But Sofia couldn't find the words. It wasn't so much the nudity, although that was embarrassing enough considering that she had only just met these people. It was also the men's... um... assets. The painting may have depicted them as innocent statues of gods but there was nothing innocent about the generous appendages both men were proudly exhibiting between their legs. Sofia wasn't much of an expert on the subject, but the two men appeared to be particularly well endowed.

"My, my, Sofia, I do believe you are blushing," Aurora said with a big grin. "Isn't the Contessa adorable, boys?" she asked.

Both men nodded, but it was the one with the light hair who allowed his eyes to crawl, lingeringly, all over their guest. It compelled Sofia to look at herself for fear that she might have something on show that shouldn't be.

"Sofia, meet Daniele and Gabriele, or Daniel and Gabriel, if you prefer," Aurora declared, pointing at the two men in turn. "Aren't they fine specimens?" she asked conspiratorially.

All Sofia could do was nod.

"Oh, my divine girl!" Aurora declared suddenly. "My absolute favourite!" She was greedily eying the bottle Sofia had forgotten she was carrying.

"Really?"

"Absolutely. But so expensive. Are you sure you want to part with it?"

"I...um..." Sofia looked at the bottle.

"Not much of an expert, eh?" Aurora said, allowing the

northern origins of her accent to make an appearance, suddenly making her even more approachable. "You won't get much change from a thousand dollars, I'd say."

"What?" Sofia's eyes widened and she yelped when she almost dropped the thing. Aurora shrieked with laughter once more.

"Okay, boys," she said. "That'll be all for now. We'll pick this up again later. Now that our guest is here, it's time for supper. Take the bottle through too, but don't open it in case Sofia changes her mind. We'll be there shortly."

The men jumped up from their positions and confidently swung past Sofia, forcing her to avert her gaze once more. Daniele though, the fairest of the two men, turned back to her, sporting a mischievous smile. Sofia wasn't sure if the heat was in her cheeks or emanating from the man's nakedness. Then, slowly, he lifted a hand to her.

"May I?" he said, smile still intact.

Sofia wasn't sure what the man wanted and was about to give him her hand when she realised. He wanted the bottle. She handed it to him, and the man finally walked away.

"Are you offended by nakedness, Sofia?" Aurora asked.

Sofia was surprised by the question and unsure how to answer it. "Well, not really. It's just—"

"Just big cocks, eh?" Aurora laughed, her voice husky. The woman was obviously teasing.

Thank God it's dark in here.

"You know, my mother used to always say, 'Rora, if you're gonna have one, have a biggun'.' She was ya typical Northern lass." The words were spoken with a perfect Yorkshire dialect that sounded odd coming from the glamorous woman's lips. "You still seem surprised?" she asked, as if she had read Sofia's thoughts.

"I would never have pegged you as a Northern lass."

The woman leaned in. "Shh... let that be our secret," she said, placing a long bony finger on her cherry lips. Then she left her stool and stood, the velvet fabric of her kaftan falling around her slender frame and to the floor, as if it was being poured over her. "Please, join me," she said, extending a hand to her guest.

Sofia allowed herself to be led out of the room, into the hallway and through pools of light. Her host moved with the grace of royalty, the velvet caressing her every curve while the shadows appeared to stir, grow, and dissipate like smoke in her presence, a phenomenon that Sofia attributed to the candlelight.

She followed Aurora down the corridor, past the staircase, across the entrance, and into a large rectangular room.

A black chandelier laden with red candles hung over a heavy blackwood dining table. It featured two more ornately carved candelabras and a veritable banquet of food. From roast piglet to stuffed birds, from pies to a cornucopia of fruit. Crystal glasses, wine carafes, and silverware winked under the amber glow. There was no tablecloth, just a decorative grape and gold-coloured runner.

Aurora headed for a throne chair of heavy-set wood at the top of the table and paused.

"Is something wrong?" she asked when she spotted that her guest had stopped in the doorway where she had left her.

Sofia was barely able to articulate anything and choked, "Um…no…this…wow. This is amazing!"

Aurora smiled. "Yes, the boys have their uses," she said with a wink. "Please. Come sit." She gestured to a chair to the side of her.

Sofia stepped forward causing the wooden floor to creak loudly underfoot. It was an odd sensation, but it felt like she was stepping on something that was alive. A strange notion, of course, which she instantly explained away. Something to do with the fact that everything in this place seemed naturally formed from wood. In the dim light, she was able to discern that it still contained its natural grain, that it hadn't been refined but simply angled and shaped into something functional. And that vibration she felt upon arrival was still present, humming through her body. Delicately. Seductively.

Her chair was heavy and, like everything else in this place, it was unconventionally made. It was a hollowed-out trunk, fashioned into a high back chair with a plush cushion for a seat.

"Your home is stunning," Sofia said breathlessly, pulling out her chair with a loud scrape and then taking her seat at the banquet table. "All of this natural wood furniture. It's like you've brought the woods indoors."

"You're too kind. It's a humble way to live, but I wouldn't want to live any other way. You see, Sofia, modern society continues polluting not only itself but also our planet. They build these poison-belching power stations that contaminate the water we drink and the food we eat, all in their obsessive quest to generate energy. But what they fail to realise is that there's an abundance of natural renewable energy already available to us courtesy of she."

Sofia cocked her head.

"Mother Nature," Aurora clarified.

Sofia smiled.

"You don't agree?"

"Oh no, I do. It's just you sound like a friend of mine. She lives in a place like this."

"Oh, really?"

"Yes, she feels the same way. You know, Mother Nature, energy...

"And you don't?"

"I do. I just... well, I've never really had a strong opinion on the subject, but if you were to ask..." Sofia shrugged. She had no idea what she was talking about and yet, "...if you were to ask me, I'd agree that being at one with nature is wonderful. I love it, but..."

"But?"

"Well, there's also the practical element. Unless we all revert to living like this..." Sofia shrugged, unsure where exactly her words were coming from and acutely conscious of the fact that she didn't want to offend her host.

"Please, speak freely," Aurora prompted, as if she had read her thoughts.

"Well, there's a practical element, isn't there? I mean, most people would like to live like this. And yet we still need to heat our homes, power industry, conduct commerce, fuel progression, satisfy demand, and feed the world. We can't just turn off the power stations without an alternate infrastructure in place." Sofia knew she had spoken the words, but they sounded as if they had come from the mouth of somebody else. What was she talking about? And how could she be so rude?

Aurora maintained her gaze for several seconds before breaking into a smile. "You're absolutely right, my dear Sofia. Somebody needs to take care of all of that so we can enjoy the finer things in life. Speaking of which, how are you settling into the palazzo?" She unfurled her napkin as she waited for a reply.

Sofia mirrored the action and then nodded. "Yes. It's lovely." She allowed herself a nervous laugh. "Takes some getting used to though."

"Of course. You're a contessa now."

Sofia pulled a face and rocked her head. "I know."

"You should embrace your heritage, Sofia. It's nothing to be ashamed of."

"I know. It's just... well, it's a bit overwhelming."

The soft scuffle of feet on wood announced the return of the two men. They were both dressed now, in elegant designer suits and cravats with perfectly styled hair, like models just off the runway. Except, from the sound of skin on wood, they both still had bare feet.

Daniele stopped by her side to pick up the decanter.

"Vino, Sofia?"

"Oh, actually, I—"

"Of course she would like some. You wouldn't let me drink alone, would you?" Aurora asked. "Besides, this is our own special brew. You're going to love it."

Sofia hesitated. She hadn't eaten and wasn't much of a drinker. But she was still reeling from her comments.

"Maybe a little," she said, looking up into a pair of piercing sapphire eyes that appeared to shimmer in the gloom of the room. He was looking right at her. No, not right at her, right into her. She had to avert her gaze from the intensity and feign interest in how the wine fell into her glass.

She could smell him. She couldn't place the fragrance, but it was good. Musky. Masculine. Almost as delicious as the food aroma that was making her tummy rumble.

She glanced across the table. Gabriele was expertly carving the piglet and Sofia felt a stab of sorrow as she watched him slice at the dead creature, its lifeless eyes looking up at her as if imploring against a fate it had already suffered.

Gabriele looked up from the task in hand, his dark eyes brooding in the light.

"Would you like some meat, Sofia?" he asked in an accent she couldn't place but had to admit was as sexy as the mischievous smile that accompanied it.

Daniele sniggered.

"Now, now, Gabriel, behave," Aurora admonished through a smile. Then she turned to her guest. "He's a terrible flirt. You'll get used to him."

Both the boys chuckled.

"See what you've done, you've made her cheeks go rosy all over again."

Sofia hadn't noticed the burn until her hostess pointed it out.

She wished she hadn't.

"It's all right, Sofia. I do like that name for you. It suits. Don't you agree, boys?"

Both men made approving noises.

Sofia shuffled in her seat. "Thank you."

Aurora leaned closer to her. "You're such a pretty thing. Isn't she just the prettiest little thing, boys?" Both men smiled and nodded as they served food onto her plate. "You must have had a lot of attention back in England."

Sofia laughed awkwardly. "I can't say it's something I really noticed. My life back in England was…" she hesitated, unable to find the words, "…difficult sometimes."

Aurora looked pained. "Oh, sounds horrendous. Is that why you're here?"

Sofia laughed, unsure how to respond, her host's directness driving the tide of saliva from her mouth. She took a sip from her glass, bracing herself for the acidity of the wine, and yet there was none. The beverage was sweet. Juicy. Delicious. It was nothing like what she had expected. It tasted more like freshly squeezed grape juice that hadn't yet undergone fermentation. Rich and vibrant, like a mash-up of grapes, figs, blueberries, and raspberries.

"Oh, wow, this wine is sweet," she said, licking her lips and rolling her tongue around her mouth to savour the flavour.

"You don't like it?" Aurora asked.

"Oh no, I love it. It's just not what I expected."

"Isn't that divine? Receiving something that was completely unexpected?" Aurora asked, glancing at Gabriele. He lifted an eyebrow before walking over and serving Sofia sliced chicken breast from a silver platter.

"You prefer the chicken, Sofia?" he asked in that deep, smooth tone of his.

She averted her gaze. Her pulse quickened instinctively, and this annoyed her. It annoyed her that she was so easily affected by everything. By this man who smelt every bit as good as his companion and whom, at least to her ears, was incapable of uttering a word without it sounding seductive.

And yes, she did prefer the chicken. After looking at the little pig's eyes she would have struggled to eat it and that would have appeared rude. Even now, she was making a point of avoiding contact with its sad, judgemental gaze.

"This spread is amazing, Aurora. You really shouldn't have gone to so much trouble, though."

Aurora drank from her glass and shook her head. "It was no trouble. I just get these darlings to do it," she said, as Gabriele moved over to her side of the table and leaned forward so she could serve herself.

She smiled up at him. He was tall enough for his crotch to be close to her face. Then, shockingly, she nuzzled against the mound of fabric, as a cat would against one's leg, making the man smile.

Sofia pretended not to notice by taking another long sip from her glass, enjoying its sticky sweetness, and ignoring the burn in her cheeks once more as she attempted not to acknowledge what she had just witnessed or dwell on the memory of the man's actual nakedness.

"Everything all right, Sofia?" Gabriele asked with his wry smile.

"Oh yes, of course, thank you," she said, holding up her glass. "Just lovely. Just wonderful."

"You may want to go easy with that, Sofia. It's not as innocent as it may seem," Aurora warned.

The two men chuckled again. It was odd because they weren't standing anywhere near her and yet they sounded so close.

There was a giggle. It was her. She took in a breath to speak, to reassure her host that she was perfectly fine when she became aware of it. Something. At the back of her mind. Something emerging from the deep recesses. Something that she had never been aware of before. Something that, like a bolted door, had just been opened, releasing first the buzz of the alcohol—merry, giddy—and then something else. Something much more potent.

Uninhibition. It flowed through her veins and like delicate fingers stroked, caressed, and probed erogenous areas she didn't even know she possessed. This and the persistent thrum of the building provoked an involuntary gasp.

"I…um…phew! You're right, Aurora, that wine is something else."

"Like most things, darling, best consumed in moderation. At least until you get used to it. Now eat up. That will help."

Sofia complied, picking up her knife and fork.

"So, what are you planning on doing with yourself? Aurora asked. "Have you been shopping yet? Some of the boutiques here are divine."

"Oh, I would love that, but I wouldn't know where to start."

"Well, we'd be happy to show you around, wouldn't we, boys?"

"It would be our pleasure," Daniele responded.

"Oh, that's very kind of you. It's just that I'm, well… The palazzo is lovely and everything, but I…um…" Sofia trailed off here not because she couldn't find the words this time, but because she could. Suddenly, she felt more than happy sharing.

Meanwhile, Aurora had paused eating and was looking at her expectantly.

"Well, as strange as this is going to sound, I think I need to get a job," Sofia said with a chuckle, popping food into her mouth.

"A job?" Aurora echoed.

Sofia nodded, still unable to quite reconcile it herself. She was now living in a palace that came with a title but had barely any money to her name.

"It's a long story." She sighed.

"Perfect!" Aurora declared. "Because the night is young. Daniele, perhaps you should top up Sofia's glass after all."

6

THE INTERVIEW

THURSDAY. EARLY MORNING.

Nine days left.

Sofia took a deep breath and then looked at her hands. They were shaking. She didn't recall ever being this nervous before an interview, and she had attended several.

It occurred to her that, for all its failings, the airport was the only job she'd stuck at. She reasoned that it was because every day had been different; different people to meet and different problems to solve. She had liked that.

This job might be the same. Maybe better.

Well, it would be. For many reasons. Not least because Steve wouldn't be there.

Whatever it was, she hoped it would be customer-facing. She was good with people or at least that's what she'd been told.

Mr Alexakis—the image of the dead man's glassy eyes staring up at her from the wet tarmac, blood frothing from his mouth, barged its way into her mind, sending a shiver through her. Oh yeah, you're really good with people.

Piazza San Marco was uncannily deserted. It was surreal when compared to the hordes that filled the space yesterday. Many of the shops and cafés that had been teeming with activity, music, and laughter now had their grey metal shutters closed like the eyelids of the slumbering tourists that would no doubt be swarming this place once more in just a few hours.

Sofia had to remind herself that, unlike them, she was not a tourist, no matter how much she felt like one. She was home.

Home. This is my home! You are one of my neighbours, she thought as she passed lonely pigeons pecking for food and cooing loudly in the quiet.

What appeared to be rain had washed and glossed the world. The square was shiny like a scene that had been reset, ready for a new take. But Sofia knew better.

Acqua Alta, or High Water in English, was a tourist attraction for many but a major threat to La Serenissima. The scourge dated back centuries and saw the city temporarily flooded at various times throughout the year when the Adriatic Sea tides rose. One of the first places to flood, of course, was Piazza San Marco, since it was effectively at sea level. Ambitious plans to literally hold back the tide had been underway for decades, but whether they would succeed in preventing the city from sinking back into its lagoons, like the fabled city of Atlantis, remained to be seen.

Overhead, blue metal clouds bubbled and spilled so low, Sofia felt she could climb the Campanile and touch them.

Straight ahead, a gargantuan black banner replaced part of the façade of the Doge's Palace, once the seat of Venetian government. Now, it was the city's most popular tourist attraction. She made a point of remembering this fact in case a relevant question was raised during the interview.

The banner featured two green cat eyes and read:

FOLKLORE AND SUPERSTITION
An exclusive exhibition by Palazzo Ducale
in collaboration with Karlson Enterprises.
OPENING SOON

Sofia's heart skipped a beat and she had to pause for a few seconds to absorb the words. Karlson. That name. She wished she could ignore it and pass off its insertion into her life as a cruel coincidence. That she could tell herself that it had nothing to do with what happened in England. But something at the back of her mind wouldn't let her push the thought away.

Focus!

Nervously, she swallowed and resumed her journey across the square, her shoes clacking with each step, the sound her only companion in this beautiful yet alien place.

Clanging and scraping drew her attention as she passed Café Florian. The ubiquitous café overlooking the square was notorious for its expensive beverages yet was regularly patronised by many who sought to catalogue the unique experience that it offered.

A young man in black trousers and waistcoat was busy setting out chairs and tables for the coming day. He was whistling but stopped when he saw her, and smiled.

My home. My neighbour.

Sofia smiled back and waved confidently before a rattle and rumble drew her attention. A street merchant noisily wheeling a rustic wooden cart laden with wares passed in front of her.

"Buongiorno, signorina," the old man said with a smile.

"Buongiorno," she said brightly. Confidently.

Then, like the opening of a curtain before a performance, the departing cart revealed the decorative façade of the palace before her.

Her stomach lurched. She placed her hands on her sides, wishing away the queasiness that had suddenly washed over her like the waves she could hear lapping against stone.

Bong!

The clock tower announced the seventh hour of the day. It was a sight to behold. She had learned that tourists climb numerous steps of the palazzo just to witness the marvel, but all she could do was try to steady her breathing. She was surrounded by three of the most iconic landmarks of one of the most beautiful cities in the world—the clock, the palace, and the marble stone columns overlooking the lagoon—and all she could do was try not to spew.

She knew why, and the thought of it brought a smile to her face. Yes, a smile. Because, for once, she wasn't feeling anxious because of some inexplicable neurosis or some weird obsessive compulsion, but because she was understandably nervous about attending an interview for what could most likely turn out to be her dream job.

Thanks to her new neighbour's connections, if she pulled herself together and didn't screw things up, with a bit of luck the view of this glorious tower of rusty red bricks, appearing to glow in the gloom of the disgruntled morn, would become a feature of her regular commute, and these people setting out their stalls for the day would be her fellow commuters.

Not quite the gridlock of the M11 motorway.

She hurried the rest of the way, splashing through the water that was already sloshing over the stone slabs.

Acqua Alta.

She rushed through the south wing column tunnel and turned onto the east wing where there was a spectacular view of the lagoon. She eventually found a small door over which a large mauve placard read, I Musei di Piazza San Marco. Then, underneath, in thick bold letters, PALAZZO DUCALE with the subscript translation of Doge's Palace.

Her heart skipped another beat.

Okay. She paused for a few seconds, breathing deeply. "You can do this," she told herself. "You can do this, Sofia. Come on, then, get in there. Get in there and get this job!"

She pressed a button mounted next to the door. As she waited for a response, it occurred to her that she hadn't taken her pills for days now and she'd been mingling with the crowds yesterday without any problems. It begged the question of whether they were really of any help. She'd been on those things for years.

Movement through the door window caught her attention. A thin man in a navy-blue uniform with an identity tag on a lanyard around his neck smiled at her from the other side of the glass.

She straightened herself and returned the smile as he swiped his card, tapped numbers on a keypad, and pulled the door open for her.

"Buongiorno," she said, ignoring the warmth in her cheeks. She was committed now.

"Buongiorno," the man responded. He was in his thirties, with unusually fair skin, thinning blond hair, and a smattering of freckles, like hers. He had freakishly fair eyebrows and looked more Scottish than Italian. "Are you here for the interview, signorina?" he asked with a grin.

He was Scottish. The accent was subtle, but clear.

She felt her nervousness melt a little. Another Brit. Another ally.

"How did you know?" she asked with a sigh, looking at herself, touching her hair as if she could see it.

"Ah, you know, just a guess." he said, smile as wide as the Cheshire Cat's in his small face. "For the record," he read from a clipboard he was holding, "you're Sofia DaTerra?"

"Yes, I am," she said with too much enthusiasm. She swallowed, straightened, and repeated. "I am. I have an interview at seven."

"Aye, you do, with Maria Bacciabella and Georgina Pellegrino." He pulled a face after the last name.

"Oh, no good?"

She thought the interview was with one person, Maria. She didn't realise there'd be someone else. Aurora had only arranged this meeting for her last night. She was friends with the curator and knew that she was looking for someone. When Sofia explained why she needed a job, Aurora immediately offered to help.

"Maria's the curator. She's lovely," the man offered.

"Right, and Georgina?"

He wrinkled his face again.

"Great." She smoothed her blouse subconsciously.

"Don't worry. Her bite is worse than her bark."

Sofia breathed a sigh of relief and then realising what he had just said, added, "Wait. What?"

"Sign in, please," the man said, leading her over to a desk and thrusting a book and pen at her. "Don't worry. You're going to be fine. Just speak up. Be confident." He leaned in. "She likes to try and rattle people, so don't let her detect any blood in the proverbial water. She can be a bit of a shark."

"Okay, I know you're trying to help, but—"

"You best be on your way. You're already a wee bit tardy."

"Right." She looked around the ticket hall.

"Just beyond the cordon, on the other side of the room, past the ticket machines, up the golden staircase, to the left. Knock on the door marked 'Private'."

"Okay." Sofia smoothed her clothes again. "Wait, the golden stairs. The golden staircase?"

"Good luck," the man said, tapping his watch.

Sofia hurried across the room that, despite the modern ticketing machines and crowd management ropes, still exuded unequivocal medieval opulence.

But it was nothing when compared to the Scala D'oro. Sofia recognised it immediately. She'd seen it in pictures before but even if she hadn't, a helpful small plaque was affixed to the wall to remind her. This was the egress to the palace, the steps formerly used only by those of standing. It featured a resplendent vaulted ceiling of golden stucco with ornate detail that dated back to the 16th century.

Sofia had marvelled at photographs of these very steps. Now, she was climbing them on her way to a job interview! It was all overwhelmingly surreal and all thanks to her new friend and neighbour, Aurora. She made a mental note to buy her flowers no matter what today's outcome turned out to be.

At the top of the stairs, when she failed to turn as instructed, a Scottish accent called out in a loud whisper, "Up the stairs, turn left!"

She crossed the landing and stopped in front of a heavy wooden door and, with one final shrug of self-encouragement, knocked.

"Avanti!" was the muffled response from the other side.

Sofia turned the handle and pushed. The door creaked with medieval reminiscence.

She stepped into a large room that continued the pervasive Venetian theme of stucco vaulted ceiling, but this time it was of white plaster that contrasted beautifully with ornate wine-coloured wallpaper that was adorned by an array of portrait paintings and religious iconography.

It was like stepping into an art gallery. Only this one had a large conference table and chairs at one end, behind which were three women.

Great.

Sofia's heels seemed to click annoyingly loudly now as she made her way across the marble floor and presented herself to the panel.

"Buongiorno," she said, conjuring her best smile.

All of them responded, but the only person who returned the smile was a diminutive woman with wispy grey hair, wearing a flowery patterned scarf. "Or good morning," the woman smiled again. She spoke with a rounded pronunciation, like she had marbles in her mouth.

"Yes. Good morning. I'm Sofia DaTerra."

"I'm Maria Bacciabella, the museum's curator. It's a pleasure to meet you, Sofia. Please take a seat." She gestured to a chair in front of the table. "And this is our chief of staff, Georgina Pellegrino, and our chief events coordinator, Raffaela D'Amosta."

Both of the women forced tight smiles that were more of an acknowledgement of their introduction than a greeting. And, even if they hadn't just been introduced, Sofia reckoned she could have plucked Raffaella from a line up. She had skeletal features shrink-wrapped in fair skin, wrinkle free though Sofia estimated that she must be in her late forties. There were no laughing lines around those grey eyes, possibly because the woman appeared to be economical with her smiles. Her hair was dark brown and cut short above the shoulders and her eyebrows thin and arched, as if permanently surprised. She was scowling, which made Sofia wonder if she'd already pissed the woman off without even opening her mouth. Or perhaps she was made of stone. That faint smirk from a few seconds ago was still imprinted on her face. Her eyes scrutinized but rarely blinked.

Her colleague, Georgina, looked as if she had been replaced by a mannequin replica and was joining via remote video conference. Enshrouded in sun-bleached blonde hair that was immaculately combed and smoothed over her head, her silicon face looked more like a mask with generous yet meticulously applied makeup. She sat straight, like she'd been to finishing school, and wore her navy-blue uniform and security lanyard like she meant it.

Sofia handed over her hastily handwritten resume and then perched more than sat in the chair. It looked like an antique and she feared it might collapse underneath her.

She had barely parked herself before the mannequin when the woman pounced on the sheet of paper in front of her and spoke through a small round mouth.

"So, Sofia," she began. "There is already one thing I would like to clear up with you." Her tone was clipped and her accent thick as she addressed her like a head teacher might an unruly child.

"Of course," Sofia responded with a smile, inching a bit further onto her seat and wishing she hadn't agreed to attend an interview so soon. She would have preferred to have at least had the time to get her handwritten scrawl typed and printed.

"I think there must be a mistake with your resume, yes? It says your address is Palazzo Rosso, Via Irregolare."

"Yes, that's right," Sofia nodded, with a smile. "It's just off the Canale Grande."

Georgina let out a hollow laugh, unimpressed by Sofia's use of the Italian language. "Palazzo Rosso is, what you say, a listed building. Built centuries ago. If you live there, you not need be applying for a job here," the woman said dismissively.

"Why not?" Sofia countered. She retained the trace of a smile because she didn't want to come across as combative, not that she thought the woman would care. She gave Sofia the impression that she enjoyed nothing more than a good scrap.

The chief of staff didn't appear to have an immediate response for the impertinent little girl—which is how she made Sofia feel—but Maria assisted.

"I think what Georgina is trying to say, Sofia, is that Palazzo Rosso is worth a considerable amount of money. The presumption is…" she paused and glanced at her colleague, "…is that if you live there, then you shouldn't need to work here."

"I inherited the place," Sofia explained, "on the understanding that I wouldn't sell it."

All three women observed her for several seconds, but it was Maria again who broke the silence.

"I see," she nodded. "Well, Sofia, you do realise that as you are the incumbent owner of Palazzo Rosso, that makes you a—"

"Contessa, yes." Sofia felt that dreaded heat rush to her cheeks. She'd made a point of omitting the ridiculous title from her hastily written notes to avoid this silly discussion and yet here they were. Worse, something told her that she'd just plummeted even further down Georgina's wrinkled nose of disapproval.

Sofia glanced at Raffaella, the events coordinator. She seemed interested in the conversation, but her demeanour remained amused yet impassive.

"It takes some getting used to," Sofia added, although she really wanted to say that the title was a load of rubbish as evidenced by the fact that she was sat there being condescended to by all of them.

Okay. So now she'd developed a short fuse out of nowhere.

Apparently not one to be deterred from belittling her, Georgina continued. "Your, um… notes say you've moved around a lot."

"Moved around?"

"Yes, changed your jobs."

"Oh, yes."

"Why is that?"

"Um, well, you know, as they say, variety is the spice of life!"

She followed that up with a nervous chuckle. She had no idea why she had responded with that stupid line because nobody across the desk was sharing her amusement.

The truth was she hadn't liked those jobs. She hadn't taken them by choice but necessity. It was the same core reason why she was there now, cringing through this interview, even if this job might actually be one that she wanted. Part of her wanted to tell them that, but the other was shouting that it would make the completely wrong impression. It would suggest that she didn't take any of her roles seriously and imply that she wasn't serious about this role either. But she was.

"None of those roles really interested me. They were more about necessity than job satisfaction." Oh well.

"And would this job satisfy you?"

"Oh, yes, absolutely," she said quickly, feeling her eyes light up with enthusiasm. "Working somewhere like the palazzo would be a dream job for me. I've always loved the leisure industry and, of course, Venice. Dealing with the public is what I'm about. As you can see," she continued excitedly, nodding at the sheet of paper on the desk, "my longest lasting positions were Thorpe Park and Stansted Airport."

"Thorpe Park?" Georgina repeated.

"Yes, it's a theme park, just outside of London."

"A theme park?" the woman echoed, that disgruntled nose seemingly elongating so she could wrinkle and look down it some more. "You worked there as an usher?"

"Yes."

"Il Palazzo Ducale is not a theme park," she retorted, enunciating and clipping each word.

"No, of course not," Sofia said, trying to recover.

"It's an international site of historic importance."

"Of course."

The room fell silent as the sounds of a new Venetian day

pushed their way through the gap in the lead windows. The noise of motorboat engines, gondola operators, tourists, and seagulls all reminded Sofia that there was a beautiful world outside of this room that, as magnificent as it was, was fast becoming grim and terrifying, like the setting of some kind of trial.

Someone cleared their throat and then the chief of staff continued. "There isn't much work history on your resume before you were twenty and I see no record of college or university. Why is that?"

Sofia's heart skipped a beat. As dreaded, the woman was venturing into an area of her past she had not wished to dwell on.

"Um… It's a part of my life that I don't normally discuss." The words fell out of her mouth.

"Why not?"

"It was a difficult time for me," she said, adding a conciliatory smile.

"Difficult how?"

Maria glanced at her chief of staff, but the woman was undeterred.

Sofia bit her lip. "Um… It was a hard time, personally."

"Why?"

"If it's all right with you, I'd rather not talk about it."

"Why not?" the woman persisted.

"It's just a part of my life I don't talk about, don't discuss."

"If it is in the past, why wouldn't you discuss it?"

"Georgina…" Maria jumped in.

Georgina turned to the curator and spoke as if Sofia was not sitting right in front of them. "I don't understand why she doesn't want to talk about it. It's very important for us to review both personal and professional history as this helps us determine if a candidate—"

"I was having some problems," Sofia jumped in hastily. She shook as she was reminded, once again, of how much even thinking about that time made her heart quicken and her insides turn. She swallowed the lump in her throat and continued. "My mother left, and I didn't take it very well. I developed some issues."

"What kind of issues?" Georgina asked flatly.

Sofia paused, stilled by the woman's insistence in raking up the worst part of her life. But she knew she had a choice. Either tell her to stick her job and walk out or persevere to try to win the placement she desperately needed.

"I…um…struggled with depression and anxiety. I became a bit of an obsessive compulsive, though, believe it or not, my therapist says that is a good thing because when I apply myself to something, I do so obsessively!"

That last bit was supposed to be a joke, the same joke her therapist made in her weakest moments. She owed that man. But the only person to react was the curator, who did so with a surreptitious grin.

Several seconds passed. Someone sang somewhere outside.

"You don't have any of the experience we're looking for. What makes you think you'd be good for this job?" Georgina ploughed on.

"I…well…um…" Sofia fumbled because she didn't know what to say. The woman in front of her had already derided all her work as well as her personal history. And yet she cleared her throat and continued. "My role as a passenger experience agent at Stansted Airport. I was there for a long time and the position requires a lot of skill dealing with the public who are often unhappy about—"

"Yes, this was your last job, correct?" Georgina interrupted.

"Yes, that's right."

"You don't say why you left there?"

"Sorry?"

"Why did you leave your last job?"

"I…" Sofia's heart hammered in her chest, urging her to run screaming from the room. Even if she ignored the fact that her father had always insisted that honesty was the best policy she knew that there was a good chance this woman would check up on her. And if she did, there was no doubt that Steve would have nothing nice to say. She had no choice but to be honest.

"There was an accident."

"An accident?" the woman echoed.

Sofia nodded. "One of the passengers was in an accident and I… I was suspended pending an investigation." She watched the woman sit back in her chair as if she'd rested her case. "But it wasn't my fault."

"No? So, you haven't been suspended?"

"No. I mean, yes, but it wasn't my fault. Maybe if you let me explain, I—"

"Sofia," Maria interjected. Her voice was calm. Rational. As if those words weren't still hanging in the air.

Sofia swallowed the dry sand that was the back of her throat, pressed trembling hands to her thighs so nobody would notice them shake, and looked at the curator.

"For clarity, this role does not require you to interact with the general public. Instead, you would be dealing directly with some of our benefactors, many of whom are very important to this museum."

Sofia frowned. "I… right…" She cleared her throat again as she attempted to process what she was hearing. She then looked at her interviewers in turn, but Georgina and the mute were busy glaring at Maria who, undaunted, continued. "We have a new, very exciting and very important exhibition coming up. We could use an additional pair of hands in the events planning department."

"Eh, un momento, Maria." Raffaella, the mute, found her tongue.

"Do you think that's something you'd be interested in?" Maria spoke over her subordinate with the most wonderful Isabella Rossellini intonation. At least, that's how it sounded to Sofia.

"I would absolutely love that!" she gushed, unable to mask her enthusiasm.

"Very well. Why don't you go wait for us outside?" Maria said. "I get the impression my colleagues would like to have some words with me." Maria made knowing eyes at Sofia, who immediately sprang up from her seat, nodded at the other two women, and hurried out of there.

She had barely managed to close the door behind her when she heard the verbal onslaught begin. The Italian chatter was fast, loud, and definitely angry.

Sofia leaned against the wood and listened to the drone like wasps in a jar.

"How did it go?"

The voice startled her, and she yelped, face burning as if she'd just been caught snooping.

It was the man in the navy-blue uniform. "Sorry, I didn't mean to scare ya. Although, I am a wee bit surprised that you could be scared of anything after surviving that," he said with a wry smile.

Sofia breathed deeply. "Yeah, well, I get the feeling I just made it worse. If that's even possible."

"Ah, don't take it personally, lass. She doesn't hate ya. Well, not you specifically. She hates everyone."

"Oh good. That makes me feel much better. Thanks. What exactly is her problem?" Sofia asked in a hushed tone.

"Well, I could give ya an answer, but I refuse to do so on the grounds I might be branded sexist."

"You're not helping."

"No, really. She lives alone in one of the most romantic cities in the world. I defy anyone not to be resentful. Take me for example. I can't stand anyone."

His wide grin coaxed a smile from her. "Thanks."

"You're welcome. I'm Cameron, by the way," he added with a wink.

He was cute in a brotherly kind of way. Sofia estimated that he was in his early thirties, but he still looked boyish, with fair skin, fiery red hair, and unusually large ears.

"So, what did Maria say?"

"Not much. But she was the only nice one in there."

"Well, you'll find that, generally speaking, if Maria wants something around here, it tends to happen."

"Really?"

Cameron nodded.

The news was like a warm hug to Sofia, who had already concluded that there was no way they were going to hire her. She felt an overwhelming desire to actually hug the man in return.

"How did you end up here?" The words just came out because, somehow, she already felt comfortable around him.

"Ah, that's a long story."

"Well, by the sounds of it, I've got plenty of time."

"Yeah, but I haven't. If I'm not back at my post before the dragon comes out, you might end up with my job. Don't worry, we'll have plenty of time to share stories and espressos once you get started. I mean at one of the bars, of course. I'm not coming on t'ya or anything… don't want ya getting the wrong idea... oh jeez." The last part of his sentence was a jumble of words and those fair cheeks looked rosy-centred like those of a Russian doll.

Sofia laughed just as the door opened and a sour-faced Raffaella appeared.

"We're ready for you," she snapped.

Sofia took a deep breath then followed the woman back inside.

7

INDUCTION

THURSDAY MORNING

Sofia could not believe her luck. Several days ago, she felt it was the end of her world. Today, she felt on top of it. She'd been in Italy barely a day and had already moved into a palace fit for a fairy-tale princess, discovered a wonderful next-door neighbour and hopefully new friend, and had landed herself a dream job.

Everything was moving so wonderfully fast that, as juvenile as it was, she felt compelled to pinch herself a couple of times just to make sure she wasn't trapped in one of her dreams.

She wasn't.

After an hour or so of formalities such as filling out forms, reviewing the employee handbook, and basic orientation, she was now being led by Raffaella through another door and across another palatial space. She felt giddy. As if she were walking through the canvases of history. She was enveloped by so much artistic beauty that after a while she felt intoxicated by it, barely able to absorb the words being machine-gunned out of Raffaella's mouth.

She did take on board that the woman was also British. Born in England of Italian parents, she was from Birmingham, to be precise. She married an Italian, she had explained, and followed him back to his homeland, eventually landing herself a job at one of Italy's most famous tourist attractions. She had been quick to point out that the job hadn't landed in her lap, that she'd had to work hard for it. That, unlike Sofia, she had a history degree, had garnered years of experience in the hospitality industry, and, also unlike her, spoke fluent Italian and French.

"You won't last long in this job if you don't know how to keep your mouth shut," she was saying, as she led Sofia through another door and another magnificent room.

Sofia agreed with her. Silently, of course. She'd already seen a demonstration of what the woman meant at her interview. She had kept quiet and thus non-committal until the curator had broadsided them by offering Sofia the job. Then both of her new colleagues had a lot to say.

She felt so deliriously excited as they moved through what resembled yet another movie set, lavish enough for the grandest of period dramas.

As if reading her mind, Raffaella—who hadn't stopped talking since her thunderous face barked *walk with me*—casually imparted that the tour would have to be short since she had a meeting with Hollywood executives about a major motion picture that was currently in production. The movie was partially set in Venice and the producers wanted to shoot an exterior scene out in the courtyard. When Sofia looked perplexed, since she had no clue which courtyard the woman was referring to, Raffaella rolled her eyes, and when she made the fatal mistake of admitting that she'd never heard of the lead actor, she invoked another exasperated sigh from her guide.

"This is the Chamber—"

"Of the Great Council," Sofia breathed as they stepped into yet another grand room, of reds and golds with ceilings and walls adorned by gargantuan works of art laid out in immaculate detail.

"Oh, so you've actually heard of it then?" Raffaella said, lifting one of her arched eyebrows even higher.

"Who hasn't? It's one of Europe's largest rooms," Sofia said, gawking up at the immenseness of the gilded wooden frames of paintings on canvas that made up the ceiling. "The painter, Tintoretto, was entrusted with the canvas that covers the entire back wall. It is the largest canvas in the world. It's called *Il Paradiso.*"

Sofia looked over but the view was blocked by a partial construction of black panels and metal struts.

"What's this?" she gasped, as she watched workmen mill back and forth. It looked like a giant soundstage.

"It's our special interactive exhibit on superstitions. It opens at a special gala in just over a week to coincide with the arrival of the comet. VIPs and dignitaries will be able to walk through it and experience first-hand a selection of different folklores from around the world," Raffaella said dreamily, as if she'd designed the experience personally.

"Arrival of the comet?"

Raffaella rolled her eyes. "Don't you watch the news? The comet, it's either going to burn up or burn us in just over a week. Depending on who you believe."

A cheer went up from the group of workers as if they had heard Raffaella's words, but the men were cheering the fact that they had managed to successfully erect a giant black banner with two green cat eyes to the front of the exhibit. Underneath, it read:

FOLKLORE & SUPERSTITION
An Interactive Exhibit.
Dare you enter?

"Andiamo!" Raffaella snapped. "We haven't got time for the guided bloody tour," she said suddenly, hurrying forward, clutching her folder to her chest.

Sofia ripped her eyes away from the banner and hurried after her just in time for the verbal onslaught to continue.

"When the executives arrive, you'll stay in the office. If the phone rings, you're to answer and take messages only. Do you understand?"

"Um… right…" Sofia said.

The woman stopped so abruptly that Sofia almost crashed into her. "Is there a problem?" she demanded.

Recomposing herself, Sofia said, "No, not really. I didn't realise that I was actually starting today. I thought it was just like an induction, you know. And answering the phone… my Italian…"

"Your Italian what? Look, if any of this is a problem, I can always tell Maria that the post wasn't for you after all," Raffaella said.

"No, no. It's not that. It's just—"

"What?"

"I um, I wasn't expecting it. That's all."

"Well, that makes two of us, *Contessa*," Raffaella scoffed, eyes roving over the newbie with such disdain, Sofia had to make a conscious effort not to check herself for wardrobe malfunctions. She was already feeling self-conscious in her skirt, blouse, and heels.

"Raffaella, look," she eventually managed, "I know I wasn't your first choice for—"

"No, you weren't. My cousin was. She's probably forgotten more about this place than you'll ever learn," she said haughtily.

"Oh, Raffaella. I didn't realise that—"

"Well, you're here now and I haven't got all day to chat. So, are you coming or what?"

"Of course."

Sofia followed her new supervisor through a set of double doors, up a flight of stairs, and through another set of doors.

"This is administration. You'll be spending most of your time back here," Raffaella continued as they walked down a narrow corridor with uneven white stone walls and creaky wooden floors in stark contrast to the rest of the building. To their left, most of the wall had been transformed into a series of windows. They gave a spectacular view of a glistening lagoon festooned with boats and gondolas, bobbing in the sun.

Sofia paused, unable to take her eyes off the scene. This was the view from her office. She could not wait to show Janay and Victoria a picture.

"...and as I've already said, the exhibit you just saw out there is important. It is sponsored by one of the museum's biggest and newest benefactors, Samael Karlson. You most likely have never heard of him either, I imagine, because, well, why would you?"

She stopped again.

"Is there something wrong?" she snapped.

Sofia was still staring at the scene beyond the glass. It was mesmerising. "No. Nothing's wrong. I was just... this view... there's something about it. I feel as if—"

"Were you even listening to a word I said?"

Sofia turned to her. "Yes, of course. You...um...you were talking about the exhibition being really important, about Sam...Samael Karlson." That name again.

Raffaella must have seen the look on Sofia's face because she instantly rolled her eyes.

"Of course, you've no bloody clue who he is," she said before resuming their journey. "He's now one of the world's wealthiest men, and quite young. He owns many of the properties in Venice, if not the whole of Italy. He is the guest of honour at the exhibition."

Raffaella paused and stepped forward, her dull, serious eyes finally flashing some life. "You'll have nothing to do with him. Do you understand?"

Sofia nodded instinctively, although she didn't imagine she would have the opportunity to have any contact with the man anyway. Nor did she want to.

"He is very important to this museum," Raffaella continued, "have I mentioned that? Do you know that his ancestors actually saved many of the paintings from the ransacking of that French dwarf, Napoleon?"

Sofia went to speak but the question was obviously rhetorical.

"Anyway, he can only be handled by a professional and that obviously isn't you. *You* are not even to look at him without my say-so. Am I making myself clear?" She held up a bony finger.

Sofia looked at the long pointy thing. It resembled an anaemic letter I with bright red nail varnish on the end. She wanted to snap it but nodded instead.

The woman eyed her as if she didn't believe her. Then, satisfied she'd marked her territory, like some kind of wild cat, she turned. "Now come on. I've wasted enough time as it is."

She walked further down the corridor and stopped in front of a door with a metal plaque affixed to it that read EVENTS MANAGEMENT. Then she turned the loop handle and pushed the door open.

Considering the size of the palace, the events management office was tiny. It barely had room for the two desks and filing cabinet that occupied it. The stone walls and ceiling were washed white with occasional dark slashes of wood struts. To Sofia, it could have been one of the many Tudor-style houses she had visited back in England, were it not for the view through a portal window of an azure lagoon and the island of San Giovanni in the distance.

"This is my desk," Raffaella declared, dumping her folder on it. "That's yours."

She nodded at the desk opposite. It was stacked with boxes, lever arch and manila folders, as well as an array of lanyards and expired passes.

"Those passes need to be shredded. That box is full of invoices that need to be filed in lever arch folders in alphabetical order. While you're at it, you can give this room a tidy and a polish. We have a cleaner, but they can't really get much done in here because of all of this crap. As you can imagine, someone in my position is way too busy to have time for any of that. That's why you're here.

"From now on, you'll be responsible for keeping this office spick-and-span. You can inform sanitation that they no longer need to bother with this office since you'll be handling it. Their details are in the directory on the computer. Speaking of which, I'm supposed to get you set up with a computer. God knows why. You're not really going to need it for much.

"Anyway, once you've tidied and filed everything into those folders, you can put this year's on top of that filing cabinet. The rest goes into the *cantina*." When Sofia squinted, Raffaella gave her another customary roll of the eyes, then added, "The cellar. The door's over there. I should warn you that the steps are steep, built more for practicality than comfort. The cellar used to be a dungeon many years ago. A lot of men died down there. Drowned when the tide came in. Of course, the viaducts have been sealed now, but back then they'd be chained down there while the guards waited up here, in this little palace."

She smiled knowingly and Sofia couldn't help but wonder if Raffaella was imaging an alternate universe where she was herself a guard and Sofia one of the unfortunate prisoners.

"Once you're done reorganising and cleaning in here, I want you to start doing the same down there. Don't worry. Nobody lives down there anymore, apart from the spiders, of course, and a few rats. Maybe a couple of ghosts." She followed this up with a chortle.

Sofia closed her eyes and swallowed the protestation that had already formed at the back of her throat. Dungeons? Spiders? Drowned men?

Raffaella savoured the look of dread on the recruit's face before snapping, "Chop chop! You're not going to get anything done by standing there. Oh, before you get started, I'd love a coffee. You'll find what you need through there."

She pointed to a small adjoining room as her desk phone rang. She turned and snatched it up. *"Pronto?"* Her face creased into some weird terminator-like smile. *"Ciao, bello. Come stai?"* She clicked her fingers at Sofia, indicating that she was still waiting for her drink, and then took a seat behind her desk.

"No. Just busy showing someone around. No, nobody important. Only an intern. Oh well, you can imagine what it's like, but, hey, someone's got to do it. Anyway, what can I do for you?"

Mercifully, the woman's voice faded a little as Sofia moved into a small alcove that had been made into a kitchenette. It consisted of a sink, a small fridge, and an ostentatious coffee machine. She looked around for a mug and found some handsome looking black ones with the palace's insignia on it. She rinsed it in the sink and, as she did so, she caught sight of another morsel of a view. It was a portal window that teased with a desaturated moving image of a sailboat drifting on choppy waters. Overhead, dark wintry clouds drifted in to occupy the pale blue sky.

Oh, so she was in Venice after all and hadn't been consigned to purgatory for stealing somebody else's job, thrown into a dungeon with old happy features in there as one of her shackles.

"Um, hello? Are you picking those beans or what?" came the sound of the woman's belligerent voice.

8

THE WITCHES

THURSDAY EVENING

It had been a long day. Sofia had spent most of it tidying, organising, filing, as well as disposing of the rubbish Raffaella had allowed to accumulate in the dumping ground of her office. Mercifully, she had not had to venture into the cellar today, but she knew it was only a matter of time before everything that she'd organised would need to be stored away.

The heels that Sofia didn't enjoy wearing at the best of times had given her blisters. She felt grimy and exhausted. Yet she had never been happier. She had no idea why, but this job made her feel good. Yes, it had its obvious downsides, but she had put up with Steve during her time at the airport. Raffaella would have to go some way to make her feel as miserable as he did, although she appeared to be giving it a good try.

The only drawback was having to return to the palazzo on her own, as ungrateful as that felt. The vastness of the space only seemed to accentuate her sense of isolation. The silence was truly deafening. Every creak. Every sigh. Every melancholic lap of water was a reminder that her loneliness was as palpable and as frigid as the building's walls.

Thinking positively, she had really enjoyed her evening with Aurora and the lads the night before. When Aurora had first mentioned the boys, Sofia had assumed that she was referring to her children. Obviously not, though she still didn't have any idea of what the setup was there. But, in Venice, that didn't seem to matter.

What mattered is that she felt good in the company of her new neighbour. Free to be herself and to express herself in whichever way she wanted without fear of it being interpreted, analysed, and regurgitated back to her in the form of yet another question. That was how it had always been in Doctor Krauss's office. Here, she was able to reminisce about her mother and talk about her father. When the tears inevitably came, both her next-door neighbour and her two male companions had put comforting arms around her. In some uncanny way, they drew the grief from her body to such an extent that she had been left feeling euphoric and peculiarly serene.

Then they had laughed for the rest of the evening as her hosts regaled her with humorous stories of life, love, and sex in Venezia. And yes, even the latter made for a delightful discussion. Not taboo but natural.

At one point, relaxed and uninhibited from the vino, Sofia lamented aloud how, at the mature age of twenty-one, she had no tales of any sexual escapades of her own to share with the group.

She had never dwelled on the thought much before, but suddenly her virginity had lain heavily upon her, as though she were enrobed in a thick gown meant for modesty that only itched and suffocated.

This realisation could have made her feel bad, as if there was something wrong with her because she had spent wasted years untouched on the proverbial shelf of carnal pleasure. But she was not made to feel that way. If anything, her dinner companions complimented her virtuous lifestyle and celebrated it even, before going on to reassure her of how gloriously delicious it would be when the time was right.

Then talk simply turned onto other subjects, and when they stumbled upon Sofia's financial dilemma once more, Aurora told her she was going to make the phone call that struck her guest momentarily dumb. Not least because, given the absence of any obvious electronic devices, Sofia was surprised to learn that the Aurora even possessed a phone. That, and when she revealed that she was close friends with Maria Bacciabella.

Sofia had still been grinning as she slid between the satin sheets of her ostentatious bed. She'd found the carved faces surrounding her nowhere near as creepy as she'd first thought. Then, under the influence of Aurora's magic brew, they had felt more like companions, watching over her as she closed her eyes and dreamt of a presence in her room, of ghostly faces and whispering, moments before a tidal wave of freezing water burst through the door, drowning her as she lay in her bed until her eyes bulged and her body twitched and spasmed in the bluish hue.

That's when she had awoken, gasping and spluttering for air as she reached over to snap on the bedside lamp. Even then, she could have sworn she could still hear whispering.

It had ceased the instant the light came on and commanded back the shadows. She was alone but for the dead eyes of the strangers that had been carved all around her.

It had then taken an hour or so of listening to the sleepless creaks and sighs of the building and the lullaby of the lapping water to coax her back into a fitful sleep. Yet when the alarm had gone off on her useless phone, urging her to get up for her interview that morning, she felt relatively rested.

Unsettled though, which was probably why she'd had a moment while putting on her makeup. She had been sitting at the vanity desk, where she could see the reflection of the bed in the background. It was when she was applying her lipstick that she could have sworn she saw one of the little boys, normally looking out towards the balcony doors, turn and look directly at her.

Yet when she yelped and snapped her head around, everything was as it should be. But the incident had still spooked her, and she'd hurried out of the house without a look back.

Of course, as soon as she had made it out into the fresh air, she explained it away, blaming her overactive imagination once more and turning her focus to the interview.

But now that the workday was over and she thought of returning to the palazzo, she realised that she wasn't in any particular hurry to go back there. She knew avoidance was a terrible way to approach the issue and that the more she built on those feelings, the harder it would be to go back to her new home. And yet…

What had happened to Armando anyway? He seemed to have disappeared. And what of the creepy housekeeper? Sofia had no idea how to contact either of them. Where did they even live? Was it nearby? They might even be ensconced somewhere in the house for all she knew. Ugh. The thought that she may have got herself into an accidental house share with a pair of complete strangers only made her feel worse. She tried to dismiss the idea only for it to settle back on her like unwanted house dust.

Maybe she'd pop round to Aurora's later. Take her a gift to

thank her for organizing the job interview. Tell her how much she appreciated her help.

You can't go over there all the time.

She had left the office and was now making her way through the palace towards the main exit. Raffaella had said she was going to do her a favour and let her leave early because they had VIPs coming in for an exclusive preview of the exhibit tonight and she didn't want her getting in the way. She was sure to add an ominous warning that she would be expecting her to make a start on *the dungeons* tomorrow *so don't bother dressing up.* She had followed that up with her trademark velociraptor smile. Well, at least that was how Sofia was categorising it now.

She descended the stairs and stepped through the first set of double fire doors. She jumped as they pulled themselves shut behind her, producing a loud slam in the hollow of the corridor.

Darkness was already pressing on the windows, and all the overhead lights were dead.

She glanced at her watch. It was almost six in the evening.

She had learned that the palace used to have its own private cisterns and wells to meet its water requirements. It also benefited from an early central heating system, powered by a collection of wood burning stoves that used to be located in the palace's underground tunnels. Today, management was working towards carbon neutrality and thus was investing in renewable energy sources, such as a new revolutionary tidal generator. In the meantime, most of the lighting in corridors and hallways was controlled by motion and thermal sensors, with the exception of the exhibits.

Straight ahead through another set of double doors led to the grand hall, but if she continued down the corridor, she could visit some of the main exhibits. And, since some of these were still lit, Sofia decided to take a quick detour.

As she walked through dimly lit rooms with nothing but the

uncannily loud clicking of her footsteps for company, she quickly began to regret her decision. After all, she knew that the palazzo, for all its majestic beauty, was also a place of darkness, of suffering, torture, and murder.

Thousands of people died here.

She hurried as best she could through another chamber, stalked by shadows, the clacking of her shoes echoing all around to emphasise that she was alone in the vastness. On the other hand, she wasn't sure how she would react to the sound of another pair of footsteps following her, so perhaps there was also comfort in the sound of her solitude.

Shut up! You're creeping yourself out. There's nobody here but you.

Exactly! That's what worries me.

She considered turning back but she was committed and was now moving through the private galleries—a series of chambers where the more valuable paintings were exhibited almost exclusively for private owners and donors, only occasionally available to the public. If she recalled correctly from her brief orientation that morning, it was just another couple of rooms until the doors would lead her back round to reception and outside.

However, it was as she reached the opposite end of the space that she noticed something through the corner of her eye.

A painting, different to all the rest.

Unlike the other works of art, this one was lit, and the solitary canvas brought her to a stop. She didn't know if it was because it was standing out in the black like a beacon, or if it was the subject matter, but something about it intrigued her.

She took a step closer, squinting into the light as she scrutinized it. She glanced around and confirmed she was still alone. This curious thing appeared to have illuminated just for her and the thought gave her a surprising thrill. Being up close and personal, exclusively, to such a work of art was something she had never experienced before. It was peculiarly intimate. She felt as if she was being absorbed into it, into the colour, into the brushstrokes that were giving life to a time, a moment, a meaning.

Sofia was no art critic by any stretch of the imagination, but there was something about this piece that fascinated her.

The painting was of three semi-naked females wearing long pointy Wicca hats. They were suspended in mid-air, a few feet above the ground. Between them, also in mid-flight, was the naked body of a man. He was either being kissed or eaten by the women, she couldn't tell. Below them, on the ground, was another man holding a blanket over his head, presumably in some kind of juvenile attempt to hide from all that was happening above him. Sofia could not take her eyes off the scene.

England. Greenfields. The forest.

The detail was so immersive, so compelling, that she couldn't help but lift a hand to touch, to feel it…

Fire. A baby crying. Witches. Victoria.

The memories, the cold of that night and the fear she had felt blew through her like the wind as she lifted her fingers closer, just inches away…

"Vuelo de Brujas."

The voice startled her out of her daze. It was smooth, deep and spoke with perfect Spanish pronunciation.

Sofia snapped her head left and then right. But, for as far as she could see, she was alone with the shadows. The painting and its overspill was the single island of light in an ocean of darkness.

"It's Francisco Goya," the voice added, now in perfect English. The voice had moved closer, and Sofia could just about discern the outline of a man. "Beautiful, isn't it?" he asked.

But Sofia was unable to respond. Her tongue was frozen to the roof of her mouth while her racing heart appeared to have much to say. Not because she was afraid but for other reasons she was unable to fathom. There was something about this man and his voice that was magnetising.

She drew a sharp breath when two flickering flames suddenly moved through the dark towards her, metamorphosing into a pair of green eyes that glinted as the stranger stepped into the light.

He had sculpted features with short black hair shaped into a sideswept crew cut. His ears were small and neatly pinned to the sides of his handsome face. His lips were thick, adorned by a speckled stubble, and those eyes… Oh, his eyes were the shape of diamonds and were accented by tidily trimmed eyebrows that curved upward and gave him a faint natural scowl. He was wearing a black suit tailored to his athletic body and had such a dark brooding way about him that Sofia imagined he must be Spanish or Italian.

"It's you," Sofia whispered under her breath, the words slipping through her lips, eager to make their way over to him.

She retreated instinctively from the painting as the man stepped closer, as if she wasn't meant to be there. Blood rushing behind her ears. Breaths deep and full. It felt as if the world moved into slow motion. Gravity eased. Everything was floating.

"I'm sorry?" he said, his accent giving nothing away of his origin. "I didn't mean to startle you."

"Oh, you didn't… I wasn't… I should…" Words failed her as his ardent gaze melted her ability to think straight.

"I…um…" she swallowed, her throat suddenly sandy dry. "Are you lost?"

"No, I think I'm exactly where I need to be," he said, a faint smile gracing those thick lips once more.

Sofia giggled nervously. The words were so obviously meant to provoke a reaction in her, and they did, warming the colour in her cheeks and awakening a flutter in her tummy. She knew this man even though she had never met him before. It was a peculiar realisation yet was true nonetheless. The familiarity was warm and intimate as if they were friends of old. It was absolutely barmy and made her giggle once more.

He smiled with her. "I came to see the painting," he said, taking a step forward in immaculately polished shoes. "It's one of my favourites."

"The Flight of the Witches. I can't say it's my favourite, but I can see the attraction," she said, suddenly becoming the critic she knew she wasn't as she fiddled with a strand of her hair and realised, to her dread, that she must look a mess.

"It's from Goya's famous six-part series on witchcraft," he said. "The original for this particular one, painted in oil, was finished in 1798. It's been described as one of Goya's most powerful works." It was as if their roles had been reversed. As if it were *he* who worked there.

While wrestling with the urge to fix her hair, Sofia noticed how imposing his height was. He must have been six foot-something. She could see that now that he was standing closer to her.

Unable to find any other words, she pointed at the plaque mounted beneath the painting. "You're right," she said. "It says so right here."

He stepped closer to her, his intensity as radiant as sunshine. "Do you work here?"

"Um… kind of."

"Why aren't you with the group?" he asked, looking over his shoulder as if there were people standing behind him.

"I've only just started. Can't be trusted with the important people yet," she said with a forced smile.

"Is that so?" he asked, turning his back on the painting completely to give all his attention to her, as if she were food and he ravenous.

She cringed inside and instinctively touched her hair, which was probably manky and full of cobwebs, given the state of the office today.

"Why?" he continued. "How dangerous are you?"

Sofia laughed and was rummaging around for a quip of her own when the lights clicked on.

"Sam. There you are. I thought we'd lost you."

It was Maria Bacciabella, dressed in a blue trouser suit with matching flowery necktie and novelty gold earrings shaped like St Mark's Campanile. There was a group of other businesspeople with her as well as…

"Sofia? I thought I told you to go home." It was Raffaella, who appeared to have made an extra special effort with her hair and makeup. Her tone was cordial in light of the visitors, but the darkness in her eyes told Sofia she was seething.

"Sofia?" the man said.

"Apologies, I presumed you'd both met already. Samael Karlson, this is *Contessa* Sofia DaTerra," Maria said with an emphasis, Sofia noticed, on her title, as if she were a proud mother introducing her own daughter.

Samael smiled and bowed his head as if he'd just been introduced to royalty.

"Samael Karlson?" Sofia repeated, stomach dropping.

"At your service, Countess," he answered, extending a manicured hand.

"I was sorry to hear about your father," Sofia said, meaning it, the words just fluttering out of her mouth.

Samael nodded. "Thank you," he said sadly. "Means a lot."

"Sam. We really need to get going," said one of the group members from behind him.

"Right," he said, eyes still on Sofia as he extended his hand. "Well, it was a pleasure, Countess Sofia."

If he was wondering what a countess would be doing working in the events department of a tourist attraction, he did not show it.

Sofia shook his hand and nodded before the man made his way back to the rest of his group.

"So, as you can see, Sam, things are coming along nicely for the gala. We really want the event to make Karlson Enterprises proud of their sponsorship," Raffaella began immediately, steering the man away.

Maria on the other hand lingered a while to give Sofia a smile. "See you tomorrow," she said.

Sofia lifted a hand, pensively. "See you tomorrow."

9

LUXURIOUS SOLITUDE

THURSDAY EVENING

Sofia enjoyed her walk back to the palazzo.

Home.

She had to remind herself every time she thought about it, but she knew it was going to take a while. There was way too much architecture, history, and festivity in this beautiful city for her not to feel as if she was on some kind of extended holiday. Not to mention the fact that she could barely string a few sentences of Italian together.

But then perhaps this was exactly how she should treat this new chapter in her life. As an extended holiday. Stop piling on the pressure to fit in, to adapt, and just take each day as it came.

Samael.

She would accept the fact that she was going to feel unsettled and a little lonely rattling around in a whole palace on her own. No. *Townhouse.* Exactly. It was all about terminology. If she approached this in the right way, she'd undoubtedly end up having much more fun.

Karlson.

That was, of course, if she could get over the sight of the creepy doorknocker that she did her best to avoid every time she put the key in the lock. And what was with that anyway? She needed a bag just to carry the huge key around. It weighed a ton. There had to be a much more practical way. Maybe she could find a hiding place and leave it there. See? Those were the things she needed to focus on. Useful things.

Samael Karlson.

Stop it!

She couldn't get the man out of her mind. No matter how hard she tried, like a boomerang, her thoughts just kept coming back to him.

Was he the one? The man of her dreams? There had to be something about him. After all, he was the head of the company that owned their house on Meadow Lane. That couldn't be a coincidence, could it? What were the chances of her flying all the way to Italy only to bump into this guy barely a day later? It was definitely some kind of fate thing. Like they were destined to meet.

She missed Victoria. A lot. She'd be all over this. She was more frustrated than ever that her phone wasn't working and didn't have a clue about where to go to get the bloody thing fixed!

She jumped as the door slammed shut behind her and thrummed around the entrance.

It didn't feel as cold inside as it had when she first arrived. It was as if someone had turned on the heating, yet given the size of the place, Sofia couldn't imagine how that would work.

She paused as she realised. The lights were on. She didn't remember leaving them on this morning. But then again, she didn't remember turning them off either. When she examined the walls, she discovered the most peculiar thing. There were no light switches. Anywhere. Maybe they were motion activated or something. Although plausible, it was unlikely. Motion activated lights in a place like this?

She rolled her eyes. She hoped this wasn't a sign of things to come. That her life would be so empty she was reduced to agonizing over bloody light switches.

She moved from the hallway into the ballroom, shoes clacking loudly as she went. She considered taking them off, but somehow that didn't feel right. It wasn't that cosy kind of place. Yet it didn't feel as inhospitable as it had at first either. It was as if the house, the walls, and the history confined within them had all grown accustomed to her and were now open to accepting her into their fold.

The lights were on in the ballroom too and so were the ones that illuminated the stairwell. In fact, the lights were on everywhere as far as she could tell. Her first thought was that it was a waste. It wasn't exactly environmentally friendly, not to mention how much it must cost to—

Sofia!

She interrupted herself. She sounded like a right old fart. Banging on about chilly houses and bloody utility bills. She knew what she was doing. She hated the idea of being in this massive place on her own. Truth be told, she was apprehensive with a good dollop of scared. She'd never been in this situation before. Dad had always been there.

Dad. I miss you.

And that house was so much smaller than this castle.

On the other hand, somebody had turned on these lights. Somebody else was probably still here. The housekeeper, maybe?

"Hello?!" she called out to the empty space. But the only sound was her own voice.

She moved over to the foot of the stairs and called again. Nothing but the creak and sigh of the building, a draft blowing eerily through a gap somewhere, and the now omnipresent hum of boats on the water.

The lights were on in the dining room too, so she walked over to the archway, and threw a hand to her mouth. The scene was beyond anything she had ever witnessed or could possibly imagine.

The dining room was aglow with candlelight, casting a warm and inviting hue on the grand banquet table. It appeared to be set for one with the finest porcelain and silverware, sparkling in the soft amber radiance.

At one end of the table, the drapes were drawn back to reveal giant balcony doors that led to the expansive terrace that stretched out over the water. It provided an unobstructed view of a giant moon overlooking the mesmerizing Venetian nightscape, spotlighting the canal and the boats drifting on it as constellations shimmered in the water.

The table was covered with the finest white linen and adorned with a lavish spread of food and drink. Succulent meats, crisp vegetables, and crusty breads were arrayed along the centre, served on gleaming silver platters, surrounded by sparkling glasses and bottles of wine.

Sofia stepped forward in stupefied wonder as a medley of tantalizing aromas teased her tastebuds. She was so overwhelmed by the beauty of it all that she could feel her eyes misting up.

The table was indeed set for one. She hadn't imagined it, but could it be true? Could all of this be for… her?

She looked around. There was nobody else here.

Gingerly, she pulled the heavy chair out from under the table and sat with wide eyes, breathing in the bounty that stretched before her and grinning from ear to ear. Janay was going to freak out when she heard about this!

The table's centrepiece was a magnificent arrangement of exotic flowers and a cornucopia of fruits, adding an alluring splash of colour to the scene.

Now emboldened, Sofia lifted the first cloche to reveal a decadent antipasti platter, featuring a variety of cured meats and marinated vegetables. The next revealed a hearty serving of seafood risotto, cooked to perfection with plump prawns, succulent scallops, and juicy mussels. Then it was dessert, which was a beautiful arrangement of Venetian cannoli sitting on a silver plate, their golden-brown shells glistening in the candlelight with a filling of creamy ricotta, cinnamon, and vanilla, sprinkled with tiny chips of dark chocolate. To accompany the sweet treat were glasses of sparkling Moscato d'Asti, which was a sublime effervescent touch to the jaw-dropping spread.

Sofia ate. Tentatively at first, like a Goldilocks who had taken a wrong turn to the palace, and then with gusto, filled suddenly by ravenous hunger. She ate much more than she ever thought she could, yet there was still plenty left over.

There was a moment or two when she couldn't help but consider the inevitable melancholy that comes with dining alone, especially in the presence of such an opulent spread, laid with such magnificence. But she forced herself to put the feeling aside, rationalising that she would always mourn for what she did not have—and perhaps what she never would—but she had to try to not let it overwhelm her. There was happiness to be had still, no matter her loneliness.

After dinner she tried to work out what the etiquette might be in such a situation. Did one take the dirty dishes downstairs to the kitchen? Hunt down the dishwasher? Would a place like this even have one? Or should she test this new arrangement and see if the spread miraculously vanished just as it had inexplicably appeared?

Given the absence of anyone who might judge her, she chose the latter. Worst case, she'd tidy up later. Besides, she was worn out. It had been a physically and mentally taxing day and, if Raffaella had her way, tomorrow wasn't going to be any different.

She made her way up the staircase and paused at the top of the stairs. The quiet of the place was so unnerving that she was desperate to turn on a television or something, but from what she'd seen, there were no televisions in any of the rooms. Not even a radio, either. It seemed that, with the exception of her phone, there was nothing inside the building that could transmit or receive a signal. Strike that, she thought, her phone was rubbish at sending signals too. So, basically nothing. She was in the middle of one of the most cosmopolitan cities in the world and yet it felt as if she was stuck in the 18th century.

She needed to change that.

But for now, she made her way down the hallway, as floorboards creaked loudly underfoot, and entered her bedroom.

Like elsewhere in the palace, the lights were on in here too, supplemented by the flicker and crackle of the fire that had been lit in the fireplace. It transformed the atmosphere from a cold medieval castle to a quaint and snug country manor.

And yet there was nothing quaint about this room with its wallpaper of rich green hues and gold embellishments. They looked more like symbols, glowing in the firelight. The furniture that had appeared black and heavy by day just appeared sturdy now, the solid dark wood exuding a sense of strength and durability. The intricate design was obviously handcrafted and whittled into the wood, accentuating its natural state, and highlighting the artistic talent of the craftsman. It didn't look depressing at all but full of character, with its distinctive knots and gnarls telling a story of its life as a tree.

Then there was the large decorative archway, the circular space it created serving as a portal-like entrance to the lavish realm of the giant bed that sat on its elevation like a queen atop her throne. It was the epitome of opulence in a room that appeared to shimmer aquamarine blue, as if birthed from the loins of the Adriatic and then encased in this intricate four-poster canopy of wood mastery.

Yes, those faces carved all around were still creepy but at the same time comforting. Company in her otherwise lonesome chamber.

She felt herself drawn to them, tracing fingers over the contours of chubby cheeks, pixie noses, slender fingers, and muscular arms. This wasn't a bed but an astounding exhibit of sumptuous crimson silk pillows and a mattress as soft as lambswool. It was beckoning to her now, seducing her into stripping out of her clothes to slip between its thighs of silky velvet.

So she did, and before long, Sofia DaTerra sank so deep into her slumber that she didn't even notice the presence that stealthily entered her room and glowered down upon her.

10

SUBTERRANEAN

FRIDAY MORNING

Eight days left.

Sofia couldn't help but pause to marvel at the view from the glass corridor, across the lagoon to what looked like infinity. Of all the beauty in Venice—of which there was much—for reasons unknown to her, this perspective was her favourite.

When she entered the office, she found Raffaella leaning against her desk, with a young woman she didn't recognise.

They were laughing but stopped the moment she entered the room which, of course, made her suspect that they were laughing about her. Nonetheless, she greeted them with a cheery, "Good morning."

"Good morning, Sofia," Raffaella replied with that raptor smile of hers. Then she looked at her friend and nodded in Sofia's direction as if to say *this is the one.*

Sofia pretended that she didn't notice as she shrugged off her coat and hung it on the back of her chair.

"Would you like some coffee?" Sofia asked brightly.

"No thanks," was Raffaella's reply. Her mute friend just shook her head.

Sofia turned to go make herself a drink when Raffaella called her name and stepped forward.

"I wanted to ask you something," she said.

"Sure, what is it?"

"Well," Raffaella began, walking up to her, "I was just talking to my friend, Valentina, about this and would appreciate your input." Her black eyes suddenly roved all over her. "New outfit?" she asked with a grimace.

"Yes," Sofia said happily. She was wearing her jeans again but had decided to pair it with one of the blouses she'd found in the wardrobe. It was a compromise. She wanted to dress up for the day, but knew she was going to end up down in the cantina at some point so decided to wear her trainers. But now that Raffaella had cared to mention it she concluded that it probably hadn't been a good idea.

"At some stage, we'll need to discuss your wardrobe," she said, compounding Sofia's concern. Especially when her new supervisor then turned to her friend, sharing a look.

"Yeah, so anyway. I've lived here a few years now, as you know, and I was wondering if my accent had gotten stronger. You know, lost my brummy vowels and developed an Italiano accent that was much harder to understand?" She appeared to ask her question in all sincerity.

Sofia half smiled, secretly grateful that Raffaella had deigned to ask her such a question. It would make the whole experience of coming to work so much more enjoyable if they were able to get along, maybe even become friends. And she could so use more friends right now. That, and analysing accents was her thing!

"No," she began, shaking her head. "I would say that there's definitely still a bit of brummy there, though when you speak Italian, it sounds flawless. Not like an English person speaking Italian, do you know what—"

"I don't care," Raffaella said sharply, holding up her hand and closing it into a fist so that Sofia knew to shut her mouth. "The only thing I care about right now is that you can understand me because we appear to have a communication problem."

Sofia lost her smile.

"I thought I had made myself perfectly clear that you were not to have any contact with our benefactors. Do you remember that? Do you remember me *specifically* telling you that?"

Sofia squinted as she tried to work out what Raffaella was talking about. "I, um…"

And then she remembered. In the gallery. Last night. It seemed so long ago. *Samael.*

"You mean that thing in the gallery? I didn't talk to him. He came over—"

Raffaella made that hand gesture again and closed her eyes with exasperation, as one might when dealing with a persistently unruly child. Sofia wasn't a child, and yet Raffaella seemed determined to treat her like one.

"I don't care if he chased you through the fucking halls," she hissed, eyes bulging, "I told you that you're to have no contact with our benefactors, especially the likes of Samael Karlson. Have I made myself clear?"

Samael. Just hearing his name. Sofia remembered the moment he emerged from the dark, those eyes so vibrant that she believed they were flames. The thought must have put a smile on her face because Raffaella instantly picked up on it.

She scoffed. "Wait, you don't think you've actually got a chance with him, do you?" she said, looking at her friend and back at Sofia again, her voice brimming with derision.

Sofia recomposed herself. She felt like she was melting under the glare of her supervisor's disdain. She wanted to say something. Deny the accusation. Make a quip. Something. But she couldn't because words were once again failing her.

"I wouldn't get your hopes up, love. I mean, do you even have any idea who he is? He wouldn't look at the likes of you twice. I'm surprised he even noticed you," Raffaella said, glancing at her friend.

Sofia maintained the woman's gaze, her defiance surprising even herself. If Raffaella was expecting her eyes to start brimming with tears, she was going to be sorely disappointed. She wanted to cry. At least it felt as if she did, and the vitriol in the woman's words was certainly bitter enough, but she wasn't going to give her the satisfaction. She might break down somewhere in private. But not now and certainly not with the mute friend watching.

Instead, she asked, "Is that everything?"

Raffaella observed her for the longest time, as if realising that this nut was going to be much tougher to crack than she had hoped.

"Yes. As long as you've finally understood, then fine."

Sofia turned and left.

"And I'd like you to make a start on the cantina," Raffaella threw after her. "Now."

Fifteen minutes later, Sofia was reluctantly pulling the bolt on the thick wooden door and allowing it to swing open with an eerie creak.

When she first arrived at Palazzo Rosso, this was the kind of thing she expected to be doing on her first day of exploration when, as it turns out, she'd barely ventured to the lower floors.

All she'd seen down there during her brief check was the massive kitchen. It reminded her of the big kitchens seen in one of those period dramas, like *Downton Abbey*. She imagined a time when Palazzo Rosso had servants and they all congregated down there. But not anymore. Now the kitchen was a barren and scrubbed utilitarian place, with just a slit window for natural light, and it gave her the creeps. Not least because she half expected the housekeeper to come running out at any moment, brandishing a rolling pin, screaming at her for daring to venture into her inner sanctum. She'd run straight back up the stairs and hadn't returned since.

Sofia wished she could do the same now as she flipped the switch. A naked lightbulb dangling from a wire burned weakly to life in front of her, revealing sombre medieval grey stone walls and narrow steps with uneven edges leading down into an ocean of darkness. The frigid air was dank with decay and thick with a sense of historic oppression, as if the very atmosphere were infused with the palpable weight of all the untold horrors that had transpired within the dungeon's walls.

Thankfully, Raffaella was too busy on the phone to notice her hesitation. She hadn't even crossed the threshold and was already overwhelmed with a peculiar sense of unease, to the point where she considered turning back to refuse to carry out Raffaella's orders, taking her chances with the consequences.

But then what would she do if she lost this job? She could love it, she was sure—present task and obnoxious colleague excluded.

Come on, Sofia. There's nothing down there but history.

She heard a lull in Raffaella's conversation and could already imagine her looking over, enjoying her discomfort. So, she turned around, picked up two of the boxes from her desk, bulkier than they were heavy, and carried them into the gloom.

It was like stepping into a parallel world. Gone was the lavish resplendence of the palace chambers and in its place was a drab grey stone wall with what looked like the original mortar. She gingerly placed one foot in front of the other as she slowly descended steps that had quite clearly been worn away with time.

She paused and glanced back at the open doorway and then down at her feet once more. She wanted to turn around so badly, but she knew that if she did it would be the end of a great opportunity. There was no way that Raffaella would let her get away with a dereliction of her so-called duties. She pressed forward and forever downward.

Raffaella had told her that there were approximately fifteen to twenty steps before she'd reach the bottom. She was also sure to warn her not to venture too close to the metal handguard as it had been reported that the thing was coming loose in places, and it was at least ten or fifteen feet to the stone slabs below. It was unlikely a person would survive the fall. Her words were delivered coldly, deliberately, clearly intended to scare the crap out of her.

It worked. Sofia stayed over to the left, close to the wall. So close that she almost grazed her face against the rough stone as she sucked in the dust of the decomposing, archaic mortar trapped between each layer of rock.

She squealed when something touched her face, jumped back and then squealed again when she realised what it was. Cobwebs. Sheets of them hanging down the walls like grim medieval tapestries. The mere thought of the size of their eight-legged weavers smothered her with revulsion.

Eventually she felt her foot hit the rock bottom and shivered. Not only was it pitch black down here—the light of that solitary bulb above refusing to venture too far into the abyss—but it was colder, much colder, the air damp and ripe with the smell of stagnant water, earth, and seaweed. It felt as if she had descended into the bowels of the earth. An otherworldly place where humans should fear to tread.

She did.

Which is why she hurriedly juggled the boxes into one arm, supported against her chest, while feeling the wall for the light switch. It took her a while, but then she felt the small lever under her fingers and flicked it.

There was a loud clicking sound as each of the lamps came on, lighting up like an airport runway to reveal a long subterranean tunnel with cells on either side.

It reminded Sofia of one of those archaeological digs where past and present fuse to become the discovery site of ages. In this case, the lights hammered into the ceiling were encased in waterproof metal and hard plastic that diffused the light into an eerie cold blue hue. Cracks ran along the walls and there were chunks missing in places. Water dripped steadily from the ceiling to form small puddles on the stone floor. The place seemed to be collapsing in on itself, slowly devoured by the earth.

Drip…drip…drip. The echoey sound plucked at the string of Sofia's nerves.

People died down here.

It was as if she could feel the suffering. Taste the death. But for the thick wire and those modern lights she would have felt as if she'd been transported back in time, half expecting to hear the agonised wailing of—

She froze. *Drip…drip…drip.*

Did she just hear something? It was faint, but it sounded like a haunted lament. She squinted down the corridor now guarded by giant shadows that dwelled on the periphery of the lights.

Drip…drip…drip.

It's all in your mind! You were just thinking about it and you conjured it up. Just get rid of the boxes and get out of here!

There was something about the place. It was as palpable as that boggy smell of decay. A sense of something despotic that raked up the small hairs on the back of her neck.

This is what she wanted. This is how she wanted you to feel.

Sofia hurried over to the first cell. It was surreal. There was a black iron gate and damp stone walls from centuries ago, yet inside there were cardboard boxes stacked on top of each other and covered with a plastic sheet.

Raffaella hadn't told her where to put the boxes she was carrying, but she knew they contained brochures and various printed marketing materials. It didn't look like they belonged in here.

She stepped across to the opposite cell, being careful not to step in the puddle on the floor, but then yelping when she saw her reflection pass over it.

This cell was decked out with metal racking, bowing under the weight of lever arch files full of accounting paperwork. It was covered with more plastic tarpaulin that crinkled at her arrival.

The next cell was crowd control: pop-up banners, metal posts, and red ropes.

Drip...drip...drip...splash!

Sofia froze. She had just turned to inspect the contents of the cell on the opposite side when she heard the change in sound. The eerie drip had included a splash, as if someone had just stepped into one of the puddles further down the corridor.

She looked down the runway of light that glowed down from the ceiling, glistening off walls and reflecting in the occasional puddles that faded into the gloom in the distance.

Did she just imagine that?

The corridor was empty as far as her eyes could see. She turned towards the safety of the steps that led back up and out to the sanctuary of the office, then back down the corridor once more.

There was nothing there.

She hurried across to the next cell. This had plastic sheets affixed to the ceiling and wall, creating a bizarre cocoon in this place where some may have drawn their last breath. The thought sent a shiver rippling through her.

Drip... Drip... Drip...

Stored inside the cocoon were various oil paintings of different sizes and colours. They featured portraits of dour characters in expensive robes who must have once been people of importance to the palace. Perhaps the former Doge himself. She had no clue. And nor did she care to know right now.

Some of the canvases were also wrapped in brown paper. One of the larger ones was sitting on the stone slabs of the floor in front of the others, with part of the paper torn away.

There was something about it that caught Sofia's attention. She didn't know what. It was a fairly unremarkable biblical image of a semi-naked muscular man. He had giant black wings against a backdrop of blue sky and white clouds and was walking on a hilltop holding the hands of two children: a boy and a girl.

Drip... Drip... Drip... SPLASH!

Sofia stepped out of the cell and looked down the corridor once more. The lights were still burning. The place was still empty.

Then why did she no longer feel alone?

Why did she feel that someone—or some*thing*—had joined her deep in the catacombs, and why had her skin started to crawl?

She hurried out of the cell and into the next, and screamed when a group of sleepy ghosts gazed back at her.

"Shhhhhit!"

She sighed a second later when she realised. They weren't ghosts, but marble or stone sculptures of different shapes and sizes, covered in sheets.

Okay. She was done. She was going to deposit the boxes and then she was leaving right this minute and she didn't care what Raffaella—

What was that? There. It was a statue. Much shorter than the others, its head was partially hidden under the sheet covering a taller statue. It was red under the light. Maybe crimson. About the only splash of colour in the whole gloomy place. She felt like it was beckoning her, urging her to take a look. A quick peek. Nobody would know. Take a look, she thought. Take a quick look.

Slowly, she put the boxes down and stepped forward, both eager and apprehensive in equal measure. *Come take a look. A quick peek. You won't regret it.* It was the most bizarre thing she'd ever experienced. It was as if whatever it was were speaking to her.

Closer…

What was that? They looked like petals. Red petals. No, they were leaves. Red leaves, peeking out from under the cloth.

Closer…

She was inches away now. Hand reaching out.

DRIP…DRIP…DRIP…

The sheet was diffusing the overhead light as she reached for it and lifted the material. She squealed and leapt backward when something rattled loudly at her.

She tripped over the boxes and crashed down onto them, twisting away from a sharp pain in her side before yelping again when she caught sight of what was staring back at her.

An imp. Sculpted from wood with man-like features, a hooked nose, sharp triangular jaw, and a lascivious grin that revealed razor sharp teeth. It was painted the vibrant colours of a court jester and wore a necklace of dark red leaves that rattled like a snake when touched.

Sofia recoiled in disgust. It was that *Burlone* thing from the Palazzo Rosso. The doorknocker she hated. But she barely had time to register this when she felt the light overhead shift and stir as if someone had just moved nearby. She looked up and gaped at the silhouette towering over her. It was a giant muscular beast with horns.

Sofia screamed and tried to find her feet. Skidding on the slippery floor, she attempted to gain purchase, continuing to scream until she was finally able to jump up.

Then she was running, out of the cell and up the stairs as fast as her legs would carry her.

She ran face first into one of the cobwebs, prompting more screams as she felt its maker scuttle across her face. She climbed the steps two at a time without looking back until she burst out of the office door, shaking and spluttering, wiping her hands over her face and body as she jumped up and down in a cloud of dusty cobwebs. This ritual went on for a least a minute until she was finally satisfied that she had peeled the last of the sticky residue off of her body and seen the recently evicted inhabitant scuttle under one of the desks.

When her attention returned to her surroundings, she found two people gawking at her. One of them had a grin on his face and asked, “Is this a bad time?”

11

THE MORTIFICATION

FRIDAY NIGHT

Mortified is how Sofia had felt the moment she caught sight of Raffaella and the man standing next to her. Both had been watching throughout her arachnophobic fit, which included watching her rip off the buttons of her blouse in her blind panic, exposing her bra while Samael Karlson—one of the world's most handsome men—pretended not to notice.

Mortifying is how it felt every time she replayed that scene in her sadistic mind.

Things only got worse when the man had casually asked if it would be okay to have a word, seemingly oblivious of the fact that she must have looked like she'd been dragged through a hedge backward.

Of course, in her daze, Sofia had replied that it would be perfectly fine, completely ignoring what she had been told by Raffaella barely ten minutes before, and feeling the woman's glare burning holes in her back as they both left the room.

They had stepped out into the glass corridor where the view unfolded with its usual breathtaking panorama. The blue sky was as if painted by the masterful hand of a Renaissance artist, with giant white clouds, soft and billowy as the finest silk, casting fleeting shadows upon that shimmering sheet of water where vessels ploughed their way through tranquil waters…

…and then there was Sofia. She had stood in front of the man of her dreams, her hair like a bird's nest as she clutched her ripped blouse together, trying to act as if everything were normal.

Then things had reached a whole new level of madness as she caught him taking a playful glance at her partially exposed body before stepping closer and asking, "Do you fancy having lunch with me tomorrow?"

Sofia couldn't help but giggle, partly from the pain of her embarrassment and partly from the pleasure she flushed with in reaction to his surprising request. As her mind raced with the implications of his question and grappled with the lingering indignity of the moment, he had reached out…

"May I?" he had asked, plucking a clump of web from her hair, complete with desiccated dead insect.

Now, as she readied for bed, she shook her head and then held it in her hands. She must have looked like a complete idiot. Especially when she wouldn't stop bloody giggling like a silly little girl.

She shook her head again.

On the bright side, she had come home to a palazzo that felt warm and cosy again. She noticed it the moment she came through the door. The atmosphere inside felt different on her skin. Warmer. Conditioned.

She reasoned that the change had nothing to do with the palace and everything to do with the excited agony of that moment when Samael Karlson had asked her to lunch. Each and every time she thought of it the thrill washed over her in warm waves.

On the other hand, yesterday's dishes had been cleared away as she had hoped—she could really get used to that—and the table laid once more for tonight's feast, courtesy of the mysterious housekeeper who still hadn't made an appearance since she'd startled Sofia in the bathroom on the first day she arrived. She wanted to thank her for the wonderful spread.

Tonight, it was pan-seared scallops with lemon butter sauce served with a wedge of lemon. Then it was fettucine alfredo for main course and chocolate lava cake for dessert.

"Thank you! It was delicious!" Sofia called out to the walls when she was done. She hadn't eaten much, though. She couldn't. She felt giddy from running the gauntlet of her feelings. The excited humiliation of her encounter in the office. And the hideous experience down in the cantina. Both were nerve-wracking but in different ways.

She reasoned that the latter was—yet again—the product of her wild imagination. Creepy place. Backlit statue of whatever that man-beast-thing was. Then full-sized imp version of that ugly thing she already hated down in one of the world's most miserable places. All of that was enough to conjure delusions in anybody. After all, there was a reason Raffaella wanted her to go down there, and it wasn't for her health. She knew what that place was like. And Sofia had given her the entertainment she had wanted.

But then Samael had shown up and dulled the impact of her machinations.

Sofia smiled as she pulled back the covers.

Things were looking up. Of course, she had expected that there would be a period of transition when she moved here, but among all of the variables one thing was for sure. If she really wanted to make it work, then she needed to keep her head screwed on properly. She needed to master her own destiny in the real sense of the word. Nobody else was going to do it for her. Her dad was gone. She was on her own. The sooner she got used to that and recognised she wasn't a helpless teenager any longer, the better.

She had tried to make contact with Janay again—she so desperately wanted to tell her about everything that had happened—but her mobile phone definitely wasn't working. There were no phones in the palazzo, she had checked. And she couldn't call from work because there was no way Raffaella was going to let her do anything like that. Plus, making international calls? She didn't want to give Raffaella any more ammunition.

Ugh. Raffaella. She'd barely spoken to her for the rest of the day beyond grunting when Sofia asked if she could borrow a black staff t-shirt she'd found during her clear out. She imagined that this was due to the fact that when Sofia had finally finished her ridiculous giggling and absorbed exactly what the man was asking her, she had somehow had the presence of mind to tell him that she had to work. She would never have dared to ask for the day off—she was sure there was no way Raffaella would approve that—but he hadn't even given her the chance to agonize over it because he quickly followed up his invite with the bombshell that he'd already cleared it with Maria. Raffaella must have hated that she had no way to refuse it.

And then he had watched her, his green eyes sparkling in the sunshine that flooded in through that window. It was only when he asked, "So?" that she realised she was gawping at him.

"So…?"

"What's your answer?"

"Oh yes, of course," she had replied, as if she were agreeing to a business lunch. Well, that's what it was. Wasn't it? Why else would one of the world's most eligible men ask her to lunch? He probably just wanted to talk about the new exhibit or the gala.

But he would talk to Maria or Raffaella about that, surely.

I don't know!

Whatever his reasons, it couldn't be because he liked her. Could it? Nobody had ever been interested in her that way before. Or more specifically, she had never wanted anybody to be interested in her that way before.

Except for Christopher Darrington, of course. But she tried not to think about him.

No. She felt different with Samael. Why? What was it about him? Was he *the one?*

These questions were still nagging her when she eventually fell into a blissful slumber.

***

Sofia stopped at the edge of the pier then turned and waved at Janay who was watching and blowing kisses to her from the ballroom balcony. She was still in her dressing gown.

Sofia knew that her friend hadn't bothered to dress yet because she believed it irritated the housekeeper who, apparently, had run into her in the hallway and glared at the sight of her bare legs like she was some kind of brazen hussy.

"I love you!" she shouted as she waved to her friend.

"Wait! Sofia! Wait! I've got a surprise for you!" Janay yelled.

"What kind of surprise?"

She followed her friend's gaze down from the balcony to the terrace and her eyes widened. Could it really be him, dressed in jeans and blue shirt to complement those gorgeous eyes of his?

"Chris?"

He grinned at her. "Hello, gorgeous," he said, walking up to her. "How's it going?"

"All the better for seeing you."

He hugged her. The embrace was strong and felt of home.

"Wow, I needed that," she said, breaking the hug and grinning up at him. "What are you doing here?"

"I came to see you. To make sure you're okay."

"Oh, I'm fine," she said, placing a hand on her chest. Her heart was thumping. *Thump…thump…thump.* She could feel it. Hear it. She was so excited to see him. Much more than she expected she would be.

"That's so sweet of you to make the journey all the way from England to see me. How ever is the legal world coping without you?" she asked.

But it was small talk. All of a sudden it didn't feel natural, and she knew why. She knew it was because she needed to be somewhere else, with someone else. And the thought of that made her feel bad. Like she was being unfaithful.

"Sofia, are you sure everything's okay?"

"Yes, I'm sure. Everything's fine. Perfectly fine."

Should she tell him? Would he be upset? She didn't want to hurt him.

He was looking down at her again, blue eyes sparkling in the early morning light just as they had on the street in Cambridge that day.

Chris, are you the one?

The one?

"No. Hold on. This isn't right."

"What do you mean?"

"Why are you here, Chris? And why are you calling me Sofia? You don't know me by that name."

He chuckled. "Of course I do."

"No, you don't. What are you doing here?"

"I came to warn you."

"Warn me? Warn me about what?"

Chris opened his mouth to speak but froze when a giant shadow fell over them. "Sophie…" he began, spraying her with spittle.

"Eww, Chris! That's disgusting!" she complained, wiping her face then realising it wasn't saliva.

It was blood!

She looked back at him and screamed when, suddenly, she saw a bloody circle appear around his neck, as if it had just been slashed with a knife. She watched, frozen, as those beautiful eyes rolled up into the back of his head.

"Noooooo!" she shrieked. "NOOOOOO!"

She could do nothing but watch in stupefied horror as invisible hands tugged and jerked at his beautiful head—rocking it violently from side to side, back and forth, eliciting a series of horrifying ripping and squelching sounds—before it was suddenly separated from those broad shoulders, releasing a fountain of blood into the air.

Sofia screamed as those same invisible hands then proceeded to shake the head up and down making it rattle like the tail of a snake.

Shhhhhh…Shhhhhh…Shhhhhh

"Noooooo!" Sofia screamed, bolting upright. She was in bed at the palazzo. Heart racing. Breath panting.

It was a nightmare. Just a nightmare. She gulped on a sandy throat. *Just a nightmare.*

Her forehead and face felt damp and for one horrifying moment she thought it was blood. She felt her cheek and then looked at her hand in the dregs of light from the street and the red-hot embers in the fireplace. She couldn't see a dark substance. It was perspiration or maybe even tears.

She sighed then clutched her chest.

"Chris."

She suddenly felt a longing to talk to him.

Shhhhhh…

What was that? Did she just imagine it? That sound. She recognised it now. That thing in the cellar. That's the noise its necklace made when it moved!

Her heart jumped into higher gear as she squinted at the foot of the bed. There was nothing there.

She looked across to the other side of the room, and then scanned the rest of the space… Nothing moving. No shadow people. Nothing.

Then, she slowly leaned over to the side of the bed and… what was that?! Something there. She just caught a fleeting sight of something as it scuttled around the bed.

She yelped, reached for the lamp switch, and flicked it on. Then she threw back the covers and raced around the front of the bed.

But there was nothing there.

And yet she could sense it, the telltale displacement of air telling her something had just been there.

"IS ANYBODY BLOODY HERE?" she yelled. "Well?"

Creaking. Lapping water. But nothing else.

And yet she planned to sleep with the lights on tonight.

12

THE DATE

SATURDAY MORNING

Seven days left.

Sofia stopped at the edge of the pier then turned and looked at the empty balcony. There was nobody standing there. Just the impenetrable blackness of those giant doors, lifelessly watching her. She looked across the orchard. Christopher Darrington wasn't smiling at her either.

That's because it was a dream. Only a dream.

No. It was one of the worst nightmares she'd had in a while. Not since her dad's funeral had a dream felt so hideously real, so visceral.

It had ignited a longing in her both for her friend and for a man she barely knew. Clearly, he had managed to make more of an impression on her than she cared to admit. In contrast, he probably hadn't given her a passing thought since she abandoned him on that Cambridge Street. He most likely thought she had a screw loose, and who could blame him?

She resolved to call England that night, no matter what. She would either find a phone shop to sort out her mobile or a public phone to call Janay. She wouldn't call Chris because… well, that would just be weird.

Hi, it's me, Sophie, just calling you out of the blue. Have you got time for a chat in between whichever flirtation you might have lined up this week?

Ugh. She'd forgotten about that. It was a silly, romantic idea to think someone like him could ever be interested in someone like her, even in some alternate life where she had not left the country. No. She needed to forget that stupid fantasy and get on with her day. Focus on the here and now. On reality.

She had eventually fallen back to sleep the night before, her fears coddled by the lights she left shining. They were still burning brightly when she heard someone calling to her.

"*Sofia, svegliati...svegliati, Sofia...*"

It sounded like a child's voice, but she knew that was highly unlikely. Nonetheless, "I'm awake… I'm awake…" she mumbled before opening her eyes, half expecting someone to be standing over her. But there was nobody but the carved faces, their presence filling her with the feeling that they only stilled and averted their gaze when she looked at them, otherwise free to move when in the corners of her vision. They didn't, of course.

Still, it certainly felt as though they had a life of their own, somewhere in the unseen.

She languished a few seconds longer until the memories asserted themselves, then snatched up her phone from the side and looked at the time. That's all the thing was good for now. She gasped in panic, shocked to see she had less than an hour to get ready.

She threw herself out of the bed and into the bathroom. In abject terror, she realised she hadn't even sorted out an outfit for the day. What was she going to do?

She washed quickly then hurried out of the shower, dripping water all over the floor and hastily wrapping a towel around her head. She wondered if she had time to go out to buy something new to wear. Maybe she could ask Aurora.

Yes, on top of everything else she's done for you.

Maybe not.

She yanked the wardrobe doors open instinctively, despite already knowing that none of the dresses were going to be suitable. She paused instantly. She couldn't believe what she was seeing. Was it there before, hanging to one side as if pulled out deliberately, specifically for the day? If so, she hadn't noticed it. But then again, she hadn't been going on a date then.

A date? Don't mind if I do.

Now, with a smile, she pulled on her black gloves and slipped on sunglasses. Sofia DaTerra had never felt this confident before. She was wearing a cream sweater dress that hugged her curves in all the right places and had paired it with a matching button-front cardigan and black beret. The look was completed with a deliciously soft crimson scarf that she had wrapped around her neck with a flourish. She had even taken her time—not that she had much of it left—to apply her lipstick the way Victoria had shown her once, by drawing a line and then filling in with colour.

Victoria. Her other best friend was also going to receive a telephone call tonight. Like it or not.

It was during that thought that Sofia became aware of the speedboat coasting towards her. She was no expert, but the thirteen-or-so metre vessel of gleaming mahogany, with its leather chairs and silver finishes that glinted in the early morning sun, looked luxuriously beautiful and very expensive.

It came with a driver who stepped over to help her aboard before turning back to the controls. He slowly steered them away from the dock, up the Grand Canal, and then out across the azure of the open water.

With one hand on her hat and the other on the rail, Sofia breathed in the salty sea air as the Riva speedboat sliced through the surf with ease, leaving a sparkling sunshine trail in its wake. Then, after several minutes, it turned on itself in a semi-circle before heading for a small, lush island.

Sofia had no clue where they were going and the idea of that was as terrifying as it was exhilarating. She had never felt this way before and the fact that it was somebody else motivating this, leading her on an adventure, only fuelled her excitement.

After a few more minutes she felt the momentum of the boat relax as they approached a high dock. The captain expertly moored the vessel before aiding her onto the pontoon and then gestured with a smile at the seven or so steps up to land.

Sofia thanked the man before taking the steps upward. At the top, her heart leapt into her mouth. Before her was what looked like a miniature airfield with a small hangar and office building. In front of it, several yards away, wasn't a runway, but a helipad, and on it sat a single engine helicopter, its black shell gleaming in the wintry sunshine, the large K for Karlson logo shimmering in gold.

Was this it? Was this Samael's surprise? Her legs felt weak as she made her way towards the craft, with some trepidation but great anticipation. She had never been in a helicopter before.

Her nerves didn't improve any when Samael emerged from behind it, dressed in jeans and a blazer. He was also wearing aviator sunglasses which he removed as he approached.

"Good morning, Contessa," he said with a smile as bright as

the sun. He looked good enough to eat. He was freshly shaven. Short black hair immaculate. Eyes glinting in the light as they did the night they met.

Sofia's cheeks burned. There was something about the way he said her title that gave her chills.

"Good morning," she said.

He opened the passenger door and extended his hand. "After you."

"Thank you," she said, climbing into her seat. Then, in an attempt to appear perfectly at ease, she asked, "So, is this yours? Does it belong to your company, I mean?"

He nodded. "Yes," he said. Then, rocking his head, as if humility forbade it, he added, "So does the hangar, that building, and pretty much the whole of this island."

Sofia's eyes widened. She wanted to say something, but words failed her. Samael politely filled in. "So, are you ready to see Venice from a whole different perspective?" he asked.

She nodded enthusiastically.

"Great. We'll get going as soon as the pilot gets here," he said, looking at his watch.

"Oh good," she said, with a sigh of relief, and finally finding her tongue, "For a second there I thought you were going to go all Christian Grey on me and fly it yourself."

"No idea who that is," he said, before pushing the door and making sure it was securely shut behind her.

Sofia marvelled at the interior of the craft, remaining as still as possible for fear of touching something she shouldn't. The helicopter looked small from the outside, but inside the cabin was spacious and luxuriously kitted out with polished wood with gleaming metal accents, as well as plush leather seats and LCD entertainment screens.

Then the pilot's door opened, and Samael climbed in, closing it behind him.

"Do you mind?" he asked, motioning to her leather seatbelt. Sofia shook her head because her tongue abandoned her once more as he leaned into her. He was so close she could smell him. Ocean breeze and cedarwood. She could feel heat emanating from his body. She gasped as he tugged on the strap. "There we go," he said with a smile. "All strapped in." Then he sat back and fastened his own seatbelt before flipping switches that prompted the engine to whirr to life.

"Samael?" Sofia said warily.

"It's Sam, by the way. Oh, and you're going to need this," he said, retrieving a headset from a nearby hook, "so we can talk to each other." Sofia removed her beret and allowed him to gently place the headphones over her ears. She was looking straight into his green eyes now, set like emeralds in that amazingly symmetrical face. But the moment only lasted a second before he retreated into his seat.

"Don't worry," he said, placing his own headset over his head and donning his shades once more. "I'm fully certified. Got my license a few days ago." He followed that up with a wink. Then he spoke into the microphone of his headset in perfect Italian before flipping more switches. The noise of the engine increased as it whirred and whined.

Moments later, he told her to hold on as he pulled on the controls and the helicopter gently lifted off the ground.

Sofia squeaked and clung onto anything she could find as the tarmac rapidly fell away. They ascended high into the sky before banking right, out over the water.

The helicopter's blades sliced through the crisp winter air as Venice and its lagoon transformed into a glittering tapestry of terracotta rooftops and winding canals. Sofia swiftly made the transition from being so terrified she could barely open her eyes as they ascended, to almost pressing her nose to the glass as she marvelled at the historical slideshow beneath them.

Sam was smiling at the wonder on her face when she turned and declared, breathlessly, "It's stunning!" her voice rebounding back to her in her headset.

"I know," he agreed, watching her, and there was something about his gaze that told her that he might not actually be referring to the canvas below but to her. The mere notion brought that familiar glow back to her cheeks.

"Oh, look!"

It was the Basilica San Marco, its domes glinting in the morning sun. Then Ponte di Rialto, the oldest and most famous bridge spanning the Grand Canal. And there, like a jewel in the crown, Palazzo Rosso.

Sam expertly piloted the helicopter over to the outskirts of the city and the Venetian lagoon, where a giant orange stripe sliced through the waters of the Adriatic.

"The MOSE project," Sam narrated over the headset.

"Oh, I've heard of this," Sofia breathed, awestruck. She knew there was a plan in place to develop technological advances to defend the city from rising water levels, but she never knew it was as impressive as what she now saw below. "Wow, it looks much bigger than I imagined," she added, as they circled the giant metal structure. It looked like a mechanical spine running the length of the lagoon.

"The gates are connected by a network of hydraulic and electrical systems. That row of giant pontoons you see there, floating in the water, are ready to be inflated and used to support the gates when they are raised. This entire project is a testament to human ingenuity. A complex system designed specifically to safeguard one of the world's most precious and endangered cities."

"It's amazing," Sofia breathed. "Sad that there's been so much controversy around it."

"Yes. But Karlson has stepped in now. We're working with

stakeholders to make sure that the original dream is realised, and that Venice is saved. It's what my father wanted," he added thoughtfully.

Sofia turned to him. She detected sadness in his voice even over the whirr of the engine and the tinny distillation of the headset. Now it was his turn to catch her looking. He smiled at her. "Ready for the next leg of your tour?"

"There's a next leg?"

He pulled a face. "Yeah, of course," he added. "Hold on."

Sofia felt the helicopter bank and tilt. It was like one of those theme park rides, the only difference being that she was no longer afraid.

They travelled north for thirty or so minutes as blue waters gave way to the greyness of industrialism and then the lush green of the countryside, the land beneath them dotted with small farmhouses, villages, and church spires before revealing the rugged peaks of the Dolomites dusted in snow.

They glided over evergreen pine trees for several minutes before reaching a clearing with a lake and a small cabin nestled on a hillside, smoke curling lazily from its chimney. The chopper circled and then slowly began its descent, its blades whipping up a whirlwind of leaves and snow as they touched down.

As the engine and rotors slowed, Sofia could barely get her harness off fast enough before she was pulling on the door and spilling out into the quiet.

It was otherworldly.

The air was mountain fresh with a hint of pine and woodsmoke. The sky was a deep shade of blue, with clouds as white as marshmallow.

It was like stepping into a painting.

Sofia sighed with contentment.

"The air is lighter at this altitude. It's possible you may feel a little lightheaded," Sam said, "but it's perfectly normal."

He was right. That's exactly how she felt, only she didn't think it was the altitude. It was everything else.

When she shivered, Sam said, "Yeah, don't let the glorious sunshine fool you. It can get really chilly up here. Come on. Let's go inside," he said, extending his hand. When she looked at it, he added, "I wouldn't want you to slip over."

She let him take her hand in his and, as the helicopter's hum faded and the bird chorus took over, they made their way inside.

The log cabin was sumptuously snug with warm rugs and throws and a roaring fire. A wide picture window gave a stunning view over the lake and the mountains beyond.

Sitting in front of the window was a wooden table set for two, restaurant-style.

Sofia gawked at her host. "Please," he said, pulling her chair out for her.

They dined on pan-seared Venetian-style duck breast with a balsamic reduction, served with creamy polenta and sautéed wild mushrooms. For dessert they indulged in the classic Italian sweet, tiramisu, which happened to be Sofia's favourite. The food had been left ready in a warmer. She imagined it had been prepped by staff prior to their arrival since she didn't sense there was anybody else at the cabin but them.

After lunch, it was coffee and conversation by the fire. Sofia could not remember ever feeling so relaxed with someone in her entire life, to the point where, if asked, she might even have contemplated staying the night. But then she felt naughty just for having the thought.

"So, what's it like living at Palazzo Rosso?" Sam asked, sipping from his cup.

Sofia rocked her head. "Oh, you know, it's a big place. Lots of history. If I'm perfectly honest, it's a tad intimidating."

"Ah, you know what the secret to that is, don't you?" He waited for a reply, but when Sofia offered nothing but a blank expression, he said, "Make it your own. Instead of trying to live in the imprint of the people that lived there before, you need to just make it your own."

"Huh…" She thought about this. "You know, you may have a point. Although, I'd have no clue where to start."

"Well, I know a few designers. Happy to send them over to you for a consultation. You know, just to give you some ideas," he added quickly.

"Oh, good," she laughed, "because I doubt there's any way I could afford them."

He toasted her with his coffee cup. "If you don't like something, change it. That's what Dad always says… sorry, what Dad used to say," he corrected.

Sofia noticed the flicker of sadness behind those vibrant eyes again. He had obviously been as close to his dad as she had been to hers. And she felt a certain kinship in that.

Silence followed as she considered what to say, filled in by the crackle of the fire. "I used to be the same, you know. Always thinking and talking about Dad in the present tense. I'm told it gets easier though."

He nodded and then promptly changed the subject. "So, your dad was Italian, but you lived in England?"

Sofia laughed. "Oh no, my dad was a true Englishman, and proud."

Sam's right eyebrow lifted. It was something she noticed he did when unsure about something. It was cute. And she was obviously high from all the thin air because she barely knew the man and yet she felt as if she'd known him for months. The familiarity was laced with the inimitable thrill of getting to know and be known by someone for the first time.

"It's… um… complicated."

Sam sat forward, listening. Sofia explained what she had recently discovered, and he reacted with a widening of the eyes.

"Yeah, I know. It was a bit of a shock for me too. I used to be Sophie Cooper, but then Dad died, and I found out that I was actually somebody else."

"Yeah, I know what that's like," Sam said thoughtfully.

"You do?" she asked equivocally.

He shook his head. "Oh, figure of speech," he said.

She wished she could read his mind. That she could understand what thoughts were going on beyond that gaze of his that made her feel as if they were the only two people left in the world.

"I'm sorry," she said with a forced laugh. "I've been babbling on."

"You don't have to apologise, Sofia. I understand." He spoke in such a way that she thought he was going to recount his own story, but he didn't. His voice was masculine yet soft, and dripped in so much auditory honey she imagined him reading poems to her.

She straightened herself in her chair. "What about you, Sam? What about that voice?"

"My voice?"

"Your accent. I mean, you don't have one. No inflection. No… nothing. It's like you don't belong anywhere, yet I heard you speak flawless Italian today. It's weird because that's my forte you know, guessing accents. I used to work at an airport. Anyway, what's the deal with you?" she asked, putting down her cup and leaning on her elbow.

"Well, there's not much to tell. I travelled a lot as a kid, you know, with my dad. I actually went to school in England, then had private tutors. Spent a lot of time in the States too. You know, learning the ropes with my dad and all that. And of course, Italy. We have interests here. Well, we have interests all over the world, really. So, I'm a bit of a vagabond, which is probably why you can't detect a specific accent."

Interests everywhere. Sofia was reminded of the house on Meadow Lane. The fact that it was owned by Karlson, Inc., no longer sounded as mysterious.

"And what about your mum? You haven't mentioned her," she asked.

"Oh, I didn't really know her. It's just been me and my dad."

"And what about girlfriends?"

What?!

The words just flew from her lips across to him. Now she had no choice but to follow through. "Well, you're one of those eligible bachelor people. You know, magazines write about you. World's sexiest man and all that."

"You've been googling me?"

"I may have."

He shrugged and shook his head pensively. "That's just media stuff."

"Maybe. But you must be beating girls away with a stick. Or men for that matter. I mean you could be gay, I suppose," she said. Then, "You're not, are you?"

Realising her words, she put a hand over her mouth.

"God, I'm sorry. I'm so sorry… not that there's anything wrong with that, of course. There's nothing wrong with that, I just—"

"Sofia, relax," he said with a chuckle. "I'm not gay," he said, leaning forward. "And no, there isn't anything wrong with that. I have friends who are. I…" He thought about this for a few seconds. "I just haven't found the right girl yet. You know? For me. I've always felt that most people go through life and relationships in the hope of finding the right one somewhere along the way. Me, I'd rather skip all that and wait until I find that special one. You know, so I can experience it all for real. I know that sounds trite—at least my friends think it does—but that's just how I am. A bit old-fashioned, I suppose. My dad always said, 'Don't chase love, let love chase you,' and I happen to think he was right." He squinted at her. "Does that make me soft? That makes me soft, right?"

Sofia shook her head because that's all she could do. She was captivated by this man. And did he just mention the one?

"…and, of course, because of that, everyone expects me to be like Mr bloody Darcy, all scowly and stuff. But I think you can be assertive without being a dick to people. And, again, I was raised to treat the janitor as you would a CEO."

She was leaning on her hand again, closer towards him, drawn to the strong lines of his jaw, the way his voice dipped and rose, the way his gaze lingered on her. It was as if he were unwrapping her with his eyes, and she could feel that flush rising to her cheeks again as she imagined what it would feel like to be pressed against him, to feel the weight of his desire.

"…so when Maria asked if I would give you a tour of the city, I was more than happy to—"

"Wait, what? Maria?"

"Yeah. Maria Bacciabella. She said that you were new to the city and asked if I would show you around. And so, I thought what better way than a bird's eye view. So here we are."

"Maria? Maria asked you to ask me out?"

"Yeah. Why?"

Sofia's heart sank. Suddenly, she felt foolish. Every thought. Every ridiculously ridiculous fantasy that she had allowed to enter her head was replayed unhelpfully for her embarrassed mind and she felt like a complete idiot. Gazing into the man's eyes like a lovestruck bloody teen! What the hell had she been thinking?

She sat up. "Oh, well, that was really nice of her," she said.

"Yeah. I quite like Maria. She's been doing some incredible stuff at the palace."

"Yeah, she has," Sofia said, sure it was true but mainly for something to say.

Sam must have noticed a shift in her demeanour because he asked, "You okay?"

"Yes. Absolutely fine. Just a bit lightheaded," she said, fanning herself and looking outside. "Um, it's getting late. We should probably head back," she said.

"Oh, are you sure?"

"Yes, I'm sure."

She jumped up from her seat, chair scraping loudly behind her, and moved to the door, where the cold air immediately slapped her in the face the second she opened it. She was instantly giddy.

"Sofia! Wait!"

She shook her head in an effort to dispel the sensation, but her breath was coming shallow and fast again. Heart thumping in her chest. Beads of perspiration pushing at her brow. She was finding it difficult to breathe. She couldn't breathe!

A panic attack? It had been a while. She had hoped she was moving past these things. And yet she could feel that familiar straitjacket of anxiety squeezing around her, tighter and tighter.

"Sofia?" He was calling to her. "Sofia?"

But she didn't hear him. She just kept moving forward, footsteps crunching loudly as the cold sunk its fangs into her skin, draining the air from her body. She clutched her chest.

"I…c...ant...br…eathe…I…c...ant...br…eathe…"

And then the world went dark.

13

TEARS FOR FEAR

SATURDAY NIGHT

For the first time since she had arrived in Venice, Sofia was actually glad to be back in the palace. There was none of that angst. None of that apprehension of being alone in the vast space. Nothing but abject sorrow.

When she entered the ballroom, the flickering light of the dining room beckoned to her, but she wasn't in the mood for food. Instead, she made her way up the staircase and to her bedroom, where the fire roared and crackled enthusiastically, making the room feel warm and snug. The air was rich with a rose fragrance although there were no flowers.

If Sofia were in any other state of mind, she might have appreciated these details. Not least the fact that it felt as if the palace itself was attempting to cheer her. But she was so busy trying not to think about her day that she ended up wandering around in a stupor.

And yet it was after she had finished brushing her teeth and was shuffling back to her bed that she allowed her memory to stray back to that now familiar place of mortification. As if she hadn't done her stint there already, but no, she decides to bring on a bloody panic attack and pass out in front of the bloody man too. He'd had to carry her back inside the cabin to lay her down on the couch like some bloody helpless damsel in distress. When she'd come around, feeling groggy and disoriented, her vision had focussed on that face of his, etched with what had appeared to be genuine concern, and those eyes, green like the leaves of the forest at first dawn. The colour was so intense, she wanted to be absorbed by them and discover the secret garden beyond.

And then she remembered.

The air up here... He hadn't finished the sentence and didn't need to because she had already said it for him in her head. *...the air is thinner up here.*

What he didn't know was that she had a history of this. A history of hyperventilating whenever things got too stressful, inducing an attack until she passed out. It was only when she started working at the airport that she was able to manage it more effectively with the help of Doctor Krauss.

Oh, Doctor Krauss, come back! All is forgiven!

She'd jumped up then, like she hadn't already made a complete tit of herself, and said that she was fine. *I'm fine.*

Except she wasn't. She was still sulking like a big kid. Sulking that he hadn't asked her on a date because he had fallen madly in love with her, but because Maria Baccia-bloody-bella had asked him to. Now why would she do that? Why would she make her think that love had finally come knocking and not only had she finally met *the one* but that he was bloody perfect?

Chris, are you the one?

The one?

Every time she thought about those words, she couldn't help but think about the man she'd abandoned on the street that day, wondering what he might be doing right then, and then felt like even more of a prat for running off like that.

The flight home was nothing like the one out there. She barely spoke. Each time Sam said something she would only offer perfunctory one-line answers. And when he would ask if everything was all right, she would lie and tell him that she was just tired and a little woozy still from the ordeal at the cabin.

Ugh. She hated herself. Especially because she knew how she was behaving. It was the kind of behaviour that her dad would reprimand her for. She was being ungracious, ungrateful, *and quite frankly rude, Sophie.*

Yeah, well, he had abandoned her, so he no longer had a say.

The goodbye hadn't been much better. Even when he asked if she had had a good day—the part where she collapsed into the snow excepted—and tried to have light banter with her, all she could muster was a weak, petulant smile that was a woefully unenthusiastic thanks for the day. She'd then walked off without offering so much as a peck on the man's gorgeous cheek.

She had simmered right up until the moment the driver, a polite middle-aged man who removed his hat when he saw her, dropped her back at Palazzo Rosso.

Then she was alone once more to stew in her misery.

Well, of course, that wouldn't do. Misery loves company. So, she decided to traipse the streets of Venice until she found a public payphone that accepted bankcards instead of coins so she could call England. She rang Janay but there was no answer at home or on her mobile. So, she rang again. Again, and again until she slammed the receiver down in frustration. Then she tried Victoria, all the while girding herself against potential cold treatment, but all she got was *the number you have dialled is no longer in service. If you believe you have reached this number in error, please hang up and try again.*

She tried sending text messages on her useless phone, but they kept failing. So, then she had searched for an internet café, logged onto her email, and sent messages:

I HAVE BEEN TRYING TO REACH YOU. HAVE BEEN HAVING TROUBLE WITH MY BLOODY PHONE!! WILL TRY AGAIN AS SOON AS I'VE GOT IT SORTED. LOVE YOU. XXX

She could have vented in the email, but it probably would have taken her all night and she didn't want their first communication since her departure to be her unloading all her problems, so she decided against it.

She probably should have, but she didn't wait to see if the emails delivered successfully. If they bounced, the reason would only be known to the cosmos and the gods of electronic communication.

And it wasn't like the rest of her day hadn't already turned to shit. Feet aching, she'd decided to walk back home. It was as she was doing this that the steam from her pressure cooker of frustrations started to dissipate, and by the time she was walking through the door of Palazzo Rosso, she had worked through everything and was able to evaluate her behaviour. She wasn't proud. Her father certainly wouldn't have been.

Sorry, Dad.

Now, as she sat in the still of her bedroom with nothing but the crackling of the fire and the occasional lap of water against stone for company, the most peculiar thing happened. A drop of water plopped onto her nose. She looked up. It seemed to be coming through the wood canopy, but she wasn't sure that was possible. It looked like one solid thing.

She lifted herself onto her knees so that she was closer to its underside. She looked all around but could only see one leak. So she stood up, wobbling a little as her feet sank into the plushness of the bed, but eventually managing to regain her balance.

She lifted herself as high as she could, raising herself up onto her toes so she was just inches away from the moisture that had formed on the wood. She gasped when she realised what she was seeing. Droplets of water appeared to be forming on the surface. In itself, that wasn't so odd, but what was strange was the fact that the liquid appeared to have emerged from the eye of one of the figurines. One of the mature female siblings.

Sofia reached out for it as if to confirm what her eyes were seeing but sank further into the bed, losing her balance and crashing to the floor with a loud thump. It took her a few seconds to recover from the shock of the fall. When she tried to get back to her feet, she felt a sharp pain in her wrist. *Of course.* All she needed was an injury to complete her day.

Eventually, she managed to stand. She went into the bathroom and ran her wrist under the cold tap. It hissed loudly as she held the throbbing joint under the stream for a minute or so, until the ache subsided. And it was there, under the hiss, that she thought she heard another sound.

Shhhh…

She stopped to listen. Nothing but the sound of the running water.

Shhhh…

She shut the tap off and listened again. Nothing. Just the creak of timber.

Shhhh…

There! That sound. That unmistakable sound. It shoved an icicle of revulsion into her spine.

Slowly, she left the bathroom and peered around the corner.

Empty room. Crackling fire. And yet there was that spine-tingling feeling again, that the air had somehow shifted and been tainted. No longer fresh as roses but foul with decay.

"Hello?" she called out loudly. Partly because she wanted to be heard and partly because she wanted to scare off any would-be intruder. "Is anybody here?"

Nothing. Just the flame shadows licking at the walls.

She walked further into the room and frowned. The bedroom door was open, but she was sure she'd closed it. She hated the idea of it being open, exposed to the corridor and the rest of the building beyond.

She moved forward and yelped when she saw a figure in the mirror before realising that it was her.

"Shit."

Her heart was wide awake now too, throbbing in her chest, and that didn't help.

She went over to the door and shoved it shut, turned the key, and then tested it. Locked.

She turned, glancing at herself in the full-length mirror. She froze. She could see the reflection of the bed, and in that reflection, she could see, to her stupefied terror, that all of the faces had moved. They were looking down, under the bed. And when she followed their gaze, she could see it, skulking under there. The rouge of its collar protruding from the dark into the overspill of the light. Its black, lifeless eyes glaring at her.

She screamed and woke up. She was lying on the floor, crumpled against the wall. Her wrist and neck were aching, and she had the most terrible headache, but she was otherwise all right.

Then, the memories came. She instantly sat up and peered under the bed. It was empty. Then up. The figurines were all as they should be. But it was when she looked at the rest of the room, and then the door, that she felt an ice-cold bucket of fear tip down her spine. The door was unlocked and wide open.

14

SUPERSTITIONS

MONDAY EVENING

Five days left.

Sofia spent most of Sunday exploring the less touristy side of the city, by foot mostly, so as to not spend money she didn't have. She decided to go on the exploration not only because she felt she needed to know more about her new hometown, but because, after the freak happenings of the night before, she didn't fancy being in the palace alone.

Although, technically, she wasn't alone. She wasn't sure about Armando; she got the feeling he had a place of his own away from the palazzo, although she didn't know where. The housekeeper, on the other hand, had to be a live-in. The creepy part was that Sofia had no idea where her quarters might be. It was reasonable to assume that in order for the woman to be on hand to prep food at appropriate times, she must maintain some idea of Sofia's movements in and out of the palace.

The big question was, did she have access to Sofia's bedroom? Probably. She needed to, to clean it regularly and build the fires. Did that mean she just came and went as she pleased? Sofia would prioritise having a conversation with her about it at the earliest opportunity. The palace was already creepy enough without the help skulking around the place.

The help?

Ugh. She'd noticed this about herself. While she remained very much shy Sophie Cooper on the inside, there were aspects of a more assertive Sofia creeping into her everyday life. She'd so easily settled into the whole dinner arrangement without continuing to concern herself with how the dishes would be cleared away. Nor was she bothered about finding out where the hoover, the mop, or even a duster was, for that matter. The place always looked immaculate and yet she'd hardly paused to wonder how exactly it stayed that way. That wasn't how she was raised.

But should she worry about it? She was supposed to be a contessa now, after all.

Ugh. Every time she heard herself think like that, she rolled her eyes, dwelling on all the other ridiculous thoughts she had had recently too. She couldn't get Saturday's trip and the embarrassing assumption she had made about it out of her mind. It was obvious it was too good to be true, especially for someone like her.

She should have thought herself lucky. How many people dreamt of that kind of adventure? It was the experience of a lifetime. And what was the part she remembered the most about it? Being told that Sam, said handsome gazillionaire, had only invited her because somebody else asked him too.

I was nothing more than a charity case.

Ugh. And on it went.

Monday could not have come soon enough. She was actually looking forward to taking Raffaella's crap, hoping it would keep her so busy she wouldn't be able to think about her weekend any longer.

And thus, her wish was granted. There was more filing and cleaning, as well as more trips down to the hellish cantina. But for some reason, it wasn't anywhere near as intimidating the second time around, although she did little more than hastily deposit her boxes before running back up the stairs, taking the final few calmly and casually, so she could stride out with unflustered confidence for Raffaella's sake. She refused to give her the satisfaction of a repeat performance from the other day.

At lunchtime, Raffaella had left her with strict instructions to take messages only. Although, yet again, she didn't give Sofia the chance to explain that her Italian was patchy at best. Luckily, she only had a couple of calls and both callers spoke English.

Maria Bacciabella also made a surprise visit and asked how Sofia was settling in and about her weekend. Sofia explained that everything was going well, recounting how wonderfully exciting the weekend had been, and how she would be forever grateful to Maria and Samael Karlson for the unique experience.

Yes, she was a fraud. She knew that. But then her father used to always say, *if you haven't got anything nice to say, then say nothing.* So, she limited herself to nice things.

By home time, she felt grimy and exhausted once again. It was an oddly satisfying feeling, like she'd achieved something. Raffaella didn't seem to think so. She said she thought Sofia could have made more progress and couldn't help but wonder what she did with most of her time.

"If I didn't know better, I'd say you spent most of your day chatting to friends, but then you haven't really made many of those since you started here, have you?"

It was a ridiculous comment. Raffaella could see from her desk that Sofia went nowhere but up and down to and from the cantina—Who was she supposed to have made friends with? The spiders?—but she had said it anyway, delivering the insult with that reptilian smile of hers. Sofia could have quite cheerfully slapped it off her face but instead satisfied herself by offering a tactical apology. Perhaps she had lost track of time; her private lunch meeting with Maria Bacciabella had overrun. Well, Raffaella didn't need to know the details.

On her way out, she made a point of exiting through the great hall because she wanted to see how the themed exhibition was coming along. She half expected the workers to still be there, but they appeared to have left for the day. The vast space was deserted.

They had made good progress though. The exhibition looked completely different to how it had that morning. The exterior was now atmospherically lit with red uplights that cast shadows over what looked like a giant demonic face with slanted eyes, as well as two flickering mock torches that appeared to burn like the real thing. They reminded Sofia of the torches outside Aurora's house.

The entrance to the exhibition was no longer a square gap but a wide angry mouth from which a red carpet extended. It slithered across the floor towards the main entrance like a long tongue. It looked very effective, Sofia thought.

After a quick glance around, she detoured for a closer look, the high heels she had worn to satisfy Raffaella's implied dress code clacking painfully loud in the hollow. It was so noisy she considered taken them off, but she didn't like the idea of dirtying her feet on the floor and then later placing them back inside her new shoes. So she ignored the burn of the blisters that had been growing all day and hobbled over as quietly as possible until she reached the red carpet. She paused and imagined herself there on opening night, dressed in her finery on the arm of some handsome stranger, waving at photographers and laughing with the other guests.

She stopped and looked up into the giant face towering over her, like it was a mountain she was about to scale. The monstrous thing looked much bigger and more intimidating up close, albeit not as grotesque as the two human-sized sculptures placed at either side of the entrance, where the light caught them in meticulous detail.

The first was of an ugly demonic creature with wide slanted eyes. It had a balding and pitted scalp with tufts of hair sprouting from it like weeds from cracks in the pavement. It had a tiny, bony nose and a wide face full of serrated teeth. Its withered humanoid body was wrapped around the naked form of a female, its long, clawed fingers on her breast and its slithering tongue snaking around her neck. The visceral depiction of the way the thing took erotic pleasure in its victim's terror induced shudders of disgust.

The second sculpture on the opposite side featured a naked muscular man with a similar creature wrapped around him, only with its claw over his genitals.

Sofia was sickened by both of them. The hideous glee of the evil things sent a shiver down her spine.

She considered turning away and hurrying out of there, but she refused to give in to her feelings. Besides, Raffaella had all but told her that she would not be invited to the gala. The grand unveiling was for dignitaries, special guests, and senior staff only. This could be her only chance to take a look.

After another furtive glance around, she stepped through the giant mouth and into a narrow passageway, the darkness only lit by red lowlights that stretched her to long eerie shadows over the walls.

It smelt new inside. Of silicon and fresh wood.

Clack. Clack. Clack. Her heels knocked loudly on the wooden boards underfoot until the corridor opened to a cubicle. It featured a tableau of a black cat with glowing green eyes, backlit by a giant light in the shape of a moon.

Next to it, an illuminated plaque read:

BLACK CAT.

Black cats are believed to be the common companions of witches. A black cat crossing in front of you is also considered bad luck in most parts of the world but good luck in the UK and JAPAN.

Sudden sounds of loud caterwauling and hissing made Sofia jump and instinctively throw a hand to her chest. When she realised it was part of the show, she felt silly and promptly moved on to the next display.

13 or 17?

This was the question posed via giant numbers that appeared to be suspended in mid-air over a hotel room door. There was no number on the door itself. The illuminated plaque read:

UNLUCKY NUMBERS?

The number 13 is bad luck in some countries and good luck in others. In Italy, 17 is considered bad luck since an anagram of XVII (17 in Roman numerals) is VIXI, which means 'I have lived'. This implies death or imminent death. Generally, in Italy, you will not find the number 17 in hotels or on aeroplane seats for this reason.

Sofia was considering this when the sound of a loud door slamming startled her once more and she swore under her breath.

She chuckled nervously, calming herself again, rationalising that each exhibit must work on some kind of proximity sensor and time delay, generating a sound a short time after a spectator stepped nearby. She smiled to herself and vowed to be ready for the next one.

It was of a giant green eye. The plaque read:

MALLOCHIO (EVIL EYE).

All cultures attribute great power to the eye but none so much as the Italians. They believe in the ability to curse someone with an envious or 'bad' look that can bring great misfortune on the unlucky victim. Ward off the harm by making horns with your pinkie, thumb and forefinger, or wear amulets shaped like horns.

That's when Sofia noticed them. There were at least a dozen suspended around the eye by invisible threads.

Horns. They looked like red peppers, shaped just like the amulet she had received from the old lady at the airport. Mia, had that been her name? Maja? She'd almost forgotten about it, but now remembered how at the time she had thought it looked like a chilli.

She clutched her neck but there was nothing there. It occurred to her that she had no idea where the thing was. She was sure she had packed it.

It was with this thought that she moved on to the next exhibit. It presented her with the inverted V of an open ladder.

DARE YOU?

The triangle was a sacred symbol for the Egyptians. For the Christians, it's figurative of the Holy Trinity. Breaching the boundaries of the space within by walking under the ladder will undoubtedly bring bad fortune. Dare you?

The exhibit then offered either a route under the ladder or one around it. Sofia stepped around it. She figured she'd already had her fair share of bad luck without courting more.

She moved forward and heard rain before a shower of it materialised from the ceiling, falling onto a black umbrella and dropping into a grate in the floor.

She smiled. It was impressive. It looked like the water was coming out of thin air.

UMBRELLAS.

Umbrella stands outside of your home are essential if you don't want to risk bringing misfortune upon yourself. Opening an umbrella inside your home is for sure a forecast for financial ruin!

Finally, Sofia had learned the silly meaning behind her father's insistence that she never open an umbrella in the house. She smiled fondly at the memory and continued on.

She yelped when she saw her own reflection in a large hanging mirror. Wow. She looked worse than she thought, and she immediately attempted to rearrange strands of her dishevelled hair.

MIRRORS.

Breaking a mirror, no matter its size, is for sure to bring bad luck. But worse, a mirror that cracks on its own is a portent of doom, for either the one in its reflection or someone close to them.

It was a dark thought. She felt as if she had already lost her friends. Not being able to make contact with them already made her feel depressed. She couldn't imagine losing them forever.

Today, when her latest attempt to send a message to both Victoria and Janay had failed yet again, she'd given serious thought to using the phone on Raffaella's desk. But she'd chickened out. The idea of being caught making a long distance call on the office phone was just too uncomfortable for her. Instead, this evening she was going to check, once and for all, if the palazzo had a landline hidden somewhere. If it didn't, she was going to try another public phone and ring all night if she had to. She wanted, no, she *needed* to make contact with home.

Home?

She was considering this as she studied her reflection in the mirror, while at the same time bracing herself for the loud sound effect of smashing glass.

None came.

Just as well. She'd had enough scares for the day. Now, all she wanted was—

"Shit!" she hissed and whirled around.

Somebody had been standing behind her. It had only been for a split second, but there had definitely been somebody there. She had seen the reflection. A dark shape several feet down the corridor.

And yet it was empty.

Did she imagine it? Was the exhibit starting to get to her? Maybe that was its purpose. The low lighting, the sound effects, the plaques, all designed specifically to influence unsuspecting minds and heighten the experience.

"Hello?" she called, her voice reverberating around her.

Silence.

"Who's there? Is there somebody there?"

Silence.

This was a mistake. Coming in here was a big mistake.

She was already feeling jittery because of the strange

happenings at the house and walking through this spectacle of superstition alone in the dark hadn't helped her nerves any. Now she was seeing things and—

The strangled caterwaul of the cat reached out of the gloom and raked icy claws of fear down her spine. She hadn't imagined it. Someone *was* in the exhibit with her, and they'd just visited the black cat display.

So why didn't they answer her?

She drew a breath to call out but decided against it. For some reason, she was suddenly afraid of drawing attention to herself.

Slam!

The slamming door sound effect of the hotel room. Whoever was there with her was now at the unlucky numbers exhibit and was heading her way. She stepped around the mirror, her footsteps horrifyingly loud on the wooden floor, and moved forward, past another exhibit.

...A hat...A bed. *Priests hearing final confessions would lay their hats on the bed... signifying eternal rest...*

She picked up the pace, ignoring other displays, eager to reach the exit now. She staggered to a halt when she saw the light up ahead darken, as if a presence had blocked the path at the opposite end of the passageway.

And then, what was that? It sounded like the hissing sibilance of people whispering to each other. Was this another special effect? If so, she hated it. She hated it because it sounded just like the whispering she'd heard back at the palazzo.

"Hello?" she shouted, frustrated, confused. Was this really happening, or was it all part of the experience?

A painting of *The Last Supper* to her left was swinging, as if it had been disturbed by something.

*Creak...Creak...Creak...*it squealed as it rocked back and forth... *THIRTEEN. The thirteenth guest at Jesus Christ's table was Judas Iscariot. So, if you ever find yourself seated with another twelve* *people, you'd best watch...*

Sofia turned towards the exit once more but jumped back when she felt the air shift in front of her. If felt like something solid was blocking her path. But there was nothing there! She could see through to the next cubicle.

Heart hammering in her chest... breaths coming fast and shallow, she slowly lifted a shaky hand up in front of her, reached out and...

Impossible! She *touched* the air in front of her. Suddenly, the heel of her shoe gave way, slicing through the moment. She shrieked, both at what she had just experienced and the fact that she had now almost fallen to the floor.

Yet she couldn't linger. She scuffled on, broken heel be damned, rushing back towards the entrance.

Thump! Clack! Thump! Clack! Thump! Clack! was the nerve-jangling sound she made as she half ran, half stumbled forward, screaming as she went, hands outstretched in front of her both to feel for anything that may be in front of her, unseen, and to stop herself falling over. Were she not so racked with terror, she would have stopped to kick off her shoes, but she didn't dare slow down or look back.

Faster. Past the umbrella, the ladder and the other spectacles that screeched out as she flurried by them before falling out of the demon's mouth and into somebody's arms where she continued to cry out hysterically. The sound of her voice filling the cavernous space as tight arms encircled her was horrifyingly reminiscent of the two statues either side of her.

"NOO! NOOOO!" she yelled. "NOOOOO!"

"Sofi...Sofi...Sofia! It's me, it's me! Sofia! Calm down! You're all right! You're okay. You're all right. You're okay."

The voice repeated itself over and over, becoming calmer and calmer, until, eventually, she became aware of its gentleness and the soft hands that held her.

"Cameron?"

"Yes, it's me."

"You scared the shit out of me!" she complained, pulling away, pushing the hair off her face, and recomposing herself as best she could.

"*I* scared the shit out of *you*? I think you've already scared the shit out of yourself by the look of you," the Scot said with a chuckle. "Did you not enjoy the exhibit?"

"I saw something in there," she said quickly, stepping away and pulling off her shoe. The damage had already been done.

"You did, aye. That's kind of the point."

"No, I mean I saw something in there. Something…"

She turned her gaze back to the entrance, as if expecting whatever she had been running from to come screeching out after her at any moment.

"Something invisible," she said quietly, knowing how it sounded.

"You saw something creepy inside an exhibition about creepy things and it freaked you out? Sounds pretty cool to me," he added with a wry smile.

Sofia scowled. "Not quite how I would describe it," she said with a sigh. "It seemed so… real."

"Aye, it does. I helped design some of the exhibits, ya know?"

"Really?"

"Aye. I was gonnae offer to take you on the tour and then out for a drink, but you've snuck in before I've had the chance to, like a wee cheeky one."

"A drink?"

"Don't worry. It's not a date or anything. Strictly celebratory, with you surviving the first day of the week and all."

Barely.

Sofia sighed again, the engine of her heart humming back to normal now she had company.

"Or we could go back inside, and I'll give you a proper tour of—" Cameron began, faltering when he noticed the frown on her face.

"I am *not* going back in there," she said emphatically.

"That good, eh?"

She rocked her head. "I thought the idea was to entertain the visitors, not scare the crap out of them," she said, finally allowing herself a smile, but it soon disappeared the moment her eyes fell on the two sculptures guarding the entrance once more. "Ugh," she said, turning away from them.

"What, ya don't like them? I helped design them too."

She nodded knowingly. Somehow that didn't surprise her. She imagined that if she had a brother, he'd probably be just like the man standing before her. Trouble, but in a good way.

"Oh, come on. You've got to admit, they're fascinating things. I mean the detail is excellent," he said, stepping closer to one of them and patting it on the head. The action went some way in dissolving its ugliness.

Sofia pulled a face. "Grotesque is more the word I would use. What are they supposed to be anyway?"

Cameron made an exaggerated face of melodramatic shock. "What, ya don't know?"

Sofia shot him a pointed look.

"Well, it's Incubus and Succubus," he said. When she continued to look perplexed, he added, "Don't you know your demons, Sofia?"

"Can't say I'm an expert, no."

"Allow me to explain," the guide said gleefully, playing into that irritating brother role she'd already assigned him. He pointed at the first sculpture. "Incubus. Also known as the demon of sex. It's believed to visit its victim in the dead of night and use them for… well, ya know… jiggy jiggy. That one over there is Succubus, the female equivalent, as in it visits men for sex in much the same way. Although, technically, they don't tend to stick to fixed gender stereotypes. It's kind of a free for all, if you know what I mean," he said with a lift of an eyebrow.

Sofia shook her head.

"No? Okay. Tough crowd. Anyhoo, once the incubus has chosen its intended partner slash victim, it attaches itself to them—a sexual parasite if you will—visiting them regularly for its own gratification."

"Great. Now they disgust me even more," Sofia chimed in. The thought of that ugly thing touching her made her stomach turn.

Amused by Sofia's reaction, Cameron continued. "Yeah, I see what ya mean. If it's any consolation, most of the time the victims aren't even aware of their nocturnal visitor. You know, on account of them being asleep. To them, the whole encounter is nothing but a wet dream. The incubus is also known to be a shapeshifter, so it can appear as anything it wants to. Whatever it needs to be to facilitate the deed, as it were. It could be the object of the victim's desire or, if the demon's in a mischievous mood, a work colleague or even a relative."

"Eww." Sofia cringed at the very idea.

"The point is that, to the victim, the net effect is only that they wake up hot, bothered, and possibly a bit exhausted. You know, as if they've actually done the biz. And often, they kind of have." When Sofia pulled another disgusted face, he added. "No? More about that later, I suppose. The worst part is that sometimes, though rarely, mind, some people emerge from deep REM a little prematurely. That's when it gets kind of messed up."

Sofia cocked her head. "Messed up?"

"Well, you must have heard about sleep paralysis, right?"

"Like night terrors?"

"Kinda. Have you heard the story of the old hag? That's where people say they woke up to find themselves paralysed with an unknown presence in the room."

Sofia swallowed hard as her heart's engine fired up once more. "Presence?"

"Well, the stories vary from person to person, but the general theme tends to be the same. Some report seeing an ugly imp sitting on their chest, its weight crushing them to the point they can't breathe. Others have reported other entities like the old hag or even shadow spectres. You know those times when you think you've seen something move from the corner of your eye? I mean, nobody truly knows if …"

Cameron trailed off when he noticed the look on Sofia's face. "Hey, ya all right? You're looking a wee bit pale even in this light."

"I'm fine."

"I mean, you know I'm just messing with ya, right? This is just folklore shite fused with a bit of actual science."

"I know. Of course, I know," Sofia said with a casual shrug. And it would have been easy for her to end the conversation there, but there was something about the things Cameron was explaining that both repulsed and intrigued her. "Please finish what you were saying."

Cameron eyed her curiously, thrusting his hands in his pockets. "Well, there's not much more to say, really. The incubus is just one of the more fascinating entities. At least I think so. There's none of that *Exorcist* pea soup stuff for a start. They don't possess you or anything. They just enjoy amusing themselves at their victim's expense. They're like morally challenged children who can't help but squeeze their pets to death. I mean, don't get me wrong, they can be charming too. As shapeshifters, they sometimes make an effort to look gorgeous for their victims. I wanted to include them in the exhibit itself, you know, instead of sticking to the usual black cat shite only. I think it would have been so interesting and made more sense. Imagine these beasties straddling a model of a life-sized female. I suggested we make one based on Megan Fox but, well, Maria wasn't keen," Cameron added forlornly.

Sofia couldn't tell if he was serious, but it made her smile. Although something about what he said stood out to her. "Why would it have made more sense?"

"Eh?"

"You said it would have made more sense to include the incubus and succubus as a full exhibit. What do you mean?"

"Well, that whole black cat witches' companion thing is a load of bollocks really. Pardon my French."

"Why?"

"Because witches, like a lot of people, both today and throughout history, like to keep cats as pets. And some of them, of course, are black. But a real witch's pet isn't a true furry ball of fluff but is actually an incubus. At least it is in my opinion. They hang around covens like woodlice under rocks, often doing their bidding in exchange for sexual favours."

"Sexual favours?"

"Yeah, a kind of you-scratch-my-back-and-I-scratch-yours situation. Collecting samples and whatnot."

"Samples?" Sofia asked, reluctantly and already vaguely disgusted, rubbing at the chill that had suddenly settled on her arms.

"Yeah, you know, collecting… um, ya know…"

Sofia looked at him and cocked her head. It was the first time since meeting him that the Scot had looked uncomfortable.

He stepped closer, glancing around to make sure they were still alone, and then added in a loud whisper, "You know. The lifeforce. The seed."

Sofia squinted at him.

"You know. Sperm."

"Eww! Cameron!" Sofia slapped the man on the arm. "That's gross!"

"No, seriously! Well, as serious as you can be when talking about mythical beings. Women are seen as the vessels of life and man's sperm as the seed. Witches use it in spells a lot. With its ability to start life, it's considered extremely potent."

"You know that's absolutely disgusting, right?"

"Hey, I didn't write the rules of witchcraft," Cameron said with a shrug.

"Yeah, but you also said these things can be cute. They sound like violent rapists to me."

Cameron rocked his head. "You've got a point. But as long as they get their way, incubi are otherwise fairly innocuous."

"And if they don't?"

"Well, they are demons after all, and they revert to type. They might torture their victim at first, playing games with them to make them think that they're losing their mind. For example, they might visit during the night, while the object of their desire is asleep, and move stuff around the place. Ya know, make a mess, hide things, leave doors or windows open. Sometimes, they'll even braid or cut hair. Imagine that, eh? Waking up to find all your hair shorn off. And they like to take their time. This stuff can happen over weeks. Slowly squeezing their pet, like I said. Squeezing it until it can't breathe anymore..."

Sofia felt her chest tighten and her mouth run dry as she remembered that night at Greenfields. That morning in the barn.

"... and even mimicking the things they say."

"What did you say?" Sofia asked.

"What did you say?" Cameron mimicked Sofia's voice as closely as he could.

"What?"

"What?"

Sofia frowned. "Stop."

"Stop."

"Cameron, stop doing that," she said, heart throbbing.

"Cameron, stop doing that," he said with a playful inflection.

"Cameron!" Breaths coming rapid and shallow.

"Cameron!"

"Cameron, I mean it, stop it!" she yelled, tears welling in her eyes.

"Cameron, I mean it, stop it!"

As her tears broke free, Sofia DaTerra turned and ran as fast as her feet would carry her, Cameron's mocking voice chasing after.

15

FRIENDSHIPS

MONDAY NIGHT

The sky had shaken off a cloak of aggravated rain clouds and laid bare the beauty of the constellations. As Sofia burst out of the Doge's Palace and hurried across the promenade, her naked feet splashed loudly through the cold water. The moon, eager to assert its dominance, had already turned the tide. The Adriatic was no longer lapping against the stone façade of Piazza San Marco but was now washing over it in gentle strokes, creating an oscillating mirror in which the city admired itself.

"Sofi! Sofia!"

It was Cameron, chasing her as she took the long route around the square where the water was presently at its shallowest.

Eventually, as she drank the fresh air into her lungs and became aware of the freedom of the open space, Sofia slowed, content that she had put enough distance between herself, the exhibition, and Cameron's words.

"Sofia, I'm sorry. I'm really sorry. I didn't mean to upset ya," Cameron said breathlessly, as he finally caught up with her.

After swiping at the tears on her face, she still couldn't find the words, so she shook her head in response. Sofia had no idea how to deal with what she'd just learned. In fact, now that she was out in the fresh air, she wondered if she might have somehow misinterpreted Cameron's words, but she knew she was only telling herself that because she wished it to be so. Deep down, she knew. She'd been denying the truth of her senses for a while now and, as convenient as it would be to continue to write off everything frightening as a fabrication of her mind, she had to accept that it wasn't. Not all of it, anyway. What Cameron had described bore an uncanny similarity to what she had experienced back at Greenfields.

What was she supposed to do with this realisation? Who could she talk to about it? Doctor Krauss? He'd twist her words in the usual way until she came to the usual conclusion; her mind was making this shit up, this time because of the additional stress she'd put herself through by uprooting her life and moving to a foreign fucking land!

She was angry, frustrated, confused.

Afraid.

She couldn't talk to the girls about this even if she could get in contact with them. She had done a spectacularly good job of alienating one and abandoning the other, despite her protestation.

And so, ironically, the most useful person to her right now, who might be open-minded or interested enough to listen without treating her like she'd lost her mind, was already walking beside her.

Together, they silently dodged the hordes of tourists and assorted Carnevale characters, many of them dressed in a range of spectral colours with costume designs that seemed to glow under the night lights.

"It's fine. I'm fine," she said eventually, averting her gaze as she stepped up onto an elevated plank runway that lifted them up and over the wash. She needed some time to recover and was afraid that he might read something in her eyes. "I'm just feeling a little sensitive right now," she lied. She couldn't think of how to raise the subject without sounding ridiculous.

"No, I'm the one who should be sorry. I get too excited about this stuff, and I act imbecilically. Most of the people here who aren't tourists would sooner pay me to shut up than hear me drone on about it. You showed some interest, which was all the encouragement I needed, but still, I took it too far. My bad. I'm sorry, Sofia. Truly."

Since they were forced to walk in single file as they trudged glumly along their side of the platform, Sofia still couldn't see his face, but she could hear his sincerity.

They walked in silence for several seconds, while, conversely, the night revellers travelling in the opposite direction whooped and hollered, thrilled to be participating in one of the world's most celebrated forms of ostentatious hedonism.

Tonight, anything goes.

A pair of flamboyant men in 18th century costumes and masks wolf-whistled at her as they passed.

"Buona sera, signorina," they said appreciatively.

Sofia couldn't see their faces, but their tone said it all. She made a conscious effort to smile at them before finally stepping off the runway and down onto the stone slabs, wincing at the cold and rough surface.

“Imbecilically?” she said suddenly, glancing at the tour guide. “Is that a word?”

“I think so. I hope so, or I’m gonnae look like even more of a plonker, aren’t I?”

Sofia smiled. “It’s really okay. I’m just… I…” No, she still wasn’t sure how to explain it and searched for something else to say.

“It’s the move and everything, you know? It’s all new to me. And this city. The history. The secrets. It takes some getting used to. If you’d seen what I’ve seen and where I live now, you’d know exactly what I mean. And why all that stuff about demons scared me shitless.”

“Why? Have you just moved into *Palazzo Dario*?” Cameron asked seriously, as they descended steps that led off the main thoroughfare to the quiet of the back passages and canals.

Sofia looked across at him with a furrowing of her eyebrows.

“You haven’t heard of the curse of Palazzo Dario? It’s probably one of the most haunted places in the world. Also known as *the house that kills.* People who have had anything to do with that house have either gone bankrupt, been murdered, committed suicide. Some say that…”

Cameron trailed off when Sofia stopped suddenly to give him another pointed look. “Oh, shite. I’m sorry. I’m an idiot,” he said. “I’m doing it again. I told you. No bloody filter.”

Sofia shook her head and smiled. The man obviously could not help himself. “You can’t help acting *imbecilically*, you mean.”

“You know, this is precisely why you need to let me buy you a drink,” he said, suddenly changing the subject. “As I say, not in a creepy hit-on-ya-new-work-colleague-after-you’ve-terrified-her-by-talking-about-demons kind of way. That would be inappropriate and you’re not even my type. Not that you’re ugly or anything. You’re really hot, just the wrong kind of sexy, if ya know what I mean? Oh, shite, I'm making a right pig's ear of this, aren't I? All right then, two. We'll make it two drinks."

Sofia didn't answer but give him an amused smile.

"Alrighty, alrighty, you drive a hard bargain. Let's call it three. Three drinks is the most compensation I ever pay for opening me big trap!"

Sofia laughed. "You're on. But not tonight. Tonight, I'd settle for you walking me home so I can soak these feet in a hot—"

Sofia yelped suddenly as they rounded a corner and skidded to a stop. Several steps down from them a group of three people, who were all wearing steam punk versions of the plague doctor costume, huddled together looking skywards. The comet appeared to burn brighter tonight. At the sound of her startled arrival, the black stares behind their large ocular cavities of repurposed gas masks and their melted, curved beaks turned menacingly in her direction.

Sofia threw a hand to her mouth as she sensed Cameron step close behind her.

"Under the fiery glow of a malevolent star, the spawn of Satan shall emerge from the depths of the earth to enslave all of humanity, reducing mankind to nothing more than mere slaves to his dark rule," he whispered ominously.

Several terrifying seconds of standoff were finally interrupted by a pair of 18th century noblemen in ornate costumes of cobalt blue with white wigs, who appeared from around the side of a building, laughing. One of the plague doctors turned back to them to speak.

"Eh, ma quanto tempo ci vuole per prepararsi. Saremo in ritardo adesso! Andiamo! Andiamo!" he said, clapping his hands together and shaking them up and down in exasperation, before he, the other doctors, and the noblemen all looked up the steps at the duo gawking down at them.

"Cameron?" Sofia whispered. "What did he just say?"

Cameron hesitated dramatically before responding, "He said, how bloody long does it take yous to get ready? We're gonnae be late."

Sofia turned to him and rolled her eyes. He shrugged. Then they both watched the group file past them, each with a pleasantly surreal salutation: *Buona sera! Buona sera. Buona sera, bella. Buona sera, signorina. Buon Carnevale!*

Sofia and Cameron mumbled a response, both of them frozen to the spot for several moments until the revellers' animated voices faded into the rest of the night's celebrations.

"Cameron," Sofia began, without turning to him.

"Yeah?"

"Did you just stand behind me to hide from the scary masks?"

"No, no, no. What makes you say that?" he asked, stepping alongside her once more.

Sofia turned to him and shook her head before they moved on, slowly now, feet frozen numb and the stone steps beginning to hurt. "Remind me never to wander the streets alone with you at night again."

She smiled to herself. She liked Cameron. He obviously wasn't much of a hero, but there was something about him, despite all his misguided enthusiasm, that rang true to her. She felt like she knew where she stood with him. He was comfortable. Safe.

When they reached the steps to Via Irregolare, Sofia froze. Her mind continued to play tricks on her, it seemed.

Cameron sidled up beside her. "What's wrong? Why have we stopped?"

"This is where I live," she said.

"Where?" Cameron surveyed the houses surrounding the quaint courtyard, their windows aglow with amber light and the vintage streetlamps nearby dispelling the darkness.

"Up there," she said, nodding to the top of the steps where a couple was talking animatedly under one of the lights.

"Up there?" Cameron scoffed. "That's Palazzo Rosso. The Red Palace. I mean, clue's in the name, Sofia. You can't live there because if you lived there that would make you the lady of the house. And if you were the lady of the house that would make you Contessa of Palazzo Rosso. And if you were the contessa then you would be living—"

"Cameron, if you tell me something horrific about the house I've just inherited that I already think is creepy, I swear to God, I will push you into the canal."

"Right. I hear ya," the Scot said, dragging his fingers across his lips as if zipping them shut.

"Now, I need you to tell me something. It's really important. Can you see those two people up there?" Sofia asked, pointing.

"Top of the steps? Aye," Cameron said with a confused frown, looking up and then back at her. "Why?"

"And is one of them—"

"Oh my God, Soph! Sophie, is that you?"

The unmistakable voice rang out like a bell calling her home, instantly tugging on Sofia's emotions, pumping tears to her eyes.

Like in a movie scene, Sofia ran up the steps as Janay ran down them. They met in the middle and fell into a hug, wrapping their arms tightly around each other.

When they had emerged from the embrace, Sofia looked at her friend, still not able to accept what she was seeing. "I can't believe it, Janay. What are you doing here?"

"What do you think? I'm here to see you."

"Yes, but, I mean, what happened? Are you all right? Is Damon okay? Where is he?" she asked, looking around as if the little boy was going to crawl out from underneath his mother's skirt. Except it wasn't a skirt, she realised, but wide palazzo pants. Janay wore them with a light jacket like it was the middle of summer.

"He's fine. He's at home with Mum. I just video chatted with him."

"You did? Blimey, I can't even send a text and you're video chatting. I've been trying to contact you ever since I got here."

Janay cocked her head sceptically.

"I have, I swear! I don't know what's happening with my service, but I haven't been able to call or send messages to you or Victoria."

"Victoria?"

"Yes. I know things got weird between me and her, but I've missed you both so much since getting here and—"

"No, Soph, it's not that. It's… I mean, don't you know?"

"Know what?"

"Good evening, Sofia. I do hope you no mind me talking to Janay while she wait for you," Daniele said. "She look lost and I was coming out of the house so I stop, you know, and keep company with her. I explain about your new job. I hope this okay?"

"He was my knight in shining armour," Janay added with a grin, shooting a surreptitious wink her friend's way.

Sofia recognised that look on her face. Eyes wide and fake lashes fluttering.

Daniele shrugged like it was nothing. As if that was how he interacted with all women.

"Hello? Sorry to interrupt the reunion and everything…" Cameron moved closer into the group.

"Sorry, Cameron, this is my best friend, Janay. She's just arrived from Cambridge… I can't believe you've come all the way here… and this is my neighbour, Daniele, part of the team that helped get me the interview last week."

Cameron nodded and smiled at both.

"So, shall we go inside?" Sofia suggested.

"Actually, Soph, Daniele has invited me… us… out for a drink. We can see some of the sights too," she said with a squeal of excitement. "Apparently, you're just minutes from St Mark's Square and I'm dying to see it."

"Oh, right" was all Sofia could muster.

"I sorry if not okay, Sofia," Daniele jumped in, placing an apologetic hand on his heart. "I understand you may wish to… how you say… um, become reacquainted with your friend instead. This no problem if you wish to postpone, this no problem at all."

"Oh, no, we don't want to postpone, do we, Soph?" Janay said quickly.

"Actually, we were thinking of going for a drink anyway, weren't we, *Soph,*" Cameron replied with a grin.

"Oh, *were* you now?" Janay asked with an intrigued widening of her eyes.

Sofia shook her head. "It's nothing like that."

"God, no. She'd drive me potty. Have you met her?" Cameron asked.

Half an hour later, after Sofia had changed her outfit to one that actually included shoes, the foursome made the journey to Piazza San Marco. It was heaving with celebrants as well as performers. They stayed for a while, absorbing the Carnevale atmosphere from the costumes, lights, music, and colours. Most of the activity took place on rudimentary platforms of wood or floating pontoons as the tide was at its highest.

Then they moved on to some of the back streets, stopping off at the world-famous Harry's Bar. It was mainly for Janay's benefit; she insisted that it was something she wanted to tick off her bucket list. Daniele and Cameron, as the experienced locals, did the gentlemanly thing and refrained from verbalising what they were clearly both thinking, sharing knowing, patient smiles with each other instead. Sofia had read that the place was all hype and of no substance, that no true Venetian would venture anywhere near it. They quickly saw why and didn't linger.

Instead, they headed down stone steps to a lagoon, to an example of one of Venice's more unique eateries. It was set aboard one of the city's last flat-bottomed sailing boats that Cameron explained was called a *bragozzo*. Built in the forties, the old fishing vessel had been converted into a popular restaurant. Daniele made getting a table for four look easy, but the disappointment of other would-be diners nearby made it clear that reservations there were highly sought after and hard to get.

They ate and drank, with Cameron and Daniele playing perfect hosts and drawing a fair few laughs. After dinner, they shared further rounds of drinks in some of the lesser-known taverns situated on the back canals, the view of the city's festivities they offered, the hosts explained, providing a more authentic Venetian experience.

The *birreria* in Cannaregio was a popular destination for discerning locals. The sounds of thumping beats and the lively chatter of the clientele created an atmosphere that was both hip and electric. The establishment served a diverse selection of craft brews as well as *ciccheti* and hearty sandwiches. Cameron was lucky and secured them seats on the outdoor benches that overlooked the vibrant canal. The area bustled with people and the waterway was alive with twinkling lights.

Throughout the evening, it became clear to Sofia that her best friend was already smitten with Daniele. She didn't have the heart to explain to her that he was somehow, although she wasn't exactly sure, spoken for, since his relationship with Aurora was still somewhat of a mystery to her.

As she took a rare break from flirting with him, an inebriated Janay nudged Sofia. "Soph, don't look, but I think that fine bit of stuff over there with the black sweater and white shirt is giving you the eye."

Of course, the first thing Sofia did was scan the crowd to see who Janay was referring to. At first, she had dismissed it as her friend having one too many drinks. But then she caught sight of a black sweater wrapped around muscular arms and those small, neat ears. He laughed at something one of the men he was with said before turning to look in her direction again.

"Oh shit!" Sofia hissed, averting her face, and hiding it behind a shielding hand.

"What's wrong? You don't know him, do you?"

Cameron looked over and grinned. "Aye, she knows him all right. Everybody knows him. It's Samael Karlson."

Janay frowned. "I don't." Then she smiled. "But I'd like to."

"You should go say hi, Sofia," Cameron teased.

Sofia glared at him.

"Sorry, what am I missing?" Janay asked.

"It's a long story," Sofia said dismissively.

"Well, we've got plenty of time," Janay said, not letting it drop.

"Well, actually, you don't. He's coming over," Cameron said.

"Good evening, everyone."

It was his voice all right. Her heart recognised it immediately, despite the alcohol coursing through her veins, already responding to his proximity.

"Hello, Sofia," he said.

Janay turned to look at her friend with a surprised smirk. Sofia finally emerged from behind her hand to look at the handsome man in front of them, who had seemingly been poured into his clothes when he dressed that evening.

"Hello, Samael."

"Sofia, could I have a word?" Then, to everyone else, he added, "If it's okay with you guys. I promise I won't keep her long."

Her companions nodded in agreement, silenced, in awe. Cameron seemed particularly dumbstruck. He had seen the man at the palace a few times, as well as on television and in magazines. He was, after all, a bit of a celebrity.

Sofia blushed at the realisation, and at the fact that said celebrity had asked to speak with her. And yet, "Well, actually, Sam, I'm out with my friends," she said, the words just tumbling ridiculously out of her mouth. She'd had way too much to drink.

Everybody else all but gasped. Janay looked bemused, not only because she had no clue what was going on but because she clearly thought the man looked *mighty fine,* as she would say. Sofia could almost hear her telepathic chastisement. *Are you mad?*

She practically pushed Sofia off the bench. "No, it's fine, no problem. We'll be waiting right here for you, babe. Won't we, lads?" Janay said.

The two men nodded obediently.

Sofia threw her friend a look and then, drawing her coat around her, got to her feet and followed the man through the crowd to a clearing that gave a different view of the canal.

The city was a kaleidoscope of colours. As the chill of the night settled in, the surface of the water shimmered like a sheet of black glass reflecting a glittering sky, the moon and its ubiquitous companion gleaming both down and up at them.

The music was loud and the revellers even louder. Samael had to raise his voice when he spoke. "How are you doing?"

"I'm fine. Thanks for asking."

"Would you like a drink?"

"No thanks. I have a perfectly good drink back at my table with my friends."

Her words came out more clipped than she had intended.

Samael frowned. "Sofia, is everything okay?"

She cocked her head. "Yes, as I said, everything's fine."

"Between us, I mean," he said, gesturing back and forth at the space that divided them.

She saw a look in those eyes as they sparkled in the canal lights. He'd let his stubble grow and his hair wasn't flicked back at the front but seemed shorter and fluffier. He looked so beautiful, yet that only intensified her frustration. Each and every time she looked at him, she was reminded that he wasn't interested in her. That he wasn't hers.

She'd faced reality. She'd accepted that the whole overblown romantic experience the other day wasn't something he had designed specifically to woo her. It was just something he did. It was something all rich people did, flying off in helicopters to have lunch in some far-flung place and not thinking anything of it. Just like it wouldn't have meant anything to Sam. Certainly not as much as it had meant to her.

"Seriously, everything's fine, Sam. But look, you've done your bit now. You no longer need to feel beholden to your promise to Maria. I'm fine. I have my friends. My *best* friend is actually here all the way from England, and I should really be with her. So…" She thought about her next words, her mind fuzzy both from the alcohol and his presence. "So, you no longer need to feel obligated."

"What? I don't feel obligated," he said.

"Well, that's good. I'm glad. Now that we've settled that, I need to get back," she said. "It was nice seeing you again." She turned to leave.

"No, wait, Sofia," he said, moving to catch her arm, but instead he knocked a drink out of someone's hand, the man spilling it over his friend.

"Scusate," Sam said.

But the man squared up to him. *"Ma che cazzo fai? La ragazza oviamente non vuole parlare con te."*

"The girl obviously not want to talk to you," somebody else said. Clearly the man had overheard their conversation and gotten Sofia's message better than Sam had himself.

Sam's expression darkened. "Mind your own business," he barked back.

"It my business! You throw drink at my friend!" the stranger continued in broken English. Sam tried to pull away, but the man grabbed him. "Hey, I talk to you!"

Sam shrugged him off, but the man latched on and was quickly joined by his friends.

Sofia watched as the two men Samael had been talking to earlier pushed through the throng of people to reach his side. The growing gathering of men quickly escalated the argument into a fight. Then, Sofia felt a gentle hand pull her away from the surging crowd as fists shot out in punches.

16

THE NIGHTMARE

TUESDAY. EARLY HOURS.

Four days left.

Sofia didn't witness the brawl. As soon as trouble broke out, Daniele urged them all away from there before the police came.

Instead, they headed home where, after bidding goodnight to the men, Sofia gave Janay a whirlwind tour of her new abode. The whole affair was filled with slurred words and giggles. Neither of them was in any fit state to negotiate stairs, lacking in any capacity to admire the frescos, no matter how much Janay enjoyed pretending as if she were in an art gallery.

It was past one in the morning when Sofia finally showed her friend to her room. She had to be up for work in a few hours, but she didn't care. She was thrilled to have her friend stay. They must have hugged and squealed at least ten times. And it was like a tonic for her soul. Anything to stop her thoughts drifting back to her encounter with Samael.

The young women had much to talk about but agreed that it should wait until they'd both slept off the booze.

Which was good. Sofia was exhausted. It had been a long day, which meant that when sleep came to claim her, she welcomed it with open arms.

Janay was still buzzing with energy, despite her intoxication. She hadn't stopped grinning from the moment she arrived in Venice. There was just something about the place that made her happy. And her friend's new life as a princess in the city was like something out of a fairy tale. She still couldn't get her head around it.

It was as she was brushing her teeth that she allowed herself the fantasy of moving to Venice too. Wouldn't it be wonderful? How would Damon react to the idea? He'd enjoy floating around on all the boats, that was for sure. Maybe Daniele would take him fishing. He would absolutely love that! She imagined the excited look on that little face of his and it made her grin.

But then she spat out toothpaste and let the silly idea wash away with it down the sink. She was due back at work in a few days. The reality of that stung much more than she expected. She hated her job, but she'd left school early and, with the pregnancy and the trials of motherhood that followed, hadn't done much else with herself since. Now, waitressing and domestic cleaning were all she could do to pay the bills.

Still, she wasn't hurting anybody if she allowed herself to

daydream a little. Imagine, she thought to herself, being wooed by handsome young Italians, born of nobility, that would take her away from her hand-to-mouth existence and whisk her off to another land. After all, Sofia's life had changed out of nowhere. Why couldn't it happen to her too?

Yeah, but she discovered her long lost dad. You didn't. You're lumbered with the piece of shit one you have. Don't think about him! Think of Daniele.

She liked the Italian pronunciation, it sounded posher, she thought while slathering moisturiser on her elbows and ankles and imagining that the touch of her fingers were his lips.

She chuckled. She never had time for any kind of beauty regime at home. She was way too knackered at the end of the day for that. Especially after a few drinks when she'd just flop into bed. But tonight, it made her feel good, sexy, as she slid between the silk sheets.

"Daniele," she sighed as the thought of him followed her into blissful sleep.

Janay was thrilled to discover that he hadn't left her at the front door after all and that they had snuck into her bedroom like naughty teenagers where they drank limoncello and laughed some more.

She gazed into eyes that seemed much darker in the low light of the room, like deep chocolate. Delectable. Irresistible. They set her taste buds tingling. Each and every time he looked at her it felt as if the intensity of his gaze was able to burn through her skin and set her senses crackling with fire.

Oh, this is bloody mad, she thought. Absolutely mad. But of course it was. She had never experienced anything like it. Had never felt this way. About anyone. Ever.

Janay had always been overweight but was probably her heaviest when she was a teenager. While other girls reached puberty and began to experiment with sex, she had been overlooked.

Until one day.

It was with an older boy, called Marcus, and her first time happened somewhat unceremoniously over the bonnet of his car. He had told her that he loved her. That just the sight of her turned him on and that his passion for her burned so hot that he had to have her there, then, and in that way.

Janay later learned that her maiden sexual encounter was actually part of a dare. The position Marcus had chosen had nothing to do with any burning desire either, but choreographed to ensure he would not have to look her in the eyes while his friends filmed everything they did.

The video went viral, at least around her school and her neighbourhood. Already often the butt of many jokes, Janay was ridiculed beyond anything she thought she could survive, with the endless taunts then more varied and cruel.

The experience affected her. She withdrew and rarely left the house, spending much of her time lost in dark thoughts. Things only got worse one day when her mother returned from work, seething. She had been shown the video by one of her work colleagues and was incandescent with rage. Her daughter hadn't just humiliated herself but the family. How could she be so naive? So careless? So disrespectful?

Unable to deal with the shame, a distraught Janay had begged her mother to move them away from London.

And go where? You don't get stronger by running away from hardship, Janay, you become stronger by facing it. That's what I did when your dad left. I had to face it and now you will too.

So, she sent her back to school and Janay endured. She faced the taunts. The mash-up animal videos. The simulated sex sounds. The explicit graffiti in the toilet cubicles bearing her name, as well as the crude biro art on her school bag. Until one day when it all suddenly stopped.

You don't get stronger by running away from hardship.

You don't. So, when another girl fell afoul of the same dare, Janay decided enough was enough. For once in her life, her weight was her strength. Taking full advantage of her bulk, she used it to power a fist into the soft belly of the mean little shit to whom she too had lost her virginity. This event was filmed also. *It* went viral, and not just around their school. It became a meme, a video that stood for standing up to all bullies, and Janay blazed as a paragon of righteous defiance. Her life inched back to normal.

That's when she discovered she was pregnant. Everything else became secondary because she wasn't going to give up her baby. She was going to be a mother.

Janay left school, took on multiple part-time jobs, and had worked ever since. Now in her early twenties, her personality might have evolved into that of a sassy, brash straight-talker, but her relationships had remained stilted. They would always come after her need to provide for her boy, but there had been a few liaisons. Nothing of substance, and most fizzled out to nothing, generally on her terms. And she was fine with that.

Until now.

This encounter was unlike anything she had ever experienced before. This man was different. Beguiling. And she wanted more of him.

They were on the bed now, laughing about something, when he suddenly broke off and kissed her. No, it wasn't exactly a kiss, but a tease. A brush of lips like cotton on skin, it was warm, plump, delicious, and sent an erotic current buzzing through her.

She felt desired and that made her feel sexy. Confident.

She leaned in, eager to savour him, but he pulled back and smiled, mischievously, as if he didn't want this. But he did. The lust in those smouldering eyes of flickering flames was unmistakable. And yet he kept toying with her with that velvet mouth of his. The anticipation was sublime.

She offered him her neck as if he were a vampire and she his prey. Only instead of the delirium and pain of penetration, he planted a chain of kisses down to her shoulders and then her chest, sending her heart into a frenzy.

He smelt good. It wasn't a specific fragrance but more of a natural, masculine musk. It fuelled her desire, and she ran her fingers through his hair while absorbing the heat of his body. He was real. *This* was real.

She had been in Venice only a few hours and this gorgeous, seductive stud of a man was already into her. The strange reality of it brought tears to her eyes; she had never experienced a wanting quite like this. To be wanted and—who knows—eventually loved by this man, who was delicately tracing kisses into the deep valley of her breasts, was more pleasurable than she thought she could bear.

She was lying on her back now. Naked.

Naked?! It's okay. The lights are out. He can't see me.

He was teasing again, his head buried in her chest, his tongue trailing over sensitive places. As he nipped and kissed, pain and pleasure made her screw her eyes shut, bite her lip, and surrender to the tantric titillation, the fuel of his yearning fanning the flames of her arousal.

She felt his tongue trailing down the disgusting mound of her belly. His focus on her chubbier parts invoked a cringe of self-loathing—she tugged his head away to areas that were less humiliating.

And yet, instead of complying, his strong hands slowly resisted her as he travelled back down her midriff.

"Shhhh…" she heard him whisper. "Shhhh..."

Reluctantly, she kept her trembling hands over her head as his tongue recommenced its journey. The silky sheets slid off her body, exposing her to the chill of the room.

The action distracted her. She wanted the warmth of his skin on hers once more and emitted a playful, pitiful sound, begging for his return. Begging to feel his lips on hers again.

Instead, both to her excitement and dismay, she felt his mouth travel down between her thighs. His tongue flicked back and forth with such intimate precision, it sent shockwaves of ecstatic pleasure rushing through her body, washing over the goose pimples of her skin, flooding her brain.

She gasped. Eyes shut tight. Fingers buried in the pillows above.

His tongue continued its sensual massage. Tweaking and jerking, tweaking and jerking, setting off a procession of orgasmic tsunamis that made her squeal then scream, then open her eyes.

But for the shadows resurrected by the moon peeking in through the balcony doors, Janay was alone in her bedroom. She felt them watching and mocking her like belligerent peeping toms. Outside, water sloshed apathetically against the stone wall.

She was shivering. Yet her plump cheeks, already flushed and hot to the touch, now burned with the shame of realisation. It *was* all a dream. He hadn't followed her into the palazzo. He hadn't throbbed with desire for her. Quite the contrary. She had longed for him so much, she'd conjured him in a dream.

A wet dream at that. She could still feel the sticky dampness between her legs. The sensation disgusted her, screwing up her face and squeezing bitter tears from her eyes.

She hated herself. Cold. Ashamed.

You're a fat pig! She could hear the voices from her past. *Fat pig! I'm a fat pig.*

It didn't matter what she projected to the rest of the world. The wit, the sassiness, the charisma. It was all a façade. Inside, she was still the insecure, vulnerable little girl she'd always been. And now, her ugliness juxtaposed with this beautiful room, this beautiful city, and its beautiful people, she felt even uglier.

The chattering of her teeth finally spurred her into action. She reached to pull the covers back over her, but they were nowhere to be found.

She crawled to one side of the bed and peered over. Nothing.

She moved to the opposite side. Nothing.

She turned towards the foot of the bed and could just about make out a small mound in the gloom. The sight startled her. It resembled a small child, standing there, watching her, as Damon had done many times before. The first time it happened, it had scared the life out of her.

Damon?

The bed was so large that the tangle of white, red, and gold fabric appeared to be on the far side of the room. It was at least eight or nine feet away, which made her wonder how exactly she'd managed to kick the sheets so far.

She shuddered as she pictured herself writhing around alone on the bed like a horny hippo. The image was so disgusting, the urge to cover herself became desperate.

She started to move from the bed but paused, squinting. Did she just imagine that? The mound of fabric, was it quivering in the gloom?

She leaned across to the nightstand and flicked on the lamp.

Nothing happened.

She flicked the switch again.

Still nothing.

She looked across at the strange formation. Had it grown? Slowly, she turned and crawled forward along the bed, her heavy breasts hanging and swaying beneath her. She was just a few feet away when she yelped and scurried back.

Did it just twitch? Did that mound just twitch? No, of course not. It couldn't have.

She blinked and squinted again but it didn't help. The shape just sat there. She looked towards the door. She considered going over there to turn on the overhead lights, but movement caught her eye.

There's something under there.

Stop being stupid! It's just a trick of the light, of the darkness.

No. There *was* something under there. She could hear it. It was breathing. Slow deep breaths. *In…out…in…out.*

She backed away until she was pressed up against the headboard and attempted to gather her thoughts. Could it be an animal? Maybe Sofia had inherited a pet too.

She glanced towards the door again. There was enough light spilling in through the balcony for her to make out that it was still closed, just as she had left it.

Naked, vulnerable, and now on high alert, she turned back to the lamp once more. A noxious vapour suddenly overwhelmed her, so foul it made her eyes water.

Putrefaction. Rotting meat. She'd been exposed to that stench so many times on her trips to the skip at the back of the café where she worked, the odour was unmistakable. She had seen it too. The instant the smell hit her nostrils, a tangle of wriggling maggots and a cloud of buzzing flies filled her mind.

She didn't have time to process it. The mound was shifting. Growing before her very eyes to form a bizarre humanoid shape out of cloth.

She pulled herself into a tight ball on the bed, her arms cradling her naked body. She could hear it now. There was no mistaking it. Throaty, rattling rasps filled the room as it breathed in and out… in and out… the sheet fabric billowing back and forth in front of what she imagined was its mouth.

She finally found her voice and started to scream but was silenced as a sheet flew across the room and a weight as heavy as the world collided with her, knocking her onto her back once more.

She cried out as her legs twisted awkwardly underneath her as the immense weight of the intruder pressed her into the softness of the mattress, squeezing the air from her lungs, crushing them so tightly they could barely expand. Breaths coming in short, ragged gasps.

The sheet that she had longed for moments before was now cocooning her, a helpless meal in a spider's web. It spun her onto her front so that her face was pressed into the pillow, smothering any would-be screams for help at birth.

The stench was much worse now and, but for the thin veil of the silk sheet, she could feel the cold yet hairy coarseness of the *thing* on her back, jostling for the best position behind her.

Eyes bulging, face overheating, mind numb with terror, Janay struggled to comprehend what was happening to her. Was it a man? A beast? A corpse? A dream?

The stink was so malodorous that it had to be the latter. This had to be a nightmare. There. That made sense. A hideously disgusting nightmare from which she could wake. Any second now she was going to open her eyes to winter sunshine and the languid lapping of water outside. The slosh and hum of boats as they sailed by her window, and it would be beautiful, so beautiful, and she would...

Her thoughts were cut off by the sound of ripping fabric. Cold air crawled over her buttocks before a sudden searing pain of clammy, claw-like hands dug into her fleshy cheeks, the intruder groping and manhandling her.

She screamed, but her mouth was buried deep in the pillow and the sounds came out as nothing but moans. "N....n....ooo. n.. oooo!" she tried again, in vain.

Then it happened. Searing like lightning and freezing like a giant icicle. Brutally. Savagely. She wasn't human but a piece of flesh to be torn, violated. The malicious act sent shards of scorching pain tearing through her nervous system, shunting a stake of abject horror into her brain, numbing her into blind submission.

Hot tears of terror were absorbed into the pillow as her broken body was viciously rocked back and forth. Endlessly. Frenetically. Whatever it was, Janay was sure now it was not of this world. It puffed, slobbered, and expelled hot air, blowing at her hair like an arid draft.

Eventually, after minutes that felt like hours, it shuddered and twitched, grunting like a truffle-hunting pig as it came to a halt. The weight was suddenly lifted from her brutalised body and the bed, then she sensed the thing disappear back into the shadows.

Janay lay still for several seconds before the horror of what had just happened found its way up through her belly, her chest, her gullet, and to her mouth. When her screams came, they were so loud, they echoed throughout the building.

17

RECOVERY

TUESDAY. EARLY MORNING.

Ospedale San Giovanni e Paolo was approximately fifteen minutes from Palazzo Rosso, but their journey there had felt so much longer. Time had continued to drag all morning, each long minute since they had wheeled a catatonic Janay into a side ward passing like a day.

In fact, it had been three hours precisely. Three hours during which it did not matter how many times Sofia asked, begged, and yelled for information from the nurses, all ignored her, each seemingly preoccupied with somebody else's life rather than her friend's.

Not only was she filled with frustration and fear, but she loathed the place. It seemed as though she had been transported back in time by centuries. The thought of all the lives that must have been lost there made her heart heavy. The atmosphere was suffused with a sense of haunting, as if the walls had witnessed too much death and were still bearing witness to it.

The two ambivalent men in bright fluorescent jackets arrived after she called from Janay's phone, coming on an orange speedboat with faded white lettering that read AMBULANZA, making it clear who they were. Yet, as she looked at their destination, she couldn't help but wonder if they had made a wrong turn to some kind of historic attraction. It didn't look like somewhere her friend was supposed to receive treatment at all, if not for the doctors and nurses hurrying back and forth.

The hospital was cold and characterless. Ornate yet depressing. Palatial yet impractical. The ceiling was so high it had the acoustics of a cathedral, with everything seeming to echo. The scuffling shoes of the medical staff. The clacking heels of visitors. The squeal and slam of the doors down the corridor. Yet somehow the announcements the faceless receptionist made still came out tinny and annoying, the radio crackling like the place was an ancient church converted into a makeshift field hospital.

And she prayed. Oh, how Sofia prayed. In her moment of desperation, with no one else to turn to, she cried out to the intangible spirit she had left behind so many years ago. In this temple of medical care, she implored God to spare the life of her friend, break the hold of her frozen gaze, and bring life back to her eyes. She begged for a voice, one that could explain what had happened to her. Why Sofia had found her friend huddled on the cold marble floor, trembling and covered in bloody scratches and bruises. And why she tried so desperately to escape through the bedroom door that she had broken each of her fingernails, reducing them to raw bloody stumps.

Sofia shuddered at the memory and drank from a plastic cup. The strong, inky coffee that had the consistency and taste of liquid tar had gone cold.

She grimaced at the bitterness, then spilt the liquid over her hand when an inhuman screech echoed down the hallway. She turned to see an orderly hastily wheeling a rattling gurney past her while a pair of nurses attempted to subdue a thrashing creature strapped to it. It looked like an old lady, with wild grey hair and black eyes.

The creature paused for a few seconds to stare at Sofia as if she were the devil incarnate, before recommencing its wailing even louder. *"E'qua! E'arivato! E'chi ucide tutti! Tutti! Tutti! Tutti!"*

Sofia gawked at the spectacle until the gurney disappeared down the hall, leaving only the echoes of the demented woman's screams behind. Sofia didn't know what all the words meant. But she understood *Here!* and *Death* and *Kill Everyone!*

She was shivering now. Unsettled. Alone. Afraid.

Then she heard them, their footsteps beating their way down the empty and interminably long corridor towards her. The sight of those familiar faces wrapped her with all the comfort of a warm blanket.

Aurora was dressed immaculately, even for such a grim and ghostly setting. The boys, as always, looked like they'd just abandoned a photoshoot. Sofia wished she had their style. Maybe when this was over and Janay was feeling better, they could spend some time with this sophisticated woman and soak up some tips. Janay would love that. She adored anything to do with fashion and was always reading about that stuff, watching those shows.

Aurora held out comforting arms. "Oh, Sofia, my dearest," she said, her voice sensitive yet full of anguish. Sofia allowed herself to be enveloped into an embrace. "I am so terribly sorry," the woman continued. "We came as soon as we could."

It felt odd. Sofia wasn't one for spontaneous displays of

affection, reserving her expressions of love for what had been her own sacred trinity: her father, Victoria, Janay. She barely knew this lady and yet a cuddle from her was as warm and welcoming as that of a mother.

"Oh, my poor, poor girl," Aurora continued cooing. "My poor, poor girl. How dreadful."

Sofia fought back tears. It was one thing to allow this stranger to act so maternally towards her and another to disintegrate in her arms.

She retained the hug for as long as pride would permit. When she pulled away, she saw Daniele and Gabriele smiling at her with soft sympathy. Daniele reached out and gently rubbed her arm.

"What can we do for you?" he asked, his accent strong.

"If it wouldn't be too much trouble, you could get me a decent cup of coffee" was her immediate response. She liked the boys, but she could do without an audience right now.

"Of course," he said, turning on his heels at once, closely followed by Gabriele.

"How is she?" Aurora asked. "Any news?"

Sofia shook her head, and said, "No, nothing. I seem to be invisible. Nobody's seen or talked to me since I got here." She looked up and down the empty corridor. Still, no one came her way.

"Don't worry. We'll get answers for you as soon as someone… ah, *scusate! Scusatemi!*" Aurora called to a nurse she saw emerging from one of the side rooms.

Sofia watched as Aurora walked over to the woman and said something in Italian. She felt the usual frustration. She couldn't understand everything that was being said, only a few words. In this case it was *ragazza Inglese* which meant *English girl* and *aspettare* which she knew meant *wait.*

She watched Aurora's face crease in a way she didn't think was possible. The beauty seemed to possess such smooth and youthful skin that Sofia had suspected botox, but the frown and the creases that now accompanied the forceful dialect of her words confirmed she might be naturally blessed after all.

Aurora was obviously giving the nurse a piece of her mind, no doubt telling her that her friend had been waiting for a very long time with no news. What kind of impression were they making on these English tourists, these new residents? At least, that's what she hoped she was saying.

Either way, Sofia was grateful she had somebody there to talk for her, to stand up for her. Someone who was on her side. Because she needed it and needed it badly, as she was suddenly crushed by homesickness. She had been beyond stupid to traipse off to a foreign land like this. Who was she fooling? She had barely been able to hold herself together in England. How could she think for one second that she could make it out here alone? And now she'd dragged Janay into it. God forbid the worst happened to her. She couldn't bring herself to consider the thought. All she could see was Damon's tear-stricken face.

She held trembling fingers to leaky eyes. She wanted to go home. In fact, if she had the money, she'd hire a helicopter right now and fly both herself and her friend back to Cambridge. She'd happily clean toilets and live in a dingy little house share if it meant she finally got some control over her life.

New beginnings. What a joke. What a fucking joke! *You're a fucking joke!*

Aurora returned. Sofia greeted her with keen, hopeful eyes.

"Don't worry. She promised to get us some news as soon as possible," she said encouragingly.

"You seemed to be having a right go," Sofia said.

The eccentric beauty rocked her head and the black wide hat that was sitting on it. "Oh, well, you know. This is Italy. They tend to respond best to impassioned discourse," she said with a smile. "So, tell me what happened." Aurora took Sofia's arm and guided her to a nearby bench.

Sofia shook her head as she recalled. "I don't really know," she said. "I was asleep one minute and the next I was woken up by the sound of screaming. I ran to her room and... I...I couldn't get in. The door wouldn't open at first, but then, I pushed harder and..."

She broke off, the words catching in her throat as she recalled the image of her friend on the cold floor, smeared in blood. "I found her there. Behind the door. Naked. Covered in blood." The last words were whispered as if the empty corridor might be interested in what she had to say.

Aurora's hand fluttered to her mouth as her face creased into a motherly frown of concern. She slid an arm around Sofia, whose eyes were brimming with tears once more.

"I've never seen her like that. I never seen anything like that," she continued, her voice atremble.

The boys returned. Gabriele was wearing an unusually solemn face as he handed Sofia a fresh plastic cup of hot coffee. She took the drink with shaky hands and sipped at it. Eyes wide like a frightened animal, she searched up and down the corridor once more, willing someone to walk in their direction.

"How long does it bloody take?" she grumbled angrily.

"She did say that..."

Aurora was interrupted by the thump of a swing door smacking shut and echoing down the corridor. A short man in doctor's scrubs with a gleaming bald head and round spectacles made his way towards them. The rubber soles of his medical clogs whispered quietly beneath him.

Sofia jumped up from her seat, nearly spilling her coffee once more. Gabriele sprang into action and, like a dutiful servant, took it from her.

"Miss DaTerra?" the doctor asked, looking at both women.

Aurora gestured to Sofia. "Contessa DaTerra," she corrected, and then asked, *"Parla Inglese? Lei é Inglese."*

If he was surprised by the young girl's title, the weary-looking man, who was somewhere in his forties, didn't show it. "A little," he replied, referring to his command of the English language. "I'm Doctor Bianchi," he said. His voice was deep for such a diminutive man. Smooth. Silky. Authoritative.

"Is Janay okay?" Sofia asked, holding on to his proffered hand with both of hers rather than shaking it, as though afraid he might walk off again and leave her still without answers.

"Ah, she in stable condition now, yes," the man said.

Sofia sighed with relief. "Does that mean she's going to be all right?"

The man nodded. "She experience much trauma, and has needed stitches, but I believe she can make full recovery."

His accent was strong, but his words were so reassuring that Sofia spontaneously threw her arms around him and squeezed him in thanks.

He responded with a polite but awkward smile as the others watched on.

After a few seconds, Sofia pulled back and wiped a tear from her cheek. "I'm sorry, Doctor. It's just that, well, we're kind of like sisters. She means a lot to me."

"I understand," the man said softly, sympathetically. He had helped her to feel better and she was grateful. She didn't know if it was the calmness in his voice or his kind brown eyes, and she didn't care. Janay was going to be all right and that alone was enough to calm the twin rivers of panic and worry that had been coursing through her all morning.

"I do have some question," the doctor said. "I'm sorry if my English not good," he added.

Sofia shook her head. "No problem at all. Please, ask."

"Can you tell me more what happened?"

"I already told the nurse all I know, really."

"Yes, she shared. Um, you say you find her like this? In her bedroom this morning, correct?"

Sofia nodded like an emotional child, almost feeling her lower lip tremble. Her tongue became thick every time she pictured the scene.

"Yes. And, um…" The doctor shifted his weight. "How do you say? She have a boyfriend last night?"

Although Sofia had heard the man's words perfectly clearly, she thought she had misunderstood them. She squinted. "I'm sorry?"

"Your friend, she have *il sesso?*" He looked at Aurora when he spoke the Italian word for it in the hope that she might be able to assist with the translation.

But she didn't need to. Sofia somehow understood what he meant. "Sex? Did she have sex? No!" she said, with an emphatic shake of the head.

The doctor pulled a face. He looked around to make sure no one could overhear before stepping closer. That act alone sent an unwelcome chill through Sofia. What further terror was there for him to tell? Just when her nerves had started to calm, he'd shaken them awake once more.

"I'm sorry, Contessa, but… um… your friend, she, um… she have serious marks. You know, damage." His words were quiet. Discreet.

"Damage? What do you mean? What kind of damage?" Sofia pictured the patches of discoloration on her friend's body but didn't know what else the doctor could be referring to. Now that she thought about it, she hadn't even paused to examine Janay. Why would she? She had wrapped her in a blanket and called the ambulance as quickly as she could.

"She have the marks on her arms, her… how you say, backside?… all over her body and, um…" He struggled with the word. "Her private part."

Sofia shook her head, stunned. "I don't understand," she muttered. She had interpreted him perfectly. There was no hope to be found in the possibility of miscommunication. And yet, her brain refused to process what she was hearing. "What do you mean, she has marks?"

The doctor rocked his head.

"Dottore, dillo a me." Aurora stepped forward and sought a more detailed explanation in the doctor's own tongue.

"È stata violentata. Gravemente. Abbiamo dovuto suturare lacerazioni che lei ha sostenuto," the man said, quickly and confidently.

Aurora drew in a sharp breath, hand moving to her mouth as if to stifle a scream.

Alarmed, Sofia demanded, "What? What did he say?"

Aurora's eyes were moist with tears and full of compassion when she turned to Sofia. She started to speak but hesitated.

"What? Tell me!" She urged.

"He…he's saying she was raped."

A waterfall of icy realisation cascaded down Sofia's back, her shoulders juddering, her stomach flipping. "But that's impossible. How?"

"He said it was so brutal she needed stitches. That's why they took so long. Who was she with last night?" Aurora asked.

Sofia looked around as though she could find an answer under one of the benches. Then, her mind reeling, "She wasn't with anybody," she said. "We went out for a few drinks with a colleague from work."

"And she didn't meet or talk with anybody else?"

Sofia shook her head. "No. Nobody. I mean, Daniele was there with us. You didn't see anybody, did you?"

Daniele shook his head.

"What about when you came home?"

"No, no one. Daniele and Cameron walked us back to the

palazzo and then we were alone. The doors were locked and bolted. I made sure of it. So, logically, this can't be true. I mean, are you sure, Doctor?"

He cocked his head. *I've spent the best part of two hours sewing the woman up. What do you think?* At least, that's what Sofia saw behind his eyes. But she still couldn't understand how it could be possible. Did that mean someone came into the house? That someone could *still* be in the house? And they broke into Janay's room?

"I can't see how this is possible. It isn't possible," she stated once more, as if by saying it enough times, she could make it true. The alternative was too horrible to contemplate.

She felt like she was going to empty everything out of the tumultuous pit of her stomach, bringing up the tar coffee she'd been running off like oil, spattering the doctor's clean scrubs and ruining Aurora's immaculate red dress that, like everything she wore, moulded itself to her perfectly formed body.

And there Sofia was wearing her usual trainers and jeans. Suddenly, she felt underdressed again, like the penniless orphan she was. Maybe she wasn't really a contessa. Maybe it had all been a fever dream and she was a vagrant who had wandered into this palace by the water, lost, and decided to call it home. Her appearance couldn't belie the truth, and it revealed her as unworthy.

Because that's what she was, unworthy. Unworthy of a friend like Janay. Perhaps she should have dressed up for the occasion or at least put on some makeup. Shown some respect to the seriousness of the situation. She'd probably be coping with all of this much more gracefully if she looked graceful herself. She'd probably be able to handle the news that someone had been in her home last night and had attacked her friend while she slept in the next room.

Soundly. Peacefully. Like the dead. She'd *slept* while her friend was tortured into a non-responsive state by person or persons unknown. But how had they got in? She remembered pulling back the bolts and turning the big key in the lock when the paramedics hammered on the door. Maybe they got in some other way. Through the balcony? The roof? There might even be some kind of secret passage for all she knew. The palazzo was certainly old and ostentatious enough.

You should know, Contessa!

What a fucking joke! The countess who couldn't even save her friend. The countess who—

A sound sliced through her thoughts. At first, she told herself she had imagined it, but she knew she hadn't. It had been as clear as the sound of her friend's rasping, supplicating breaths.

Snickering.

She turned and gaped at Daniele, who looked back at her with his arms folded across his chest. That's when she saw. Most of it had been diluted, slipping back into a look of devastation. Only the dregs remained, but it was enough. A smile. No. Not a smile.

A smirk.

"Are you okay, Sofia?" he asked, unfolding his arms, his face etched with concern.

"You think it's funny?" she growled.

"What?" he asked, glancing at the others, as if there was something he had mistranslated from her English to the Italian in his head and they could explain her question for him.

"Sofia," Aurora began.

"You think it's funny that my friend's in the hospital and that someone did this to her?"

"No, of course not," he protested, his face bewildered.

"Then why are you laughing? Why the *fuck* are you laughing?"

"I wasn't! I'm not!"

"You were! I saw you. I *fucking* saw you!"

"Please, let's all stay calm," Aurora continued.

"Get the fuck out of here!" Sofia yelled suddenly, her voice ringing off the vaulted ceiling. "Get out! GET OUT! GET THE FUCK OUT!"

Daniele held up his hands in bewildered surrender and staggered away from her as if her voice had physically punched him. The light spilling in from the giant cathedral windows dimmed.

"Please, Sofia, please," Aurora said, glancing at a pair of nurses who had stopped to observe the commotion.

But Sofia kept her eyes on Daniele until he disappeared down the hallway, with Gabriele following closely behind him.

Seconds ticked by. A door slam broke the silence that was still haunted by the echoes of Sofia's outburst.

The doctor, somehow maintaining his cool despite the heated exchange, said, "Miss…um, Contessa—"

"Please, stop calling me that," Sofia said, holding up a hand, pushing the title away with the air. She gave a hollow laugh. "I'm not a bloody countess. Jesus Christ, didn't you just hear my foul language? I don't even have the money for your medical bill. I had to give you a bloody credit card that I'm going to have to repay with money I don't have. So, please, stop calling me a fucking contessa!" Shadows shifted uncomfortably over the walls as she yelled.

The doctor shrugged sympathetically and, with emphasis, said, "*Miss* DaTerra. Your friend injuries. They are serious assault. I must report it to police."

Sofia nodded before swiping away a fresh tear. "Can I see her?"

"She rest now. It not a good—"

"Please. I promise I won't disturb her. Please, I need to see her."

"I really don't—"

"Doctor, please!" she supplicated, grabbing the man's hand once more.

He hesitated, then nodded reluctantly. "But, signorina, I must insist you not disturb—"

"I promise," she interrupted, forcing a smile. "Thank you. Thank you so much."

Janay was on a ward now, a long narrow atrium with rows of beds separated by curtains. Sofia imagined the space would have been stunning once upon a time, with its extensive views of the city and giant window to the heavens. But kitted out in the accessories of illness under the dark spotlight of an aggravated sky, there was little beauty to be found there now.

Sofia slipped into the chair by Janay's bed. For some reason, she was wearing some kind of skull cap. Her dark hair was attempting an escape from its confines like the audacious tendrils of a climbing plant.

"Wake up," Sofia whispered as tears filled her eyes.

A heart monitor connected to a patient in one of the other beds began to beep anxiously.

"Wake up, Janay. Wake up. These Italian weirdos have stuck your hair in what looks like a bloody swimming cap, if you can believe it. They obviously don't know you. If they did, they'd know that you wouldn't be seen dead in one of these things. You'd be throwing a fit because your big hair wouldn't be distracting people from your double chin. But you don't need a distraction, Jan. You look beautiful to me."

Sofia reached out and caressed the scratches on her friend's face while her own contorted. She wanted to hold back the tears for as long as she could. She'd already shed enough of them.

Yet Sofia felt how alone in the world she was. Victoria had turned on her, and the only other person she considered family was lying in the bed in front of her. Tubes coming out her nose. Wires attached to her body.

Sofia squeezed her friend's hand as the tears broke free and ran in rivulets from her eyes when a sudden wailing from the next bed over made her jump.

"É qui! É qui! É tornato! É tornato!" the voice wailed as the urgent beep of the heart monitor ascended to a frenzied crescendo. Then there was the scuffling of shoes, the swish of clothing, and bursts of urgent Italian until everything stopped, and a persistent tone sounded. Flatline.

Outside of the privacy curtain that had been drawn around them, Aurora watched a partial view of the reluctant contessa through a gap in the material when footsteps drew her attention.

She turned as Daniele and Gabriele joined her. Gabriele stood to one side and watched on as Daniele stopped in front of her with his head bowed.

Aurora looked around to make sure she was not being overheard before turning to him, seething. "What did you do?"

18

TWISTED

WEDNESDAY. LATE MORNING.

Three days left.

Sofia ran under a rageful, blood red sky that groaned and spat at her as she stumbled through the boggy marsh. She was standing on the bed of the lagoon. All the water had been drained away, revealing drowned carcasses tangled in the weeds, the decomposing corpses of humans and animals.

Mud sucked at her feet as she trudged forward, yet the more she struggled, the more she sank deeper and deeper. Something was following her. She couldn't hear or see it, but she knew that it was evil, that it was death itself, and if she didn't make it to the red river she would die.

She ducked instinctively when thunder rumbled overhead. No, it wasn't thunder but giant hoofs smashing down into the earth.

BANG! BANG! BANG!

She wrenched up her feet, but the stubborn mud held on, as if there were claws beneath the surface, anchoring her in place so that *it* could get her. But she refused to give in. Not yet. Not now. She screamed through gritted teeth as she strained and tugged at her trapped limbs, spittle dribbling from her mouth, veins popping in her forehead. Pulling. Yanking. Pulling. Yanking. Desperately, painfully struggling to free herself as the presence inched closer and closer.

BANG!

Closer…

BANG! BANG! BANG!

Closer…

Then its claws were on her. Grabbing and shaking her.

"NO!"

Grabbing and shaking.

"NO!"

Sofia opened her eyes and instantly shrank back into her pillow in horror. A craggy face with one filmy white eye and a hairy mole towered over her in a cloud of garlic breath.

She sat up, clutching the covers to her chest defensively, her modesty already preserved by a t-shirt. "Bloody hell! You scared me to death!" she complained.

The housekeeper was unphased but took a step back. She stood ramrod straight with aged white hands wringing in front of her, her indignant face as sour as chewed lemon.

Silence reigned. Motorboats purred outside. It was morning but Sofia felt like she'd only just collapsed in bed. Yesterday started as one of the most hideous days of her life and had only marginally improved by the time it ended, like she was being punished for all the merriment of the night before.

When a Trunchbull of a nurse evicted Sofia from her friend's bedside late yesterday morning, she had been escorted home by Aurora. Her elegant neighbour had invited her back to hers for tea and company, but Sofia declined. She had been overwhelmed by a crushing sense of loneliness and yet needed to be by herself. She needed time to process everything that had happened. To think. She had learned a lot over the past few days. Awful, disturbing things that defied logic. No matter how much she tried to rationalise them, a thorn prick of doubt at the back of her mind would not let her.

And yet she'd barely managed to get bathed and dressed before the sound of the door knocker had echoed throughout the building. The sour-faced housekeeper, aloof until now, had suddenly reappeared and announced that the caller was for her with an expression that suggested she found dealing with visitors a personal inconvenience.

It was Cameron who had called, bringing levity to the cold, damp gloom of the grey day. Apparently Raffaella was on a warpath because Sofia hadn't shown up for work without so much as a phone call.

Oh shit! Work! With everything that had been going on, she'd completely forgotten that she'd only just started a new job.

Eventually, once she was able to get a word in edgeways, and while giving her colleague a whistlestop tour of the infamous palazzo at his behest, she explained what had happened. It was the first time since she'd met him that the Scot was rendered truly speechless. His face turned to ash before her.

They debated the very same things that Sofia had already been processing endlessly without resolve—How? Who? Why?—before the tour guide announced that he needed to get back to work. He'd promised to explain to the wicked witch of the palace without going into too much detail.

As he was leaving though, Sofia had felt a distressing pang of abandonment.

"Cameron, would you come with me to visit her tonight? I know it's a lot to ask but—"

"Of course," he had reassured her.

Darkness had easily devoured the miserable greyness of the day by the time they had arrived at the hospital. Visiting hours were nearly over, the nurse had told them, so Sofia was only allowed ten minutes with her friend.

Rain was pelting the glass when they had entered the curtained cubicle. It felt as small as a prison cell. The ward was decorated like one too, with a basic institutional aesthetic of whitewashed walls and metal-framed beds. It was cold and no more than functional. Sofia could not wait to get her friend out of there.

She had brought flowers to add some cheer to the sombre place. Cameron had kindly offered to hunt down a vase while she made the most of her visit.

Sofia had barely sat down in the plastic chair next to the bed when her friend's hiss startled her.

"Sophie."

"Hey," she had said softly, tenderly. "I didn't realise you were awake. How are you feeling?"

But Janay hadn't seemed to be listening. Her moist wild eyes were busy searching the shadows of the tiny space.

"Jan?"

"You didn't see it, did you?" her friend had asked without looking at her, eyeballs darting all around.

"See what?"

"It was in the room. Hiding in the shadows. Watching us."

A lead ball fell to the pit of Sofia's stomach.

Janay finally turned to her friend, eyes wide and haunted with terror and tears.

"I want to go home. I want to go home. I want to go home. I want Damon. I need to see him. I want to go home. I want to go home. Take me home," she had cried over and over.

Sofia had grabbed her friend's hand and squeezed it.

"Of course, of course," she had said, tears brimming in her own eyes. "As soon as you're well enough."

"You too, Sophie. Please tell me you'll come too! Please, Sophie, please. You too. Please, you too, Soph. Or you'll die here. you'll die here!"

"Of course me too. The both of us," she had said, ignoring the chills scuttling down her spine.

"Promise me. Promise me. Please. Please. Please!" her friend had chanted in rapid succession. "Please. Please. Please."

"I promise."

Sofia had believed that Venice was going to be a fresh start, but so far it had proven to be more of the same. Doctor Krauss was right. Her troubles would follow her wherever she went. And part of that, at least, was undoubtedly down to her.

But right now, Sofia needed to deal with the crotchety housekeeper. She was still hovering nearby, frowning as if indignant that Sofia should oversleep in her own bed. But she had a point. Sofia was going to lose her job before she'd even found her feet if she didn't get a move on. But then, did she even care if she was thinking of going home?

To what though?

Sofia tucked her hair behind her ears and composed herself. She was never going to get used to having hired help in the house and concluded that she would be much happier without it. Somehow, she was going to send the woman packing.

In the meantime, she rubbed her face some more as though she could erase the dregs of yesterday's misery and the nightmare that still clung to her like sodden clothes. She could feel the seeds of a migraine sprouting at her temple.

The housekeeper, seemingly satisfied that Sofia was finally stirring, moved to the other side of the room and dragged the curtains open. The view revealed another disgruntled Venetian sky that did little to illuminate the cavern of the room.

When the woman was done rearranging the curtains, she turned to observe Sofia once more, her hands folded in front of her.

"What? What's the matter? What do you want?" Sofia snapped, before realising. "Oh, um, che…um…cosa vuoi*?*" She scraped the words together and hoped for the best.

The woman sighed then retorted, *"Ma la Polizia ancora ti aspetta."*

At first Sofia thought she must have misheard but there was something about the exasperated look on the woman's face that told her that she hadn't. "Polizia? The police? For me?"

"Si. Ti aspetta da fuori."

"They're waiting for me? Outside?"

It was about time. This was obviously something to do with Janay, Sofia thought, and she was about to pull back the covers when she became aware of the fact that the woman still stood there. There was no doubt that she was used to seeing her charges in their underwear, perhaps even naked, but Sofia wasn't used to such familiarity.

"Okay, well, then…um… Grazie," she croaked. Her mouth was dry and tasted bitter, like she'd been eating fried food before bed and had forgotten to brush her teeth. She hadn't, but still, she could use a drink. Yet when she looked up, the woman had already taken her cue and quietly left the room as if she'd never been there.

That was something else. The woman's ninja stealth creeped her out. Sofia sighed. She wished her Italian was better so that she might have a serious chat with her imposed help and her unsettling ways.

She pulled back the covers and instantly regretted it. The cold inside the palace often felt as vast as its emptiness. Being surrounded by water on one side obviously wasn't helping.

She pulled on socks and a dressing gown that looked more like a smoking jacket that she'd found hanging in the giant wardrobe. It smelt musty as if it had been stored there for a few years, but the chill necessitated it. She probably looked a state but who was going to care?

She felt fatigued. Like she needed at least a few more hours in bed, but a glance at the clock told her that it was nearly eleven o'clock. No wonder the housekeeper and her mole were so judgemental.

With a deep breath and, after painting a smile on her face, she descended the stairs to what Cameron explained was the *soggiorno*—a room in a house used for guests. More commonly known as a *temporary stay in a place*—but Sofia preferred ballroom because that's what it looked like to her. And that ballroom was empty. The only thing that greeted her was a weak shard of light through the balcony doors, cheerlessly doing its best to pierce the seemingly impregnable gloom.

"Hello?" she called out to nowhere in particular. The only response was the sound from the rest of La Serenissima as it went about another day.

"Hello?" Sofia yelled.

Still nothing. She turned to go find the housekeeper and yelped when she found her standing directly behind her.

Sofia placed a hand on her chest. "Jesus Christ, you have got to stop doing that!" she hissed.

The woman observed her with her one good eye as if she were something she'd scraped off her shoe. Her hands were not neatly folded in front of her this time but clutching a faded kitchen towel.

"What is your name anyway?" Sofia said, tucking her hair

behind her ear as the woman stared at her blankly. "Your name..." she repeated slowly. "Nome. Tuo nome," she said, pointing.

The woman didn't even blink.

"Oh, forget it. Where's the policeman? Polizia?" she said loudly, like the woman was deaf and not Italian, while holding up inquisitive hands.

"Fuori. Ho detto fuori," the housekeeper responded, pointing towards the entrance hall.

"Outside? You mean you left him outside?" Sofia asked, hunching her shoulders. The cold seemed to be getting worse. That's when movement across the room caught her attention. The balcony doors were actually open, with their curtains rising and falling, the winter chill busily making itself at home. *Why would she do that?*

"Si. Fuori," the woman said. With an exasperated shrug, she turned on her heels and disappeared down the stairs towards the kitchen.

Sofia pulled the gown tighter around herself and then made her way down the entrance hall to the front door where she turned the giant loop handle and tugged it open. It squealed like a stuck pig, pulling on her last nerve.

"Buongiorno. Contessa?" asked a tall, uniformed officer. He must have been over six feet tall and was looking down at her.

That title again. She stopped short of rolling her eyes and squinted into the daylight like she'd just emerged from a subterranean lair. She gave him a bewildered nod.

He was handsome in a brooding kind of way with thick eyebrows and chestnut eyes. Of course, she must be imagining it, but it seemed that every young Italian man she'd seen so far appeared to have some kind of attractive attribute. Was she really that desperate?

Nonetheless, she found herself shifting to stand straighter as she instinctively touched her hair, fiddling with it as she tried to work out exactly who he was. Her instincts told her that he was an ordinary police officer, but the black uniform he was wearing made him look like he was military. Not that she was an expert.

A hubbub of voices outside caught her attention and she took a step out of the front door, but the officer restrained her with a strong but gentle hand. *"Prego,"* he said. He obviously did not want her to leave the building.

She frowned at him momentarily, unable to find the words to ask him what the hell was going on. The cold was encouraging the ache that still lingered in her head and made it grow.

The officer turned away and looked down the steps before reaching for the radio affixed to his chest. When he talked into it the only response was static. He tried again.

As he did so, Sofia observed him through a hazy break of most welcome sunshine. He looked immaculate. He had neatly shaved sideburns peeking out from under his hat and wore a pristine white shirt with black tie. His trousers had a red stripe running down the seam into his shiny black boots. She noticed he was also carrying a gun in a white leather sash he wore over his black jacket. Combined with his height, it made him look intimidating. She hadn't really seen an armed police officer before, at least not outside of the airport, and she was both afraid and excited by it.

What's wrong with you? She had no idea, but she wasn't feeling herself.

She watched as the uniformed man left the front door and descended a couple of steps as he attempted to contact someone via his radio once more.

Static.

Sofia followed his gaze, but, from her position, it was difficult to see anything. She shuffled forward, stepping out of the palazzo. Now she could see that a group of people had gathered at the foot of the steps, some dressed in the same uniform as her visitor. More police. Others wore white jumpsuits with hats and masks.

She drew a sharp breath and crept further forward for a better view.

"Contessa, si prega," the officer said, looking back at her.

"What happened?" she asked.

"Please. Stay!" he said, holding up another halting hand before returning to his radio, tapping it and talking into it.

Just static.

Defeated, he resorted to more traditional methods.

"EH!" he yelled, following it up with a loud whistle while pointing at the people below. But nobody was listening.

He descended a couple of steps more and repeated the process. When it still had no effect, he muttered what was presumably some kind of a swear word and then descended further.

'O sole mio sta 'nfronte a te! 'O sole, 'o sole mio
Sta 'nfronte a te... sta 'nfronte a te...

The dulcet tones of a crooning gondolier drifted up to her. Seagulls joined in with their own rendition overhead. And yet still she could hear the ominous buzz of voices coming from the gathering below.

She watched the officer as he stepped down towards it. At one point, he stopped, glancing back at her to make sure she wasn't following, the barricade of his palm held out to her once more.

But the action had the opposite effect; the more he tried to keep her back, the more she wanted to see what was going on. And yes, he was cute, but telling her to stay like a dog was beginning to grate. Besides, as a resident, she believed she had a right to know what was taking place outside her front door.

So, she followed him to the crest of the steps where a bitter chill rushed up to fondle her hair. She looked down, cocking her head from side to side in order to get a better look at the scene, but two people in the white jumpsuits were blocking her view with their backs as they crouched over something, while other officers stood in a chain together to create a privacy screen around them.

Her heart was curious too because it was tapping at her chest now, as she was reminded of that last night on Meadow Lane. It was like the commotion outside her neighbour Lucy's house. Something had obviously happened. Why else would they be circling and leaning over whatever it was down there?

Two more steps.

The chatter was loud now, and she could see them on the other side of the bridge. People. Spectators and more *Carabinieri,* as well as the *Polizia* blocking access across the canal.

Another step. Then another.

The officer had almost reached the gathering below and she knew it would only be a matter of time before he turned her way once more.

She moved forward, faster now, as she attempted to get close enough for a glimpse before she was discovered.

She watched the officer reach the bottom and talk to a man in a blue suit with thick salt and pepper hair.

She was still about ten steps away when someone moved, and she saw it. The sight sent a shockwave through her.

A shoe. Brown. Leather. Expensive. Seemingly brand new. It was on its side, sitting in a pool of dark gloop, marinating in it.

Then she heard somebody scream. It was a high-pitched, breathless sound that she assumed must have originated from a member of the public. It was only when the group in front of her parted to look her way that she realised the scream was coming from her.

Now she had a clear line of sight to the spectacle they were congregated around.

It was a body. A mangled body.

It was sitting upright with its back to her, but its arms were twisted and folded backward, each resting on the other. And its head...

Oh, dear God, what happened to his head?

It had been grotesquely rotated; the skin twisted in folds at the neck. It was looking at her with glassy, dead eyes.

No, not *it*, but he.

Daniele.

It was Daniele, and he was gazing at her lifelessly. Even now, in death, she could swear he still had the dregs of that furtive grin on his face.

The contessa started screaming once more. This time she knew it was her, as did all the other residents when her voice resonated all around them.

19

AN INSPECTOR CALLS

WEDNESDAY. EARLY AFTERNOON.

The housekeeper had uncheerfully fetched coffees for the unwanted guests and had made it so strong and bitter it would normally have made Sofia gag. But not today. Today, she had the presence of mind to add four cubes of sugar, courtesy of the man sitting in the chair across from her. He was the man in the blue suit who had introduced himself as Ispettore Gianni Puglisi of the *Carabinieri*.

Eager to talk about anything other than what she had witnessed an hour or so earlier, Sofia found herself asking what the difference was between the Carabinieri and the Polizia that she'd already seen on the streets of Venice. Puglisi explained that, like the police, the Carabinieri were responsible for upholding civil law but that they also had military training.

Sofia didn't understand what the point of that was and she didn't particularly care as she wiped away yet another tear with shaking hands, taking sharp, shallow breaths. Her whole life tilted as she drank from a glass of water that had been hastily handed to her by someone—she couldn't say who—as if it somehow contained tranquilising properties and was all she needed to set her world back on its axis.

The police officer, who she now knew went by the name of Verrastro, was standing to attention nearby. He hadn't been introduced to her, but she'd become aware of his name shortly after she was exposed to the hideous sight of Daniele's corpse. The ispettore had started yelling at the officer in front of everyone, presumably because he had been made responsible for keeping her in the palazzo and had failed to do so.

Verrastro looked suitably sheepish now and avoided eye contact with his boss, which meant he didn't notice him grit his teeth and glare at him when he saw the state Sofia had been reduced to.

"Contessa," Puglisi began slowly. *"Mi dispiace..."* He stopped himself and lifted a hand. "*Scusi*... I'm sorry, my English, it not very good. I learn from the American movies, you know, like *Die Hard*. I make point of—"

"Sofia," she said blankly.

"Scusi?"

"My name's Sofia. Not Contessa."

Puglisi frowned but obviously thought better than to question it, at least not at that moment. "I very sorry you see that, Sofia."

She didn't respond. She was still wrestling with more tears as images of the body, with its head twisted the wrong way around, paraded themselves in her mind like a macabre fashion show.

Realistically, she shouldn't be so devastated. She hadn't known Daniele that long, but every time she thought about how he must have suffered her vision blurred in a wash of water. It made her miss Cambridge. She wanted to go home, to leave Venice right now, never to return.

Home? This is your home now, she thought miserably. *Even if it doesn't feel like it.*

There was nothing left for her back in England. No parents. No house. But at least her friends would be there, and if she could somehow get things back to the way they were between them before all of this, then she was confident that she wouldn't feel so isolated, so vulnerable, so frightened.

But what about Aurora? How must she be feeling? Oh God. Poor Aurora. She hoped that she, at least, had not witnessed what had happened to her companion.

She must be in pieces. I should go see her.

"Sofia."

She refocussed on the tanned, weathered skin of the man sitting in front of her.

He had a kind, round face and was likely in his late forties. He carried it well, with the refined elegance typical of Tuscany vintages. The only indication of his age were the few lines around his astute grey eyes.

He was looking at her with interest, like he was genuinely concerned for her welfare, but she imagined this was just part of his act.

"Sofia?" he repeated softly.

She met his gaze. "Yes?"

"Are you alrighta, signorina?" he asked, with his strong Italian inflection.

"What do you think? My friend was attacked in my house and my neighbour fell down the steps just outside it." The sprinklers of her eyes wanted to burst on again, but she swallowed and squeezed the valve of her eyelids shut.

The inspector nodded. "I very sorry for your loss."

Sofia sniffed and then asked her own question. She wanted answers too. "So, are you here because of what happened to… um… what happened out there or what happened to Janay?"

He watched her for the longest time, as though he could tell that she wasn't really in control of herself. That he knew it was like she was being kept together with flour and water.

Flour and water. It was the homemade glue she used to make when working on school projects. The homemade potion that she used to create her first art piece, Princess Sally. The doll had been made from clothes pegs, fabric from an old t-shirt, and lots of gloopy white flour glue.

Sophie hadn't followed all of the teacher's instructions; she was too eager to see the result of her hard work. She layered her soggy newspapers over and over on the pegs, until she had created Sally's torso, arms, and legs. Then she painted her smiley face and big red cheeks, created a mop of hair from strands of a yellow duster, and made a golden crown from wine bottle seals. There she was. Her own Frankenstein creation. She had been so proud. She had made Sally all on her own, without any help from anybody, and she was beautiful. So beautiful.

Then presentation day came. Sophie almost skipped to the front of the class; her smile as big as her creation's.

"Sally. Princess Sally!" she had declared, lifting her pride and joy up to the class. She was grinning from ear to ear until Princess Sally's arm fell off, then the other, and then a leg. She remained standing where she was until the whole class started laughing.

Plop! Plop! Plop! went the sound of Princess Sally's limbs as they hit the hard floor tiles. *Plop! Plop! Plop!* went the sound of her falling apart. In her pride, she didn't even notice what had happened, but everybody else had. Everybody else noticed and knew that, like Humpty Dumpty, there would be no putting

Princess Sally together again.

"Signorina Sofia?"

She shivered and rubbed her arms. The temperature in the room seemed to have dropped even further and Sofia wasn't sure if it was her imagination, but what little light was coming in through the balcony doors was already fading.

"I said I'm fine. You still haven't answered my question," she said flatly.

Puglisi glanced at the officer and back at Sofia, then cleared his throat. "Like I just say, signorina, I need you answer my questions first, please."

Sofia looked at the man through sore and puffy eyes. "Ask your questions," she said tersely, as she suddenly felt worse. Her stomach was griping. Her head pounding. She could do without this inquisition right now.

"Very well." The inspector put his hand out and Verrastro placed a notepad into it. He opened the cover, squinted, and then rolled his eyes. *"Ma che e questo, Verrastro? La scrittura di un bambino?"*

Sofia wasn't sure but it sounded like the inspector was asking the man if the scribblings were that of a child. Sofia noticed that the police officer's cheeks had changed to a bright shade of rouge as he leaned in to look at the page. He obviously had her problem too.

"Che cosa dice questa parola?" the inspector asked, with all the scorn of a disappointed teacher.

Sofia had no idea what they were saying now but from the interaction it seemed that Puglisi was unable to read the officer's handwriting. She glanced at the balcony. The curtains were still billowing lazily. No wonder she was cold.

"... Violentata," the officer whispered.

"You call that la V? *Mamma mia*," the man lamented as Sofia considered walking over to close the doors and maybe getting a blanket to wrap around herself.

The inspector waved the officer away and back to attention.

"So, uh, your friend," the man resumed, looking at her, glancing at the notepad and frowning. "Uh, you tell doctor that she was attacked?"

"No, he told me. I didn't find out until we were at the hospital." She gulped down the lump in her throat.

"And your friend, this Jan…Janay, she had boyfriend, yes?"

"No. She's only just got here."

"And nobody come back to house with her?"

"No."

"And what about you? You have boyfriend, yes?"

"No. No boyfriends. Neither of us has a bloody boyfriend!" Sofia snapped. Her reaction was a mixture of irritation and embarrassment. The former she understood, but the latter? She glanced at Verrastro, who was listening impassively.

"But you were drinking Monday night, *corretto*?"

"Yes. So?"

"How much you drink?"

"A little. My friend had just arrived. We were celebrating."

"So, is it possible you forget the man?"

Sofia gaped at him. "Are you serious?"

He met her gaze. "Yes, of course I serious. I always serious when I talk about such things, Miss Sofia," the man responded drily. "You know what it like when in *vacanza*. You know, vacation. You have one drink, then another then another, and *boh*," he shrugged, "before you know it, your friend carry you home."

She sat forward. "Well, firstly, I'm not on holiday or on *vacanza,* as you put it, Inspector. I live here now. Secondly, my friend was with me and while we may have had a few, we certainly were able to carry ourselves home. Now, I told you, there was no boyfriend except for…" She trailed off as realisation dawned.

"Except for?" the inspector prompted.

Sofia cocked her head. "Well, except for Daniele."

"Daniele?"

She pointed at the door as if he was standing out there, as the memory of him stung her eyes with more tears. "He showed us around a few places in Venice, you know, for food and drinks."

"Where? Which place?" Puglisi asked, handing the notepad back to the officer, who produced a pen and promptly resumed taking notes.

"I can't remember, exactly. There was Harry's, then some other place off the piazza, and then we went to have food on a boat."

"See? Very easy to forget important thing when going out with *il vino*," Puglisi said knowingly.

So much for the Columbo act, she thought.

"So, you had drinks with the... um... what you say... the victim?" he asked, eyebrows arching with curiosity.

"Victim? What do you mean, victim? He fell down the stairs, didn't he?"

"*Prego, signorina*, if you allow me to ask the questions, this will be faster," Puglisi said as Sofia frowned. "So, you have drinks with Daniele and then come back here with him?"

She glanced at the curtains moving in the breeze and nodded distractedly. Then, realising what she was saying, she quickly corrected herself. "No. Not *with* him. He lives next door. He and my colleague from work walked us home and then went home themselves."

"One moment, please. Colleague?"

"Yes, Cameron, he's a work colleague. He was with us."

"*Mannaggia... Signorina, per piacere,* please. This is much quicker if you tell me everything firsta time."

"I told you everything. I didn't know if you had already talked to him. Cameron is his name, he—"

"And his surname?"

Sofia shook her head as she realised she didn't know it, and then swallowed her irritation. "He works at the Doge's Palace, Inspettore, and is Scottish. I doubt it'll be too hard for you to find him. He was with us the whole evening, but then he went home too. So, we were *alone*."

"Alone?"

"Yes. I told you we were alone."

"No, I mean Daniele and this Cameron, they go home alone or together?"

Sofia sighed. "No, Inspettore. Daniele lives across the way. He went home alone as did Cameron who… well, I don't know where he lives, but it isn't here. They both said goodnight and went bloody home!"

Sofia rose from her seat as she snapped then crossed over to the balcony doors and shoved them shut. They protested by squealing and then clanging loudly. The relief, however, was instant. It was still cold in the building but at least the gelid air was no longer blowing at her legs.

Sofia rubbed at her arms and then crossed them before reluctantly making her way back to her seat. She just wanted the men to leave now. Her headache was getting worse. She wondered where the housekeeper might be so she could ask if there were any pills in the place.

"You saw them leave?" the man continued casually.

Sofia bit her lip, partly because she was annoyed and partly because she was trying to remember. "Um, yes, I saw him go across the way and Cameron started to go down the steps."

"But you didn't see Daniele walk into the house?"

"No, Inspettore, I didn't see him walk into the house! I was with my friend. My attention was on her and not on him."

Puglisi nodded. "Hmm," he grunted pensively. "Also, signorina, if you don't mind. It is *I*-spettore. There is no *en*."

Sofia threw him a look of annoyance.

The man straightened in his chair. "So, when you had drinks with Daniele, what did you talk about?"

She took a few seconds to think about this. "Nothing in particular. Just what it was like to live here. But a lot of the time I was talking to Cameron about work. I've just started a new job at Palazzo Ducale, and he was telling me about the place, the history; he's a bit of an expert. Janay talked to Daniele."

"Why not?"

"Why not what?"

"Why not you talk with him? He's your neighbour and you no talk with him?"

Sofia hesitated because she knew where this was going. "We did talk, *I*-spettore. But my friend quite liked him, so I gave them the chance to chat. And as I told you, I was talking to Cameron."

"Aha!" Puglisi said, like he truly was on the set of a Columbo movie.

"Aha? What do you mean, aha?"

"So, she *did* like him. She *did* want him to be boyfriend."

"Inspector, I don't know about here, but in England, just because we like someone, it doesn't automatically make them a boyfriend."

"No? What does it make them then?" he asked seriously.

She thought about this, then, "Look, I've told you all I know," she said, eager to get it over and done with. There was something about this line of questioning that was ridiculous. "And now that's all I have to say about that. Inspector, I'm sorry for Daniele, I really am, but I would like to know what you're doing about what happened to my friend." Sofia was surprised by her own assertiveness.

"You mean how she... what do you say... was *violentata* in her bedroom behind the locked door?"

"Yes, exactly that. No, wait, what?"

"Signorina, forgive me, as I say, my English not very good, but you tell me that you and your friend come home, alone…"

"Yes…"

"That Daniele take you to the front door and that he then leave, and he go home, is this *corretto*?"

"Yes, I told you—"

"And that this Cameron, your work friend, he also go home?"

"Yes, that's right, so?"

"Well, if what you say is true, then why your housekeeper tell me that your friend… how you say, *sgattaiolare*?" The inspector looked up at the policeman who dropped his eyes to look at his boss. *"Come si dice… sgattaiolare?"* he asked with a shrug. *"Boh."*

"Um, *non lo so.* Um… sneak!" the officer declared like he was on a bloody gameshow and was winning himself a prize. The farce irritated Sofia, as did the growing gloom in the room. It was deepening by the second as if the world outside were being swallowed up by some cosmic black hole.

"Yes, she *sneak* Daniele into her bedroom! Why would your housekeeper say this?"

Sofia's stomach lurched. "What? No," she protested. "That isn't what happened."

"No?"

"No."

"How can you be so sure? Did you spend the night with your friend?" the man asked, raising his thick eyebrows.

"No. Of course not."

"Then how do you know?"

"I would have… she… um… I would have known. We left Daniele outside," Sofia reiterated, waving a shaky finger at the hallway. "She came in with me. We talked. I showed her around."

"For how long?"

"A little while. We were both dr-…" she reselected her choice of words, "...tipsy, and tired. We were both looking forward to going to bed."

"So it seem," the inspector said, rocking his head.

Sofia leaned forward in her seat. "I don't know what you think you know, Inspector, but my friend didn't and *wouldn't* invite Daniele in without me knowing."

"And I hear what you say, but you cannot tell me how you so sure, can you?"

Sofia paused. She couldn't. "She would have said something."

"So you say your housekeeper is lying?"

"That's exactly what I am saying," Sofia said loudly, looking over her shoulder as if the woman might be standing there. She wasn't, but Sofia hoped she would hear from whichever shadow she was skulking in.

"Why would she do that?"

"I don't know. Because she hates me?"

Puglisi thought about this for a few seconds. "Why she hate you? You only just come here. That is *corretto*, no? You just make your *permesso di soggiorno*. Your visa?"

"Yes..."

"You leave *Inghilterra*, England, and live in this very expensiva palazzo in Venice."

"Yes, and?"

"With housekeeper who doesn't like you? Why is that?"

"I don't know. You need to ask her."

Sofia thought he was going to react to her words, but instead the man nodded as if that sounded perfectly reasonable, before changing his line of questioning. "Miss Sofia, can you tell me why you move to Venezia?"

Sofia frowned at the irrelevancy, but at least she had an easy answer to offer. "Inheritance."

"You inherit this place, yes?"

"Yes."

"Mannaggia..." The inspector shook his hand like he had

burned it and gave out a faint whistle before exchanging a look with his subordinate. "You're very lucky, signorina, inheriting a multimillion-euro palazzo," he said, looking around. "But is this the only reason why you're here?"

"What do you mean?"

"Is there no other reason why you leave your home, your country, to come and stay in *Italia*?"

"No, why would there be?"

"No?"

"No. I already told you. I inherited this place."

"So, you didn't leave England because of what happen at your job?"

Sofia felt another boulder drop into the pit of her stomach. "Who told you about that?"

"Please, signorina, allow me to ask the questions."

Sofia shrugged. "In part, yes."

"You were suspended from your job, yes?"

Sofia hesitated, rubbing at the pressure in her skull. "Yes."

"Why is that?"

"What do you mean?"

"Why you were suspended?"

Her heart was throbbing once more. "I really don't understand—"

"Signorina, *prego*, please, answer my question."

The tide had left Sofia's mouth, leaving nothing but dry words in its wake. "I really don't want to talk about it right now," she said, using both hands to push strands of hair behind her ears.

"No?"

"No."

"Oh, well thatsa no problem, signorina. I can arrange for you to answer my questions at police station at a better time for you if you wish."

Sofia glared at him. "Something happened."

"What happened?"

"Somebody died."

"A passenger, yes? A passenger that *you* were responsible for, *corretto*?"

"It's not as simple as that."

"No. But you make it simple, no? You just send your boss letter and no go back. *Boh*," the man shrugged. "I wish I could send letter to my boss, and he, Verrastro, he wish he can send letter to me every day, no?"

He glanced up at the officer who was allowing himself a fleeting smile.

"He just says, I am tired of Puglisi bullshit, I send him emaila or letter and that it!" The man swiped his hands together as if washing them and pulled a face. "*Bimma, bamma*, no more work."

"It wasn't like that."

"No?"

"No."

"What about what happen to your neighbour?" the man said suddenly and seriously. Sofia's eyes widened.

"Daniele?"

"No. Not your neighbour here, signorina, but your neighbour in *Inghilterra*. Dead, no?"

Lucy.

"Please—"

"Your other neighbour across de street, he also very unlucky. Dead."

Sofia could feel pressure building behind her eyes and closed them.

"Then more neighbours, they lose baby…"

Her stomach churned and she clutched at it.

"Gone!"

"Please. I'm not feeling well," she groaned.

"No? I understand. *Mamma mia…* I not feel well either if all this death happen around me, Signorina Sofia. Phew, eh?"

The floor stretched up and she thought she was going to topple onto it, but, mercifully, it receded once more as Puglisi continued his verbal assault. "Then, your best friend and her husband. Same day you run away and come in Venezia. Dead. And then, you here not even one week and Signore Daniele dead. Ma, signorina, you must understand how this look. It is *una grande coincidenza*, no?"

"W…what did you say?" Sofia asked, eyes bulging and head swirling as a ball of bile slithered up her throat.

"Coincidence, no? That not how you say it?" the man pressed.

"No, before. About my friend and her husband."

Puglisi observed her for the longest time as if trying to read the truth in her eyes. "Why you leave England so suddenly, signorina?"

"What?"

"What make you run from your country to come and live in a place where you can't speak the language?"

"I told you," she groaned, desperate to get her answer. "I inherited this place. I didn't run away."

"No?"

"No! Now tell me about my friend!"

Puglisi didn't respond. He simply nodded and then stood. "*Allora,* please, signorina, I must ask you make no more sudden journeys withouta speaking to me first, you understand?"

"What? Why?"

"Otherwise, I will have no choice but to take your *passaport. Capisci*?"

"No, I don't bloody capisci! You have no right to keep me here. I haven't done anything wrong," Sofia protested.

"You should know your own police in England, they already make a warrant for your arrest. If you don't wish me to do the same, you do as I ask."

"No! Wait! What?" Sofia cried. She jumped up from her chair but as she did so, the room began to spin. "Wait!" She swallowed back the lump in her throat and closed her eyes as she was overwhelmed with queasiness.

The inspector paused and turned to her.

"P…please," she mumbled. "Wait… My friend and her husband… You didn't tell me what happened to them."

But Puglisi offered no reaction.

"WHAT HAPPENED TO THEM?" she screamed.

The man scrutinized her for several seconds before announcing, "They're dead, signorina. In fire. But you say you know nothing about this either, *corretto*?"

BANG! BANG! BANG!

Sofia felt her legs buckle beneath her and she collapsed back onto the sofa as someone started hammering on the balcony doors. Each impact was so powerful it rattled the glass, threatening to shatter it.

Sofia yelped and shrank back into her seat while the officer instinctively crouched and drew his weapon. Puglisi froze and all eyes turned to the giant doors.

Daylight had been devoured by darkness. It was as if an eclipse that nobody had known was coming was taking place.

The housekeeper rushed in clutching the obligatory kitchen towel but stopped abruptly in front of the view outside. Then, she slowly backed away, crossing herself, when she realised what was happening.

BANG! SHAKE! BANG! SHAKE! BANG! SHAKE!

The officer warily moved forward, weapon raised in his outstretched hand, and yet he'd barely reached beyond the sofa when it happened.

Suddenly.

Loudly.

Violently.

The glass on both giant balcony doors imploded. A shower of jagged fragments was catapulted into the house along with a clutch of tennis-ball-sized hailstones, smashing onto the floor and skidding to various corners of the room.

Then silence.

The wind that had aggravated Sofia just moments earlier had calmed, along with the sound of the rest of the world, until a distant scream pierced the quiet. Then another and another.

Puglisi slowly emerged from behind the corner of the sofa while the officer, who had thrown himself over Sofia as a protective barrier, slowly lifted himself from on top of her. Glass slid from him and tinkled to the floor.

"*Tutto bene?* Okay?" he asked, his brown eyes full of concern as he looked down at her. Sofia could only nod.

He slowly peeled himself off and winced. He was wounded, with a series of small shards embedded in his jacket. Yet he paused to offer Sofia his hand and help her sit up.

"Attenzione!" he said abruptly, but then qualified it with a gentle, "Careful, glass."

He looked over to his boss. *"Apposto?"* he asked, but he only received a distracted nod from the man who was focussed on something behind the officer. Both he and Sofia followed his line of sight.

The housekeeper was still standing with her back to them. She couldn't be certain, but it sounded as if the woman was mumbling something. It was hard to tell since the sound was mostly hisses and esses, now being upstaged by the wailing and screaming that was taking place beyond what was left of the balcony doors.

"Signora? Eh! Signora!" It was Verrastro again who, despite his own wounds, stepped forward to assist the housekeeper. He stopped in his tracks when the woman slowly turned around. Sofia heard a horrified shriek escape from her own mouth.

The woman was no longer recognisable. Her face was streaked in the blood that was dribbling down it, off her chin and to the floor. Large angry shards protruded from her eyes, cheeks, and chest, while her pleas for help were reduced to nothing more than a gagged gargle by the chunk of glass pinning her top lip and chin together.

Outside, and all over Venice, hundreds of boats and gondolas had been damaged, as if they had been stoned, and were sinking into the canals which were now stained crimson with the blood of passengers. High above, the sky had been transformed into a peculiar and ominous shelf of rageful blackness. A patchwork quilt of grey mammatus clouds hung from it in giant pouches and pockets, like boils from necrotic skin.

The time was nigh.

20

LIES

WEDNESDAY AFTERNOON

Sofia had spent the rest of the afternoon lying. The worst part about it was that she had been raised with the strict moral principle that peace could only be found in truthfulness. Yes, it was ironic that, as it turned out, the person who had brought her up that way had lied to her for her entire life. Still, a talent for deceit must run in the family, she thought, for she was surprised to find that she was quite adept at it.

First, she lied to the police by telling them that she was fine after her housekeeper had become a pincushion for shards of flying glass. She wasn't though. Far from it. How could anyone who wasn't made of stone be fine after witnessing something so horrific?

Yet she told the police that she was okay, that all she needed was to get some clothes on and visit her friend at the hospital. Reluctantly, Puglisi released her from his charge but only on the understanding that she would not make any significant journeys either around or out of the country while the investigation was ongoing.

That is when she told them her second lie.

After, she spent an hour or so in front of a cold latte at one of the bars overlooking the Grand Canal. She watched as a steady stream of damaged boats of all sizes buzzed sadly in front of her like battle weary soldiers.

Though the sky was calmer now, the hailstorm of her own mind was torrential. Her thoughts churned in her brain like the wake behind those vessels, but just like them, they eventually fizzled out to nothing. She still had no real answers to any of it.

What about Victoria? Had she somehow misheard? She wanted to hope so but knew she hadn't, and not only because of what the policeman had told her. Now that she thought about it, she remembered the look on Janay's face the night she had arrived. She had started to tell her something about Victoria but then they were interrupted. She didn't notice it at the time, but now it all made perfect sense.

The disgusting truth was that she didn't *feel* anything. She was numb, as if she was totally unaffected by it. How was that even possible? She would have expected a few tears, at least. Those things seemed to be with her in abundance lately. And yet nothing.

She told herself it was because she was in shock still. She hadn't allowed herself time to absorb the information which she had received in the midst of so many other horrors. Yes, of course, that was the reason. That was why she was feeling like all those years they had spent together as inseparable friends had never happened.

But no matter how much she tried to deny it to herself, when she paused, cleared her mind, and allowed it to stray deeper, behind the façade of social decencies, she knew that it was the truth. That somehow, however it had happened, the fate that had befallen her old friend was right and proper.

Right and proper?

Those were the words that formed in her mind like a metastasizing cancer. She didn't even use the expression and yet there it was, ringing around her head. It was the most peculiar sense of detachment, like Victoria had barely been a passing acquaintance.

How strange it was. Yet this was nonetheless how she felt.

Something had changed in her. She didn't know when or how exactly. Maybe it was sometime back in England. Maybe it was the moment her father died. Or perhaps when she discovered the truth about her parents. It could have been the housekeeper's coldness or even the moment she'd caught Daniele snickering at the hospital. She didn't know when, but all of it did feel *right and proper.*

Now, as she stood at the stern of the vaporetto and travelled under a dark sky that seemed ambivalent to the carnage it had caused, Sofia DaTerra reached a decision. If that involved telling more lies, so be it.

She arrived at the hospital to discover that the police had already taken Janay's statement. If Sofia's visit was anything to go by, she wouldn't have given them much. As soon as she strayed remotely close to the topic of what happened in that bedroom, there was a visible shift in her friend's demeanour, her body stiffening, her eyes widening.

So, Sofia kept the focus of the conversation on more cheerful subjects, such as Damon. Janay had spoken to her son and explained that she'd had an accident, that it was nothing serious and she would be home soon.

This led conveniently to Sofia's next series of lies. She omitted the real events of the morning and instead told her that she had spoken to police and that they were investigating what had happened and were hoping for a breakthrough soon. She then apologised to her friend as if she had been personally responsible for her pain.

They cried together.

After that, Sofia implemented the next part of her plan. She told Janay that she'd spoken to the lawyer in England about getting the palazzo sold as soon as possible and that she was going to use the money to buy herself a nice place back home. And, although there was no commitment and she wasn't expecting her to make any decisions right away, she would be happy to look at buying somewhere big enough for the three of them. But only if she wanted to, of course. There was no pressure.

When Janay looked at her with more tears welling in her eyes, Sofia simply hugged her friend tightly and told her to think about it, in her own time. She would always be there, if ever and whenever she was ready.

Sofia also told her friend that she'd spoken to the doctor, and, after another night's observation, he couldn't see any reason why she shouldn't be discharged in the morning. She would book her a ticket home shortly after.

When Janay grabbed her hand, Sofia quickly told her next lie. "Not to worry. I'll be right behind you. As soon as I settle everything with the house."

It was kind of true. She hadn't talked to Roger Mitchell, the lawyer, yet, and she had no idea if anything could be done. The lawyer had been quite specific on the subject of selling Palazzo Rosso, but this didn't mean she wasn't going to try.

Lying to her friend was a necessary evil to get her to leave the city without her. Otherwise, all they'd do is argue about it, and Sofia couldn't have that. Her priority was to get Janay home to her son and safety. Nothing else mattered.

After promising to collect her first thing in the morning, Sofia made her way back, but not to Palazzo Rosso. No, first, she had decided, she needed answers.

21

THE STAR OF THE MORNING

WEDNESDAY. LATE AFTERNOON.

The thunderous sky glowered as Sofia made her way across the city, the square, through the pools of light in the courtyard, and then into the place she had called work for less than a week.

The beauty of her surroundings still wasn't lost on her, although she was busy pondering other matters now, which superseded everything else. When she finally found Cameron giving a guided tour to a group of tourists in the splendour of the Council Chamber, she barely paused to look.

"...Two branches of power met in this very room: one that

dealt with all maritime matters relating to the Venetian empire, and the other that dealt with all mainland affairs. They were called the *Savi* and the *Signoria.* This artwork was designed and commissioned after the great fire of 1574 and—"

"Cameron."

"Sofia? What are you doing here?"

"I need to speak to you."

"I'm… um… just in the middle of a—"

"Now," Sofia insisted through gritted teeth beneath a fake smile for the sightseers.

"Okay. Right, so…" Cameron turned his attention back to the group. "Why don't you all take a wee look around and I'll be right with ya for any questions," he said brightly before turning to Sofia and stepping out of earshot. "I thought you weren't coming in today."

"I'm not. I haven't."

"Well, you probably shouldn't. Raffaella's seriously got it in for you. She's already spoken to Bacciabella."

"I don't care about that. Something else has happened, Cam."

"What? With Janay?"

"No. Something else. Listen, I need you to tell me everything you know about the palace." The guide frowned, so Sofia added an explanation, "No. Not this one. Palazzo Rosso… what? What is it?" She had noticed how the guide's eyes flicked away from her. There was something there. Something in that action. "Cameron? Tell me."

"Sofia," he said, taking a step back to make a space between them. "You told me you were gonnae push me in the canal the last time I tried to tell you anything. What's changed?"

"It doesn't matter. I just want you to tell me what you know."

"Sofia—"

"I need to know," she insisted forcefully. She had spoken so loudly that a couple of curious tourists loitering nearby turned their way. They obviously suspected some kind of domestic drama and were lingering.

"Sofia, I cannae tell ya."

"Why?"

"Because you'll hate me, that's why."

"Well, I'm going to hate you if you don't, so you may as well spill it."

He led her further away from the eavesdropping tourists before dropping his voice to little more than a whisper when he spoke. "You know this stuff doesn't mean anything, right? It's just urban legend, fables passed down through the years. People like to tell stories, that's all, and the scarier the better."

"Right. So, you *do* know something then?"

The Scot glanced away.

"Cam?" Sofia prompted. His trepidation told her that what she was about to hear could be much worse than she had anticipated, and now she definitely needed to know.

The guide still hesitated, looked around, and then continued in his hushed tone. "Put it this way, the Palazzo Rosso name has nothing to do with the colour of its walls and everything to do with what went on there."

Sofia met him with a blank stare, so Cameron took a deep breath and continued. "Okay, do you know the story of the Star of the Morning?"

Sofia shook her head.

"Right. So, the Star of the Morning was one of God's most prized angels. A chief angel, if you will, blessed with unrivalled beauty and wisdom. But after a while, not unlike most aesthetically gifted people today, this chief angel started to develop a bit of a chip on his shoulder. He literally thought he was *God's gift,* hence the expression, because he was endowed with what most others lacked. Because of this, he felt he shouldn't have to worship God but instead wanted to be worshipped as a god himself. He became proud and, in God's eyes, corrupted by his own splendour. God had no choice but to evict him and all his cohorts from the lap of Heaven and threw them to Earth.

"Which is why, many centuries ago, when the place we now know as Venice was just a boggy swamp and thousands fled here to escape the tyranny of Attila the Hun, they received a warm welcome. For this is where the Star of the Morning had built his own church. They worshipped and sacrificed to him in exchange for his wisdom, leadership, and of course, his protection. Before long, a major settlement was established that many years later would emerge as the country of Venetia, which was eventually assimilated and Romanised. Under the Romans, Venetia and its capital Padua became extremely wealthy. An empire was born, and it ruled the world."

Sofia pulled a face. "Okay, Cam. Great history lesson, but not quite what I was after."

The guide smiled. "Sofia, while it's certainly undergone many alterations, the church of the Star of the Morning *is* Palazzo Rosso. That's why it commands prime position on the Grand Canal. It's quite literally stood there for centuries."

"Right. Palazzo Rosso used to be a church. So what?"

"Not just any church, Sofia. *His* church."

"This morning star angel person?"

"Star of the Morning."

"Yes, him. Is that it?"

"Do you know who the Star of the Morning became better known as?"

"I have no—"

"Lucifer, Sofia," Cameron threw out. "He became better known as Lucifer, the Prince of Darkness, and whichever other name you'd care to affix to the being who professed himself to be the very antithesis of God."

Sofia let out a laugh. "Right. Good and evil. That old

chestnut. Got it," she said with a smirk.

"It's no joke. Some awful things have happened there over the years, Sofia. Terrible things," Cameron added seriously.

Sofia stopped smiling. "Okay, Cam. Just so you know, you're doing that thing you do and are starting to creep me out. I mean, you're acting like I've moved into some kind of satanic temple or something."

Cameron looked at her like he was about to say something further but then thought better of it.

"What?" she prompted.

"It doesn't matter."

"Cameron..." she warned. She didn't particularly want to hear more, but she needed to. The tour guide was now shifting the weight on his feet, his eyes darting every which way but at her. She had to know.

"Sofia, nobody just moves into Palazzo Rosso," he said gravely, his voice barely above a whisper.

"What do you mean?" she said, stiffening as her body reacted to the tone of his voice and what it might mean.

Cameron hesitated and was about to continue with his story when...

"Sofia?"

They both turned to watch Maria Bacciabella walk up to them. As always, she looked stylish in a black pantsuit wrapped in a longline petrol-colour sweater.

"What a wonderful surprise," she said, joining them. "We weren't expecting you today. Is everything all right?"

"Oh yes. Sorry, I wasn't planning on coming in but then I realised that I needed to talk to Cameron about something."

"Oh. I see." Bacciabella looked at the guide and then glanced at the group of tourists milling about behind him.

The action did not require words. Instantly, Cameron said, "Well, I best get back to me tour. It was nice seeing you, Sofia.

Give my best to Janay, won't ya?" He nodded at Bacciabella then hurried away.

"How are you, Sofia?" the curator asked, reaching out and gently touching her new recruit on the arm. "Is everything all right?" There was kindness and sympathy in her eyes, as if she were feeling Sofia's pain.

"Oh yes, much better now, thank you," Sofia said, both masking her disappointment that her conversation with Cameron had been cut short and thinking of ways to avoid being dragged into small talk with her new boss. She didn't want to appear ungrateful. The lady had been good to her, but she needed time to process everything she had learned today, and that couldn't happen while she was here. She needed to get away.

"Things seem to be coming together for the gala. Raffaella has done a wonderful job with the exhibit. We're very much looking forward to it. Are you?"

Sofia squinted. "Um… not really. Raffaella said it was senior staff only."

"Nonsense. Everybody's excited to meet you."

"Everybody?"

"Of course."

"Um, well, actually, Maria, I—"

"Yes?" the woman asked eagerly.

"I…I don't have anything to wear."

"Why, my dear child, even Cinderella managed to make it to the ball, no?"

Sofia didn't know how to take that. Cinderella had a fairy godmother, someone she could definitely use but was sorely lacking. Of course, it was just the woman's way of telling her to be creative. Nonetheless, it reminded her of how lonely she was, despite the curator's good intentions.

"Of course," she said with a smile. It didn't matter anyway. The gala was in a few days, and by then, all being well, she wouldn't even be in Venice anymore.

22

INTO THE VOID

WEDNESDAY. EARLY EVENING.

By the time Sofia returned to Palazzo Rosso, the blackened sky had been roused from its slumber. A thundering flotilla of heavy charcoal rain clouds drizzled their intention to unleash a watery payload on a city already drowning in *Acqua Alta*.

Although Cameron hadn't managed to go into the specifics, he had said enough to crank her imagination into gear. Since she had left him, she had done nothing but think about the apparently satanic nature of the temple she had adopted as her home. Though, in truth, she realised, it was more as if it had adopted her.

It was all ludicrous, of course. As he said, it was just one of those urban legends that had been handed down through the generations. She truly believed it must be so, she told herself. It had to be. Still, her own reassurances did nothing to dilute the images of Daniele at the foot of those steps and the punctured eye sockets of her housekeeper.

No. There was no way she was staying there tonight. She didn't have any money, but she did have a credit card and a goal. She would use the card to check in to the first available hotel, where she planned to soak in a hot bath as she processed everything that had happened. And, after a good night's sleep, she was going to collect her friend from the hospital.

She had no idea what she was going to do after that because anything beyond picking up Janay would see her move from law abiding citizen to fugitive.

You should know your own police in England, they already make a warrant your arrest. Puglisi's stumbling words echoed in her mind.

A warrant for her arrest? That was insane! She hadn't done anything wrong. The image of a couple of burly officers clapping handcuffs on her the moment she walked through the arrivals gate threw itself at her.

At the bridge over the canal, she paused to catch her breath and looked across. From her position, she could not see anything of the fate that had befallen Daniele, apart from a patch of dark discoloration on the washed stone.

Blood. His blood.

Overturned shoe. His head facing his back. The faint smile on his lips. A trainload of grotesque images rattled along the tracks of her mind, as they had ever since she had witnessed the scene. She wished she could reach into her brain and scrub them away, but she knew they would haunt her for the rest of her days. Some horrors could never be forgotten.

What had she become? Moving to Italy was supposed to be a fresh start for her, but it had turned out to be an ugly continuation of what had started back in England. Maybe the police were onto something. Maybe all of this somehow had something to do with her. But how? She was a nobody.

Contessa of Palazzo Rosso.

Now, as the storm clouds gathered overhead and thunder rumbled to unleash a wintry gale until it howled through the passageways and swarmed all around her, that title took on a whole new meaning.

Contessa of the Temple of Lucifer.

No. She definitely could not stay there. Not tonight, not now, and certainly not alone.

She hastily climbed the steps, her eyes averted from the large, smudged stain. She paused at the top and looked towards Aurora's house. She needed to go and see her, as uncomfortable as that meeting was going to be. It was the right and proper thing to do.

Right and proper. Those words again. In the light of everything that had happened, the world appeared to be anything but, yet the feeling she had about the phrase remained the same. She would visit Aurora as soon as she was done collecting Janay's things.

She turned to the door and frowned. That ugly appendage of a doorknocker watched her with its grin and those dead eyes. She wanted to smash it. If she had an axe to hand right now, that is exactly what she would do. She would swing it and she would swing it until there was nothing left of the little monster. Instead, she looked away, as she had always done since she first saw it, turned the key in the lock, and entered.

As much as she didn't want to shut herself inside, she let the door go. It swung slowly, heavily, creakily shut, with a loud thud that echoed around her.

The entrance hall had its usual cold and inhospitable atmosphere. It was like she'd stepped into the lair of a thousand malignant spirits seeking justice for the many wrongs done to them. The house somehow felt more unwelcoming than it had earlier in the day, even colder and bleaker. She supposed her imagination wasn't helping any, fuelled by what she'd learned since. It wasn't surprising. Of course she was going to sense more malevolence in the place than was rational, in the light of the history Cameron had illuminated, but at the end of the day it was just bricks and mortar. Stone and… glass. She thought about the housekeeper's eyes and shivered.

It's just a building, Sofia! It is only what you make of it. Satan's temple?! If it wasn't so bloody creepy it would be laughable.

The germ of her self-comforting smile was sterilised the moment she heard the sounds drifting to her from deep within the belly of the palazzo. Thumping… Whispering…

At first she thought she was imagining it, but then she stopped and held her breath. Yes, there! There were voices coming from up ahead, from inside the ballroom.

Hell bloody no. She considered turning around and heading straight back out the front door but then heard another sound. Was that laughter?

She waited then took a step forward.

More laughter. Yes, she could definitely hear it now. It wasn't ghostly whisperings at all, but people talking in Italian.

What the hell was going on? She hurried forward, each step an indignant stride until she saw him.

Armando. She let go of the breath she was holding when she saw what he was doing. The handyman had plugged the gaping holes of the balcony doors with plywood, blocking out what little daylight was left as well as the beauty of the view outside that had so captivated her when she first arrived. God, it felt like a lifetime ago and yet had only just been a week.

The handyman had also enlisted the help of a few of his friends. They were busy cleaning and polishing away every trace of what had happened there with meticulous attention. One of the six men was even on his hands and knees, scrubbing in between the gaps of the floor tiles with a tiny brush.

The moment they sensed her presence, the whole crew jumped to their feet. Like Armando, they promptly removed their hats and turned their eyes to the floor. The scene was reminiscent of an officer arriving for a hut inspection at a concentration camp.

She hoped that wasn't how they saw her and hated herself for having such a bizarre thought. She acknowledged the men with a feeble smile.

Eyes still to his feet, one man spoke. *"Domani,"* he said, making a circular gesture with his finger. *"Domani ripariamo il vetro."*

Sofia nodded vacantly. She thought she caught the gist of what the man was saying. *Domani* meant tomorrow. And *vetro*... She knew of a company called Vetro, and they specialised almost exclusively in glass tables. It wasn't much of a leap to conclude that the man was talking about replacing the glass in the balcony doors tomorrow.

She didn't know if she even cared about that right now. What she did care about was that there was a group of mature but handy men in the building. That made her feel better. Safer. In fact, she wanted them to stay while she did whatever she needed to, not that she could communicate that to them. Besides, even if she could, she didn't want to come across as a silly little girl that was afraid of being in her own house by herself, especially in the face of such deference.

So, she simply smiled again before hurrying up the stairs. With a bit of luck, she'd be able to collect all of Janay's things and some items for herself before the men downstairs were done.

Sofia was about to enter Janay's room when she heard a *creak.* It was coming from the opposite end of the floor, near her room.

The gallery was steeped in shadows. The gold candelabra sconces hanging at intervals from the wall struggled to pierce the gloom. One of them seemed to be flickering. Or was it her imagination?

Sofia wasn't sure, but the creak she thought she had heard had sounded like weight shifting on floorboards. Like somebody was down there and had just stepped out of sight.

"Hello?" She spoke the word reluctantly as if she didn't want to hear a reply. Which was good because the only response was from the sound of the men working downstairs. And it was reassuring.

There was nothing down there, nothing she could see, yet a sinister feeling of being watched crawled over her skin like the tickle of insect legs.

She hesitated a few more seconds then sighed. The more she did this to herself, the worse things were going to seem. The seed had been planted now. Every single sound and movement and shimmer of light was going to seem bloody creepy from here on out because she had put herself in this situation. Things were already bad enough. She should never have visited Cameron and learned what he knew.

What's done is done. She needed to focus.

She turned, hurried across to Janay's room, and paused outside as the sound of her screams replayed in her mind. She felt the wall for the light and clicked it on for what it was worth, but it did little to illuminate the space. It seemed like the lightbulbs all over the building had suddenly become fatigued from all their years of service and no longer had the verve to continue performing their function.

She took in the desolate room. Just a few days before, she and

Janay had entered this space and filled it with drunken giggles and lively chatter. Now, Janay's suitcase lay abandoned on the floor and her clothes were discarded on a nearby chair. The bed was naked but for a new fitted sheet. The housekeeper must have replaced it some time since. *The housekeeper.* Dead. Every time she thought about her, all she could see was those shards of glass.

She hurried forward, opened the suitcase, and then started to collect Janay's clothing and other items. Questions about what actually took place there chased her around the room. She dodged obvious responses, but they came at her relentlessly. Her friend *did* have a lot to drink. The housekeeper testified that Janay *had snuck* Daniele into her room. Why would she lie? But why would Janay lie? There was no denying that she had been attacked, that much was obvious and corroborated by her doctors.

Sofia shook her head as if attempting to shrug off the thought of even momentarily doubting her friend. She switched on the bathroom light and hurried inside, avoiding her reflection in the mirror. She'd only seen a few horror movies, but she knew the drill. If she looked directly into the mirror, there was a good chance she would see the reflection of an ugly vampiric creature glaring back at her.

No thank you.

Instead, she collected Janay's toothbrush and other assorted items, placed them back inside her washbag and then attempted to zip the whole thing up as she hurried back towards the bedroom. In her haste, the zip snagged and when she attempted to yank it up, she tugged the whole bag from her own grasp. It fell to the marble floor with a loud thud, spilling and scattering its contents across the room.

Sofia swore. She considered leaving everything as it lay. She would pick it up tomorrow or even just replace it. But Janay had been quite specific about needing this stuff. And what exactly was her problem? Why exactly was she allowing herself to be chased—

Her thought was interrupted by the creak of the door. She could do nothing but watch as it slowly and loudly screeched forward as if it was about to close.

It didn't, but the fact that it had moved at all was enough to shift the thumping of her heart into a new gear. She crouched down, snatched up the nearby toothbrush, and shoved it back in the bag. Next, she retrieved the errant moisturiser, miniature perfume bottles, and lipstick.

It was when she moved to the far corner of the room to retrieve a runaway compact that she felt a draft brush against the back of her hand. She looked up and was startled to see wild-looking eyes staring back at her.

Her own.

She was gazing into a full-length mirror, housed in an ornate frame. She instantly wanted to look away for the same reason she wanted to avoid the mirror in the bathroom but lingered for several seconds as the air around her face shifted. Slowly, she moved forward, turning her cheek to her reflection. Yes! There!

Cold air. She could feel it blowing at her cheek. But how was that possible? She was staring at a mirror on the—

No.

She interrupted her own thought and slowly rose to her feet, lifting a trembling hand and holding it out in front of her. Yes. She could feel it. There was a draft coming from the mirror or somewhere around it.

She stepped forward and examined the back of it. It was hanging from the wall via giant hooks. She waved her hand all around it like one of those airport scanner wands as she attempted to detect the—

What was that? Just behind the edge of the mirror. Was that a hairline crack in the wall? It was difficult to tell, as gloomy as it was in the room. She pulled her phone out of her jeans. The thing had been pretty useless the whole time she had owned it as far as making calls were concerned, so it could at least prove itself useful in other ways.

She tapped a few times, and the LED light came on. She checked the battery. It was low. *Of course.* But then she hadn't bothered charging it and it would still do for now.

She trained the light over the wall. It *was* a crack, barely detectible and almost parallel with the edge of the frame in such a way as to appear as if it were part of the mirror.

A secret passageway of some kind.

"Shit!" she hissed, stepping away from her reflection as if it were contagious.

"Shit!"

What should she do? She checked around the room. She half expected someone to be standing behind her, as villains often were when protagonists uncovered such things. This had to be it. This had to be how whoever it was had managed to enter Janay's room and how they could still be entering the house unimpeded. The thought of that stabbed at her heart with a blade of cold fear. Whoever it was could be in there with her right now.

She looked around the room again. Eyes darting everywhere, she threw the washbag onto the bed and rushed back into the corridor. She knew what she would do. She would call Dad's Army from downstairs to help her investigate behind the mirror. Then, if they found that it was what she suspected it to be, she would call the police.

"Arm—" she began to call down the stairs but cut herself off.

What are you doing?

What *was* she doing? For all she knew, it could be one of them. Maybe even Armando himself. Maybe nobody knew the place better than he did. There's no doubt that if anyone knew about any secret passageway, it would be him. And if it wasn't him, there was a good chance he was on the take, facilitating somebody else's entry to the palace.

Paranoid now too?

She should call the police then. Have them investigate. *Investigate what? You haven't found anything yet.* Her inner critic had a point.

"Shit!" she hissed again. She was bloody confused.

Scared, more like it, she thought. She was without a doubt. But if she couldn't call the men because they were prime suspects, and she couldn't call the police because, well, she didn't know what she was calling them about, then there was only one other option.

She returned to the bedroom. She scanned the space and saw nothing, but the hideous sensation that she was being watched still clung to her alongside the chill in the room.

She shone the light of the phone all around. It was just bright enough to see into the corners. She savoured the power of driving back the dark with a mere flick of her mobile.

Satisfied she was alone, Sofia trained the light on the mirror. As if she needed more proof, she held up her hand and let it travel around the edge once more. Yes. It was still there, that faint cold draft. She replaced her hand with her cheek. It appeared much more sensitive to the cold. That confirmed it. There was definitely something behind there.

She began pressing and prodding, hoping something would just pop out of place or swing open. There was no obvious handle or mechanism of any kind, which meant that it had to work on some kind of push catch, like one of those sleek kitchen cabinets that had no knob.

But she pushed, tapped, thumped, and pulled at the frame, and nothing opened or revealed itself to her. Finally, when she reached the middle section and pressed roughly where a door handle and lock would be, there was a loud clunk and the whole mirror sprung at her.

Sofia yelped, almost dropping her phone, and jumped back

from the thing, hand cradling her heart to stop it from punching its way out of her chest.

The draft was much stronger now, whistling through the gap that had appeared between the mirror and wall, bringing with it the smell of stagnant water.

She took a beat, her mind racing, her pulse throbbing, her breaths short and fast. She was scared. For all she knew the person that attacked Janay might live behind there, like one of those home invasion people that secretly ensconce themselves in other people's attics. It could lead to anything or anyone, even something from Cameron's hideous historic tale. That's probably what frightened her the most; the reality that her discovery might have no basis in the supernatural but in the real world. It was easier to hold a fear that was implausible.

She looked at the exit back into the corridor. Part of her wanted to leave, to go and get help with the secret passageway. Because that was all it was. No so-called smoking gun, but a theory on how someone may have entered Janay's room. It still didn't prove anything.

And yet she remained, as the mirror creaked back and forth in the draft, beckoning her inside.

23

THE STAIRCASE

WEDNESDAY EVENING

Sofia's hand trembled as she reached for the mirror and pulled it open. It felt heavier than she expected, yet it swung open with relative ease and hardly any sound. That wasn't lost on her. If somebody wanted to enter the palace undetected, this would certainly be a good way to do it.

She shivered. The very thought of that made her want to turn and run screaming from the room. But she couldn't. It was as if the dark were calling to her, beckoning her to its black heart with the promise of truth. In it lay the answers to what had happened there, it seemed to say, and retribution against those who had perpetrated it.

She aimed the phone light at the cavity and drew in a sharp breath when she thought it revealed the black outline of a person. It was only as the whole structure became clear under the powerful LED light that she could see that it wasn't a person at all but a staircase, a metal one, spiralling downward.

Sofia gasped when she realised that she was still holding her breath, unconsciously not wanting to make a sound for fear of disturbing whatever might be lurking in the void where the air smelt musty and damp, as if it had been trapped there for centuries.

As she stepped forward, she could feel the cold clamminess of the place on her skin and, as the light beam rushed ahead of her, she could see why. The metal steps twisted down and then disappeared into the blackness of the earth.

Her heart attempted to talk some sense into her by pounding against her chest. There was no way she could or should go down there, at least not without an escort. Her work was done. She'd proven there was access to the room and now it was for the police to investigate. Simple. She needed to stop shining her phone in front of her like some kind of amateur detective and start dialling.

Go on. Stop shining and start dialling.

It took several more seconds for her to overcome her sudden fascination with the unknown before she finally stepped back towards the bedroom. But then she heard it…

Whispering. Down there, in the dark, someone was whispering. They must have seen the light beam travelling over the steps of the staircase, and yet still they continued talking, muttering under their breath.

Was it someone? Some*thing*?

She stepped forward, the light carving shadows out of the dark then scaring them off over the stone walls. She had no clue where exactly she could be. She was inside some kind of cavity within the palace itself. The wall she was looking at directly behind the stairwell was most likely the external wall, but she wasn't sure. What she did know is that she was thinking about this technicality because she was trying to avoid the thought of imminent danger that was attempting to assert itself in her mind.

But she couldn't help herself. She had to know. She shone the beam of light onto the steps and moved further towards them so she could listen to the sound more closely.

She waited. Silently.

It wasn't whispering after all but something else. Something that sounded like whispering. Talking, maybe?

Heart in her throat, and with one final glance at the sanctuary of the bedroom, Sofia DaTerra stepped onto the stair. She expected it to shake and squeal, threatening to collapse under her weight, but it didn't. It barely moved. The structure felt much more robust than she anticipated. Cast iron hammered into the walls, maybe. It felt safe. Enticing. Reassuring. It was *safe* for her to descend the steps to God only knew where. After all, where could it possibly lead to if not downstairs?

Silly. What else could it be but a shortcut to the dining room or one of the other rooms below. The vast kitchen, probably. It was most likely an old servants' staircase that had been forgotten. It was hardly going to lead into one of the canals. The sound she could hear was probably the men talking in the ballroom.

At least she hoped it was as she descended one of the steps, then another and another. There were probably around fifteen or twenty in total. She wasn't sure. She was too busy focussing on the sounds that were drifting up to her along with the pungent smell of stagnation. The further she descended into the frigid darkness, the more it became obvious to her that the stairs were leading nowhere but into a stone well. At least that is what it felt like when she stepped off the last one and placed her foot on the rough, slimy surface of stone at the bottom.

She shivered, her breathing short and ragged in the cold air. She had no business being down there alone. And yet, it was the most peculiar compulsion; something continued to push her forward. Something that would see her neglect all urges for self-preservation in favour of discovery.

Because you're insane!

There was that, of course.

The whispering had metamorphosed into the sound of dripping and trickling water. She wasn't in the palace anymore after all. At least it didn't feel that way. It felt like she was somewhere else. Somewhere she wasn't meant to be.

She looked upwards towards the faint glow of light, towards the sanctuary of the bedroom, and, as her heart thundered in her chest, considered turning back.

But the thought was momentary before she allowed the light beam to drift down the wet wall opposite until part of it fell away to reveal a narrow tunnel made of slick stone.

This must be some kind of secret passageway in and out of the palace.

It made sense. She knew enough about history to know that private escape routes weren't uncommon in this type of grand home. The only question was, where did it lead?

The walls were pocked and damp, with water trickling down the surface in thin streams. Patches of mould and mildew had taken hold in the crevices, and cobwebs stretched from one end of the wall to the other, as if knit together by some unseen hand. Ahead, an uneven path paved with stone and the occasional puddles of water led into darkness.

As she considered navigating the pools of water, she caught a faint scent. At first, it was barely noticeable against the musty smell of water-logged decay. However, as a cold draft swept through the tunnel, the scent grew stronger, as if the opening of the mirror had created some kind of flue-like effect. The fragrance was sweet and flowery. Joss sticks? Incense?

She aimed the light forward. The scent seemed to be coming from the other side of the tunnel.

So it did lead outside after all. To people celebrating masquerade? To a nearby souvenir shop perhaps? To the busy streets crowded with performers?

A drop of water dripped and dribbled down her face. She yelped and almost stumbled on the uneven surface, light beam slicing around the dark. She straightened herself and without thinking further, walked forward. She wanted out of the damp and cold catacomb now and she didn't care how.

But the stones were slippery, the tread of her trainers seemingly powerless in the face of the green, muddy slime that had accumulated down there. She had no choice but to slow down and proceed with caution.

After ten or so feet the fragrance grew stronger, as did the sound of sloshing water. It wasn't inside the tunnel but somewhere outside. She was unable to work out where; she felt as if she had descended down to water level and yet the sound appeared to be coming from beneath her.

It was difficult to gain her bearings in the dark. The feeling worsened when the light on her phone suddenly weakened. She turned the screen over and gawked at it, thinking for one horrifying moment that the battery was dead. She was both relieved and dismayed to discover that it wasn't quite dead but definitely dying. It had dimmed when the remaining power reached ten percent, the phone automatically switching mode to save energy.

She needed to hurry. She knew that. The last thing she wanted was to be stranded down here in the dark. The thought of that filled her with a sudden claustrophobic terror.

She looked up and was about to resume her journey when she spotted something up ahead. Something that sent a wave of relief washing through her, reducing the tension in her body.

Light. The weak amber glow of a streetlight.

I must be close. I must almost be out of this bloody tunnel.

She hastened her pace, navigating the treacherous path with caution. Soon, the dim light grew brighter and the scent in the air grew stronger. However, the muffled sounds of the city and the sound of the water lapping beneath her remained distant, echoing beyond the stone walls.

It was at this point that Sofia began to suspect that she wasn't emerging onto the street at all but to some kind of steep incline. It seemed to gradually narrow the orange light into an oblong shape roughly the size of a door, but oddly it was in the… *Is that the ceiling?* It didn't make any sense.

Until it did.

Sofia approached the opening slowly. The air was thick and heady with the incense now, except the notes had changed. It smelled of burning wood mixed with a medley of herbs and flowers. This accompanied a new sound, one she recognised immediately.

Crying.

Sobbing, in fact, muffled yet unmistakable.

Sofia was climbing now. There were just a few stone steps more and she crept up them. She paused for breath then slowly took the final step that lifted her head through a wide trapdoor opening and into the light.

It took several seconds for her eyes to become accustomed to the brighter but still subdued lighting, but when it did, her mouth fell open.

Her head was at eye level with dusty wooden floorboards. Above her loomed a circular room, dimly lit by an array of stumped candles and oil lanterns. It looked more like a burrow of some kind, as if she had tunnelled deep beneath the ground. Tree roots snaked along the floor, over and into stone walls before disappearing up into the ceiling. Cobwebs fashioned like rags of gauze hung from crevices and seemed to move as if they had things crawling through them. The moss-smothered stone seemed to glow, casting a ghostly green hue.

The space was cluttered with strange objects. Bottles of various sizes and colours sat on dilapidated shelves, filled with murky liquids, twisted plant roots. The glass was ancient, and the labels faded and worn. Some were corked while others were sealed with wax.

Strange symbols were etched into the walls. Dried leaves and herbs hung in bunches from the ceiling.

In the centre of the room, sitting on a large triangle made of cobblestone, was what looked like a giant glass demijohn filled with fire. It would have been easy to mistake it for one of those modern floating stoves that Sofia had seen on the home makeover shows she'd occasionally watch with her father. But it wasn't like that. It was different. The fire didn't just flicker, snap, and crackle; it waxed and waned with uncanny fluidity, as if it were some kind of sentient being, trapped inside a glass bubble.

Sofia was in awe. There was something otherworldly about the place. As if she wasn't here at all but trapped inside a fantastical dream.

Yet those guttural sobs were all too real. They drew her attention from the visual oddity in front of her to the other side of the room. Through a tangled curtain of gnarled roots, she could see a figure slumped over a bench. It was hard to tell in the eerie green gloom, but it looked like an old woman with long scraggly hair, her face buried in her hands.

Sudden movement on the opposite side of the room caused Sofia to duck instinctively. A figure. There was someone else in the room who had been standing quietly in the shadows the whole time. Now, they moved slowly, reluctantly, stepping over towards the old woman and under the spill of the lamplight.

Sofia's eyes widened. She recognised that handsome face. The elvish ears. The slim, defined body. The dark hair.

Gabriele.

He was dressed in what looked like riding pants and a loosely unbuttoned shirt. He reached out and placed a gentle hand on the figure's shoulder but there was a loud screech, and he was shoved so violently away that he crashed to the floorboards, his fall launching a cloud of dirt and dust into the air.

"DON'T TOUCH ME! DON'T YOU DARE TOUCH ME!" the old woman snarled, drops of spittle glinting in the candlelight. There was a whimpering sound from the floor.

"You were supposed to take care of him," the woman wailed. "Why didn't you take care of him? Why didn't you stop him? WHY? ANSWER ME!" she shrieked. The sound was so loud it shook dust from the walls.

The whimpering from the floor sounded more akin to an animal than a human being as Gabriele picked himself up onto all fours. It was difficult for Sofia to see him exactly. He'd fallen into shadows and the tangle of roots was too dense for her to see him in great detail, but she imagined his faced pained, those thick lips wrinkled into a sad frown as—

Her thought was interrupted by a dreaded familiar clicking sound and then the vision of the shadow crawling forward on all fours, like an obedient pet. *Click…click…click. Click…click…click.* It was an instant trigger for Sofia who threw her hands to her mouth to stop the scream that was attempting to flee from her, just as she wished to flee back to the bedroom sanctuary she should have never left. A gargantuan claw of horror grabbed her and squeezed her so tightly she could barely breathe as she watched *it* move under the dappled flickering light. It was the embodiment of those statues she had seen standing outside of the exhibit at the Doge's Palace. The wide and slanted eyes. The balding pitted scalp. The mouth of teeth that glinted in the flickering light. There was no mistaking it. Yet it defied reality; Sofia was sure she was having another one of her dreams and she needed to force herself awake.

Wake up now, Sofia. Wake up! Go on!

But it wasn't happening. Worse, as she gazed into the middle distance, willing her body back to reality from her somnambulistic nightmare, her attention was drawn to a giant maggot of at least five or six inches wriggling in front of her face. Luckily, she still had her hands over her mouth to stifle a scream, and as the thing came into focus, she realised that it wasn't a maggot at all. It was one of the roots, moving, in some uncanny way, like a worm as it reacted to her proximity. It compelled her to snap her head back away from it.

That's when she heard a loud guttural snarl and looked through a gap in the tangled roots towards it; the old woman was staring in her direction.

Sofia staggered back as tears of terror sprang to her eyes. She could see her now. As the candlelight danced across her features, she could see the hag's true form. The once beautiful face was now twisted and contorted, the smooth porcelain skin now craggy and lined and those large almond-shaped eyes circular and jaundice yellow, with only dots for pupils. And her hair! What had happened to that long, luscious black hair? It was straggly, clumpy, and worn away in patches.

She was barely recognisable and yet somehow Sofia knew that that thing glaring in her direction from across the room, sniffing the air like a rabid animal, was her next-door neighbour.

Aurora!

Mind numb with shock, Sofia allowed herself to fall back down the hole and into the tunnel once more as her phone tumbled out of her hands and into a puddle.

There was loud heavy scuffling and clicking overhead as Sofia lunged for the light of her phone. She snatched it up and half ran, half stumbled her way back down the stone corridor as fast as she could.

The return journey seemed much more difficult, her panic making each step treacherous. The walls were tighter and more claustrophobic as the light bobbed up and down in front of her, barely illuminating the path as she stumbled and then tripped in the dark. She threw both of her hands out to break her fall and winced when she felt the jagged rocks bite into her skin. Then something scuttled across the wall near to her face, making her yelp and start forward, only to trip once more. This time, it was her phone that bore the brunt of the impact, its feeble light snuffed out forever.

She abandoned it and hurried, slipped, and stumbled forward, arms outstretched, feeling her way as the blind person she had now become.

She could feel the witch's cold fetid breath breathing down her neck now. See the dead housekeeper—shards of glass for eyes—reaching out for her.

"No!" she screamed, slapping hysterically at the dark around her. "NO!" Her voice amplified by the deep.

Then, as her eyes became accustomed to blackness, she saw it, up ahead. It was faint yet unmistakable. Light in the dark.

She increased her pace as the amber beacon grew larger and eventually turned into a spotlight overhead. She had the fleeting thought to stop and listen for sounds behind her, but dismissed it immediately, reaching out instead for the cold iron railing of the staircase, feeling for the first step, and mounting it, then the next and then the next. The construction groaned loudly this time against her speedy assault, yet Sofia did not stop. Not until she reached the top step, stumbled into the bedroom, and then shoved the mirror shut behind her.

24

THE VISITOR

WEDNESDAY EVENING

The *Comando Provinciale Compagnia Stazione*, Venice's police headquarters, was nestled along the edge of St Mark's Lake, hidden away in a narrow passageway called *Riva Degli Schiavi*, or Shore of the Slaves. The station's unremarkable and dishevelled exterior, with its peeling terracotta walls and gloomy windows, was a stark contrast to the grandeur of the nearby Hotel Danieli. The rusty, gapped teeth of the iron bars and grills covering the glass panes only added to the building's foreboding appearance.

Inside, the station served as the base for the Carabinieri's foreign affairs department, a small and overworked group of officers who had drawn the short straw for the week and were tasked with dealing with the relentless barrage of complaints from tourists that flooded the city every year. Lost wallets, lost children, jilted lovers, and honeymoons gone awry were just a few of the issues they had to contend with on a daily basis.

Ispettore Puglisi had been responsible for the trivial concerns of Venice's visitors before being promoted to serious crime. It was a welcome change, but with limited resources and an overwhelming workload, he often found himself taking on more cases than he could handle. Still, operating under constant pressure from superiors was nothing new to him.

He sighed as he sat at his desk, surrounded by piles of paperwork. He had only been out a couple of hours and had already received fifteen new emails as well as a barrage of voicemails demanding his immediate attention. He was in the process of sifting through them when he heard a commotion in one of the nearby offices.

The station hadn't changed much in the many years since Puglisi had first joined the force. Instead of large, open-plan offices, it featured several smaller and more intimate spaces, starting with the reception area and progressing towards his office of the serious crime unit.

He couldn't let himself be distracted. The work had been piling up since the start of the week. He was not going to allow himself to be drawn into whatever antics his colleagues were currently engaged in.

At least that was the plan until Verrastro appeared in front of him. *"Eh, Puglisi, ma tu non senti?"*

"No, Verrastro, I hear you all perfectly," Puglisi said, eyes on his computer while holding his mobile phone to his ear. "But I'm drowning here, and that craziness at Palazzo Rosso today only made things worse. So, if Saluzzi is watching porno again, don't bother sending it to me because—"

"It's about the English woman. That detective from England."

"No! No! No!" the man said emphatically, pressing buttons on his phone. "Tell her I'm not here. And tell her if she keeps calling, I'll have even less time to talk to her." The man juggled his phone into the crook of his neck while tapping on his computer keyboard as he grumbled on. *"Pronto! Pronto!"* he yelled in frustration.

"Perhaps you should tell me yourself, Inspector," he heard a female voice say. It wasn't coming from his phone but from in front of him.

Puglisi closed his eyes. "*Merda. No, non parlo con te.* No, I don't talk to you!" he added into the phone before disconnecting the call and looking up.

Detective Inspector Patricia King stood in front of Ispettore Puglisi's desk with her arms crossed tightly over her chest. She was wrapped in a sleek black coat with a red scarf and matching hat that made her sapphire blue eyes pop. She looked just like her picture; black, petite, and stunningly beautiful. From her abrasive tone on the phone, he and his colleagues had imagined her differently. Like one of those prim British headmistresses whose secret life involved dressing up in a leather catsuit and whipping deviant politicians. It had become a joke around the office.

But it wasn't funny now. Her expression was tight, and it was clear that she was not in any way amused. He had been avoiding her. And now that she had overheard what he had just told Verrastro, which could only add fuel to the fire, her silence spoke volumes.

He noticed that she had her case with her, which meant she must have come straight from the airport. Puglisi glared at Verrastro, who shrugged and held up his hands as if to say *I tried to tell you.*

Puglisi sighed. "Signorina King—"

"Detective Inspector," she said, cutting him off. "I'm a detective, just like you. And you know, even if us Brits have got a reputation for being aloof and maybe even a little sour when it comes to dealing with foreigners, I'd like to think that if the roles were reversed and you asked me for assistance with a case, I would at least do you the professional courtesy of taking your phone call."

There was a cheer from across the room. If King noticed it, she didn't show it. Instead, she kept her eyes on Puglisi, who was becoming transfixed by the violet he could see in them.

"Please, sig..." Puglisi interrupted himself as his computer beeped and an instant chat message window opened on his screen. A three-second GIF started playing automatically; a dominatrix slapped a riding crop against the palm of her hand while eying the bare buttocks of a man at her feet.

Puglisi looked across the room towards the surreptitious snickering of some of his colleagues, then glared at Verrastro once more before casually clicking the chat screen closed. "Coffee, Detective King? Can I offer you a drink?"

"I didn't travel all the way here for coffee, Detective," King said flatly.

"No, of course not," Puglisi said, standing up and grabbing his jacket from the back of his chair. "But I'm Italian; we talk much better when we have food or a drink in our hands."

A bitter wind greeted them as they left the police station and made their way up the alleyway to the main thoroughfare, where the cold weather had done nothing to dampen the Carnevale spirit. The streets were alive with people dressed in vibrant costumes, their masks hiding their faces but not their excitement. The sound of laughter and chatter filled the air, mixing with the distant strains of music and the occasional burst of fireworks. The colourful lights from the street vendors illuminated the way, casting a warm glow on the faces of those around them as the smell of fried food tantalized their senses.

Some revellers, mostly tourists, were bundled up in their coats and scarves as they made the most of festivities by joining in with the dancing and singing. Spirits were high despite the chilly temperatures.

The two detectives walked in silence until Puglisi spoke. "This your first time in Venezia, Detective?" he asked, dodging around people in the crowd.

King shook her head. "No, I've been here before," is all she said without offering anything further. The reality was that she had previously been to Venice on her honeymoon and later vowed never to go back. But when she learned that Sophie Cooper had suddenly fled from the country, and with Interpol giving her the runaround, she had decided to take matters into her own hands. Of course, she was perfectly aware that she had no jurisdiction there, and, as difficult as it was to accept, she knew she needed to keep the ispettore onside.

"Look, Detective," Puglisi began, speaking loudly over the celebrations. "I 'pologise. I no mean to cause you offence."

"What are you apologising for?" King asked. "Ignoring my calls or having a laugh at my expense?"

They had stopped outside a busy café. Puglisi shrugged and, feeling somewhat sheepish, said, "Both, I think."

King observed the man. He reminded her of a younger version of the Italian actor Marcello Mastroianni. He wasn't really her type, but he was handsome in a mature kind of way. She imagined that the lines around his eyes were from laughter, though he did look tired. It had obviously been a rough week. She decided to cut him some slack.

"I know what it's like, you know. How mad it can all get. You only needed to say something. And I've worked with juvenile men my entire career. Your lot are nothing new to me," she said, stepping into the café like she knew the place.

At the bar, Puglisi was able to command expeditious attention from one of the busy barmen. *"Ciao, Massimo, un espresso per piacere,"* he shouted over the din of the other punters. The place was heaving. He looked at King. "Would you like tea? Un latte, perhaps?"

King frowned. "Espresso's just fine, thanks."

Puglisi smiled. *"Massimo, due! E portaci un piatto,"* he added. Then to King he asked, "Have you eaten today?"

"Ispettore—" she began.

"It's just food," he interrupted with a shrug. He knew she hadn't eaten and was probably tired. Clearly, she was one of those women who preferred business before pleasure. However, as an Italian, he didn't believe the two had to be mutually exclusive.

"And so, Ispettore. Sophie Cooper."

"Who?" the man asked.

King frowned. Was he trying to irritate her?

"Don't you mean DaTerra? Sofia DaTerra?"

King's eyes widened. "She's changed her name?"

"It seem that way, yes," he said. *"Grazie,"* he added as the barman first deposited their espressos before them and then a large platter filled with paninis and pastries. *"Prego,"* Puglisi said, gesturing to the counter. When King hesitated, he cocked his head and smiled.

It was obvious he wasn't going to let up, so she indulged him. At first it was because she didn't want to seem ungracious—she needed the man after all—but once she caught a whiff of the sweet fried pastry, that changed. She wheeled her case between them, loosened her scarf, and stepped up to the counter.

Satisfied that King had accepted the hospitality, Puglisi continued. "You know, this such a pleasure to be hosting a detective with such… um… experience, and of course, so beautiful."

She watched his eyes travel over her.

"It okay I say beautiful? I know it not… how you say… political correct these days."

"You can call me whatever you like as long as you take me to see the girl," King said, with a sweet smile and a bat of the eyelids. She dissolved both an instant later when she added, "And you can drop the sweet Columbo act. Nobody is buying that crap. I have been and am a pain in your backside, so why don't we just get to it, shall we?"

He chuckled. "You English… always so cynical."

"You Italians… always such romantics."

King had tacked a smile onto that too, but Puglisi knew she was serious. He liked that about her. There was something very sexy about her brooding demeanour and her tenacity. It excited him. But he knew she was out of his league. She was at least ten years younger than him for a start, and so stunning. There was also the minor detail that he was married.

25

THE DECISION

WEDNESDAY EVENING

Sofia collapsed against the mirror as she fought to catch her breath, quietly though, so she could listen for sounds behind it. There was nothing but her own anxious gasps and the blood thumping behind her ears, when what she thought was the sound of that doorknocker reverberated in the distance.

Her eyes widened. "NO!"

She jumped to her feet and raced out of the room. She bolted down the stairs, to the consternation of the workmen. They all froze, black garbage sacks and cleaning utensils in hand, as if they had just been caught doing something they shouldn't.

Armando was the first to drop what he was holding and remove his hat. The others immediately followed suit. Then, noting her distress, his eyes flickered to life as he rushed forward.

"Mamma mia! Contessa, ma che é successo?!"

He turned to one of his colleagues, who instantly hurried away towards the stairs and then down into the kitchen.

"Contessa?" Judging by the wild look in the man's eyes, he was genuinely concerned for her. "What happened?" he asked in English, looking at her and then her bloodied hands.

Sofia was still reeling from her ordeal. Her breaths came thick and fast, and her eyes darted back and forth to the front door, and yet her curiosity compelled her to utter, "You…you… sp… speak English?"

The man dropped his eyes and sheepishly replied, "Yes, when I have to." His accent was strong, but his words were clear.

"I didn't think you understood me," Sofia said, holding her wounded hands aloft. The cut didn't appear to be too deep. The stinging was mostly from the grazes on her palms.

"I learn a long time ago, Contessa," Armando continued, "that it best not speak unless spoken to." He tacked a quick faint smile onto the back of his words.

"Oh my goodness, what happened?"

At the sound of a new voice, Sofia's heart, not even yet recovered from its latest trauma, leapt into her throat.

Aurora entered the room trailed by one of Armando's colleagues. She wore a black gown with a fur wrap and looked as gorgeous as ever. She moved closer and Armando immediately shrank away.

"Oh, let me see," Aurora said, taking Sofia's hand in hers and examining it. Her touch was soft and warm, but it was all Sofia could do not to snatch away from her grasp. "Oh, you poor thing," she said, before looking up at her with arched eyebrows and a face full of pained sympathy. "What did you do?"

Sofia could do nothing but gawk at the lady whose porcelain skin was as radiant as it was tight over her cheekbones. Her makeup flawless like she'd just stepped out of an artist's chair. Could this really be the thing she thought she saw down there? It didn't make any sense.

She swallowed hard and resisted the urge to place a hand on her chest. Her frenzied heart was thumping so loudly she feared the woman standing before her might hear it.

Their eyes met. Sofia expected to see something in them. Recognition. Recrimination, perhaps. Anything. Something that confirmed that what she believed had happened barely a minute or so ago had indeed taken place and wasn't a figment of her imagination. It couldn't be. The sting in her hand proved it. Didn't it?

Yet no matter how much she searched the beauty's eyes, there appeared to be nothing but sympathy.

Mercifully, the moment was shattered by the return of Armando's colleague, breathless from rushing around. He was a short man with an uncanny brotherly resemblance to the caretaker, right down to his hat. He handed him what looked like a tea towel.

Armando looked at it and rolled his eyes.

"Ma non ho trovato altro," the man said with a shrug and a lift of his hands.

Armando dropped his eyes again and stepped forward. "I 'pologise, Contessa, ma he was unable to find anything else," he said tentatively.

He started to reach over but was intercepted by Aurora. She snatched the cloth from him then gently dabbed at and then wrapped it around one of Sofia's hands.

"Come take a seat, my darling. Over here where I can take a better look at you," the woman said, leading Sofia to one of the chaise longues at the foot of the stairs. Sofia wanted to resist but felt conflicted. Somehow, now that she was back in the palace with Armando and his men standing right there, her fear felt childish.

But Armando must have noticed something on her face because he suddenly asked, "Contessa, *ma tutto aposto*? Everything it okay? You need *ospedale*?"

"No," Aurora said sharply. "She doesn't need a hospital. She'll be fine. Won't you, love? It's just a scratch." Aurora smiled and stroked her neighbour's hand.

Sofia jumped up. "Yes… I'll…um…I'll be fine."

Armando hesitated then nodded. "Then *allora,* Contessa. We, um, we finish for day. Back *domani* to fix glass," he said, making a spinning gesture with his finger.

"Oh, right," Sofia said uncertainly, taking an awkward step forward that led nowhere. She didn't want him to go but didn't know what to say to make him stay. She didn't want to be left alone with this woman, whoever or whatever she was.

But his friends had already picked up their gear and were making their way towards the door.

"Armando?" she called after the man.

He turned immediately. "*Si*, Contessa? You need something else?"

"No, you run along home," Aurora said sweetly, standing beside Sofia once more. "The contessa is in perfectly good hands with me."

Armando glanced at the woman, then looked at Sofia before nodding. Then he replaced his hat and slowly walked away.

Seconds later, the slam of the door echoed around them.

Something moved in Sofia's peripheral vision, and she spun around to look. There was nothing there. Just the overhead lights flickering feebly, summoning and vanquishing shadows.

"Is something wrong?" Aurora asked.

"Um, no. I thought I… um… No."

"Are you sure?"

Sofia turned to her and startled. It looked like the woman had silently glided even closer to her.

"Sofia," she began, lifting a hand with rubies for fingernails and gently placing it under Sofia's chin. "Are you sure you're feeling all right? You're looking a bit peaky." The woman's deep gaze studied her intensely.

Sofia twisted away as casually as she could. "Yes, of course. I'll be fine."

"Can I get you something? A nice cup of tea perhaps?"

"No, thank you. I…" She trailed off and paused for a moment, considering. "Actually, that would be lovely," she continued. "If you're sure you don't mind."

"Of course not." The siren shrugged off her fur and then, with one last look at her, slowly disappeared down the stairs.

Sofia did not hesitate. Aurora had barely vanished from sight when she was already racing back up the stairs, down the hall, and into her bedroom.

There, she grabbed her case from the walk-in wardrobe and started throwing her things into it, mainly her own practical stuff, such as the jeans and other clothes she had brought with her. She would have to leave some things behind, and she was fine with that. She went into the bathroom, sweeping toiletries into her own washbag in a scene eerily reminiscent of the one she had played out earlier.

The action reminded her. She looked at the tea towel wrapped around her hand. It was ridiculously bulky and kept catching. The pain had subsided anyway, so she unwrapped it, and froze. *What?*

There was nothing wrong with her hand. In fact, there was nothing wrong with either of them. There was nothing there. No grazes and no pain. How was that even possible? It happened; she knew it had. She could picture everything so vividly. The sights.

The smells. Her.

That thing!

She couldn't have made that up. She knew she didn't make it up.

Sophie, you know how stress takes its toll on you.

Her former psychiatrist's voice chased her out of the bathroom and back into the bedroom, but then she yelped when she saw a silhouette standing by the balcony doors. Then she blinked and they were gone. Did she imagine that too?

Oh, what was happening to her? She checked again. There was nothing there.

She needed to leave. She needed to get out of there. She needed time to clear her head.

She stuffed the washbag into the case, but the haphazard way she'd packed the other items meant there wasn't room for much else. She pulled, pushed, and grunted angrily but the bloody thing wouldn't shut.

"Sofia?"

She screamed and whirled around.

Aurora was standing in the doorway. "Oh, *mia cara*, I'm so sorry. I called you but you didn't answer," the woman said, her eyes on the case now on the bed with Sofia's knee pressing onto it. "What are you doing?"

"Aurora… I… um… didn't hear you come in."

"Well, I did call you. Didn't you hear me?"

"Sorry, no, I didn't."

"Well, I made tea," she said, watching as Sofia struggled some more with her case. "Where are you going?"

"I'm leaving," Sofia said through gritted teeth, struggling still to close it.

"Leaving? Leaving for where?"

"I'm going back to England. I'm going home."

Aurora let out a short laugh. "England? But whatever for? You said yourself that you have nothing to go back to. This is your home now."

It irritated her that Aurora was using her words to make a point, but otherwise she didn't care. "I was wrong," she said.

"Oh," was all the woman could say. "But what about your job?"

"My job?"

"Yes, at the palace."

"I don't think it's going to work out. Raffaella hates me." She paused and considered her words for a few moments, then added, "I'm sorry. I know it doesn't look good. Especially after what you did to get me the interview in the first place. But it just isn't going well for me here. I need to go home to be with my friend."

"What about the gala?"

Sofia gawped at the woman. "The gala? Oh my God, Aurora. People are dead. Daniele is dead. Doesn't that mean anything to you?"

The woman's eyes dropped. "Well, of course it does, especially now that you mention it so casually. So… coldly."

"I'm cold? You've been gliding around here without a care in the bloody world since it happened. How is that possible?"

The beauty frowned at her next-door neighbour's insensitive tone, then swallowed and lifted her head as if to shrug it off. "Not everybody wears their grief on their sleeve, Sofia," the woman said, seemingly affronted.

The act of reserved bereavement tugged at Sofia's sympathy and guilt until the memory kicked in. *The demijohn of fire. The decrepit old lady with wild hair. That thing at her feet.* She flinched, still unable to reconcile that with the woman before her. Could she have imagined it? Perhaps fallen asleep and not realised?

"I think you should reconsider, Sofia," Aurora continued, back to her bright self. "After all, we're finally going to find out whether or not the comet is going to safely burn up in our atmosphere, or if the conspiracy theorists are right and this really is the end of the world."

"Well, it's just going to have to end without me," Sofia retorted flatly. She dragged her case off the bed and made for the door. Aurora stood in her path.

Her heart switched up a gear. "Excuse me," she said.

"Sofia—"

"Aurora, let me through," she demanded through gritted teeth. Her mind was already racing with contingency actions should the woman refuse to step out of her way. However, after several seconds, Aurora moved aside.

The lights flickered as she hurried up the hallway, Aurora following behind her.

"Sofia, please, you must reconsider," she began to babble. "Whatever it is, I'm sure we can work through it. Together."

Flicker.

"Where will you go?" the woman added, hurrying to keep up with her.

Flicker.

"I have no idea. Anywhere but here. I need time to think."

"About what?"

"About everything," Sofia threw back over her shoulder as she neared the top of the staircase.

"Sofia!"

Aurora stopped following.

"Sofia!"

The lights flickered angrily.

"SOFIA!"

The woman screeched as lightbulbs shattered all around them. Sofia felt her feet give way beneath her and she crashed to the floor.

After a few seconds of cowering under the shower of glass, Sofia spun around to see that all the lights were dead but for the one just outside her bedroom, back down the hallway. It still flicked *ON* and *OFF*. *ON* and *OFF*.

ON. She saw Aurora walking towards her.

OFF. Now it was the silhouette of a stooped figure with wild hair.

ON. Aurora.

OFF. The silhouette.

Closer…

ON. Aurora.

OFF. The silhouette!

Sofia screamed. Such was her terror, she didn't even hear the footsteps racing up the stairs until, suddenly, strong arms were around her, lifting her to her feet.

26

DEPARTURE

EARLY THURSDAY MORNING

Two days left.

Sofia barely slept a wink all night. Every noise outside and every sigh of the wind was Aurora and Gabriele, readying to storm her room and drag her by the hair kicking and screaming to their burrow. At one point she dreamt about it and woke up shrieking.

But it didn't happen. Whatever she heard or whatever she dreamt had nothing to do with her eccentric next-door neighbour.

Despite the little sleep that she did manage, her body felt weary. Her mind exhausted by the piranha thoughts snapping for attention the moment she opened her eyes.

It seemed that no matter how hard she tried to organise everything in her head and no matter how she struggled to rationalise it all, none of it made sense. Either she was losing her mind or Aurora, like Victoria before her, was some kind of a witch.

There. She'd said it. Witch. And if that were true then… there was no answer. Every time she sought to find one, she drew a blank. What did she do now? What did it mean in the real world? Should she keep it to herself? Tell someone? What should she do with this kind of information?

Continue to ignore what's right in front of your face, of course.

She couldn't allow her mind to stray there. It was just too abhorrent. Yet, no matter how hard she tried to repel the thought, she had to consider that people were dead. Both on Meadow Lane and there in Venice, things had happened. Terrible things. As much as she might want to ignore what she had seen, she had to accept that bad things had hurt real people and that her friend, Victoria, and whatever cult she was part of, had been involved.

What should she do about that? Go to the police? They would laugh at her. She had no evidence. She could already imagine their sceptical expressions. *So how long have you been receiving mental health support, Ms DaTerra? Is there anyone we can call?*

It had taken several minutes for Sofia to recover from her encounter in the hallway. Without any lights, it was particularly dark in the gallery, and it took her a while to finally focus on the face in front of her.

It was Cameron. Cameron and Armando. He had carried her down the stairs into the light and onto the chaise longue at the foot of the staircase. When he was finally able to get an answer from her, it was in the form of a hysterical stream of accusations about her stunning next-door neighbour. The beauty was gazing anxiously at her from a couple of feet away, chewing her lip and wearing an innocent expression of wide-eyed concern.

Sofia had accused her of being *a hag! An old hag!* It sounded like nothing but a simple insult until Sofia was forced to be more specific. "She's a witch! She's a fucking witch! Get her out of here! Get her out of here!" she had screamed until the lady had humbly excused herself, apologising for any distress she may have caused.

It was only after Aurora had left that Sofia, noticing the baffled look on the men's faces, had led them back up the stairs to Janay's room and the mirror. There, she had tugged, pulled, screamed, and sobbed as she attempted to yank the unrelenting mirror off the wall. Armando was forced to intervene and insist she stop for fear that she might injure herself.

"It's a doorway! It's a secret doorway!" she had screamed hysterically, but closer inspection by the two men had revealed no such thing. It was solid wall behind. There was no hairline fracture. No hollow sound when it was tapped.

No access to an underground tunnel.

"I know what you're thinking, but it was there, I swear! You've got to believe me!" She'd then proceeded to recount what she believed had happened to her, including the miraculous healing of the wounds on her hands.

"Yes! My hands! What about my hands, Armando? You saw them!"

The old man had nodded and reluctantly looked at the hands she was opening and clenching in front of him. They were indeed red, cut, and bleeding, but the wounds were straight, clearly made from her stint at trying to rip the mirror from the wall.

"They weren't like this! They were different before. They were grazed. You saw them. They were grazed!" But Armando could only bow his head, torn between loyalty to his mistress and what he actually believed he saw.

In the end, she insisted on leaving the house and going to a hotel. Anything to get out of that place.

But now, in the cold light of day, everything felt different. She was confused. Her mind ran on a loop, boarding thoughts onto various tracks but failing to reach any destination but one. The most plain and logical conclusion.

Deal with each item in turn in order of importance. That was how Doctor Krauss had taught her. *Avoid becoming overwhelmed by what you cannot control.*

And that was exactly what she planned to do.

Unfortunately, it involved doing something that she had been expressly asked not to. She had agreed not to leave the country but now she had no choice. She had to get Janay and herself away from there. Once she had some distance, she'd be able to get some perspective, she was sure.

It wasn't as if the police would have put a block on her passport or anything. Would they?

One thing at a time.

She accepted that there were many things she couldn't know or predict and resolved that she would stick with her plan and let the chips fall where they would. After all, when it came down to it, she knew she had not done anything wrong.

They were going to fly back to England today. She would have to stay with Janay until she was able to get herself sorted. She never belonged in Venice anyway. She was naive for ever thinking she could and accepted that Doctor Krauss had been right. *You can't simply move to a different place and leave everything behind. As much as we feel this to be the simplest solution, it is actually the most complex. We're merely postponing the inevitable. Since we are often our own problems, we carry them in our head.*

So why was she leaving now?

She ignored her quarrelling thoughts and decided that the doctor would be another step in her plan. Once she was settled, she would go back to seeing him. She would tell him everything and work through whatever process he felt was appropriate.

She had considered sharing everything with Janay, but she didn't even know how to start. Her friend was already dealing with a lot and there was Damon to consider too. She would see how things panned out once they were back home, once they both had had some time to forget Venice and everything that happened there.

Right now, she had other more practical concerns, such as, what were they going to do about money?

Assuming she didn't get arrested either before she left or when she landed, she needed to speak to her lawyer, Roger Mitchell, as soon as possible. She needed to know what her options were.

You can't just quit, Sofia. This isn't like one of your other jobs.

Well, she had, and he was just going to have to deal with it. She was relying on him to help her find a way out of it all. Not that she could afford him. He was obviously very expensive, and she had nothing but credit card debt to her name. If they could find a way of selling Palazzo Rosso, though, she would have plenty of money. She could retain his services and still have enough to guarantee a comfortable future, not just for herself, but for Janay and Damon too. After all, they were the only family she had now. It was up to her to take care of them.

She smiled at Janay while unconsciously rubbing the palm of her hand. They had already bid goodbye to Venice. Sofia was surprised to find that, despite everything, she felt sad as she watched the blue hues of the lagoon blend into the multicoloured greys of land.

They had taken the train to Mestre and were now riding the bus to Venice Marco Polo Airport where they'd make the two or so hour flight back to Stansted Airport. She wasn't exactly excited at the prospect of flying back to her old workplace, but if it got her out of Italy and back home, it would be worth it.

As she gazed out of the window, her thoughts turned to Sam, how things had ended awkwardly between them, and she couldn't help but wonder what could have been. She realised that it was with a heavy heart that she considered that she may never see him again.

Then she sat up straight and took a deep breath. She had some semblance of a plan, and if she wanted to get through this, she needed to stick with it.

27

THE BINDING

THURSDAY MORNING

Down beneath the narrow walkways and bridges of Venice, hidden beneath the labyrinth of stone, the figure shuffled back and forth in its lair. Shadows danced in the amber light as it went about gathering the ingredients, placing them on the bench beside the demijohn.

The scales of fish, taken from the Venetian lagoons, symbolized the city's connection to the sea and its power over it. The root of demonio, plucked from the marshes of La Serenissima, represented the ancient magic that flowed through the land and the power of the earth. The universal power of the seed and a lock of fine hair completed the necessary components.

It stood over the demijohn as the fire inside flickered and danced, then oozed and slithered like a serpent yearning for freedom. Its light played off the figure's leathery skin, stretched tightly over high cheekbones and a sharp jawline, giving the appearance of a skull. Its thin lips were curled back into a malevolent sneer.

It placed the ingredients into the bowl as its sunken and jaundiced eyes rolled back into its head, leaving only white ocular cavities to gaze into the flame. It began to murmur the incantation.

"Ex ovo universum. Ex aqua omnia. Ex terra homines. Ex igni spiritus. Ex Serenissima, ego te ligare. Ex radice demonio, ego te retinere. Ex squama piscis, ego te tenere. Ex mea voluntate, ego te manere."

With each phrase, the figure let the elements it had collected fall into the simmering mixture. The spell was strictly precautionary; the girl's fate was ordained many years before and sealed the moment she placed the iron key in the lock of the palazzo. But it could not risk failure. It knew all too well that its continued existence depended on this success.

Now, as it quivered in the stream of energy released by the spell, it became aware of something else. A presence of a different kind was approaching the palace, one that needed to be greeted.

Personally.

28

FLIGHT RISK

THURSDAY MORNING

Detective Inspector King slept better than she had anticipated. She had feared that memories of her previous life would haunt her in the solitary attic room of the guest house near the police station. But instead, sleep had claimed her the moment her head hit the pillow.

She had learned a lot during her meeting with Puglisi. Surprisingly, he was quite a charming man. Like her, he was dedicated to his work, but he seemed to have a way of seamlessly weaving his job into his life without letting it consume him. She wished she knew his secret.

She was glad she had travelled there, even if it had been

without her boss's blessing. Her instincts had been right. There was something about Sophie Cooper, or whatever she was calling herself now. Although she had no hard evidence yet, there was no doubt that the girl was in some way involved with the events of Meadow Lane and now those in Venice too.

Puglisi had agreed, which was why, under the wintry sunshine, they were now disembarking from a Carabinieri speedboat and making their way up the jetty leading to Palazzo Rosso. The air was crisp, and the sky painted in shades of pink and orange in the hue of the early morning light.

"Detective," Puglisi began. "May I ask a personal question?"

"Only if I may decline to answer it," she said.

Puglisi smiled. "Yesterday, when I ask you if you have been to Venice, you say yes, but I could not help but notice your voice."

"My voice?"

"How you say… Not excited." He waved to an old lady on the opposite side of the bridge. *"Buongiorno!"*

"Are you asking if I'm still married, Detective?" King asked. She couldn't help but wonder if the man already knew the answer.

He looked up the steps to the palace, rolled his eyes, then turned to her and shrugged. "Only if you wish to answer, of course."

"I was until recently," she said.

"I'm sorry to hear that. It very sad." He began climbing the steps. "You know, we have a saying here in Italy, *Il matrimonio è come una barca, se uno non rema, l'altro lo trascina.*" He turned to King, who was following behind. "Marriage, 'tis like a boat. If one doesn't row, the other drags."

King lifted her eyebrows. "Oh, it definitely dragged after a while," she said as they resumed their journey to the top of the steps. King stopped at the front door, then frowned when she saw the doorknocker appendage.

"It to ward off evil spirits," Puglisi offered.

"Ward them off? That thing looks like an evil spirit!"

Puglisi shrugged. She had a point, but he didn't hesitate to grab the thing by its horns and allow it to fall on the door a couple of times in quick succession.

They waited. Seagulls called overhead as Venice went about its day. When they received no reply, King stepped back and looked up. The building bore down, smothering her with its shadow.

"Mi scusi, signora. Mi dispiace disturbarla, ma ha visto la ragazza che abita qui?"

King turned to see Puglisi talking to an elegant-looking lady in a black dress with white detailing and matching hat. She was crossing the bridge towards them.

She responded in Italian. By the look on Puglisi's face, her answer wasn't good.

"Grazie tante." He turned back to King.

"What?" she asked.

"She said she saw her leaving with her suitcase." He reached for the phone in his pocket.

King rolled her eyes. "Please tell me you confiscated her passport."

But Puglisi didn't need to reply. The look on his face said it all.

29

SECURITY

THURSDAY MORNING

Marco Polo Airport is located on the mainland of Italy, about seven kilometres north of Venice. The fifth busiest air complex in Italy, it was named after the famous explorer, Marco Polo, who was born in the city. It had one terminal building and two runways, and it served as a hub for several airlines to destinations throughout Europe, as well as the Middle East, Africa, Asia, and North America.

Sofia led Janay through the hustle and bustle of the early morning passengers as they made their way to the check-in desks. The sound of wheeled luggage skimming over marble floors rumbled through the spacious concourse. The air was filled with the low hum of conversations in multiple languages as travellers either rushed or meandered through the building.

The smell of freshly brewed coffee and baked goods floated on the air, mingling with the scent of designer perfumes. The hybrid aromas transported Sofia straight back to her days working at Stansted. It had not been long since she had left, it was true, but so much had happened since that it felt like a distant memory.

It wasn't a fond one and was mercifully interrupted by Janay. "I could murder a coffee right now. Let's go and grab one before—"

"Actually, Janay," Sofia interrupted. "I'd rather we get ourselves checked in first."

Janay frowned. "All right. Are you okay?"

"Yeah, I'm fine," Sofia responded, her eyes scanning through the crowds as she checked for their flight number and check-in desk. "Oh, here. We're over here!" she said, tugging at her friend and leading her into the line. Luckily, it wasn't too long.

"Sophie…"

"Yeah?" she responded distractedly. She was looking along the queue in front of them where there were three sets of people: a middle-aged pair that were currently being dealt with, a young family of four, and a senior couple.

Experience told her that the seniors would probably have pored over their itinerary and made sure they had their documents readily available. It looked like they had a high probability of being processed quickly.

The family, however, might be a different story. The children were an unpredictable variable. There was a good chance that the parents would have been distracted by their little ones when packing or that they would be while checking in, so there was a greater chance they would take longer to handle.

"Sophie!"

"What?"

"I was calling you. What's up?"

"What do you mean, what's up?"

"You've barely said a word since we left the hospital, and every time you see a policeman you keep looking away, like you're wanted or something. Is there something I should know?"

Sofia scoffed. "Don't be silly. Of course not."

"Soph…"

Sofia widened her gaze to one of innocence. "There isn't anything, I promise. It's just that I thought Venice was going to be a fresh start for me," she lied, "but… you know." She shrugged in a performance of defeat.

Janay eyed her suspiciously for several seconds. "Is that really it?"

"Of course. But how are you? That's more to the point," Sofia said, stroking her friend's arm as a group of people filed in behind them.

"I'm fine, Soph."

"Are you sure?"

Janay nodded. She obviously wasn't fine but she was keeping it together, for now at least. That was something else Sofia had considered. Janay would benefit from seeing someone too, but telling her she needed to do that and gently encouraging her were two separate things.

One thing at a time.

It turned out that Sofia's expert judgement was already becoming rusty. The young family went through quickly while the senior couple cogitated for a long time. The man struggled to locate his ticket, prompting his wife to berate him with the fact that she had said he should have let her manage both tickets, but, of course, he wouldn't listen…

The result was a delay, but Sofia remained hopeful until she spotted two armed Carabinieri. One of them was talking into his radio as they both looked in her direction.

She averted her gaze. Thankfully, Janay was too busy looking at her mobile phone to notice that the officers were making their way towards them.

"Next, please," said the attendant.

"Soph!" Janay nudged.

"Oh, sorry," Sofia said, following Janay forward with her case.

"Did you pack your own bags today before coming to the airport?"

Janay nodded and said, "Yeah," although it wasn't true. Cameron had helped Sofia finish gathering Janay's things before she'd finally escaped Palazzo Rosso for the hotel.

"And did you leave your bags unattended at any time between then and coming to the airport?"

The answer was yes, but Janay responded, "No."

Sofia heard the crackle of a radio nearby and her stomach dropped. The policemen were standing right behind her. They were onto her already. If she was stopped, what would she do? She would have to convince Janay to go without her. *Don't be stupid! She'll never go without you. You should have told her!*

"Sophie!"

It was Janay again. Sofia looked at her. "What?"

"Your case, Soph," Janay said.

"Oh, sorry." She placed her case on the conveyor belt as the attendant with way too much makeup stretched her lipstick into a wide fake smile.

"Did you pack your bags yourself?" she asked.

Sofia nodded, her eyes on the attendant but her ears on what was happening behind her. She felt so tuned into the two men that she felt as if she could almost hear them. Not their radios, but them. Their bodies. Almost if she could hear the very whoosh and sigh of the air they drew into and then expelled from their lungs as they loitered nearby.

"Scusate, signorina." The voice was low, masculine, and terrifying. They *were* standing behind her. They *were* onto her. Sofia kept her eyes on the attendant who was still speaking, though she couldn't consciously hear a word she was saying. All she could do was look at that smile on those painted lips. They were smudged lips at that. Victoria would have something to say about her lip line. It looked like she did it in the back of the car this morning.

Victoria. She was gone.

"Sophie!" It was Janay again. Sofia looked at her and Janay made eyes behind her. "I think you're wanted," she said.

Reluctantly, Sofia turned to face the two policemen. They looked like Laurel and Hardy instead of the handsome descendants of Roman gods she had come to expect all Italian men to resemble. They were more like Little and Large.

"Yes?" she said, heart thumping as her blood rushed behind her ears.

"Hai perso questo," Lurch with the long forehead and thick eyebrows said, looking down at her. It took several seconds for Sofia to work out what he meant. When she eventually allowed her gaze to drop, she understood.

Her beanie hat. The one she'd bought on the way out here. She'd obviously dropped it.

"Oh. Right. Grazie," she said, taking the hat from the man.

He eyed her for a while. This time Sofia knew that it wasn't suspicion but appreciation. Thankfully, he didn't linger much longer but nodded at her before he and his colleague resumed their business elsewhere.

"Oooh, he likes you. What do you think, eh?" Janay said with a wink.

Sofia scowled then shook her head.

"No? No jiggy jiggy with the nice Italian policeman?" Janay teased. Sofia couldn't have loved her friend more in that moment.

She managed to make light of everything regardless of her own inner turmoil.

The attendant handed her their boarding passes. After one more bout of repressed terror when she handed over her passport and ticket to security, which they returned without further investigation, Sofia finally started to relax.

"Can we go and get that coffee now? And maybe something to eat? I'm starving," Janay said.

Sofia nodded, even though the last thing she felt like doing was eating or drinking. Her heightened nervousness had left her feeling nauseated. However, something else caught her attention that she had not noticed before. She couldn't tell if it was her imagination or not, but the cuts she had made on her hands when trying to remove the mirror from the wall now seemed to be itching, not just aching.

She dismissed it as her imagination and decided not to let it affect her. After all, if Janay could continue with their plans with as much positivity as she could muster, Sofia wouldn't let her own worries hold her back. She put on a smile she didn't feel and followed Janay in search of lattes and croissants.

30

THE CURSE

THURSDAY. LATE MORNING.

Sofia and Janay sat in the bustling departure lounge of Marco Polo Airport sipping on their lattes.

Flight 307 from Venice to London Stansted was scheduled for departure at 12:05, which meant that boarding would no doubt start imminently.

The terminal seemed particularly busy. Sofia was grateful, finding comfort in humanity as she sat in contemplative silence and simply observed. She attributed this to her time spent by herself in the palazzo. She had felt isolated and lonely, but not here. Here, the general chatter interspersed with public announcements reminded her of the busyness and sense of purpose that came with work. It reminded her of the familiarity of home.

The weather had taken a turn for the beautiful, as if trying to entice them to stay. Warm sunshine streamed in through the large windows and bathed the space with its soft golden glow.

Sofia was feeling brighter now and had rediscovered her appetite. She had devoured two ham croissants as well as a chocolate chip muffin and was considering going back for more before Janay pointed out that their flight would be called any second now.

"All right, miss food police," Sofia said with a smile.

Janay barely faked a flash of a grin in response. Her mood appeared to have grown sombre.

Sofia placed her hand over her friend's. "Are you okay?" she asked softly.

"Yeah, I'm good. I'm all right." She nodded, as if the affirmation could make it so.

"I'm here for you. Always," Sofia said with a gentle squeeze.

"I know," Janay said as a sheen formed over her eyes. "Thanks, Soph. I'm sorry this whole Venice thing didn't work out for you."

Sofia released her friend's hand and took a sip from her drink. "Don't be silly. Things have worked out fine. I have much more perspective on my life now than I ever did before I came here," she said earnestly.

"I get that, but still… it can't be easy."

Sofia wondered what her friend's reaction would be if she knew everything.

"But there is something else," Janay continued, looking away.

Sofia sat forward. "Oh?"

"There's one more favour I need to ask ya."

"What's that?" Sofia said, leaning in.

"I need you to make me a promise," Janay said, finally finding her friend's eyes. "I need you to promise me that once we step onto that plane, you and I will never talk about what happened here. Ever."

"But Janay—"

"Soph, I need you to promise me," Janay continued, her lips trembling as her eyes brimmed now with tears. "Because of my boy. He's my light, Soph. He's everything that's good in my life, and I can't take this back to him."

It was her turn to reach for Sofia's hand now, and she squeezed it tight. "Do you understand? I can't, Soph… I just c…can't." Her voice faltered but her resolve was unmistakable.

Sofia knew what her friend was like once she had made up her mind. She wanted to say more. She wanted to tell her that she didn't believe that repressing what had happened and how she felt was the way to deal with it. She knew that. But when she looked into her friend's watery eyes, she had no choice but to acquiesce, at least for now. Maybe one day, when they were settled and the opportunity arose, Janay would feel differently, but right now Sofia simply nodded. "Of course."

Janay blinked back her final tears over the matter and smiled.

Flight 307 to London Stansted is now boarding at gate five. Passengers travelling on flight 307 to London Stansted, please make your way to gate five. This flight is now boarding.

"That's us," Janay said with a lift of her brows and a grin as she swiped her eyes tidy and stood.

Sofia smiled broadly in return despite the lead weight that had dropped into the pit of her stomach. This was it. They were finally leaving. She looked around. No Puglisi. No police anywhere to be seen. Still, when she grabbed her bag and coat, she had to stop herself from running over to the gate, despite it being less than a hundred feet away.

People were already making their way past the podium and through the gateway beyond.

She looked through the glass wall at the giant nose of the craft. It was attached to the building via the boarding tunnel, like a giant umbilical cord.

"That's our plane!" Sofia said with childish excitement, like she'd never seen one before. Janay frowned at her, perplexed, but laughed, nonetheless. "Boarding pass?" she asked. Janay grinned and waved it at her as they joined the line. "Passport?"

Janay rolled her eyes. "Look, I know you used to work at one of these places, but I have flown before."

Sofia nodded sheepishly. "Yes, of course. Just checking."

There were at least ten people in front of them. Sofia scanned the departure lounge once more. Janay followed her gaze then looked back at her.

"What?" Sofia asked.

"Who are you looking for?"

"Nobody. Why?"

"I don't know. It just looks like you're looking for someone."

"Nope." Sofia said a little too brightly. "Just being nosey."

There were five people in front of them, one of whom was unable to find their boarding pass.

Sofia chewed her lip then held her belly. It was churning now. She seriously regretted the amount of food she'd eaten.

She snatched a surreptitious look behind them. There was no sign of danger, just traveller after traveller.

Have a nice flight. Thank you. Have a nice flight. Thank you.

She could hear the gate attendant now.

Three people in front.

Thank you. Have a nice flight. Thanks.

She could hear the machine whirring as boarding passes were inserted into the scanner and then spat out again.

Two people in front.

Whirr. Thank you. Have a nice flight.

Janay handed over her boarding card.

"Thanks very much. Have a wonderful flight," the gate attendant said with a wide smile, handing the ticket back to her.

Janay stepped into the tunnel, waiting. It would only be for mere seconds, yet Sofia felt a strange sense of isolation as she stood by herself on the opposite side of the podium.

Sofia grinned nervously at the attendant who looked at her with a mixture of confusion and repressed irritation. After several awkward seconds the woman said, "Boarding pass, please, madam."

"Oh!" Sofia chuckled. "Sorry. I was daydreaming. Where did I put it now?"

She frisked herself while looking at the people in the line behind her, smiling apologetically, and then glancing at the rest of the departure lounge.

There was nobody chasing her. *Relax.*

She checked her pockets. "I know I put it somewhere here."

"Soph..."

"I had it with me just a second ago..."

"Soph..."

"That's strange because—"

"Sophie!" Janay called out forcefully.

"What?"

"You put it in your bag, remember? For safe keeping," Janay said, smiling at the attendant.

"Oh, that's right," Sofia said, ignoring the knot that was tightening in her overly full stomach. What the hell had come over her? She needed to pull herself together.

Eventually, she found the pass and handed it to the attendant. Her heart throbbed in her chest, and she had broken out in a sweat. She could feel it prickling her forehead, but she didn't dare wipe it for fear of drawing attention to herself.

She watched the attendant place the card in the slot. It beeped at her, so she pulled it out and tried again. *Beep.*

"Is there something wrong?" Sofia asked quickly.

"No, I think it's just not picking up the card properly. They can be temperamental sometimes."

The woman looked at the card, bent it backward and forward to straighten it out, and then tried it with the scanner once more. This time it entered the slot but paused on the word CHECKING…

Sofia's stomach churned. She felt nauseated enough to know she would think twice before eating a ham croissant again.

Finally, the machine beeped, and the light turned green, displaying the word OK on the screen, indicating that the card had been accepted. Sofia stopped herself from performing a celebratory dance.

"Thank you. Have a wonderful flight," the gate attendant said.

"Thanks," Sofia replied with a broad smile. She reached for her card, but a searing pain suddenly burned through her fingers, prompting her to snatch her hand back. This was followed by a shriek from the mild-mannered gate attendant.

The boarding card she was holding suddenly burst into flames. She threw it to the floor, drawing cries and gasps from the other people in the line.

Sofia examined her fingers. They looked red raw, as if she had just burned them by lifting a hot pan. But before she had a chance to process this, she felt a sharp stab of pain in her belly that quickly flared up through her chest.

She screamed and clutched her body as the people in the queue behind her recoiled in horror.

Breaking free of her shocked trance, Janay rushed past the attendant, who was still nursing her own fingers, to her friend's side and put an arm on her shoulder. "What is it? What's wrong, Sophie? What's wrong?"

But Sofia, now wailing in excruciating agony, spun around, accidentally elbowing her friend to the floor before throwing her head back, retching, as what felt like a red-hot lump of coal burned its way up her throat towards her mouth.

There were screams from bystanders as they watched the young lady's throat distend. It was grotesque and unnatural. The bulge in her throat crawled under her skin like a giant parasite.

Security to gate five immediately, please. Security to gate five immediately.

Sofia's face contorted in intense suffering as tears streamed from her bulging, bloodshot eyes. She doubled over, hands grasping knees, as her body sought to expel the unnatural lump.

There were more horrified screams from onlookers as first bile then blood dribbled from her lips to the carpet, closely followed by more heaving as Janay rose to her feet and moved to help her friend.

She was too late. Sofia's body convulsed as the fluids from her mouth sprayed onto the nearby attendant. Her face was contorted in desperation as she tried to plead with her friend and anyone nearby as her mouth was forced open in a grotesque manner and her eyes rolled back into her head. She gagged as a large, gelatinous ball of bloody mucus was expelled from her mouth with a loud squelch and splattered onto the carpet.

The smell of bile and rotten flesh filled the air as the macabre voyeurs who had dared to linger in the vicinity to watch, transfixed by the horror, were now pushing each other as they scrambled to leave the scene.

Sofia collapsed to the floor and Janay hurried over, but nothing could have prepared her for what she saw.

Sofia was lying on her back, her eyes wide in terror and her mouth distended and caked with bloody drool. The arms of the sweater she was wearing appeared to have burned away, the skin left behind bubbling and blistering.

"Please… help me…" she croaked. "He…l…p me… H…e…lp me…" Sofia felt the life force slowly ebb from her body.

Nearby, the gelatinous mound writhed and wriggled. It was alive with worms made of plant roots tangled through clumps of fish scales that shimmered a multitude of colours in the sunlight.

31

CONFISCATED

FRIDAY MORNING

One day left.

Sofia ran down the stone steps, her bare feet slapping against the rough surface. Her long crimson gown billowed behind her like a sail in the wind. Above, an apocalyptic sky was the colour of coagulated blood, the clouds angry and inflamed.

At the end of the stone pier, Sofia stopped. The lagoons were dry and desolate, with boats beached and abandoned. That's when she heard the screams. They were distant at first but became louder as she finally looked up to a sight that filled her with horror.

The sky, like a bruised and festering wound, opened to reveal a blinding white light. In front of it was a giant swarm of insects. Yet when she placed a hand to her forehead to fend off the glare, she saw that they were not insects at all but…

Humans. Humans were being lifted off their feet as they flailed and screamed, sucked into the light by a mighty invisible force. Beneath her feet, the ground began to shake and crack as fissures opened to reveal a fiery chasm. She felt a hand on her shoulder and screamed.

Sofia's eyes flicked open with a gasp. The beeping heart monitor mirrored the thumping in her chest. She was in a small room that looked familiar yet was alien to her. Whitewashed walls. High vaulted ceiling. Wide, barred window looking out to a cloud-filled cerulean sky.

She was lying in a hospital bed. Her throat was sore, and her arms were tight from bandages shrouding tingling skin.

Bubbling and blistering.

She gasped again as the memory asserted itself. The airport. The burning ticket. That lump in her throat…

"Hey, hey… there she is."

Sofia looked to her right. It was Janay jumping out of a plastic chair. Her face was filled with concern.

"Janay?" Sofia rasped, her eyes instantly misting with confusion. "Wh…ere am I?"

"You're in hospital, babe," Janay said softly.

"Home?" Sofia asked hopefully, although she already knew the answer.

"No, my darling," Janay said with a pained expression. "We're back in Venice."

"Venice?" Sofia croaked, and her heart sank. She tried to sit up as the rest of the world started to fade in with this news. Boat engines purred on the water outside. She could hear people talking in quick and passionate Italian in the corridor. Tinny public announcements sounded beyond the door. She wasn't on the ward but in a small room.

My room? How am I affording this?

She felt gentle pressure on her shoulder. "You need to take it easy," Janay said. "Doctor's orders."

Sofia coughed then cringed as the rawness in her throat grated. Janay sprang into action and picked up a bottle of water from the side table. She held the straw protruding from it to Sofia's lips so that she could sip, but Sofia finished the whole bottle before settling back on her pillow.

"The doctor says you're going to be raw for a few days, but that you'll be all right."

Sofia coughed and then straightened herself into some semblance of a sitting position. As she adjusted herself, she glanced at her arms, feeling the tightness of her bandages once more.

Janay noticed and explained. "Doc doesn't think there's permanent damage but there may be some scarring."

"What… h…a..ppened?" Sofia croaked.

Janay chewed her lip. "They don't know yet for sure, but they think you might have had some kind of allergic reaction to something. They've run a bunch of tests but so far have come back with nothing."

"Th…is room?" Sofia asked, looking around.

A smile crept over Janay's lips. "Yeah, it's all right for some," she said. And then added, "Sam was here."

Sofia's eyes widened. The pace on the heart monitor quickened.

Janay glanced at it, and her smile broadened. "Oh right, okay." She nodded. "He came over as soon as he heard, Soph. He wanted to move ya to one of his private hospitals, but the doctor wasn't having any of it. So, he starts having a serious conversation with him in Italian, and the next thing I know you're being moved here."

A smile flickered across Sofia's lips. Sam. He'd sat by her bedside the whole time. Her smile diluted. "H…how…l…ong… have I been here?"

Janay hesitated. "About a day now."

Sofia's eyes widened. "D…D…Damon…"

"He's fine. Don't worry about him, he's with Mum. I said we were going to be a few more days." Janay hesitated, her eyes dropping. "Look, Soph, there's something I need to tell—"

Janay was interrupted as the door flew open and a face Sofia recognised walked in. It was the doctor from the other day. Bianchi. Janay gave the man a weak smile.

"Ah, good morning, Contessa," the doctor said. "How you feeling today?" It was a perfunctory question, like he already knew the answer.

Sofia nodded distractedly, for her attention was drawn to the woman that entered the room behind him, and the man that followed.

It was the police. The inspector from Palazzo Rosso and—it took her a few seconds to recall—that detective from England. She couldn't remember her name. What was she doing here?

"*Buongiorno,* Contessa, you remember me, yes?" Puglisi asked with a big smile.

"Ispettore…" the doctor began.

"Un momento," Puglisi said, dismissing the doctor and turning back to Sofia. "You remember me, yes?"

Sofia nodded.

"Good," he said, retaining his smile. "So, you also remember what I ask when we last meet, yes?"

"Look," Janay spoke. "She's only just woken up. Can this wait until—"

"Please, Signorina Evans, I must ask that you not interrupt,"

Puglisi snapped.

Doctor Bianchi, who was now standing next to Sofia, checking her IV drip and making notes on a clipboard, joined in with a disgruntled and animated tone, *"Ma ha ragione. Te l'ho detto, ha bisogno di tempo."*

Puglisi responded in turn, and the two men began a heated debate in Italian.

King rolled her eyes and stepped forward.

"Sophie… or is it Sofia?" King said casually. "Which one do you prefer now? I'm a bit confused. In any case, what I think the inspector wants to know is, why is it that you seem to have a habit of running from major crime scenes?" She tacked on a sarcastic smile for good measure.

"Detective, the doctor just said—" Janay began, but King glared at her. "If you're going to keep interrupting, I'm going to have to make you wait outside."

"You and whose army?" Janay began, stepping forward.

"P…p…please…stop," Sofia said with a frown. "I…w…asn't running."

"No?"

Sofia shook her head.

"Then perhaps you could explain to me why you left the country when I specifically asked you to remain available to us while our investigations were ongoing." King's tone was firm and controlled, in stark contrast to the two men who were still yapping in Italian.

"In…in…inheritance."

King lifted her eyebrows. "Your inheritance?"

Sofia nodded.

"Right, so you're saying that you were in such a hurry to claim your inheritance that you left in the dead of night without so much as a goodbye to your best friend?" King nodded in Janay's direction. "Okay. And what was your reason for trying to run away from Venice?"

Sofia held her throat as she croaked, "I…w…wasn't running."

"No?"

Sofia shook her head.

"Well, why else were you at the airport?"

"H…home."

"Home? You were just going home?"

Sofia nodded.

"Detective, please…" Bianchi had stopped arguing with Puglisi and had now turned to King.

She ignored him and continued. "You were just going home?"

Sofia nodded once more.

"Oh, right, sure. I suppose it had nothing to do with the fact that your neighbour Daniele Giordano snapped his neck and most of his limbs after being thrown down the stone steps just outside your newly inherited palace…"

Janay drew in a sharp breath.

King turned to her, "…or why, by the looks of it, you neglected to tell your friend about it."

Sofia looked at Janay. She had wanted to tell her friend about Daniele, she really had, but there was so much going on that she couldn't bring herself to say anything. All she could think about was getting her home, safe, to her little boy.

"Contessa, the doctor he say that you no remember much of what happen at the airport. *Corretto*?"

Sofia nodded.

"And you have no idea what trigger this reaction in you?"

Sofia shook her head.

Puglisi thought about this and then suddenly said, "Beh, Contessa, I must say I am trouble. I am very trouble, because I ask that you no leave Venice while my investigation it is happening. But then I find that you do exact the opposite. That you try to do now what you did back in England." He glanced at

King. “And therefore, I am afraid that your action leave me no choice but to confiscate your *passaporto* and to tell you that you must remain under house arrest for the rest of this investigation. Do you understand?”

“W…ha…t? No!” Sofia croaked, eyes wide.

“You can’t do that!” Janay protested, turning to him.

“I think you find I can,” the man said with a satisfied nod.

“She’s an English citizen! You can’t keep her here!” Janay shouted, pointing a finger at the man.

“Calm down, please.”

“No! I won’t. You can’t keep her here!” Janay yelled angrily.

“Calm down, signorina, please,” the man repeated, unaffected.

“No, I won’t bloody calm down. Who the hell do you think you are?”

“Miss Evans,” King said, taking charge of the room once more as she stepped in between them. “I suggest you do calm right down if you don’t want to be detained too.”

“What the hell is going on here?” somebody said, appearing in the doorway.

All eyes turned towards them.

32

THE ONE

FRIDAY. LATE MORNING.

When Sofia first saw Christopher Darrington in the doorway in jeans and a jacket, with a baseball hat pulled down tight and accentuating those blue eyes of his, she thought she was dreaming. She was convinced she'd slipped into unconsciousness once more and was only imagining that the man had travelled for several hours to be there.

But then she heard his deep voice, and something told her that it was real. That he was real. Her heart soared. It wasn't quite like coming home, but it felt as if a bit of home had come to her.

They hadn't seen each other or spoken since the day she

abandoned him on the street in Cambridge, but she had thought about him often. And now here he was. For her.

He wasn't taking any prisoners either. When King argued that he wasn't even a criminal lawyer, he told *her* that all she needed to do was abuse her power and he would give her a taste of how much he knew about criminal law. Then he had leaned into her and added, "Oh, but you don't have any power here though, do you, Detective? You're just a visitor like me, and the monkey to this organ grinder."

He nodded to Puglisi, who didn't care for the analogy. When Puglisi spoke up next, accusing him of not knowing the first thing about Italian law, he dared the man to find out. He was obviously convincing, because Puglisi told him he could have ten minutes to confer with his client.

Now, the three of them were in Sofia's room alone.

Chris had moved over to Sofia's bedside while Janay stood opposite.

"I c…an't believe you're here," Sofia said.

"Nor can I," he said with a smile. "But when Janay called, she sounded unusually rattled so I got the impression it was important. So here I am. How are you holding up?"

"I'm fine, I… think," Sofia said, her voice husky but her words more coherent as she soothed it with another drink of water.

"Thanks for doing this, Chris," Janay contributed, before turning back to Sofia. "I filled Chris in on everything. At least everything that you've actually told me, that is." There was a tone in Janay's voice, and Sofia knew that her friend was upset with her.

Chris shrugged. "It's no problem, but I have to level with you both," he said, lowering his voice. "They're right, you know. I don't have the faintest clue about Italian law. I do know that they can't keep you indefinitely without charge. Forty-eight hours tops, I'd say, but then I'd expect them to be able to petition the judge for extra time as long as they can justify it."

"But they can't justify it, though, can they, Soph?" Janay asked, looking at her friend, her eyes seeming to search for any other secrets she might be keeping.

"No, of course not," she said. "I didn't do anything."

"Well, you tried to leave the country when you were specifically told not to," Chris added unhelpfully. "That implies you have something to hide."

Sofia threw him a look.

"No, he's right, Soph. What the hell were you thinking? Why didn't you just tell me?"

Sofia shook her head slowly. "I'm sorry. I didn't mean to keep anything from you. I just wanted to get you home. Back to Damon, Jan. Especially after what happened."

"Why, what else has happened?" Chris asked.

"It doesn't matter," Janay said quickly. "You should have told me, Soph. I would never have kept it from you."

Janay was clearly irritated, but Sofia was all right with that; she got the sense that it was easier for Janay to be irritated than to feel the greater pain that had settled deeper within her. Besides, she was right. She should have told her.

Chris looked at them both. "Okay, what am I missing here?"

"Ask her," Janay said. "I need some coffee and some air." With that, she left the room.

"She doesn't seem very happy," Chris commented.

"No, she doesn't. She's mad at me because I kept stuff from her."

"Yeah, you've got a habit of doing that, haven't you?" Chris said with a smile.

"Don't you start," she threw back. Then paused to take him in as she was suddenly overwhelmed with a sense of fondness for the man which prompted a heartfelt, "It's good to see you, Chris. Thanks so much for being here."

He nodded. "No worries. I just wish the circumstances were different."

She looked at him but was unable to see his eyes beneath the shadow of his cap. Her heart was suddenly anxious, excited at the thought of seeing him again, yet intimidated by his closeness. Should she offer him a seat? An apology maybe? What was it about this man anyway?

She couldn't help but question her feelings. Were they so intense because she was particularly vulnerable right now, or was it something else?

Whatever it was, she felt an odd compulsion to make contact with him. To touch him in some way. But she wasn't sure how. She couldn't take his hand because, well, that would be weird. And, even if she could move them without wincing, she certainly couldn't give him a hug because, well, that suggested something more. Didn't it?

What, then? She could tell him how she had missed him. Maybe? How she had thought about him. No. He might not believe her, asking why, if it were true, she did not bother to pick up the phone or send a postcard.

Argh! She had no idea what to do. She had no experience with any of this stuff. Why was she overanalysing all of it anyway? *Just tell him how you feel!*

But what if he rejected her? As she had rejected Sam. Is that what she had done?

Chris, are you the one?

The one?

"Chris—"

"I'm going to have a chat with the inspector, see if I can convince him to at least let you leave the hospital. Unless you have anything you'd like to tell me." He gazed down into her eyes.

There was a moment. A fleeting moment where she thought he looked hopeful. It was like he wanted her to say something.

Did he? Or was she reading into this too?

"Um... no." The words fell out limply. The intensity of his gaze was just too much for her to bear.

He nodded, then turned and left the room as Janay had minutes before.

Loud rapping drew her attention to the window. Rain. Spitting at the glass as if disappointed with her performance. None more than she. She realised that when it came to anything remotely emotional, she appeared incapable of dealing with it.

An emotional cripple. It was a term she'd often heard but never truly understood, until now.

She felt miserable. Her mind was a whirlpool of questions without answers. Why was she even in this bloody place anyway? What exactly had happened to her at the airport? The detail, like a fleeting shadow, remained hidden from her. What she mostly remembered was searing pain and dazzling sunshine. And what was this about her being allergic to something? She'd never been allergic to anything in her entire life. In fact, now that she thought about it, she couldn't remember ever really being sick.

Yet more questions without answers. She was tired. Exhausted. The weight of her thoughts, like a physical burden, dragged her down, deeper and deeper, until the light began to fade, darker and darker, until there was nothing but blackness and the rain drumming against the window...

The sound wrenched her out of her sleep to a dark room and the dreaded realisation that it had happened again. Slowly, she turned her head to confirm what she already knew; the nightlight and its silhouette projections of Venice was dead. There were no people floating in gondolas. No stars over Piazza San Marco. Just darkness.

The lamp, a souvenir of her mother's, had sat in her parents' bedroom for as long as she could remember, until, one awful nightmare-filled night, her mother had offered it to her with the reassurance that it would always be her beacon in the darkest hours. And it had been, until now.

Now, it was lifeless, almost lost among the many shadows that haunted her room, with the memory of its glow resurrected only by the dirty yellow hue of the streetlight spilling in through the arched bedroom window. On nights like this, these reborn shadows took on the elongated features of a monster with high angry eyebrows and a wide jagged mouth.

She was sitting up in bed now, squinting into the gloom. Eyes wide as saucers, breath coming shallow and fast.

It was in her room again. Hiding in the shadows. She could sense it. The foul malevolent thing was watching her. Plotting. Waiting for the perfect moment to reveal itself.

Her heart was afraid too, for it was knocking on her rib cage, urging her to jump out of bed and flee. But she couldn't. She dared not move. Instead, she allowed her oval blue eyes to flick across the covers to the other side of the room to see that the door was shut. Everything appeared to be in its place and… what was that? There! In the corner of the room. A dark shape she did not recognise.

Her heart was hammering loudly in her chest now, begging to be let out, to be set free. Instinctively, her eyes flicked over to the door once more, but the closet door was wide open, like the gaping mouth of the beast itself. And she knew why. It had left its lair and was now stalking her.

Then she heard it. *Squelch…squelch…* but she daren't look. Daren't peek over the side of the bed.

"No! No! This is wrong. This isn't my room anymore. No!"

Look, Sophie. Look at me.

"No! No!"

Look at what you did to me.

"NO… NO…" she chanted. "No!" For she knew what awaited down the side of the bed. Yet no matter how hard she tried to resist, the compulsion was too strong. It pulled her, beckoned her, until slowly, reluctantly, she peeled back the covers and crawled over to the edge.

Her chest tightened. Her body shook. Her eyes welled. "No…no…"

She didn't want to see. She didn't want to see what awaited on the cold hard floor.

Look at me… Look at what you did to me…

"No," she whimpered.

Yet still she moved forward, hand following hand and then knee after knee, until she was looking over the side. Looking at the person lying on the floor…

Eyes beseeching, tears falling, Janay stared up at her, her body paralysed.

Shhhh…shhhh…shhhh…

The Burlone's red leaf collar rattled with quivering excitement as it used its claws to hold her friend's mouth open into an inhuman gaping black hole and prepared to climb inside—

Sofia was jolted out of her sleep by a tap on her shoulder. She yelped in shock and flinched sideways, only to find herself face to face with Damon. But she knew it wasn't really him. The figure sitting beside her on the bed may have had her friend's son's cute little face and may well have been wearing his pyjamas, but its eyes were not the warm brown that Sofia remembered. Instead, the sockets were as black as midnight and fixed her with an icy gaze as it declared, *"Mummy's going to die there with you."*

Sofia let out a blood-curdling scream.

"NOOOOO!"

The heart monitor beeped frantically in response to her distress. Chris, by her side, reached down and placed gentle hands on her shoulders in an effort to get her attention.

"You're okay, Sophie. You're all right," he said, trying to calm her down. "You're okay. You're all right," he repeated.

Eventually, she focussed on his face and then suddenly threw herself into his chest, sobbing. He softly folded her into an embrace. "You're okay," he continued. "You're all right."

After a minute or so, Sofia emerged from the hug with tearstained eyes and looked up at him with determination. "Chris," she said, pausing to swipe at tears, "there's something else I need to ask of you, and you're not going to like it."

33

FATE AWAITS

FRIDAY. EARLY EVENING.

There's no fate but what we make.

Sophie Cooper had always been a believer in predestination. In fate.

The concept had long been a topic of discussion and debate in various cultures and belief systems. Some believed that everything in life was predetermined, while others believed that fate was shaped by an individual's choices and actions.

The idea that everything in life was planned out has been documented in various religious texts and philosophical works throughout history.

In ancient Greek mythology, the Fates were three goddesses. They were responsible for spinning, weaving, and cutting the threads of life.

Oedipus was fated to kill his father and marry his mother. Despite his attempts to avoid this end, he ultimately fulfilled it to his downfall. The story was often cited as an example of how fate could control lives and lead people to their destiny, regardless of their own free will.

This concept of fate was also present in the works of Shakespeare, who often used the idea in his plays to add depth and meaning to the lives of his characters.

It had been easy for Sofia to think that she had a good grasp of the various philosophies about destiny, but now she realised that she hadn't truly understood it until she arrived in Venice and found not the version of herself she thought she had known, but the person she was destined to be.

While the specifics of her fate still eluded her, the knowledge she had encountered on her journey did not.

Her friendship with Victoria had taught her about ambition, obsession, and desperation. Janay had taught her about selflessness and the compulsion to put the wellbeing of others before oneself. Her foster father, Alan Cooper, had taught her about the strength of familial bonds, about being a decent human being, about righteousness. Doing unto others as you would have them do unto you.

While she may not have had much time with her foster mother, Elena Cooper, even she had influenced her. It was Elena who had introduced Sofia to Venice and to the concept that monsters might just exist, if not in real life, then in the mind.

Sofia could see it all very clearly now. There was a reason why she was unable to integrate at school or to forge other meaningful relationships with any of the other children beyond her few friends. There was a reason she struggled to lay down roots.

Her repressed sexuality, dormant for all her formative years and stifling her appetite for romance beyond the craving of her dreams, no doubt had its purpose too.

While the nature of this remained a mystery to her, she still strongly believed that it was fate that had carved a path for her to Palazzo Rosso, and everything that had happened up until her epiphany in that hospital bed had happened for a reason. To teach her. To prepare her for what awaited.

She knew this now. And she was ready.

But this was her journey. Hers alone.

She knew Christopher Darrington had moved into the house on Meadow Lane and across the street from her for a reason. It was to show her, sometimes, no matter how twee it might sound, the inner self is often reflected in one's physical appearance. Just how kindness, confidence, and compassion are often displayed in one's body language, in their smiles, and in their interactions with others.

Christopher's humanity was rooted in his need for social interaction, which allowed people to build trust, form strong bonds, and engage in positive relationships with him. Sofia was sure that this was one of the reasons why he had befriended her father; Chris knew that he was often lonely. And it was no doubt one of the reasons why her father had come to trust him, as she would now.

Sofia knew that in order to convince Janay to return to her son without her, she would need to enlist the help of somebody that her friend already liked and trusted. And she had been right.

Now, in the emptiness of the palazzo's ballroom, she was starting to wish she had found some way of going with them.

It wasn't possible. Puglisi had confiscated her passport and would have had her confined to the hospital had it not been for the intervention of Maria Bacciabella.

Somehow, she had managed to convince him that Sofia was a

crucial member of her staff and had been instrumental in organising tonight's gala. Everybody who was anybody would be there, including the mayor and police commissioner. It was imperative that the event celebrating the history of superstitions and, of course, the lost comet, proceeded without impediment.

Sofia paused at the staircase and looked towards the balcony. Like her, it had been mended, the doors repaired, and the glass replaced. It was as if the damage had never happened, and the housekeeper hadn't met her demise in such a horrific way.

Then she noticed it. Light, spilling out of the dining room, as it had every night she'd been there. The sight of it made her stomach lurch. How was that possible?

She turned and scanned the room. The hallway. Upstairs. "Hello?" she called out to the empty space. The echo of her voice was the only response.

Slowly, she made her way over to the dining room. Peering through the archway, she threw her hands up to her mouth.

The table was laid out as usual. Even the candles were burning brightly, like they were freshly lit.

Tears pricked her eyes. She had believed this was the work of the housekeeper, but she was gone now. It defied rational explanation.

"Who did this?" she yelled out into the ballroom. "WHO IS HERE?"

She drew in a sharp breath. The day she arrived she had thought she saw the frescos morphing and changing, reacting to her in some way. At the time, she decided it had been her imagination. Tonight, she knew for certain she had not been mistaken. The frescos had transformed once more.

As she gazed upward, she saw a stunning canvas of once thunderous clouds parted to reveal a sky in brilliant hues of oranges, pinks, and purples. The rising sun cast its warm and welcoming glow over the world, illuminating the clouds from within and creating a dramatic contrast with the surrounding colours.

Sofia gaped in wonder as she watched the rays shine down upon the earth with brilliant golden light, in awe of the majesty of what appeared to be a new dawn.

"Breathtaking, isn't it?"

Sofia started as Aurora appeared in the hallway. She was dressed for a ball in a plunging black gown. Her hair was swept to one side and cascaded over a generous décolletage.

Sofia felt her body stiffen as she put her guard up. Swiping a tear from her eye, she demanded, "What are you doing here? What do you want?"

"I came to see you," the woman said, advancing into the ballroom.

"And do you always just let yourself in like this?"

"Didn't you when you came to my home? Twice, if I'm not mistaken," Aurora added with a lift of the eyebrow.

"Is this you?" Sofia asked, pointing to the dining room. "Has all of this been you all along?"

The beauty scoffed. "Me? Cook? Are you mad?"

"I must be," Sofia said, shaking her head.

"You're not. What you are experiencing is perfectly natural."

"Natural? You call any of this, everything that has happened here, perfectly natural?"

Aurora thought about this and rocked her head. "Most of it, yes, though I admit there have been a few deviations along the way."

"Who are you? What do you want from me?"

The woman smiled and took another step forward. "You're not asking the right questions, Sofia. It's not a case of what I want, but of what I can do. For you."

Sofia took her own step forward. "There is nothing I would ever want you to do for me," she growled.

The lights dipped, and contrary to all her previous reactions, Sofia didn't even flinch. She kept her eyes locked on the intruder in her home.

Aurora seemed to find this development most interesting. In fact, instead of being intimidated by it, her dazzling smile suggested she was quite delighted.

"Nothing?" she asked.

"Nothing," Sofia responded, "except for getting the fuck out of my house." She may have spent most of her time in Venice fearing its unexplained shadows and wanting to escape them, but now she was hammering her flag into stone and staking her claim. Another detail that didn't go unnoticed by Aurora.

"What? Don't you even want me to help you uncover the truth? To understand the one thing that has plagued you your entire existence? All those days of therapy failed to eradicate it from your consciousness. Try as you might, no matter how much you have repressed it, you can't go even a single day without thinking about it. Wouldn't you like to finally understand?"

Sofia didn't respond but simply clenched the muscles in her jaw as she observed the woman.

But Aurora had seen the flicker in her eyes. That split second of self-doubt. It was her job to convince the girl, and the time for subtlety had long passed. The direct approach was required to bring things to their rightful conclusion.

The clock was ticking, after all.

"You can't tell me that you haven't been thinking about it, Sofia."

"Thinking about what?"

"You know what. The truth about what happened to your mother."

"I know what happened to her. She left us." Sofia said it with some conviction but not enough to convince the woman before her.

"That's true, she did. But not in the way you think."

"What are you talking about?"

"You already know. You've been hiding from it all these years. Your mother didn't choose to leave you. You know this."

Sofia shook her head. "She did. She left us. She left us because she couldn't bear to be married anymore. She couldn't bear to take care of me!"

"Who told you that? Your father? Your therapist?"

"She left," Sofia repeated, momentarily confused. She thought she'd misunderstood the woman because for the first time in her life, someone had spoken of the same incident but with their words in reverse. Someone had told her that her mother didn't leave her, but that she was taken. But that couldn't be. Why was this woman doing this? Why was she lying? And how could she possibly know?

The lights flickered again.

"Sofia, come on. The time for naivety is over. Now is the time to start opening your mind. There's a reason why you haven't been able to make contact with anybody back in England, and there's a reason why, despite everything that has happened since you arrived here, you haven't run screaming back there—at least not until you started fearing for your friend's life, and that doesn't count. It's time to accept who you really are, Sofia. Embrace your destiny."

"What do you mean, who I really am?"

Aurora rolled her eyes. "I'm not playing this game anymore." She turned to walk away, and the lights dipped again.

"Hey! No, wait! What are you talking about?"

"You know what I'm talking about, Sofia, you just won't allow yourself to see. Open your eyes."

"My eyes are open. What did you fucking say about my mother?" she growled. Somewhere, a door slammed.

"You heard what I said."

Sofia stepped closer to the lady. "I want you to say it again. Say it," she ordered through gritted teeth.

"You heard me," was the defiant response.

"But that… that isn't right. What you said isn't right. My mother left us."

"No, she didn't, Sofia. She was taken, and you know why."

Sofia shook her head. Her thoughts coming thick and fast, her mind reeling as she attempted to deprogram the mantra of her entire life.

She left us.

She was taken.

She left us.

No, she was taken!

Taken? Could it be true?

"Tell me everything you know," she said.

Aurora smiled.

34

THE ORDER

FRIDAY EVENING

Detective Inspector King had just stepped out of the shower when the alert on her laptop told her she had an incoming video call. She swore under her breath, hastily pulling on a dressing gown and wrapping a towel around her wet hair.

It was freezing in her bloody room. She planned to take it up with the front desk as soon as this call was over, but for now uncheerfully sat down to take it, still dripping.

She glanced at the clock at the bottom of her screen and then clicked on ACCEPT.

Detective Sergeant Butler lifted an eyebrow and grinned. "New fashion statement?"

"You're early," King said flatly.

Butler's grin faded as he looked at his watch. "By two minutes."

King said nothing. She didn't need to. She had made a point.

"Sorry," Butler said grumpily.

"What have you got that is so important?" King noticed the subdued lighting behind her partner and what looked like a kitchen cabinet. "Where are you calling from?"

"I'm at home."

"At home? Why? Is there something wrong with you?"

"No. I didn't want anybody at the station to overhear what I have to say."

"Okay. So, what do you have to say?"

"I think I've found something," he said.

"You *think* or you have found something?" King asked.

"I *have* found something," Butler clarified. "But it's a bit out there, so I'm going to need you to keep an open mind."

Despite herself, King was intrigued. She settled into her chair, pulling her gown around her as Butler began.

"Do you remember that we found a word burned into the walls of that bedroom in Meadow Lane?"

"Yeah, of course. What was it again? Ven…Veni…"

"Venit." Butler confirmed. "Do you remember what I said it meant?"

King thought about it. "Something about someone coming? He's coming, wasn't it?"

"Yeah, well, I've contacted a language professor at the university, and he's given me the literal translation." Butler looked down off screen. "He says it's *he, she, it* or even *they come,* depending on context."

King's interest was piqued. "Right. And?"

"Are you familiar with the story of the morning star?" Butler asked, looking into the camera again.

"The tabloid?"

"No, not the newspaper. The morning star is a reference to the fallen angel, Lucifer, also known as Satan."

King sighed. If Butler noticed, he didn't show it. Instead, he looked to the side of the screen and clicked his mouse. Seconds later, Butler's video image shrank to a thumbnail. It was replaced by a painting that depicted a dark and tempestuous sky from which a giant winged man appeared to be falling to Earth.

"In the Bible, Lucifer is described as having been cast out of Heaven after rebelling against God," Butler narrated. "In Isaiah 14:12, he is referred to as *morning star, day star,* or *shining star.* In the New Testament, Jesus also refers to Satan as *the ruler of this world.* And in the Book of Revelation, Lucifer is described as the *star that fell from the sky.*"

King sighed again while adjusting the towel on her head. "Butler, this is all very fascinating, but Bible study never was my thing."

Butler nodded. "Yeah, I know what it sounds like, and I felt the same until I started doing some digging, and…" He trailed off when he noticed that King was looking off camera. "What's up?" he asked.

King looked at the door. She wasn't sure, but for a moment she had thought she heard the handle rattling.

"Guv?"

King lingered a few more seconds and then turned back to her laptop screen. "It's all right. Go on."

"Yeah, so I did some digging. You know, ran a few queries—"

"If you're going to say that you found more cases like this in the past month, then it's hardly a surprise. Ever since that comet showed up the whole world's been going mad."

"Yeah, well that's just it. I didn't find any other cases quite like this."

King frowned.

"At least, not recently," Butler added mysteriously before clicking his mouse again. Four images appeared on the screen. The first was a colour photograph of the end of a bed, a dresser, and then a wall sporting a rash of one word: VENIT. The second image appeared to be of the same room only blurrier, and from a different angle. The third and fourth images were the same as the previous two but in black and white.

King shook her head, perplexed. "What am I looking at?" she asked, peering closer at the screen.

"What do you see?" Butler asked.

King scowled. "I see the crime scene at whatever the house number was on Meadow Lane."

"One of them shows the crime scene at number twelve Meadow Lane, yeah. But the other three don't."

Butler was way too excited for the mood King was in.

"The second one is from nine years ago, from a village in Chile. The next is from nine years before that, in the United States, and the other is Pakistan, another nine years earlier."

King took a deep breath. The crimes scenes were almost identical. "Are you sure about this?"

"Yeah. I mean, they're the only images I've found so far, but given time..."

"So, what's your theory? That it's definitely ritualistic?"

Butler rocked his head. "Yeah, but I think it's more than that."

"All right, what?"

"Do you remember the last time there was a comet in the sky for this long?"

"I have no idea."

"Nine years ago. And do you know how long it was before that?"

"Don't tell me, nine years before."

Butler nodded.

"I'm sensing a pattern," King said sarcastically, though she was starting to wonder if Butler might well be onto something. But she needed him to prove it.

"So, when Morning Star, or Lucifer, was cast out of Heaven for pissing off God, he lost everything, including his immortality."

"You do realise this isn't a superhero movie, right?" King threw in.

Butler nodded and continued. "He effectively becomes a man. Human. Which means that, just like a human, his physical body would age and die, the same as any other mere mortal. So, what's his new compulsion?"

"To inspire tedious storylines for very bad films?"

"Well, it's the same as every other human. To procreate, to spread his seed, to perpetuate his bloodline. He wants to bear children that will go forth into the world and do his bidding."

"Which is?"

"To make God's children suffer for what God did to him."

"What? Every nine years? Does he go on sabbatical the rest of the time?"

"No, he's working every minute of every day. All of the headline-grabbing bad shit that happens every day, all of the stuff that we have to deal with and everything terrible that's happening right now is happening because it is not God's will."

King leaned forward and looked directly into the camera. "Have you been drinking?"

"No. Not yet. I probably will after this though. This stuff isn't a little theory I've just come up with; it's fact, according to the Church of the Morning Star. Have you heard of it?"

"Beyond it sounding like a bad eighties song? No, I can't say I have."

Butler was on a roll now. "Neither had I until I looked them up. They aren't that well known at all. Or at least that's how they first appeared. But when I dug a little deeper, I found rumours about a secret and super powerful organisation about which hardly anything is known. And do you know why? Because that's how they want it. These people quite literally scrub any reference to themselves off the internet. Do you know how difficult it is to do that?"

"No, but I have a feeling you're going to tell me," King said, feigning boredom. Clearly Butler was motivated to do his best work when she kept him feeling like he needed to prove himself.

"It's nigh on impossible without unlimited resources," Butler continued. "I mean, these people make Scientology look like a knitting circle. The few people who have heard of them are scared. The religious expert I eventually managed to speak to about this would only talk if I swore not to mention him. *Forget the Illuminati. Forget the freemasons. There isn't any other organisation like this because the Church of the Morning Star exists for one reason and one reason alone. The conservation, preservation, and proliferation of teachings and children of the Morning Star.* At least I think that's what he said." Butler looked down at his notes. "I mean, *you* could be a member of the order and I wouldn't even know it." He leaned into the camera and with a serious face asked, "Are you?"

King wanted to laugh but chose not to. "Butler, you do realise that everything you just said is pure conjecture. I'm still none the wiser as to why you decided to bore me with it. I mean…"

Was she imagining it? It was hard to be sure. The Carnivale revellers outside her window were particularly loud tonight, but for a split second it seemed as if she'd seen the handle of her hotel room door turning, as if someone was trying to come in. But when she looked again it was perfectly still.

"Guv?"

She turned back to the screen. "Yeah, I'm listening."

"So, you wouldn't buy a whole *secret handshake* thing?"

"Scripture, secret societies, handshakes. Not exactly hard evidence, is it?"

"It gets better, I promise."

"Is this why you're calling me from home? Because you're worried about being overheard talking about this? I suppose I would be too. That lot are already a bunch of piss-takers."

"Well, it's partly that, but also because I didn't want to take any risks with what I am about to tell you." Butler's tone was serious once more.

"Okay, but if it's any more about this *church of the poisoned mind* lot, I'm closing the lid on you."

"The what?"

"You know, Culture Club?"

"Who?"

King had forgotten the age gap between them. "Never mind. Just get on with it. I'm freezing here."

"Well, I'm gonna tell you this and you can make of it what you will, but I need to put it out there, okay? This contact I spoke to said that the comet, Sekhmet or whatever its name is, is an omen. It's been exactly nine years since the last rebirth and…" Butler looked at his notes and read aloud without looking up. "*And lo, there shall come a time at the dawn of each decade where a portent shall appear in the night sky to mark the start of the ritual. And in recognition of his rebirth there shall be a celebration with feast and sacrifice.* Or words to that effect. He was talking a bit fast."

King lifted her eyebrows and sighed.

"I know what it sounds like, Guv, but think about it for a second. What's it been like since that comet arrived? And what about the *cruel and unusual* crime scenes? The words are quite literally burned on the wall. *He, it, they* is or are coming. I think there's some truth to this. I think that this morning cult lot are celebrating the so-called return of their idol and are going nuts about it."

King considered her partner's words. Satanic worship was something they had already considered, but this was something bigger than they could have ever imagined.

"And you think this has something to do with the Cooper girl?" she asked eventually.

Butler scoffed and shook his head. "No. I think that's some…th…ing…el…se."

King frowned as the lights dipped and Butler's face pixelated on screen. "Hello?"

"H...llo?"

"Butler? Are you there?"

"Y…ah. I think I am. What happened?" he asked as the video was restored once more.

"Not sure. I think we had a power cut here or something. What were you about to say?"

"That I've saved the best for last."

"Okay, well here's a tip, next time lead with that if you want to keep the interest of…" *That bloody door handle again.*

"What?" Butler asked. "What is it?"

"Hold on," she said, instinctively drawing her gown to her as she rose from her seat.

She shuddered as she realised how cold she had become. Her hands, her legs, her whole body now shivered in the chill.

"Guv, what's going on?"

But King didn't respond. Instead, teeth chattering, she walked across the room where she hesitated for a few seconds before unlocking and snatching open the door in one swift movement.

There was nobody there.

She leaned out into the corridor and looked along it. To the left: empty. To the right: also empty.

Puzzled, she stepped back inside her room and then examined

the worn doorhandle, turning it a few times. It was an antique and, like the rest of her room, had seen better times, but it still seemed firm enough.

"Guv?" Butler's tinny voice called from the computer.

King pushed the door shut and rolled the key once more. When she turned back towards the centre of the room, she froze as the lights flickered and died, and she saw it…

There… Standing in front of the window, backlit by the city beyond the glass.

The beast!

It stood over nine feet tall and had gnarled horns reaching up to the ceiling. The streetlight cast an eerie glow upon the illuminated half of its twisted features.

There was a loud bang. King yelped and fell back against the door as an explosion of multicoloured light filled the room before the overhead bulb came back on.

She blinked several times as fireworks whistled, and crowds cheered outside. There was nothing in her room. It was empty. And yet she was certain that it, whatever it was, had been standing there, right in front of the window. Or had it? She looked around the room once more. A trick of the light? It had to be.

"Guv? Hello? King, are you there? Everything all right? King? Answer me!"

After several more seconds, King returned to her seat and said, still somewhat shaken, "Hello. Yes, um… I'm here!" though her eyes still darted around the room.

"What happened? Everything went dark your side," Butler said.

"N…Nothing. It was just a power cut," she said, checking behind her once more as a shiver scuttled down her back. She shifted her chair so that she no longer had her back to the window.

"Are you sure everything's all right?"

"F…fine… just, um, just finish what you were saying," she said, unconsciously pulling the gown around her once more, the noisy crowd outside so close yet suddenly feeling so far.

"Okay, but prepare yourself. This is the reason why I'm calling you from home tonight. What I'm about to tell you will change the course of the whole investigation."

35

THE CONTESSA

FRIDAY EVENING

Two hours remaining…

Contessa Sofia DaTerra's ballgown swirled around her like a tempestuous flame, drawing the eyes of all who gazed upon her as she ascended the golden steps. The rich velvet fabric, embroidered with gold thread and adorned with sparkling jewels, hugged her slender form like a lover's embrace. The bodice, cut low to reveal her alabaster skin, was cinched tight at the waist before flaring out in a riot of cascading skirts, each layer a fiery hue of red. The sleeves long and billowy, were finished with delicate lace trim.

Her beauty was accentuated by an elaborate coiffure reminiscent of the 18th century style, with her platinum blonde locks swept up and pinned in a tumbling wave of curls and twists. An intricate set of braids was woven throughout, adorned with bright gems and glittering hairpins, with strategically released tendrils to frame her face and highlight her delicate features. She was the epitome of elegance and grace befitting a contessa.

Now, as she clutched a mask poised upon a delicate stem—its feathers and gems catching the light as she moved—she made her way through the throng of guests in the grand chamber, her every movement a symphony, every rustle of her skirt a crescendo, while many lips whispered her name.

Sofia had found the dress spread out on her bed. When she asked Aurora if she had put it there, her cryptic reply was that it had been there all along. She just didn't see it.

"We see what we want to see, Sofia," she had told her. It was ridiculous; the dress hadn't been there before. She'd have noticed it.

Aurora had then introduced her to her duo of stylists, a man and a woman who worked fast and efficiently, like they were being graded. They quickly made a masterpiece of her.

If Raffaella had been honest with herself, she would have conceded the Sofia did indeed look beautiful. Gone was the awkward tourist with the ill-fitting office wear and in her place was someone she didn't even recognise. And what was she wearing? That dress must have been designed for her, but by who? Prada? Versace? Whoever it was, they must have also designed her some class because it couldn't possibly belong to her. Sofia's hair alone was an artistic marvel compared to her own slicked-back do, plain black dress, and heels.

"Sofia!" she said, waving with a big smile for the benefit of nearby guests as she moved to intercept. When she reached her, she grabbed her by the arm and pulled her to one side, an action that should have made her cry out in pain. And yet, it did not, for Sofia no longer felt pain. She had discovered this when she told Aurora that she would not be attending the gala tonight on account of her injuries. The woman had simply smiled and asked, "What injuries?"

"Are you mad? These injuries!" she had said, thrusting up her bandaged arms. And yet, it was in that moment that she discovered that she no longer felt pain. When she unravelled the bandages, she couldn't believe her eyes. Both her arms were still marked with dark discolorations, but the blistered burns had disappeared.

"What the fuck are you doing here?" Raffaella hissed through her smile, dragging her back to the present.

"What do you mean?"

"I mean," Raffaella continued through her gritted grin, "What the fuck are you doing here? I told you explicitly that you were not required. I mean, have you any idea who any of these people are?" She looked around and smiled at a passing couple. When Sofia didn't respond, she rolled her eyes. "Exactly. You've no clue, have you? These people are the crème de la crème, the who's who of Venice, Italy, the world! Politicians, bankers, studio bosses, and titans of enterprise, for God's sake, and there's no way you're qualified to go near them. I mean, have you any idea how many years it's taken me to earn the privilege of being here tonight?"

"You don't have to worry, Raffaella. I'm not here to work," Sofia said, as assertively as she could, considering that she was shaking. She may have walked with confidence and poise, smiling at smiling faces like she knew everybody there, but that was only because it was what Aurora had told her to do. Believe you are confident, and it shall be. Whatever that was supposed to mean. But it seemed to work even though, beneath the surface, she was terrified.

She had no idea what was happening to her. And there was no doubt that something that strayed beyond the realms of reality was happening, but she had no clue what that might be. Yet, she wasn't about to let Raffaella see any of it.

"What's she doing here?"

It was Georgina, the chief of staff from her interview. She wore a red up-and-down cocktail dress that did nothing for her flat chest. With makeup that looked like it had been applied via shotgun, she looked more like a walking mannequin.

"I was just asking her the same thing," Raffaella sneered, looking around to ensure nobody was overhearing them.

The two wicked sisters looked at each other, eyebrows arching just a little further than was natural. They proceeded to drone on about something else, but Sofia wasn't listening. Her attention was elsewhere. Across the room, through the crowd dressed in their finery and masks, her eyes fell on the handsome man dressed in a black tuxedo that accentuated his muscular frame perfectly. He was holding a mask in his hand and appeared to be deep in conversation with a couple who had both lifted their disguises and rested them atop their heads.

Suddenly, he looked across at her and smiled. She felt heat rise to her cheeks and returned a smile of her own. It was as if he had sensed her looking at him.

Raffaella noticed the exchange.

"Buona sera."

The women turned to see Maria Bacciabella dressed in a sequined red gown with a black faux fur wrap around her shoulders.

"Buona sera," they responded.

Bacciabella admired Sofia. "You look positively radiant, my darling," she said with motherly pride.

Sofia felt a warm blush spread through her. "Thank you," she replied earnestly. "And thank you for speaking to Puglisi for me."

Bacciabella shrugged, as if it was all in a day's work. "Think nothing of it." Then she turned to Raffaella. "I'll be doing the speech shortly. When I do, I'd like each and every one of the delegates to have a brochure and details of the offering in their hand."

"Of course," Rafaella said cheerfully. "We're ready."

"Buona sera," said a man's voice.

A flutter of excitement filled Sofia's chest. She would recognise the timbre anywhere.

Samael.

"Ah, if it isn't the most handsome man of the hour," Bacciabella said.

Sofia looked up and their eyes met. He was clean shaven again, and with his hair combed sideways, he reminded her of a forties movie star.

"Quite a turnout," he said to Maria.

"All thanks to you," she said.

He bowed his head before looking up at Sofia and renewing that smile. "It's really good to see you back on your feet," he said, earnestly.

Sofia's heart throbbed. She wanted to talk to him. She wanted to thank him for visiting her and apologise for how she'd behaved last time they met, but she could feel the scrutiny of the other women.

"Thank you," was all she could muster. He bowed those smouldering eyes and Sofia suddenly felt that there was no need for additional words.

Then he turned to the group as a whole and said, "Ladies, if you would permit me to say it, you all look absolutely breathtaking tonight."

"Oh, you are such a smooth talker," Raffaella said with a giggle so light and girly Sofia didn't even recognise her.

Sam smiled politely before turning his eyes back to Sofia.

Noticing this, Raffaella quickly made her move to interrupt. "Oh no, I just realized!" she exclaimed with a feigned look of dismay. "We're going to be short on brochures for some of the packets." Raffaella made sure to capture Bacciabella's attention before continuing. "Sofia misunderstood my instructions and took all of the brochures down to the cantina instead of just the old ones."

"Raffaella, I'm due up at the podium any minute," Bacciabella said, her voice filled with a rare sense of urgency.

"I know, I'm sorry. I meant to get them so nobody would even notice they were taken down there but then time just ran away from me." She cast a sly look at Sofia. "Sofia, would you be so kind as to retrieve them for me while I organize the rest of the packets?" her voice cloying and saccharine.

Sofia's stomach lurched. "Me?"

"Yes. If you don't mind."

"After all, you are the one who took them down there," Georgina contributed.

"Well…um…" Sofia glanced at Maria.

"I could go if you'd like to do the packets instead," Raffaella added, knowing full well that Sofia had no clue how to put them together.

"No, it's okay. No problem. I'll go."

"If it's okay, I'd be happy to escort you," Sam said.

Sofia smiled, but it was soon wiped from her face.

"Actually, Sam," Bacciabella interjected, "there are some people I'd like to introduce you to before my speech, if that's okay. Sofia won't be long. Will you, Sofia?"

She shook her head. "No. Of course not," she said, and watched forlornly as Sam was steered away.

Raffaella waited for them to be out of earshot before snapping, "Well, go on then! Chop! Chop!"

Sofia left quickly, mostly because she felt an intense urge to punch the woman's sour face. She decided against it; she already had enough to contend with without creating a scene. For starters, how was she was going to negotiate the steps and uneven flooring of a literal dungeon in her sparkly princess shoes? She could barely walk as it was.

Still, she was happy to put some distance between herself and the bitchy duo. She could still feel their eyes on her as she teetered across the breadth of the chamber to the exit and the flight of stairs beyond.

Before long, the strings of music and chatter quieted into the distance, replaced by the still of the hollow. She kept glancing back at the merriment as she went, until the bright lights of the ball had gradually faded into shadow.

36

TRADIMENTO

FRIDAY EVENING

Detective Inspector King stepped out of her hotel and drew her coat tightly against the cold wind that was driving through passageways and sweeping across the canal. Leaves and debris swirled around her feet, as though the very earth was in turmoil. Overhead, a cantankerous sky grumbled and spat as if protesting her very existence.

Yet the weather had done nothing to deter the revellers who were eager to celebrate the last of Carnevale season before it was over for another year. The streets were filled with more merrymakers than ever, dressed in elaborate costume designs and vibrant colours.

Their cheer did little to negate King's unease. In every gloomy archway and in every blackened window, it felt like the dark was giving refuge to a thousand eyes, watching with ardent malice.

The presence in her hotel room had rattled her. It was as if the place had taken on a whole new atmosphere after the power cut, and she found herself eager to be out of there.

Of course, she had already berated herself. She was a trained professional. Throughout her career, she was conditioned to deal in facts, concrete proof, and evidence, not conspiracies, conjecture, and mumbo bloody jumbo. Yet today it had all done a pretty good job of unsettling her.

She knew why. There was something about Butler's report that rang true, something about the way his theories stacked up. It was for this reason that, instead of visiting Puglisi at the station or talking to him on the phone, she had insisted that he meet with her at a small piazza not far from her hotel. It was a quiet square she'd stumbled across when first exploring the city with her husband in a long-ago time of love and romance. She'd buried the memory of it so deeply it barely seemed real anymore.

It had started to rain now, so she increased her pace, pushing through the crowds and splashing through puddles as the precipitation pelted her like a sinner on her walk of shame. Occasionally, she felt compelled to look over her shoulder, but nobody was following her. Still, she couldn't shake off the feeling that somebody was.

She hurried over a bridge and jumped when she caught sight of her reflection in a *pasticceria* window. She looked haunted, her eyes wild, hair escaping in strands from beneath her hat.

She held a long blink and took a deep breath. She needed to pull herself together. This wasn't like her. Why was she allowing some weird trick of the light, brought on by Butler's words, to panic her heart into this frenzied palpitation?

Calm down, she breathed. *Calm d—*

She felt someone bump into her shoulder, then another, and another. Then she opened her eyes and yelped when she saw a hooded presence standing behind her. But then she saw; the person was just letting someone through the narrow lane before moving on.

She hurried away, dodging tourists and their umbrellas. She crossed another bridge and then descended steps, water tumbling down in front of her as if eager to race her to her destination.

She looked up for street markings as she attempted to find her bearings, but there were so many people streaming towards her that she was struggling to take a beat. Noblemen, noblewomen, a harlequin, and *it!*

King screamed but in a blink of an eye it was gone. She was sure she'd seen it, with its horns and everything. It was there, standing right in front of her, a monochromatic shadow amidst the rainbow surging towards her, the same thing she'd seen in her room. But there was certainly nothing there now.

It's a hallucination. You are imagining it because you have induced this state of anxiety. Pull yourself together!

She was standing in the middle of another narrow passageway, *Calle de I Fiori.* The crowd was pushing around her on what was obviously a main thoroughfare. Some of those who had witnessed her outburst paused for a second, as if concerned that she might have another episode at any moment.

That name. She recognised that name. *Fiori* meant flowers. She knew she was close. She hurried forward once more.

A thick shroud of darkness had fallen upon the city. It obscured the once vibrant buildings and streets, leaving only the faint flicker of streetlamps and the occasional burst of fireworks to guide the way.

Both her heart and mind were racing as she hurried down more stone steps and around a corner, only to crash into what felt like a wall. The impact was so powerful it knocked her off her feet and backward, flailing in the air, until she splashed down into a body of water. She hit the stone beneath so hard that it sent an electric shock of pain running through the length of her slender body and into her brain.

She arched her back in agony and cried out as she squinted up into the precipitation, and to the shadow looming over her in ominous slow motion. It was a giant of a kind she had never seen before. Dressed from head to toe in black, its eyes were bottomless pits. Its long beak was curved and menacing but its face otherwise expressionless.

DI King, who was renowned by her peers for her plucky confidence and commended by her superiors for bravery, now sat in a pool of frigid rainwater holding up defensive hands and whimpering.

"O, mio dio… ma cosa è successo? Stai bene?" a voice said. Suddenly, the figure pulled off their masked beak, revealing a young woman. Two men appeared next to her, both removing their disguises too. They extended their hands to help King up, but she was momentarily paralysed by pain and shock. The freezing cold water had seeped into her clothes and was now clinging to her skin.

"Ma sei okay?" one of the men repeated.

Eventually King was able to process what she was seeing. Young men and women. Masks. Costumes. These weren't creatures birthed from a different realm but people on a night out. She'd crashed into the one dressed as the plague doctor. She could see the mask in her hand. The sharp ugly thing still gaped at her as it hung flaccidly in the girl's grip.

She took one of the proffered hands and, cringing from the ache in her lower back, slowly got back to her feet.

The trio were babbling to each other now. She had no idea what they were saying but at one point she heard the word *ospedale.*

She shook her head. "No, grazie. No ospedale," she said, instinctively brushing herself as if that was in any way going to make a difference. "I'm fine," she said. "I'm okay."

"Eh! *Aspetta!*" one of them called, but she was already moving away from the main thoroughfare to a side passage. Above her, hammered high onto the stone wall, was a hand-painted plaque that read *Piazza del Tradimento.*

She had arrived at the archway leading to the tiny piazza. She had timed it just right, for only seconds later she saw him appear on the opposite side of the square and hurry across towards her. A plume of smoke trailed behind him under the streetlight.

It was Puglisi. He joined her under the archway but not before throwing his cigarette to the ground and stomping on it.

"I 'pologise," he said. "It a terrible habit," he added, as if he somehow had to explain himself to her. King imagined it was more a reflexive comment typically meant for his wife.

When he looked up and he saw the part of her that wasn't steeped in shadow, he drew a sharp breath.

"*Madonna mia*, Patrizia! Are you okay? What happen?" he asked, looking at her dishevelled and soaked appearance.

"It's okay," she said quickly, attempting to rearrange herself and her coat as she ignored the pain at the tip of her spine. She was thankful that she was so cold some parts of her extremities were actually numb. "I slipped and fell over, but I'm fine."

"Oh, *mamma mia.* We need to get you somewhere warm. Come. I know a place near here where you can—"

"No," King said sharply as fireworks sailed over nearby houses. She jumped as they exploded into a myriad of shades.

Mercifully, the rain was easing off now.

"Okay, you instead take my coat," he said, unbuttoning it.

King refused.

"No, I insist. You are shaking," he said, lifting his hands. He removed his coat and wrapped it around her.

The additional warmth over sodden clothes was minimal yet noticeable. It took the edge off her shivering, at least.

Puglisi's remaining layers of shirt and sweater offered limited protection against the chill, and he huddled into himself as he spoke. "Patrizia, perhaps you be so kind as to explain me why we're out here in cold with all the crazy people," he nodded at the steady stream of characters on the path several yards away, "and not in a nice warm bar somewhere?"

King looked at the man. He was partially illuminated as they stood on opposite sides of the archway at the entrance to the square, the structure offering some shelter but not fully denying them light.

"What do you know about the Church of the Morning Star?"

Puglisi cocked his head and smiled. "Dis is why you ask me here under veil of secrecy?" he chuckled.

"Can you answer the question?"

Puglisi scowled then shrugged. "Patrizia, the morning star is a tale. You know… how you say… folklore?"

"Well, I've got a crime scene back home that suggests otherwise."

"What do you mean?"

"We have images of crime scenes dating back decades, all pretty much identical to each other. All with the same M.O. Each shows a horrific death with one word left behind like graffiti all over the bloody walls. *Venit.* It means—"

"I know what it mean, Patrizia. I am Italian. I know the story of the morning star. Many Christians do. Satan is cast from Heaven and builds his church here on Earth with the plan to corrupt man and take over the world with his children, so they do as he say. I mean, can you hear that? Oh, shit. Is dis why you call me here, to discuss religion? If so, *non perdere tempo*, save your time. I get enough of dis lecture from my wife."

"No, I didn't call you here for that. I called you to tell you…" she trailed off, unsure how to proceed.

Puglisi cocked his head so that only a diagonal portion of his face could be seen under the streetlamp. The rest was steeped in the shadow of the archway. It gave him a sinister yet somehow sexy appearance, like one of those mature photo models enticing people to visit Italy for untold pleasures. At least that's what her ex-husband had fallen for when he decided to take them to Venice for their honeymoon, only the model had been young, female, and overly made up.

Puglisi broke into a smile. Although King couldn't see it in his face, she could see the sparkle in his eyes. "Oh, I see," he said knowingly. "Well, if you are going to suspect me of being a member of the Order of the Church of the Morning Star, Patrizia, can you do it while I smoke a cigarette?" He pointed at his coat. "May I?"

She nodded and he walked over. He felt the pockets of his coat over her body, his eyes locked with hers. There was something there between them: an attraction. She was far from conceited, but she could recognise when a man was drawn to her. Puglisi retrieved a cigarette and his lighter from one of the pockets and then put his hands up as he retreated back to his side of the archway.

They both turned at a sudden loud scream, as if someone had just been stabbed. But it was only a female on the main thoroughfare who had been sprayed with cold water by her male companion, who had stepped into the puddle that King had fallen into.

There was a clicking sound as Puglisi lit his cigarette, the flare of the flame momentarily highlighting his whole face before it went back to the partial eclipse King's eyes had adjusted to.

"I know it sounds ridiculous," she continued. "I felt the same when I first heard it, but if you'd seen the dossier that my colleague has compiled, you'd agree that it's quite compelling."

Puglisi scoffed as he unleashed a cloud of smoke that escaped towards the square and into the light, as if afraid of the gloom. "You mean *il demonio* returning as a comet for his rebirth through one of his children? Oh yes, very compelling."

"I was talking more about the fact that all of these crimes share a striking similarity. In addition, these supposedly random acts of violence have taken place ever since the arrival of that comet, so we have to consider that it may not be so random after all. It could be some kind of sick celebration by fanatical cult members, hellbent on sowing meaningless destruction in worship of a myth."

On cue, another rocket screamed as it was blasted into the sky. It exploded seconds later, bathing them in a surreal pink glow. Patricia tried her best not to flinch, but she was still shaking, and it wasn't all due to the fact that the chill had now burrowed down deep into her bones.

"So, you do believe is a myth, no?"

"I don't know what to believe. All I know is that we've uncovered some pretty damning leads in England and a lot of that points this way."

"What? To here? As in Venice?"

King nodded.

"What kind of leads?"

"Secret handshakes, backhanders, evidence tampering, and that's just the beginning. There's some serious shit that seems to point to people in very high places, such as law enforcement."

Puglisi scoffed. "Patrizia, I came here in the freezing rain as a professional courtesy to you and because you say it important. But when you start making wild accusations, insinuate things about me and my colleagues without any evidence, I have to draw the line. Do you understand?"

King watched the red glow fall to the floor and disappear as it was squished out by Puglisi's shoe.

"I hope you have a wonderful evening."

With that, he hunched his shoulders before walking out of the archway and into the downpour that had intensified once more.

Patricia hesitated but realised quickly that she had no choice but to take a leap of faith. "You forgot your coat!" she shouted.

The man didn't even turn around. He just waved a hand and threw back over his shoulder, "Keep it! Drop it off at the station when you no longer need. That, of course, if you trust anybody there."

"Gianni," she called, but when he didn't stop, she yelled, "Gianni, please! I'll tell you everything I know."

Puglisi finally stopped. He turned back with his hands in his pockets, cringing against the falling rain.

Behind him, the sky suddenly erupted into a kaleidoscope of colours that scattered back down to Earth, as if taking cover from the loud bang and pop that followed.

"Please," she said. "Come out of the rain."

Eventually, the man walked back and joined her again under the archway. Water dribbled off his wet hair and dripped to the ground, creating a puddle of its own.

He looked at her expectantly. She was under no illusion that she was pushing her luck with this man.

"I'm sorry, but I feel I have to be careful who I share this with," she said, feeling a pang of guilt that she'd stripped the man of his coat and then insulted him. "I know what I'm about to say is going to sound incredible, unbelievable, and maybe even painful, but I just ask that you hear me out, okay?"

He nodded.

King looked around to make sure nobody was listening. It was only after she was satisfied that they were alone that she began.

"Back in England, we found something at each of the crime scenes I have been investigating. Something that links them all together.

"And what is that?"

"An object. An unusual one, but I'll get to that. We think it's some kind of calling card. It was left at each of the murders. We missed it the first time around because of its organic nature."

"What is it, exactly?"

"Some kind of ball, made from thorns and vine."

Puglisi frowned.

"Yes, I know. We've consulted an expert. He wasn't able to identify it specifically, but he said it's the sort of thing that is used in witchcraft. You know, like voodoo dolls and effigies."

Puglisi nodded.

"Anyway, we sent it to the lab and they've come back with a match. Not one hundred percent—that's why we're running more tests and rechecking the evidence—but it's enough to make an arrest."

Puglisi stepped forward. The left side of his face was lit like an eerie author portrait inside the cover of a horror novel. "Are you serious?"

King nodded.

Puglisi's left eye widened. He seemed genuinely surprised. "Okay, then send me everything you have and let's go pick them up," he said, moving into the light as if he was going to do it that moment.

"No, hold on," King said quickly, placing a halting hand on his arm. "This is where things get tricky."

Puglisi stepped back. "What do you mean?"

"Think about it. If this is Church of the Morning Star..."

Puglisi rolled his eyes. "*Madonna mia,* Patrizia..."

"We agreed you were going to hear me out," she said. Then, stepping closer to him, she added in a subdued voice, "What if, eh? What if they have members in your office? And in mine for that matter? They could quite easily make this evidence disappear.

Do you want to take that risk?"

Puglisi shrugged then lifted his hands. "Yes, but you're assuming that such an organisation even exist, Patrizia. I told you, 'tis a lot of bullshit!"

"Yeah? Well, my first reaction was the same as yours, but then I started thinking, Gianni. I started wondering how someone like Sophie Cooper, a little girl without a penny to her name, managed to move here, and into a palace, no less, pretty much overnight."

"She inherit the place, Patrizia. We checked it out. *You* checked it. Unless you are saying that your office has been infiltrated also?"

"Well…" King shrugged, acknowledging the possibility. "My partner was spooked enough to call me from his home this evening. He said he's seen all kind of suspicious trails that lead to mysterious dead ends at various branches of power. He didn't want to take any chances."

"That may be because he is paranoid like you."

"No, it's because he's spent the past week buried in this stuff and it's all just a tad too circumstantial. Think about it. This girl practically lived next door to the neighbour that was butchered, as well as across from a mutilation and an abduction. Then…" It was King's turn to gesticulate, counting off each item as she listed it. "Then her best friend is killed, and she leaves immediately for another country. This girl literally emigrated overnight, Gianni. Who does that? Now, no offence intended, but I get the impression that your red tape is worse than ours when it comes to foreign affairs. And yet this girl managed to get a visa to stay here indefinitely pretty much at the drop of a hat."

"So? Maybe she fast track it."

"I'm telling you, somebody is helping her. Somebody powerful. Now what kind of individual do you think that might be?"

"Could be anyone at foreign affairs. It doesn't mean anything."

"Okay, but then what made her run?"

"Boh, is circumstantial. She come here to claim her inheritance."

"The night her best friend died? And let's not forget, she didn't have much of a choice because her home was being sold from under her. Do you want to know why? She didn't even own it. It was leased on her behalf through one of the many subsidiaries owned by a corporation that I understand just happens to be well known around here. Karlson, Inc. They happen to be one of your prime minister's biggest donors and an important benefactor of Venice. Now why would one of the world's most powerful companies have anything to do with this nobody girl?"

Puglisi shrugged. "You have to ask her that."

"I wanted to. But she left the country, remember?"

Puglisi shook his head. "I don't know, Patrizia. All this seem a bit flimsy to me. It sound like you think the whole world worship the devil and you have something against this Sophie Cooper."

"If you'd seen some of the heinous things I've seen, you'd start to think it was the work of the devil too," she hissed.

"Patrizia," Puglisi said, shifting into a conciliatory tone. "You're a professional. You know what this job is like. We can only deal in the facts, with the evidence, not in the conspiracy theories and hysteria."

"Gianni, I'm telling you, there's something about her. I think she's either responsible or at least involved in everything that happened in England."

"Be that as it may, Patrizia, you don't need me to tell you that none of this mean anything without evidence."

"So you think that it's a coincidence that just days after she got here, your guy ends up down a flight of stone steps with his head screwed on the wrong way?"

"And you think that little girl did that?"

"I don't know. Possibly. Either her or the members of her church."

"So, it is *her* church now?" Puglisi sighed. "I don't know. I have to say, I'm surprised. I really am. I've seen your record and it is one long list of success, yet now I hear you talk like dis and it trouble me."

King paused then frowned. "You've looked at my file?"

Puglisi closed his eyes as if he'd just been caught in a lie.

"Why?" King prompted.

"Patrizia—"

She took a step back from him. "Why were you looking into me?"

"Please, don't overreact."

"I'm not overreacting. I want to know why you were looking at my file," she said, eyes wide with distrust as she attempted to read his face, part of it still in shadow.

Puglisi hesitated and then shook his head, muttering under his breath. "It wasn't me. Well, it was, but it wasn't me who look you up. It was my colleague," he said, lowering his gaze, ashamed. "He did a Google search, and find you and think you beautiful."

King took a few seconds as her mind attempted to reconcile the compliment with the annoyance of learning he had snooped into her. But then again, she had done exactly the same thing before making the journey. She had wanted to know who she'd be dealing with. It wasn't that unusual.

"That doesn't explain why you read my file," she said anyway, too proud to back down.

Puglisi shrugged. "We… *I* wanted to know more about you then. I wanted to know who the crazy lady was that kept telephoning and send me messages."

"You mean you wanted to check if I was just a pretty face?" she corrected.

He rocked his head and shrugged once more.

"I 'pologise if it offends you in any way. That is not my intention," he said. The sombre tone of his voice accurately conveyed his regret.

King sighed. Then she suddenly said, "We have her DNA."

"What?"

"The girl's DNA. We found it on each of those objects."

Puglisi cocked his head. "Are you serious?"

King nodded. "As I say, we're running it again just to be sure, but as it stands, it puts her at all of those crime scenes."

"I can't believe it," Puglisi said. He seemed genuinely stunned. "But, if what you say can be proved, then 'tis a done deal. Let's go pick her up."

"No, this is what I'm saying to you. We can't take the risk. If that evidence falls into the wrong hands, this whole thing could fall apart," King said, looking around them.

"Well, you haven't told anybody else about it yet, have you? I mean, just you and your partner know about this, right?"

King nodded. "And the lab, obviously."

"Then we need to keep it that way," Puglisi said thoughtfully. "And if your partner emaila any of this stuff to you, you delete it immediately."

"Does this mean you believe it now?" she asked hopefully.

"No, but I don't think it hurt to take precaution," he said. "Something I wish someone remind me before I have my children."

The weak smile that King forced was illuminated by a series of red explosions overhead that merged with their reflection in the drenched cobblestone of the piazza. Puglisi looked at her under the light extravaganza. She was shivering inside his coat wrapped tightly around her body.

"Forgive me," he uttered, before lunging forward and kissing her on the mouth.

King was too shocked to react consciously but was surprised to discover that her body was receptive to it.

The fireworks were reaching their crescendo. They had merged into one continuous show of colour and their powerful percussions bounced off the buildings. Each one was accompanied by the excited cheers of those walking nearby. For a split second, King believed that they'd seen the kiss and were cheering them on. It was only when the moment ended, and Puglisi stepped back that she realised.

"I'm so sorry," he said quickly. "I 'pologise."

King smiled. "No… it…it's fine," she said as she tried to stop her teeth from chattering as her frozen mind attempted to process what had just transpired. After several seconds, she asked, "S…s… so, what now?"

Puglisi was reduced to a lovestruck teenager once more as he searched for an answer. "Well, I, um… as you know, I'm still married…"

"No, not that," King smiled, taking a calming breath to stop herself from blushing. "I mean what we've been talking about."

"Oh, yes, of course. Well, I think first thing I need to see exactly what we do and don't have. This means I need to speak to your colleague. You know, video conference to go over everything. You understand that I need to have all the facts myself before I can make a decision about how to proceed?"

King nodded. "Oh yes, of course. That's not a problem. I can set something up."

"Tonight?"

"Tonight. Yes."

"Beh… so we meet at your hotel say in one hour. Okay?"

"Okay. But where are you going now?" she asked.

"If we are doing this then I need to have someone I can trust to… what you say… watch my back. Don't worry. I've been friends with him since we were bambini. I trust him."

King gave a reluctant nod and Puglisi stepped out under the still sparking sky.

"Don't forget your jacket," she said again, half expecting him to refuse to take it back, though he didn't.

"Thank you," he said as she peeled it off her body. He watched her for a few seconds as she shivered in the gloom. She thought he was going to kiss her again, but instead she followed his gaze across to the nearby passageway. There were still a few people milling back and forth but it wasn't as busy as it was earlier. As had been the case the whole time they were there, nobody seemed interested in them.

When she looked back, she watched Puglisi brush his hand across her neck and step back out of the light. As he moved into the dark, for the first time, she saw his eyes flicker like two small flames.

The pain that slashed across her throat burned but it was the sensation of something falling onto her chest that drew her attention.

Blood.

And then she saw the blade in Puglisi's hand, glinting under the brilliance of the fireworks. In stupefied horror, she realised what had happened and threw her hands to her jugular, but she could do nothing but watch the viscous liquid of her lifeforce drain out of her body through her fingers.

She staggered backward, eyes wide with terrified bewilderment, her scream reduced to a series of gasps and gurgles, before she slammed up against the cold wall.

Puglisi stepped forward. The movement revealed only a fraction of his face, but it was enough to see that those lips that had just been pressed against hers were curved up in a smile. He was pleased, happy even, as he watched the dark stain spread through the dampness of her clothes for a few seconds, before he slipped into his coat once more, pulled up the collar and stepped away from the archway, walking calmly yet briskly across the piazza before disappearing out of sight.

Detective Inspector Patricia King, struggling for air like a suffocating fish, staggered towards the passageway of people. Nobody noticed her, not even as she stumbled out from under the arch with both hands clamped to her throat as she attempted to stem the flow of blood. She was fading fast, her head beginning to spin, her vision dimming, and before she knew it, the cold wet ground reached up to slap her in the face.

She lay there, her beating heart usurping her attempts to cling to life by pumping her blood out and into a nearby puddle.

As her light was slowly extinguished, Patricia King watched as the reddening water mirrored the beauty of the sequinned sky overhead and the irony of the street plaque nailed into the stone above: *Piazza del Tradimento*. Square of Betrayal.

37

CLAUSTROPHOBIA

FRIDAY. LATE EVENING.

One hour…

Sofia was surprised by how eager she was to get back to the party. She wanted to talk to Sam. She needed to tell him what she now knew to be true. What she could feel in every fibre of her being. It was him.

He was *the one.*

She felt it in that moment. When he looked across the room at her tonight. And she had to share this with him because she feared her heart would otherwise explode.

Sofia had always believed that her dream took place inside of some kind of theatre, but she realised now that the red carpet she kept seeing in her dream could also apply to the one that had been rolled out at tonight's gala. Suddenly, it all made perfect sense.

But what if he looked at her the way Chris had before back on the streets of Cambridge and made her feel like she was a nutter? Well, that's a bridge she would have to cross when she could. Right now, as Aurora had said, the clock was ticking. To what, exactly, she was unsure.

Aurora hadn't really told her much beyond cryptic words like fate and destiny, and that tonight, when the time was right, everything would become clear.

She had scoffed at the time, but it seemed that fate really did have plans for her, and now she was finally going to uncover its designs.

As she reached the loneliness of the empty events office, she wished she hadn't gone there but instead had the confidence to tell Raffaella what she could do with her instructions. In fact, now that she entered the room, cold and steeped in shadows, she had a good mind to turn around.

But then Sofia thought about Bacciabella. Maria had been kind to her; it wouldn't do for the museum director to make her speech only to be left red-faced because the guests didn't have all of the information they needed.

On the other hand, she knew that Raffaella *had not* told her that some of the literature was required for the event. If she had known, she would have never taken those boxes down to the cantina.

She looked at the dungeon door and remembered what it was like the first time she went down there. Maybe she should leave now, regardless of the consequences. She could go back to the party and pretend she couldn't find anything. But that was wrong. She could already hear her father's voice. *Sophie, really…*

She imagined Bacciabella delivering the speech of her life with nowhere for it to go.

...and now, if you'd like to turn to page x of your invisible brochure...

They'd made no secret of the fact that the gala's guests were very important. It would be deeply embarrassing for Maria personally, and most likely a setback for the museum.

Still...

She rolled her eyes, exasperated at herself. She teetered over to the door, pulled the bolt across, and lifted the latch. It opened with an eerie creak, and she paused on the threshold. Then, with a deep breath, she stepped inside. It was simple. Just a retrieval job. *Get the box and get out of there.*

She felt the wall, found the light switch, and flicked it on. The worn stone steps were revealed to her. Already, she could feel the cold dankness of the place pressing on her cheeks.

Come on. Just get down there and get on with it!

She placed one glittery shoe in front of the other and, being sure to stay close to the wall, slowly descended into the catacomb. She half expected to find a haunting mist creeping along the floor and up the steps to greet her, but there was nothing.

Nothing.

It was fine. It was okay. She just needed to ignore all of the crap she'd been told about the history of the place, particularly what used to happen to people who were sent down here.

Sofia shivered as she reached the bottom step and vowed never to listen to Raffaella on any topic ever again. Everything about her was toxic.

The air was its usual inhospitable self: chilly, moist, and stinky. Tonight, for extra atmosphere, the walls were weeping what seemed to be sea water, reminding her just how far down in the depths she was. For all she knew, the ancient walls might be the only thing holding back the sea. The prospect did nothing to calm her nerves.

It was fine. She was fine. She'd been down there a few times now and survived. She just needed to focus on the task at hand.

She thought back to the first time she was down there. She'd dropped the boxes in the cell after her dramatic encounter with the shadow. Then she'd stacked them to the side. They were the only boxes she remembered that had brochures in them, so they must be the ones she needed. She hoped so since there was no way of calling anybody from down there.

She hastened her footsteps, the click of her heels loud in the quiet.

Drip...drip...drip.

She hurried down the passageway, past the first cell and then over to the one containing the exhibition equipment. When she stepped closer to it, she yelped. Things had changed. A public bench made of wood had been placed there and a monster sat atop of it. With its eyes staring, its teeth bared, and its long talons outstretched, one of those *things* clung to some kind of plinth.

The incubus. The winged demon from the exhibition.

Except there were three of them. They looked different to the other ones she'd seen upstairs. Uglier, if that was even possible. As she slowly approached, she could see that one had a whole side of its face missing, its manifestation unfinished.

Statues. Prototypes, perhaps, or iterations that obviously didn't make the grade, dumped there to torment her. They agitated her heart, which was already throbbing at her throat.

They're just statues.

Still, they filled her with a palpable dread that made the vein in her neck drum.

The cell had what she imagined was the original barred gate attached to it, so she unhooked it from its moorings and pushed the thing shut. The squealing sound it made as she forced the rusty hinge to move scraped through her nervous system like the talons of those grotesques, but she was eventually rewarded with the satisfying clunk of the catch connecting.

She thought of how miserable life would have been for the poor wretches sentenced to time down there, centuries before. The noise must have felt like a bell ringing in their doom.

She moved to the next cell where she found more stored documents and exhibition equipment, and then to the next, which contained the paintings. The boxes were still where she had left them.

She went over to them, and as she reached down, she realised. She *had* inspected the contents before bringing them down there. The brochures inside were old. They were for a completely different exhibition. When Sofia had suggested throwing them out, Raffaella had procrastinated and said that they might come in handy should they choose to bring back the same set of displays, which happened sometimes.

It meant Sofia already knew that those brochures could not in any way be the ones for Maria's speech. So why send her down here?

A sound interrupted her thoughts. No, it wasn't a sound. It was a sense. The periphery of her conscious mind had noticed something, though she was yet to understand it. She stuck her head out of the cell. There was movement at the end of the corridor. One of the ceiling lights was winking intermittently, casting long bony fingers made of shadows along the walls.

She was gaping at the spectacle when a noise much closer to her made her shriek. There, in the cell, behind one of the paintings, something was moving around.

Rats?

She stepped back, heel catching in the uneven floor and threatening to topple her over. She fought to regain her balance, wailing as she did so, her shoes scuffling and echoing around her.

"Shit!" she hissed, realising how limited her movements were in her dress.

She was ready to turn back now.

Scratch! Scuttle!

It was louder this time. One of the boxes tilted forward, ready to spill over, making her yelp once again.

More movement. This time from down the tunnel. Another lightbulb was flickering like something out of one of those horror movies where the lights die and—

She screamed.

The thought had barely crossed her mind, but as one of the bulbs went out then came back on again, she saw something. She had no idea what it was but there was something down there. A shadow. Something that appeared then disappeared as the bulb cycled.

Then she heard a hissing. Or was it whispering? It was all around her, as if the very walls were stirring, the horror they had housed rousing from its ancient slumber.

There's nothing here! Nothing here. Just you!

Scratch! Scuttle! Behind her, a rat scampered off into one of the cells.

She was done with this place. But that was when she noticed. That *thing*—the Burlone with its red collar—wasn't there anymore. The paintings had been moved, the other statue was still there, though it was covered now. But that thing... *It* was nowhere to be seen. The very notion that it might be hiding somewhere nearby filled her with a dread so palpable she could feel it crawling under her skin.

She held up her skirts and hurried forward out of the cell and to the steps without looking back. She didn't want to see something that would reinforce the idea that Aurora had put in her head; it was possible that the things she had been seeing were not her mind's fabrications at all but the manifestation of a hideous but hidden dimension, existing on the fringes between reality and madness.

She was halfway up the stairs, ducking away from cobweb curtains that fluttered out in front of her like tatty knitting as she held her dress away from the grime with both hands, when the sudden sound of sniggering forced her to an abrupt stop. As she paused, she heard shoes clicking and scuffling loudly on the stone.

She looked behind her. Nothing.

She looked to the open doorway and the sanctuary of the office light beyond when…

S Q U E A L!

The loud and unmistakable screech of that cell gate reopening shocked an electric current of chills through her.

She looked back down the steps. Light bulbs flashed. Shadows appeared and disappeared.

She ran…

Up the remaining six steps that she wished she could have taken two at a time were they not so steep and were she wearing a more practical ensemble.

Three steps…

Two…

As she reached the top, just as she was about to fall back into the room above, she was confronted with the terrifying creak of the office door, slamming shut just inches from her face.

"NO!"

She threw her body against it and turned and pushed on the loop handle. It wouldn't budge.

"NO! HELP! I'M IN HERE! PLEASE! I'M IN HERE!" she yelled, hammering on the thick wood.

"HELLO? IS ANYBODY THERE? HELLO!"

She pounded on the door some more, then waited and listened, her breathing fast.

Was that giggling?!

Though muffled, she could hear it coming from the other side.

"HELLO? HEY! I'M IN HERE!" she screamed. The reality of being locked in suddenly overwhelmed her, and she started to breathe in short, sharp shocks, like a plastic bag had been tied over her head.

On the other side of the door, Georgina shushed Raffaella, who started tittering the moment they shoved the door shut. Pulling the bolt closed felt so good.

That would teach her. The bitch had waltzed in like she owned the place, stolen that job from right under their friend's nose, and now was even trying to make a move on Karlson. There was no fucking way Raffaella was going to let that happen. Who did she think she was, lording it over them with her contessa shit? Well, they were going to show her. They were going to teach her a lesson she'd never forget.

"Let's see how much the contessa enjoys spending the night in a rat-infested cellar," Georgina whispered.

Then, grinning, they hurried back to the party.

Back atop the dark staircase, Sofia was already hyperventilating at the thought of being trapped with whatever was down there.

What had made that gate swing open again?

Maybe she was just letting her imagination get the better of her. Maybe the gate always did that by itself. The hinge was rusty after all, and that could be why it had been anchored; maybe it had the tendency to swing open on its own.

She should go and see. She should go back down there and check for herself so that she could feel better.

"HEEEEEEEELP!" she screamed. "HELP! I'M IN HERE!"

She banged on the door until her hands ached and her knuckles burned. Her already tender throat was now raw again from shouting. She waited and listened for a few seconds, panting from the exertion, then, "LET ME OUT! LET ME FUCKING

OUT!" she shrieked as hysteria grabbed hold.

That was when it began, quietly and imperceptibly at first. Sofia didn't even notice the overhead light rocking back and forth.

It was only when something crashed at the foot of the steps that she stopped screaming and tuned in to the other sounds around her. Crates smashed to the floor. In the office beyond the door, she could hear things topple over. The gate below squealed as it opened and closed.

Then she felt it. For the first few seconds she thought it was her imagination, a reaction both to her predicament and the dankness of the dungeon. But then the sensation intensified, travelling through the stone, her feet, and then up the rest of her body.

It was a low rumble, swelling in power and volume until first dust and then debris began to fall from the ceiling. The slab beneath her heels shook so violently it threatened to send her tumbling down the stairs.

Sofia screamed again, helplessly, as she attempted to steady herself by holding onto the door's loop handle and the handrail. The latter wobbled unreliably, and she jumped away in the nick of time as chunks of stone and dust rained down and smashed into sections of it. The rail shook back and forth, as if being torn away by invisible hands, before crumpling in on itself and disappearing into the abyss.

Sofia was trapped, sheltering in the narrow space that remained in the corner between the door and the wet wall. Her nails snapped as she struggled to maintain her grip, her hands slipping and sliding on the jagged surface as the world around her quaked ferociously. The tremor was so powerful it removed one of her shoes and fed it to the gloomy chasm. Light bulbs popped as the building groaned like an ancient demon. Dust filled the air like smog, and rubble fell from walls.

Sofia knew that she wasn't safe perched on the steps and that she was at great risk of following her shoe over the edge. Even though every fibre of her being willed otherwise, she descended, crablike, the back of her dress scraping and tearing across the coarseness of the crumbling wall as the structure continued to fall around her.

Suddenly, she felt a weight smash into her shoulder and a searing pain hit her across the face as she was knocked down the last two steps. She smacked into the sodden floor, then everything went black.

38

THE REAPING

FRIDAY. LATE EVENING.

40 minutes...

The hall of the great council was abuzz with the nervous chatter of the assembled guests. They were still recovering from what had undoubtedly been an earthquake.

Earthquakes were recorded regularly all over Italy due to the geodynamics of its territory, but seismic activity in Venice was relatively rare. Still, the phenomenon was over before it was able to cause any major damage or panic. Indeed, by the time guests had even realised what was happening, it had passed, leaving behind nothing but a few smashed drinking glasses and swinging chandeliers.

Samael Karlson was in the middle of giving his speech when it hit and was quick to return to the microphone afterwards to thank his host for staging such a wonderful evening. The special effects were perhaps a tad too realistic for his liking, he added, to the amusement of the room.

The audience had been on edge throughout the evening, due in part to the immersive exhibit on superstitions. Conversations had inevitably turned to the hysteria surrounding the mysterious object in the sky. Although few dared to mention it, many were beginning to believe that the earthquake was a harbinger of things to come.

Samael Karlson continued his monologue like nothing had happened. He acknowledged how honoured he was to have been invited to a place of such majesty and historic significance, both for Venice and for Italy, as well as the world. Finally, he finished with a reassuring gag; the Doge's Palace had stood the ravages of time and tide and, as far as he was concerned, it was the safest place for them to be.

There was applause as he passed the microphone back to the evening's host before stepping away. He scanned the crowd for Sofia. He needed to see her. He needed to talk to her. It was time to tell her the truth.

She had been gone a while now. His heart skipped a beat. Had something happened to her during the earthquake? Was she okay?

In that moment a slamming door caught his attention. Movement. But his hopes sank. It wasn't her. It was the other duo of women that made up Maria's chief staff attendees for the evening, the two who always fawned over him every time he visited the palace. From the looks of it, they hadn't enjoyed the earthquake. They were no longer giggling and gossiping. Instead, they were silent, their faces pale and shoulders trembling. They each snatched a drink from a tray and downed them almost in one.

Meanwhile, Maria Bacciabella was eager to move on from the excitement of the tremor. It was time for the evening's main event.

The moment of truth.

Scientists had attempted to assure the public through numerous interviews and articles that any comet making it through Earth's atmosphere would break up into smaller fragments, and that those fragments might even create a meteor shower that would provide a dazzling display in the night sky. The size and velocity of the comet would ultimately determine the extent of said fragmentation upon entry.

However, some conspiracy theorists had a different perspective. They claimed that the comet was large enough to survive unbroken and become a giant meteorite that would hit the earth with cataclysmic force, triggering tsunamis that surpassed the scale of the 2004 Indonesian disaster.

Then there were the others. The few who believed the comet to be something altogether different. They were the outcasts, the heretics, the voices most rarely heard. They saw it as a portent, a sign of the rebirth of the one true deity through his offspring. They believed that on this night, a new legion of his children would be born, just as Jesus was born under the guiding light of a star. The comet, they said, would signal the arrival of those destined to rule man and the world.

Thanks to the power of social media, all opinions had received some attention, but none more so than the conspiracy theories. The theorists had gained significant traction with their ideas, spreading doubt and fear among millions.

The guests at the palace were feeling understandably rattled, both mentally and physically, as they waited for the answer to be revealed: the revelation Bacciabella had promised them.

"Please, if you'd assemble in orderly groups by the windows, the spectacle of truth is about to begin."

Having spoken the words, Maria realised that she was feeling nervous. She believed in science, yet, like many she had been subject to such a barrage of propaganda in the last few weeks that she couldn't help but wonder, *What if?* What if they were right? What if these seconds, these moments, were indeed the last for her and countless others?

The thought filled her with dread. Still, she smiled at her guests as they assembled in front of the glass, peering out at the views it offered over the lagoon.

Helpfully or not, it was a clear night. The comet was burning brighter than ever, and the marvel was mirrored on peculiarly calm waters.

It was time.

30 minutes…

It was first the beeping and then the freeze that roused Sofia from her dreamless unconsciousness.

She was lying embedded in what she first thought was a block of ice, but the persistent rumble and woosh of running water made her realise that she was in fact immersed in ferociously cold tides. What was once the stone slabs at the foot of the steps was now a shallow pool.

She lifted herself up into a sitting position, wincing at an ache in her arm. She sensed injury in the already scratched palms of her hands too, although it was difficult to tell; they had turned white and numb from the chill.

Slowly, like the water rising around her, the memory of what had happened came flooding back. She'd fallen down the rest of the steps and, by the ache on her forehead, must have hit the floor.

She groaned as she instinctively looked at her wrist. There was no watch there and no clock down in the dungeon either. She had no concept of time and thus no idea how long she'd been lying there.

Overhead and through the entire length of the corridor, panicked lights flickered. Some had already died of fright, leaving patches of dark like gapped teeth in an elongated mouth. Nearby, lit intermittently, were the broken remains of the handrail, her shoe, and several soggy cardboard boxes.

She yelped when something touched her arm. It was only one of a series of glossy brochures aquaplaning on the water towards her. Her relief was short-lived however when she realised that meant that the water was flowing in her direction from the other end of the corridor.

Shit. Oh shit!

It was all suddenly brought into focus. She had been locked in, had fallen down the steps, and was now sitting in a pool of water. The cantina was flooding! It must have been caused by the earthquake.

She kicked off the remaining shoe that was still clinging to her heel for dear life and scrambled to her feet with a groan. She had grazed her knees too, the sting of them made bearable only by the balm of the glacial water she had laid in and which was now sloshing around her.

It dripped from her body, and she began to shiver as her attention was drawn to the incessant beeping. It appeared to be coming from the flashing light of a red wall panel.

She moved over to take a closer look, feet rippling loudly through the freeze. It looked like a fire alarm panel, but for the flashing light and the two words at the bottom that read *Allarme Allagamento.*

Well, one of those words was obvious. The other was formed partly by *allaga,* which sounded very much like the word *lago* which she knew meant lake. Lake. Water.

Bloody flood alarm!

Her heart didn't like the sound of that—it began knocking inside her chest. Her urgency increased tenfold when she realised that the water that was barely an inch high just seconds ago was now covering her ankles.

Oh, God!

The cantina was flooding, and she was locked down there.

Sofia willed her cold and aching body up the stone steps and out of the wet. The relief was instant and as powerful as her will to be free.

She pushed then pummelled her frozen fists on the door, but it wouldn't budge.

"HELP! HELP ME! I'M TRAPPED IN HERE! HELP!"

She stood back and attempted to kick the door with her bare feet. The tide had already climbed three of the bottom steps and was now swirling upward towards her, rising even faster than she had feared.

"PLEASE! HELP ME!"

She couldn't keep screaming. Her voice cracked as she slapped useless hands on the door. It was pointless. There was nobody on the other side. She was alone. Nobody was going to save her, so she would have to save herself.

She took another step back to appraise the exit and yelped as something grazed her foot. It was a rock the size of a small football. It must have come loose in the quake.

She lifted it and swung it at the door.

SLAM! Once… twice… three times.

She summoned all the strength she could muster to knock the bloody thing down but to no avail. It was thick with metal bars, designed no doubt to repel potential marauders of yesteryear. There was no way she was going to smash her way out with that rock. She needed something bigger and heavier.

She looked around but there was nothing but a rising swell that reached almost halfway up the stairs. The rest of the cantina was now underwater.

She was going to die in here. She knew it. This is how she was going to meet her maker, drowned in a haunted cellar in a foreign land. She thought of her father, of what he might think of her getting herself into this mess, and tears sprung to her eyes.

"HELP ME!" she thumped once more. But there was nothing but the sound of the approaching beast of the sea, and she knew there would be no holding it back.

Then it occurred to her. Crowd control. The barrier base she previously saw should still be down in one of the cells. Those things weighed at least twenty pounds. If she could carry one up there, she could use it against the door.

She looked at the rushing tide. She'd have to swim through it and then make it back up with that weight. She could do it. She'd carried them before when she worked at the theme park.

Yes, but half frozen, shoeless, wounded, and up a dozen steep stone steps?

There was no time to think about it. She descended the steps to the water then bent down and ripped a giant slit in her dress. After taking a deep breath, she waded into the freeze once more, gasping in hypothermic shock as she went. It felt as if her chest was being squeezed as she pushed against a current that felt so much stronger now.

BUZZ! POP!

One of the bulbs exploded but she wasn't deterred. She pushed into the cell where the shiny posts stood out of the water like the futuristic pylons of a pier and was about to reach for the base weight when she realised that the unit was already assembled. She would have to carry the whole thing up there. It would be harder to move, but it would give her more leverage.

But as she placed her hand on it, there was a loud rumble and ripple as the river of the flood pushed her way.

She screamed as something touched her leg and she looked down to see a giant row of sharp jagged teeth reaching up for her. For one horrifying moment she thought that there was a creature in the water but then realised that one of the prototype statues had overturned. The grotesque incubus was lying on its side like a drowned prehistoric beast.

She moved out of the cell and back into the corridor.

BUZZ! POP! BUZZ! POP!

Something must have collapsed and cleared its path, for the surge was rising much faster.

The drowned alarm was still wailing.

Sofia hurried forward as waves of the renewed surf scurried about her like fluid talons, eager to pull her under. But she'd already reached the first step, where she half lifted and half dragged the post and its weight up as she climbed. She finally emerged at the top and was faced with the door once more.

Shivering and dripping, she stepped back and allowed the post to swing like a pendulum as she threw it forward.

SLAM!

Again. Again. Each time she lifted it higher, allowing the battering ram to arc as far and as high as her remaining strength would allow.

SLAM! SLAM!

The water was at her waist now. Her hair slapped in soggy strands around her face, as with teeth gritted and body shaking, she continued her assault on the exit.

She raged against it, screaming and grunting with each and every impact. She knew that the higher the flood climbed, the less of a swing she'd be able to muster. She had only seconds left to make this work.

SLAM! BANG! SLAM! BANG!

The water was up to her chest and the door was showing no signs of yielding. Yet she didn't stop. Though weak and feeble, and with tears in her eyes, Sofia DaTerra could not and would not desist, even if what began as a rageful assault was now no more than a whimpering tap.

As the water encircled its glacial claws around her throat, she resigned herself to the knowledge that there was nothing else she could have done. As her limbs slowly became paralysed by the freeze, she had no choice but to allow the weight to fall by her side.

The tide rose quickly to her chin. Finally, she was barely able to gasp for air as it covered her nose and then her whole head.

10 minutes…

In the great hall, all the guests had assembled by the windows and were gazing skywards. All but for Samael Karlson.

The man, who recently became one of the world's wealthiest and most powerful men after the death of his father, had left the congregation and made his way over to the exit as quietly as he could in search of Sofia. He could feel it now. Something inside told him that he needed to get to her. That he needed to tell her the truth before it was too late.

If Samael had stayed in the hall, he would have noticed one of the guests gasp and point at something beyond the glass. Something that had nothing to do with the comet. Something that was worse, much worse.

7 minutes…

Sofia attempted to hold her breath for as long as possible, but after several seconds, her body began to rebel against the restriction. The need to release it pushed against her skull with a pressure so immense, it felt as if her head was going to explode. She began to gag, inhaling salty sea water that her lungs attempted to expel in a cloud of bubbles.

Eyes wide, she scratched at the door, thrashing her head around as she desperately hunted for an escape route or miraculous air pocket, anything to prolong her life. But there was nothing, and after several more seconds of expending what little energy her body had left, she slowed as her body jerked spasmodically, beginning to accept her fate.

So this was how it was going to end for her. All of the dreams, all of the speculation, and this was how she was going to meet her demise, sealed in these godforsaken catacombs.

Accept was the word that kept sounding through her brain. *It is time... time to accept... accept your fate.*

And she did. She felt her limbs grow heavy as a strange sense of peace washed over her. Her mind slowly reconciled itself to the inevitable.

Suddenly, there was a muffled squeal followed by an almighty *whoomph!* As the door in front of her disappeared, the pressure of the surge against her back rushed her forward and she exploded into the office, washing straight into the opposite wall.

The water roared like a beast and surrounded her. Electrical outlets shorted and new alarms sounded. The surge of water flooded the room, searching for new spaces to fill and air to displace. Sofia gasped and spluttered as she was battered by the waves, her bruised and exhausted body finally coming to a stop on a perch. She was now a castaway on Raffaella's desk.

She gawked at her surroundings in a stupefied pant as her brain caught up. It seemed that by some higher grace she had survived. Death had been imminent, and the enormity of this realisation injected her with a tiny and most welcome reserve of energy.

She took in the room. Water was still gushing in as it bubbled upward from the cantina. There was no way of stopping it since the door, she realised, had imploded inward, the bolt having yielded to the immense weight of the surge that was now rapidly dominating its new terrain.

She was still in danger.

Spluttering as she recovered, Sofia sat up and reluctantly stepped back into the flood which was already foaming to her knees. She quickly waded across the room where she yanked the door open, relieved to be able to close it behind her to trap most of the water inside.

She was back in the main corridor with the long glass wall and stunning view of the lagoon directly in front of her. The same view had taken her breath away the day she first arrived here. It felt so very long ago.

Were it not for her ordeal, she would have paused to marvel at the moonlit vista of the boats and gondolas marooned on the marshy bog of the shallow tide, but she wanted out of that place and back onto dry land *now.*

She broke into a weak run but immediately skidded to a halt when an immense explosion of light lit up the world around her.

The sky was on fire.

At least it looked that way. Billions of particles of a multitude of colours streaked across it like a colossal firework display.

Sofia could only gawk at the spectacle, convinced that it was the end of days.

But wait, no. It was the comet burning up in Earth's atmosphere, exactly as scientists had predicted. The doom-mongers were wrong. They were wrong!

It took several seconds for Sofia to understand, but as she did, the warmth of it spread through her like a comforting mantle, fighting the freeze that had settled in her bones and bringing a smile of relief to her face.

It was finally over. All the negativity, all the angst she had associated with that *thing* had been blown up into an explosion so beautiful it brought tears to her eyes. This time for all the right reasons.

The glorious display continued for what felt like a couple of minutes before *they* finally caught her attention.

She had been so absorbed by the cosmic show that they didn't register at first. There were thousands of them… Fish, of all shapes and sizes, twitched, twisted, and jumped as they gasped for air. Along with assorted boats and gondolas, they had been beached the whole time.

Where was all the water? The tide had disappeared. Not slowly and languidly, but as if Neptune himself had pulled the plug in the great basin of the lagoon, draining the Adriatic, and leaving nothing behind but mud, debris, and stranded oceanic life.

"Oh my God!" is all she could gasp. This had nothing to do with the comet and everything to do with the earthquake.

That's when she heard the squeal of the door opening at the other end of the corridor.

It was him.

"Sofia!" he called.

"Samael?"

"Sofia!"

"Samael!"

He ran to her. "I've been looking for you everywhere," he began, pulling her to him. "I thought something had happened to you and… it looks like it has!"

He paused, examining her to make sure she wasn't hurt. "Are you okay? Are you all right?"

"I'm fine."

"Are you sure?"

"Yes, listen—"

"No, Sofia, please hear me out. I am sorry. I am so sorry. I have so much to tell you. I don't even know where to start, but first, I need you to know. I need you to understand that that day we spent together, that day wasn't about doing anybody a favour. I mean, it started out that way, but then it changed. Things changed for me, Sofia. They changed the moment I saw… the moment I realised that for me it was you… It was you. *You* were *the one.*"

Sofia was about to respond but was cut short by a sudden

vibration underfoot. At first, she thought it was the water gathering in the office behind them, but it soon became clear that this was something bigger and stronger.

Samael noticed the look on her face. "What? What's the matter?"

Sofia didn't respond. Instead, eyes wide, she turned to look out of the window once more. Horrifyingly lit by the lightshow in the heavens, a burgeoning wall of darkness on the horizon was headed straight for them.

Samael followed her gaze and froze. "Oh…" is all he could say as he took on her shock as his own.

30 seconds…

The boats and gondolas were floating once more as they sped towards them on a colossal tidal wave. It was so high it gradually blocked out the view of the sky.

The tsunami had begun almost a kilometre offshore, gathering size and strength as it absorbed and carried everything in its path, and it was now hurtling towards them at the speed of a jet plane.

The roar and rumble rapidly grew in intensity as Samael grabbed Sofia's hand and tugged her away.

"COME ON!" he yelled as they started forward.

But it was too late.

Seconds later the window imploded, showering them with shards of glass as the wall of water slammed into them with the force of a freight train. The rush sucked the air from their lungs and filled their ears, drowning out all other sound as they were thrown around in the churning deathroll. Bones snapped as battered bodies were carried along with chunks of debris, tossed around like ragdolls in a swirling underwater tornado that tore them from each other and carried them away in a wild frenzy.

10 seconds…

There was no pain as there was no end to the vastness of the ocean. No reprieve. Just an endlessly frigid blackness…

5 seconds…

…from which for Sophie Cooper and Samael Karlson there would be no escape.

Zero seconds.

The countdown was over. The ritual was complete.

38

THE WRATH

TWO YEARS LATER

The winter sun was strong in a cerulean sky, irradiating the great city of Venice with all the colour and warmth its tourists and locals craved.

The city hadn't yet fully recovered from the tsunami of two years earlier, but it was getting there. Homes were being rebuilt and the landmarks that needed it were being restored. Miraculously, in what most had branded an act of God, most historic sites went untouched by the killer wave. It had claimed countless lives, with numerous high-profile individuals including senior government officials and leading figures in industry among them. The loss was devastating, not for the deaths alone but also for their impact on the city's society and global economy as a whole. It had been a haunting reminder of the power and unpredictability of the sea.

Palazzo Rosso had also undergone its own refurbishments since the flood. Under the supervision of its new owner and with a generous investment, it had been lovingly restored to its former glory. In addition, a few modern touches had been conceived and implemented by some of the world's best designers and craftsmen.

In the ballroom, like a queen over her subjects, the giant canvas now showcased a new portrait. The metamorphosis appeared to happen overnight and gave a stunningly accurate representation of the incumbent lady of the house. Her hair, as white as snow, fell in long locks over slender porcelain flesh and milky white breasts. Her lips of rouge curved upward ever so slightly in a rare smile worthy of a Messina.

All the rooms had been updated. The gallery had been adapted into lounge and office zones with bookcases, a workstation, couches, and chaise longues with views over the ballroom, the Grand Canal, and the rest of the city. On the desk was a slimline computer streaming a live broadcast of an elegant lady at a podium as she addressed a mass gathering. Underneath, the red and white caption read:

LIVE: PIAZZA SAN MARCO

REMEMBERING VENICE TRAGEDY

Mayor of Venice, Maria Bacciabella

The subtitles read:

Two years ago, our beloved city was struck by a devastating tsunami that took the lives of 103,695 fellow Venetians and other members of the international community. Our hearts were shattered and the loss was felt by every single one of us. But in the face of tragedy, our city showed its strength and tenacity.

We lost so much that day, but we did not lose our spirit. With the help of the incredible organizations that came to our aid, we have been able to rebuild and begin to heal.

Indeed, it gives me great pride to say that Venice is once again thriving. We owe much of our success to the generosity and unwavering support of our benefactors. In particular, I would like to extend my heartfelt gratitude to Karlson, Inc., who have been instrumental in our recovery.

For centuries, we Venetians have lived in harmony with the Adriatic Sea. It is this unique history that has taught us resilience and the ability to rebuild so we are better and stronger. And that is exactly what we have done and shall continue to do.

We will never forget the lives that were lost in the tsunami, but today, we remember them with pride and with hope for a brighter future…

Contessa Sofia DaTerra-Karlson was dressed in a black and white tweed dress and heels as she sat on a couch holding a tablet. She was talking into the camera.

"… and how are you settling into the new place?"

Janay shook her head. "I'm lost for words, Soph, and you know that's a first for me. I am loving it! And Damon, well he's made up! There's so much space to run around. The back lawn is massive! Mum says it's bigger than the park we used to go to! I mean, seriously, can you believe it? Bigger, Soph! And of course, he's only started going on about getting a bloody dog, ain't he?"

"You should get him one. It'd do him good to have a little companion."

"Oh, don't you start. Mum keeps going on about it as well."

Sofia sipped from her espresso cup. Seagulls called outside.

"Seriously though, Soph. I don't know how to thank you for everything you've done for us."

"Janay, you really don't have to thank me every time we talk. It makes me happy. You know that."

"Yeah, but still. Thank you so much for this and, you know, that money for Damon's college as well. I mean, Soph, he'll be the first in our whole family to go to college and university. Mum can't stop crying."

"Oh, bless her. It's good, though. It's good that he gets the chance to be the best that he can be," Sofia said with a wink.

"I really love your hair like that," Janay said, peering into the screen.

"Yeah?" Sofia touched the strands of her hair with immaculately painted nails. "Thanks." When she looked up, Janay had a grin on her face. "What?"

"Nothing."

"Janay!"

"Well, I'm just in bloody awe of you, aren't I? I mean you look positively stunning, Soph. Like a bloody model or something. Your hair, your makeup, your clothes. You just look so hot! It's like a whole new you, with so much more confidence."

"That's because it *is* a whole new me."

"No, seriously. I am so proud of you. You know, after everything, you've really done well. Even landed yourself a young, fit bloke who just happens to own half of the bloody world. And the fact that you both come from similar backgrounds—you know with him being fostered too—is just so bloody cute. It's like a romance novel. Of all the people in this world, you've found your soulmate, Soph, and he's such a lovely guy. Top fella. I'm just so happy for you." Janay paused for breath as her eyes misted.

"Oh, Janay, don't. You'll get me started," Sofia said, gently dabbing the corner of her eyes to avoid smudging her mascara.

Janay laughed away her happy tears and then used a tissue to dry them. "So, anyway, what's it like being back there after what happened?"

Sofia looked around. "It's good. It feels different, you know, like I'm not even seeing it as the person I was before, but as someone else. Do you know what I mean? It feels like… home."

There was a pause. Boats droned outside. Pigeons cooed.

"Where is hot stuff anyway?"

"He's out at the square for the memorial. With Karlson leading the way with the rebuild, it was important for him to be there. I was there earlier today."

"I still can't believe you two got out of that alive, especially after what happened to everyone else. It's insane. A bloody miracle! And if you hadn't got me back to England when you did, God knows what would have happened," Janay said, eyes watering once more with the thought of orphaning her son simply too much to bear.

"I know, but it's okay. You're fine. We're all fine," Sofia said with a faint smile.

"But it's just weird, right? All of this stuff and how it happens. Fate and all that. Like those people who decide last minute not to take a plane and all that *Final Destination* shit."

"Well, I hope it isn't exactly like that," the contessa said with a laugh.

"Oh, you know what I mean. It's just one of those things that's meant to be. You know, all the stuff that happened over here and everything that made you go there in the first place at that exact time… it just makes my head explode. You know they're still making documentaries about you both. You're like gods now. The couple that survived the impossible." Janay scoffed. "Of course, there are still those weirdos who think Sam is the spawn of hell and all that."

"Really?"

"Yeah, that story's still making the rounds. Sexy devil more like!" Janay laughed. "I mean, I didn't even know Samael is actually another name for the devil. Did you?"

The contessa cocked her head. "Is it? No, I didn't know that. Huh. You learn something new every day."

A door slam and its echo interrupted the conversation. Sofia turned towards it. "Oh, I think that's him now."

"Okay, well, that's my cue. I'll leave you two love birds to get on with your holiday. Although every day's a holiday for you now, *Mrs Karlson.*"

"Um, excuse you. It's Contessa DaTerra hyphen Karlson, I'll have you know and thank you very much."

Janay stuck her tongue out at her friend. "Are you still visiting next month and coming here to stay?"

"Of course. Wouldn't miss it for the world."

"Just as well, since you own it!"

"Goodbye, you," Sofia said with a big smile, blowing kisses until the screen went black.

She put the tablet down, quickly reapplied her lip gloss, and then turned to see her husband coming up the staircase.

He was wearing a tailored navy blue suit. It was her favourite colour for him because of the way it brought out his lovely green eyes.

"Ciao, caro," she said as she walked over to him, slipped her arms around his waist, and then pressed her lips to his.

"Hmm, some greeting. You taste like cherries," he said appreciatively.

"Yeah? Do you like it?"

"I do."

"Best give you some more then," she said, kissing him again. "You've been gone a while. How was it?"

"Good," he said.

"Amazing what money can do, eh?"

Sam smiled. "It has its uses."

"It certainly does. Do you know what else has its uses?" she smiled.

Samael cocked his head.

"Finally being alone in a floating mansion in one of the

world's most romantic cities."

"Is that right?" he asked with a curious smile.

Sofia nodded, taking her husband's hand, leading him down the hallway and into the bedroom.

Voiles fluttered languidly on a cold breeze. The room smelt of lilies and sea air.

Beyond the balcony, a street merchant announced his arrival in the small piazza. On the other side of the bridge, the calle buzzed with tourists once more.

Sofia stopped in front of the bed, which was littered with clothes and metal hangers.

"Been shopping or still unpacking?" Sam asked.

"Both," she said, unbuttoning her husband's shirt, slowly revealing tanned skin, rounded pecs, and sculpted abdominal muscles. She kissed his chest, nipped one of his nipples, and then pushed him backward onto the bed, eliciting a jangle of metal.

"Oh, like that, is it?" he asked with a smile.

Sofia's only response was a nod and a grin as she pulled off her husband's shirt, unbuckled his belt, and unzipped his trousers, before tugging them off and throwing them across the room with a flourish.

He laughed and she giggled.

Sofia observed her husband for the longest time. His tall, lean body. The way he filled his white shorts. His black hair, neatly pinned ears, and that chiselled jaw.

He looked up at her. "What?"

Her eyes welled with tears. "You really are handsome," she said. "I'm so lucky."

"Come here, beautiful," he said, reaching up for her. "Ow!" he suddenly groaned.

"What's the matter?"

"Nothing," he said with a wince. "Just cramp in my arm," he laughed.

"Oh, you poor thing."

Sofia stepped out of her dress and then bent down to kiss his wrists and muscular biceps. She loved this about him. The way his body was sculpted, not artificially inflated.

She straddled him, the heels of her shoes at the end of her bare legs fuelling his arousal. She dangled the tips of her long hair to trace and tickle his chest, before leaning to kiss his face and nibble his ears. She was gentle at first, then passionate, hungry, manoeuvring her underwear and herself in such a way that required no further removal of clothing.

Then she began to rock up and down, back and forth, manipulating his body, using it in the best possible way to bring her the greatest and most intense pleasure.

He moaned. The hangers clinked and rattled.

She felt his hands slide from her rear and fall by his sides as he allowed her to take full control.

"I love you," she whispered. "I adore you." Then she repeated it. "I love you. I adore you. I love you. I adore you." Over and over, again and again with each and every thrust. Faster. Louder. Faster. Louder.

"I love you. I adore you. I love you and adore you."

Faster. Jangle.

Louder.

Faster. Jangle.

Louder.

And then, as the sensation built, as they both grappled for that moment of pressurised release, Contessa Sofia DaTerra-Karlson declared:

"...but THIS MUST BE DONE!"

She snatched up one of the metal hangers and jabbed the hook into the side of her husband's neck. As she yanked it sideways with inhuman force, it ripped his throat open with the simplicity of a knife through warm butter.

Samael Karlson's eyes snapped wide open to reveal a look of bewildered confusion as he attempted to lift his hands to stem the gushing of blood from the gash in his throat. For reasons unknown to him, he couldn't. His mind willed it, but his limbs refused, stuck in paralysis.

"Shhh… my handsome love… shh… it's okay. It's just a little concoction to numb you so you don't suffer too much," she whispered. She wiped her lips with the back of her hand and blew strands of hair from in front of her face as she continued to rock up and down, basking in the afterglow as her husband's body twitched reflexively beneath her.

High above, anchored to the wooden structure of the bed, the once serene and contemplative faces of the canopy appeared to shift and morph, twisting into expressions of shock and horror that mirrored the tragedy below as Samael Karlson's lifeblood drained from his body, pooling and seeping into the covers.

"Shhh, my darling. Shhh… it'll all be over soon," she said as his flame ebbed from those gloriously green eyes. "Shhh… your work is done. It's time for me to take over. Shhh."

Awash with her husband's blood, Sofia bent down and kissed him on the lips.

"Sleep, my darling. Sleep now," she said, momentarily blinking back tears as her face creased with agonized dismay before she wiped it away with the back of her hand once more.

Then, she dismounted from the dead man and made her way towards the bathroom, removing her soiled underwear as she went.

***

Thirty minutes later, freshly showered and dressed in a long cardigan dress with a rolltop neck and wedge sandals, the contessa descended the staircase as the front door slammed shut.

"My babies!" she squealed happily, as the twins, a boy and girl, were carried to her in his and hers carriers by Gabriele.

"Oh, Mummy has missed you," the contessa cooed as they were set down next to each other. She gave each of them a kiss before sweeping back the locks of white hair from their faces, and then looking up. "How were they?"

"They were as good as gold," Aurora replied, breezing in in a black dress and hat as if she'd just been to the races and not for a stroll by one of the canals. "How are you feeling now?" she asked with a pained expression. "Are you feeling any better?"

"Oh, much, thank you," Sofia said.

"Good. I know these things can be difficult," she said sympathetically. "But we all have our part to play in whatever role has been assigned to us."

Sofia was about to respond when the baby boy started crying. "Ah, I saw that, Seraphina," the contessa admonished. "Don't bash your brother like that. He's very precious, you know. He needs to grow up one day and do his bit to keep the family bloodline going. He can't do that if you keep beating him up, can he? Now, both of you give Mummy a big squeeze and a kiss," she said, unstrapping them both and squeezing them tight.

"Would you like me to take them?" asked Ms Whitlock as she emerged from the dining room.

"No, we're fine, thank you, Ms Whitlock. Besides, Gabriele can take care of them, can't you?"

"It's my pleasure," the man said with a bow of the head.

"Wonderful, but I want to keep them with me for a little bit first."

"Of course."

"Oh, and Ms Whitlock," the contessa began, pulling a face, "I'm afraid I made a terrible mess in the bedroom. Would you mind taking care of it for me?"

"Of course not. I'll see to it right away. How about a beverage before I get started?"

"Oh, I would love that. I could murder a cup of tea."

"What a wonderful idea," Aurora enthused. "In fact, I'll tend to the contessa's chamber, Ms Whitlock, if you want to get the kettle on."

"Oh, well, if you're sure."

"Of course. It's no bother."

As both women went their respective ways, one up to the bedroom and one down to the kitchen, Sofia pulled the balcony doors open and shivered as a cold wind blew at her face, fanning her long hair behind her. It was picking up already. She knew it would only be a matter of time.

Then it came, ringing down the hallway and the staircase like the dissonant shattering of glass, an ear-piercing shriek the reverberated around them. It was followed by another and then another. Shortly after, Aurora appeared breathless on the gallery, no longer her calm and measured self.

She grabbed the handrail and screamed, "MS WHITLOCK! MS WHITLOCK! Oh shit! Oh, fuck and shit! MS WHITLOCK! We're all gonna burn for this!" She dropped her practised inflection for her native Yorkshire accent in her panic. "We're all gonna fuckin' burn!"

She turned to Sofia. "What have you done? You stupid, stupid girl! WHAT HAVE YOU DONE?" she screamed.

"Goodness gracious," a harassed and also breathless Ms Whitlock muttered as she made her way up the stairs with a tea towel in her hand. "Whatever is the matter?"

"SHE is the matter!" Aurora declared, pointing at Sofia. "SHE! is the matter. She's only gone and killed him! SHE FUCKING KILLED HIM!" Aurora screamed before making her way down the stairs as fast as her dress would allow, grumbling, "He won't stand for this. He's gonna kill us. He's gonna kill us all!"

Ms Whitlock threw a hand to her mouth and turned to Sofia, hoping to hear her deny it.

But Sofia said nothing. Instead, she took a deep breath and, with both her babies in hand, stepped out onto the balcony as a furious wind whipped at her hair.

The thunderous sky overhead had transformed into a sickly hue the colour of an ugly bruise. In the distance, inky black storm clouds stained with threads of lightning lit up like veins of fire.

Sofia leaned into the turbulence. Catching her breath and holding firm to her resolve, she turned to her children.

"Mummy will never let you go. *Never.*"

EPILOGUE

THE NIGHT IT HAPPENED

The helicopter took off just minutes before the first surge hit the city of Venice. The paramedic who was administering care to the patient glanced out the window, his jaw slack with amazement as he saw the wave approach.

"*Guarda! Guarda giù!* (Look! Look down!)" he yelled over the whirring of the engine. A giant wave washed away the helipad they had just left and continued across the whole island, making its way towards the city.

Their patient was in a critical state and was barely clinging to life. They had been drifting in and out of consciousness. Everything was a haze inside of which there was nothing but the fleeting shadows of memories. Something bad had happened to them. Something terrible, so terrible they had lost a lot of blood.

They could smell it, taste it, and feel it draining from their body with every beat of their heart.

The prognosis wasn't good. That much was obvious. However, if by some miracle they did survive this, Detective Inspector Patricia King would find those responsible and any of their associates, and she would make them pay.

She would make them pay dearly.

If you enjoyed

MALEFIC

Please leave an Amazon / Goodreads rating
so that others may enjoy it also.

Generally, only a fraction of satisfied readers will leave a rating, so yours really will make a difference.

THANK YOU.

FOLLOW TONY

Subscribe to the blog, mailing list, or follow on social media for the latest news, special chapter previews and exclusive giveaways.

VISIT
www.tonymarturano.com

JOIN THE MAILING LIST
visit www.tonymarturano.com,
click on contact and subscriptions.

LIKE THE FACEBOOK PAGE
facebook.com/tonymarturano.author

BROWSE INSTAGRAM
instagram.com/marturanotony

FOLLOW ON TWITTER
twitter.com/tmarturano

FOLLOW ON AMAZON
to be automatically alerted of every new release.

or google tony marturano

ACKNOWLEDGEMENTS

I'm so very grateful to everyone at a Different Angle, who has supported me throughout this book's journey, from manuscript to print. A special thanks to the following who have actively contributed to its realisation.

THE TM FOCUS/READER'S GROUP

My heartfelt thanks to everyone for giving so generously of their time and opinions!

(In no particular order)
Francesca Marturano-Pratt – Anna Pratt – Renee Owens – Lisa Hall – Cheryl Green

MY EDITORS

Nicola, for helping me shape the story into the best that it can be.
Sydney, for that all-important attention to detail.

YOU, THE READER

If you're reading this book, there's a good chance you bought it. I'm obviously very grateful for that.

Thank you!

On the other hand, if you borrowed from or were gifted this book by somebody else, even better! It means they thought it was good enough to pass on.

Printed in Great Britain
by Amazon

22042664R00233